Bio-plasma boiled up from the jungle, tracing a bright blue arc across the sky.

The dropship banked starboard. The pilot had needle-sharp reactions, but despite his simulated senses, he wasn't fast enough. I heard the patter of small arms fire against the hull, saw the flash of the null-shield activating as it repelled energy-based weapons. The Cougar spat out flares and decoy drones, and fire chased us lower still.

"This is Angel One, this is Angel One," said the pilot. "We are encountering heavy resistance. All Cougars, be aware."

The Cougar launched missiles into the jungle. Krell bodies scattered, and the landscape was soon on fire. Other Cougars were dropping in behind us, clustered around the Sci-Div transports. They got the same welcome. In some cases, even worse.

By Jamie Sawyer

THE LAZARUS WAR

Artefact

Legion

Origins

Redemption (ebook novella)

THE ETERNITY WAR

Pariah

Exodus

Dominion

THE ETERNITY WAR

BOOK THREE: DOMINION

JAMIE SAWYER

orbit

www.orbitbooks.net

Copyright © 2019 by Jamie Sawyer
Excerpt from *Velocity Weapon* copyright © 2019 by Megan E. O'Keefe
Excerpt from *Fortuna* copyright © 2019 by Kristyn Merbeth

Cover design by Lauren Panepinto
Cover illustration by Ben Zweifel
Cover copyright © 2019 by Hachette Book Group, Inc.

Orbit
Hachette Book Group
1290 Avenue of the Americas
New York, NY 10104
orbitbooks.net

First Edition: November 2019
Simultaneously published in Great Britain by Orbit

Orbit is an imprint of Hachette Book Group.
The Orbit name and logo are trademarks of Little, Brown Book
Group Limited.

The publisher is not responsible for websites (or their content) that are
not owned by the publisher.

The Hachette Speakers Bureau provides a wide range of authors for
speaking events. To find out more, go to www.hachettespeakersbureau.com
or call (866) 376-6591.

Library of Congress Control Number: 2019940683

ISBNs: 978-0-316-41119-6 (mass market), 978-0-316-41118-9 (ebook)

Printed in the United States of America

OPM

10 9 8 7 6 5 4 3 2 1

To Louise, for everything

PROLOGUE

The sun relentlessly beat down on the city and its surrounding sectors. The marketplace—at the edge of the
conurbation of human structures that made up Shangri
Capital—seemed to catch its glare most of all.

There was no hiding from the sun. All day, every day.
No night, ever. There the sun was: high on the horizon,
so big that it almost filled the vista. It illuminated the
world's moons too, creating six burning discs in the sky.
In the twenty days that Daneb Riggs had been on-world,
he hadn't seen a single cloud. It was an anomaly caused
by the planet's orbit, so Riggs had heard. One face was
always to the local star, while the other was forever in
darkness. Stable weather and a warm climate on one
side. Constant night and erratic storms on the other.

The planet's name was Shangri VI, which was a reference to some Old Earth religion—a supposed Utopia.
That, Riggs figured, was typical of the parasitic mites
that had colonised this world. When they'd first settled
here, they had brought the baggage of their mythology
with them. Riggs had been like them, once. His family—
his *old* family—were Gaia Cultists. The tradition had

been generations long by the time of Riggs' birth. He hadn't known any better, and so he'd gone along with it. That thought made him bristle, and he grabbed for the bottle of beer on the table in front of him. It was a local brew, weak and warm. He swilled it down with an unhealthy dose of vitriol. He was different now. He was a True Believer, and Warlord had shown him the way.

The planet was one of many Outer Colonies, a string of systems along the Former Quarantine Zone. Although many regarded Shangri VI as heaven, to Riggs the place was far closer to hell. He looked out across the street, across from the bar in which he sat, and pondered why he despised the place so much. Riggs' feelings for Shangri VI were more complex than just about the world's proximity to its local star. The sun illuminated everything, put the world into constant sharp relief. Nothing was hidden. The blazing light exposed all imperfections.

And Riggs had many, many imperfections. Like Shangri VI, Riggs had two faces. He had tried to forget one of them, to replace it with the other. But as with Shangri, in its tidally locked orbit, Riggs knew that was impossible.

Daneb Riggs was a traitor. A deserter. A renegade. One of the most wanted men in the thirteen Alliance territories. He had turned his back on the Army, on his training, on his people. On his own Christo-damned squad... The thought of his own betrayal kept him up at night, drove him to the brink of madness. Some nights, he managed to justify the actions that he had taken—the things he had done—to himself. He had done what Warlord had wanted him to do. He had only been carrying out orders. The Alliance deserved everything they got.

But other times... Other times he wasn't so sure. There was still some shred of doubt in Riggs, and it niggled at him. A wound that wouldn't heal, the edges always tender, the infection never quite gone.

Riggs' hand, he realised, was shaking. He focused on the Spiral insignia tattooed on his forearm. It snaked around his data-port; the connection that would allow him to operate a simulant. The thought of making transition again—into a new body—pulled him back into the present.

Riggs' post on the terrace overlooked the planet's main spaceport. It was a decent vantage point, with a view across the landing pads. Further out, a refugee camp had grown up around the port. There were hundreds of tents and other temporary habitats. The noise and smell of the encampment had expanded with its size. Eager to flee from the encroaching Krell exodus, many families came to the Outer Colonies searching for asylum. There was very little assistance waiting for them, though. Resources were stretched. The military was already overworked, and aid agencies had long abandoned the worst choke points. Many refugees never left. There were stories of groups having camped in the shadow of the spaceport for months. Stranded, left behind. Forgotten. Such were easy recruits to the cause. Already, a network of Spiral agents had infiltrated the camp, and support was growing by the day. As Riggs watched, another civilian starship crossed the sun and landed on one of the pads. Riggs made a mental note of that. It was the thirteenth ship today. He had seen several hundred since his emplacement. Like many, this one was Russian. Probably another of the survival fleets from Kronstadt, from the Mu-98 system.

"Credit for the poor?" came a broken, parched voice. "Please, sir."

The figure to which the voice belonged was just as broken. A beggar. Black rags, typical of the underclass of Shangri VI, swathed the woman's body. Beneath, she wore a battered survival suit, and her head poked out of the tattered collar. She had a weathered mask of a face, streaked by complicated tattoos that were sun- and age-bleached. She sat with her back hunched, hands outstretched to all that passed by. Many such beggars crowded the bars that surrounded the spaceport.

"Credit, sir?" she asked again, calling out to Riggs. Her eyes were bright jade, her dirty silver hair plaited down her back.

Riggs sneered. "Get out of here," he mouthed.

The woman broke eye contact. She turned to eas- ier pickings, as a group of refugees stumbled by. They looked dazed and shocked—were doubtless new arriv- als. Riggs had seen that response before. It was a com- mon reaction to the sort of horror that was enveloping this sector of the galaxy.

A shadow passed in front of the table, and Riggs looked up.

"Aren't you worried that someone will recognise you?" the newcomer asked.

The man was taller than Riggs by a good degree, with a muscular bulk that verged on threatening. Without invitation, he pulled up a chair and sat opposite Riggs. He wore the full uniform of an Alliance Navy officer, a captain's rank badge on his shoulder and a service cap tucked under his arm. He ran a hand over his bald head, wiped sweat from his pate.

"Not particularly," answered Riggs. "No one cares, here. It's been months since anyone saw the local gover- nor. They say that he's fled. Anyone who's anyone has already left for the Core Systems. Law enforcement is gone, the Army's going."

"True enough," said the officer. He waved over at the serving droid—a humanoid robot with a sleek metal shell made to mimic female anatomy. "Kronstadt vodka, on the rocks."

The droid nodded and trotted back into the bar.

"You're late," Riggs muttered.

"We don't work on your timetable, Disciple Riggs."

The man's body didn't quite fit the uniform, and it showed—under the microscope, the disguise likely wouldn't pass. There was, Riggs noticed, a bloodstain on the man's sleeve. That was a reminder that the uniform hadn't been given willingly, but had been taken by force. The man saw where Riggs was looking, and grinned. The expression made the skin of his cheeks crease unpleasantly.

"What should I call you?" Riggs asked.

"You can call me Captain Mikhailov," he said. He wore photo-reactive lenses over his eyes, and they reflected Riggs' image back at him. "It's not my name, but it will do."

"I've been waiting here for twenty days," said Riggs. "What's wrong with you people?"

The waitress delivered Mikhailov's drink. He took it, knocked it back in one gulp.

"Since Kronstadt, military fill the space lanes," he said. "Organising a ship took longer than expected."

"But you have one now, I take it?"

"Of course. Why would I be here if not?"

"I have no idea."

"Have you arranged the payment?"

"Of course," mimicked Riggs.

He slid a universal credit chip across the table. Mikhailov glanced at it, then placed it under his glass. The chip contained a significant sum of money, and it had been burning a hole in Riggs' pocket since he had been tasked with the mission.

"Exactly as we agreed," Riggs said.

"Then we seal our bargain," said Mikhailov.

"It had better be a good ship, given what we're paying you."

"It is. Fast Q-drive, well armed."

"Fine."

"Why can't you use the Warlord's ship?"

"Warlord is…" Riggs paused, shook his head. "Otherwise engaged. Things are about to get interesting. Real interesting."

Mikhailov grinned again. "Interesting, I like."

There was a small tri-D viewer in the corner of the bar. The intense sunlight washed out the image it projected, but Riggs squinted to see the feed.

"*…this is despite the unparalleled number of refugees throughout the Eastern Sector,*" said the newscaster. "*Alliance Command reports huge inroads at this point and suggests a potentially decisive response to the threat. Secretary Lopez has promised a press release, to explain his long-term plan for the region…*"

The image showed ships advancing through a star system. Riggs recognised neither the ships, nor the sector. He'd heard rumours of the Navy repurposing fleets, but such talk was cheap. There was probably no truth in it. The news clip was as likely a stock image from the first Krell War, as evidence of a new deployment.

"This is your people, yes?" Mikhailov muttered.

"They're not my people any more."

"They say that Jenkins' Jackals made it out of Kronstadt," Mikhailov said. His accent was thick and Slavic, and every word that came out of his mouth had the edge of intimidation to it.

Riggs knew that the man was trying to aggravate him, and he wished that it wasn't working. "There's no proof of that."

"They escaped at Darkwater too, as I hear it."

"That wasn't my fault."

"But Warlord blames you, yes?"

"It isn't like that," Riggs said, although he knew that in truth it was exactly like that. One hand dropped to his data-ports, and he felt the urge to get into the tanks once again. He'd make this good. He'd solve this.

"Now Alliance say they can turn war. Is this right?"

"It's propaganda," Riggs declared. "Pure propaganda. They're losing, and they know it."

"Hmmm," said Mikhailov. "There are a lot of ships in this sector. Many come here."

"That doesn't mean anything."

"This is different. They are definitely planning something."

"They plan, we plan," Riggs said, with a feigned air of nonchalance. "That's the way it works. But are we going to sit around here all day, or get on with this? Time's wasting."

"Very well. Major wishes to see you."

Riggs exhaled through his nose. "Good. That's good."

He stood from the table. Rearranged his atmo hood, so that it covered almost all his face. Despite Riggs' bold talk of the Spiral's control over Shangri VI, he would rather avoid capture if at all possible. Mikhailov smoothed down his uniform but otherwise didn't move.

"You want to watch that neckline," Riggs rebuked. "Your gang markings are showing."

Mikhailov nodded and pulled at the collar of his uniform. The tip of a tattoo was visible there. Crude, not a powered marking like many proper soldiers had. Words in Cyrillic script. Riggs had seen those markings before and knew exactly what they meant. SONS OF BALASH: that was what the text translated as. Leon Novak—a member of Riggs' former squad—had once been a Son of Balash. Membership of the organisation was prohibited throughout the Alliance, and their leader had become infamous in certain circles. Riggs was eager to meet her.

"So where is she?" Riggs asked, confused by the fact that Mikhailov still sat at the table.

"She's here," Mikhailov said.

The whir of an old exo-suit's motor touched the air, and Riggs felt the hairs on the back of his neck stand on end. Something animated from the corner of his vision.

"Disciple," came a grating old voice.

The beggar from the street corner shuffled up to the table. Except that she wasn't the beggar any more. Now she stood straighter, taller. Something altogether darker replaced the lost expression on her face. The transformation was remarkable. Frightening, even.

Mikhailov's smile broadened. He appeared to be enjoying Riggs' reaction.

"I introduce the Major Mish Vasnev to you, Disciple Riggs," he said.

The old woman looked Riggs up and down. Her gaze was almost wilting in effect.

"You are younger than I expected," she said. "This is surprising."

Riggs swallowed. "Warlord wants to know that you can do this," he started, finding his voice. "He wants to know that he isn't throwing this money away."

"Since when do Spiral care for money?" the woman said.

"Why didn't you tell me you were already here?" Riggs countered. "I've been waiting for the last twenty days. I've seen you every day!"

Vasnev's face barely moved. "We make checks. My Sons, they do not work with just anybody."

"You . . . you could've been captured," Riggs said.

"Hiding in plain sight," said the old woman. "This is sometimes best way to be."

Riggs wanted to be angry, wanted to argue, but there was something completely disarming about the woman's aura. He was almost speechless in her presence. A tight knot formed in his stomach. This was what doubt felt like. But he knew that there was no going back now. The deal had been done, and whether Riggs wanted to work with these people or not, the Spiral's plan needed them. This was one pact, with one organisation. Across the Alliance, other such agreements were being made, by other Spiral agents.

It's all for a purpose, Riggs thought. *All for the greater goal.* He felt the swell of determination in his chest, and it finally swallowed his doubt. This was the only way. He was going to show Warlord what he was capable of. He was going to show them all.

"The starship is not far," Vasnev said. She placed a battered old forage cap on her head, the Russian military badge on the front polished to a sheen. "We go now."

"Come," said Mikhailov.

Major Mish Vasnev, head of the Sons of Balash, turned into the street. Mikhailov and Riggs followed in her wake. The trio disappeared into the crowd.

CHAPTER ONE

RAID ON VEKTAH MINOR

Space was bright with plasma fire.

"Is it too much to ask that you just get us down there in one piece?" I argued as the dropship made another sudden jink. Safety-harnesses held the occupants of the troop cabin in place, but we were still liberally thrown around. There was a harsh clatter as armour struck armour.

"Christo!" said the dropship's pilot. "You Sim Ops are all the same. This isn't as easy as it looks."

"Who cares?" growled Novak. "Are plenty more bodies where these came from."

Lopez shrugged, lifting a perfectly arched eyebrow behind the face-plate of her tactical-helmet. "Can't make an omelette without breaking eggs, right?"

We were somewhere in the Drift, on the outer edge of the Maelstrom, and approaching the planet Vektah Minor. An ancient Krell dynasty that Science Division had labelled the Red Claw Collective once occupied this sector. The Red Claw was one of many Collectives that had fallen to the Harbinger virus, and that was the very reason space was currently on fire.

I was in a new state-of-the-art simulant, armoured in a Class X Pathfinder combat-suit, and armed with an M125 plasma battle-rifle. Printed across my torso was my callsign CALIFORNIA, along with other miscellaneous battle-honours. Most importantly, a stylised dog-head was stencilled on my shoulder-guard.

"The orbital defences have woken up," said the co-pilot. "We can expect the drop to get hotter from here on down."

"Hot, I can take," said Feng, chewing the words around his mouth. "Scalding? Not so much."

I scanned the battle-net, both visually through the images projected onto my HUD, and mentally via my combat-suit's neural-link. The net was constantly refreshed with data from our dropship and the other nineteen ships that were also involved in the mission. Among the squads on those transports were such stalwarts of the Sim Ops Programme as Tsung's Finest, Walker's Dead, the Gallow Dancers, and even Phoenix Squad.

Our current mothership was the UAS *Providence*. The strikeship was the base of operations for this mission, and where our real bodies currently lay in state: immersed in simulator-tanks, remotely operating the simulants via neural-link. The entire strike-force—all twenty dropships, and all forty squads—was composed of simulants. Another stolen glance at the surrounding battle space made it pretty clear that simulants were a necessity for an operation like this. We were being hit, and hard.

Lopez was reviewing the same data, and she sucked her teeth. "Got to be said: when the Alliance goes to war, it puts on a damn good show."

"When *Sim Ops* goes to war," Feng corrected. "It's us doing the dying, Lopez."

"I hear that," Novak growled, rousing from his seat.

Our Cougar's cabin was tightly packed with two squads of troopers. Each wore a tactical-helmet, like mine, with the visor semi-polarised so that the wearer inside was only just visible.

These were my dogs: *Jenkins' Jackals*. My HUD showed the biological signs for each trooper, confirming that they were at optimum combat-performance. A carefully balanced cocktail of combat-drugs kept them that way.

"Is going to be fine, people," Novak drawled in his laconic Slavic accent. "Is all under control."

Private Leon Novak—callsign CONVICT—was strapped into the seat opposite me. His face was blunt and hard. In his real skin, Novak was covered in tattoos and scars. The tattoos were the reward for decades as an enforcer for the Old Earth *bratva*, while the scars were the prize for his time under my command.

Novak stroked the hilt of a sheathed knife, taped to his thigh. He carried a bewildering selection of weapons across his armour. His Pathfinder suit was covered in Cyrillic script and crude pictograms; imitations of the markings on his real skin, back on the strikeship. Novak's dark eyes widened and twitched as he tracked the Cougar's external cams. He was almost entranced by the flashes of light and explosions that populated the interior of his HUD

"Is beautiful, yes?" he said.

"Only you could describe something like this as 'beautiful', Novak," replied Lopez.

PFC Gabriella Lopez—callsign SENATOR, after her father—sat beside Novak. She too was watching the conflict, but her reaction was very different. Lopez was the daughter of Secretary of Defence Rodrigo Lopez. Some said that Lopez Senior was the greatest man in politics, while others said that he was the most dangerous. Whatever the truth, he was a serious future contender for the position of Alliance Secretary General. My Lopez was smart, sharp and pretty: another dangerous combination.

Her dark, curly hair was pulled back from her angular face; a pale moon behind the visor. Like Novak, she looked very different in her real body. She was the product of an opulent upbringing, and had enjoyed the benefit of the best skin-sculptors in human space.

There'd been a time when Lopez had struggled with military leadership, and I'd questioned whether she was taking it seriously. But now I knew who she really was. She caught my eye, through her face-plate, and gave a slight nod. That communicated everything I needed to hear from her. *I'm ready for this*, the look told me. *I'm hungry for this.* Lopez had a Widowmaker sidearm holstered on her thigh, and she kept one hand there, the other on the strap of her seat, prepared to disengage when the moment came.

The Cougar shuddered again. In no sort of formation, the dropships made hard thrust towards the objective, moving at maximum velocity. They were streaks of light against the blackness of space; engines firing on all cylinders. Each laid down a blistering wall of weapons-fire as the battlegroup advanced, filling near-space with missiles and defensive flak-gun fire.

"Hey, what warheads are you carrying?"

The question was directed at the Cougar's crew, but it pulled me back into the cabin. It came from PFC Chu Feng—callsign CHINO, former Directorate clone-trooper, latterly turned Alliance simulant operator. Of all the Jackals, Feng's simulants looked most similar to his real skin. He was muscular and broad, which made his boyish-looking face almost out of place. Feng had been custom-grown in an Asiatic Directorate military creche, and his features were a handsome South Asian mix.

"Banshee-type 3As," said the pilot. "For the air-to-air, at least."

"What about for ground targets?" asked Feng, leaning forward in his seat.

The co-pilot clucked his tongue. "This guy knows his stuff, right? We've got Delta 3s, cluster munition. That satisfy you?"

"Interested to see how they work out, is all," said Feng.

There were two flyboys in the pit. I'd never flown with them before, but they were both veterans, and operating next-generation simulants.

"Ah, ma'am," asked another voice. "Permission to speak freely?"

I swivelled my head and searched for the speaker. The name REED, PIERRE and the rank CORPORAL flashed up on my HUD, by way of identification. Reed was from the other squad being dropped in our Cougar: Reed's Rippers. Unfortunately, the squad name appeared to be ironic, because the Rippers were about as green as they came. They were fresh meat for the grinder, wearing recon-suits that denoted their junior role on the operation.

Corporal Reed looked very young; his ruddy complexion visible through his face-plate. The simulant tech is weird like that. The cloning process was supposed to capture the operator in his or her prime, and to breed a sim that represented the best that a user could be, but so many operators coming up through the ranks were barely in their prime. Reed was such an example; his simulant's nose was freckled, and he looked too young to be playing soldiers.

"Go on, kid," I offered.

"Is it true? What they say about the Jackals, I mean?"

Now *that* was a question. People said a lot of things about the Jackals. Some good, others not so much.

The kid could've been referring to our achievements in the war to date. The Jackals had rescued the Pariah from North Star Station. We'd been on Kronstadt in the hours before it fell. We'd secured vital intelligence on a third alien species, the so-called Aeon.

On the other hand, the Jackals had gone rogue. We'd disobeyed standing orders by not returning to Unity Base after our mission into the Gyre. My Jackals had even worked against the Alliance on Darkwater Farm, under the auspices of former Lieutenant-Colonel Harris, the legend also known as Lazarus.

And that wasn't even the worst of it. Reed eyed up Feng, sidelong, reminding me that there was still hostility towards the trooper. Through no fault of his own, Feng's loyalty to the Alliance had faltered during the closing stages of the Kronstadt operation. He had been "activated" as an enemy agent by his creator, Surgeon-Major Tang. Science Division had removed the control module from Feng's skull, and given him a clean bill of health, but that wasn't exactly reassuring. They'd done just the same prior to his activation: no one had even realised that Feng was carrying around Directorate tech in his skull until it was too late.

It was Lopez who spoke in Feng's defence. She narrowed her eyes.

"What exactly *have* you heard, trooper?" she asked, pointedly.

Reed looked nervous, as though he was worried he'd insulted us.

"That y'all have done this before," he said. "That you've seen infected Krell, up close."

I was relieved that we weren't going to have a situation here.

Lopez nodded and answered for the squad. "It's true. No big deal. They die just like anything else."

"Is this your first transition, Corporal?" I asked.

Reed's squad nodded in unity.

"First combat transition, ma'am," Reed said. "We're damn glad to be going in with the Jackals."

Novak made another grunting sound, which he probably intended to be a laugh. Lopez provided some encouragement.

"Everyone has to start somewhere," she said. "We've all been through it."

There was a chime over the joint battle-net.

"Stow it, troopers," I said. "Incoming comm." I thought-activated my suit's communications-system and accepted the transmission. "This is California. We read you, Command."

"This is *Providence* SOC," came the response. "You're looking good, Jackals. Your feeds are clear."

I recognised the voice. Zero—Sergeant Zoe Campbell—was the squad's intelligence handler. She was currently aboard the UAS *Providence*, in orbit around Vektah Minor, manning the Simulant Operations Centre. From there, she watched the op via our combat-suit video-feeds, and monitored intelligence provided by other Alliance assets in the theatre. Zero was the squad's lynchpin and a great intel officer.

"Looks hot and heavy down there," Zero said. I could sense the smile in her voice, and imagine her poised over the vid-terminals, hungrily drinking in every aspect of the mission.

"Just how the LT likes it," Feng added.

"Just how *you* like it, if the rumours are to be believed," Lopez countered. "Or that's what Zero says after a few drinks, anyhow."

Feng blushed and fell silent. He and Zero were having some sort of relationship—the details of which weren't really known to me, and to be honest, I didn't really want to know. Zero and I went way back, and we were friends more than anything else, but she was a big girl now and she had to make her own mistakes . . .

Zero was a little too professional to take Lopez's bait, and she ignored the comment.

"Standby for mission update," she said. "Captain Heinrich wants to give a further briefing."

"Captain wants to give us briefing *now*?" Novak probed. "We have fiery ass!"

Lopez sighed. "You mean we have fire *on* our ass, right?"

"Is what I said," Novak muttered.

"We're ready to receive, Zero," I said.

Putting it as neutrally as I could, Captain Heinrich was a piece of work. His face appeared as a transparent blue holo, right in front of mine, and he scowled critically. Even though he was addressing the entire strike-force, I couldn't help but feel that the expression was directed at me. Heinrich and I had never got along, and the Jackals' most recent foray into the Maelstrom hadn't changed that. Although I'd travelled light-years to escape Heinrich's command, history had a funny way of repeating itself, and Jenkins' Jackals had fallen back under his leadership.

Heinrich had a youthful appearance; more boy than officer, and the moustache that graced his upper lip was blond and thin, somehow making him look younger still, although it was obvious that the opposite had been his intention. He wore formal Alliance Army uniform, which bristled with accolades and badges, and his bright blue eyes peered out from beneath an officer's cap. Although he seemed to know an awful lot about it, Heinrich had never actually been in combat. He was the epitome of a desk jockey; a real REMF. Heinrich held a senior post in the Simulant Operations Programme, but he wasn't actually *operational*: he wasn't even capable of operating a sim.

He solemnly pursed his lips, and I had no doubt that he was assessing the data-feeds, tracking the progress of every dropship individually. "Micro-management" was Heinrich's middle name.

"Listen up, troopers," he said. "This is Captain Heinrich, aboard the *Providence*." He paused dramatically. "You all have your orders, but you can expect the LZ to be hot. The Krell down there are infected, and this place is crawling with the Harbinger virus."

"Tell us something we do not already know," Novak muttered.

Heinrich neither heard nor responded to him. I'd muted Novak's line so that he couldn't communicate with Command.

"There can be no deviation from your orders. Follow them to the letter. In the case of extraction, we have further dropships ready for launch. You'll be sent back into the fray until we can secure the objective. In T minus two minutes, the spearhead will breach Vektah's orbital defences. That's when things are really going to get dangerous."

Across the cabin, Reed's squad collectively grimaced. The Jackals remained cool. We'd all heard this sort of spiel from Heinrich before. He had a way with words, to say the least.

"The Science Division ships are to be protected at all costs," Heinrich said.

On the external cams, those ships towards the centre of our flight group were highlighted. They were heavier, bulkier craft; up-armoured, much bigger than the Cougars. They reminded me of civilian cargo haulers, except these ships were equipped with null-shields and carried automatic cannons on their noses. Their grey camouflaged hulls were plastered with the Science Division badge.

"Exfiltration of the target requires that the Science

Division transports get down to the surface. Once the spearhead makes planetfall, I want a foothold established. The primary objective is to secure a specimen.

"For those squads with special orders, you know what to do," Heinrich said. That was obviously directed at the Jackals. We had the most special order of all. "Support assets are inbound."

There was only one asset that mattered. Despite myself, I thought-activated my scanner and watched its progress. Even without checking the battle-net, I knew that the asset was still alive.

"No slip-ups," Heinrich said. "I want this done by the book. Do me proud. For the Alliance."

His words were echoed over the channel, both from our ship and across the whole strike-force.

"One final reminder," Heinrich said. "You all know the protocol. Last man standing initiates the hammer fall. Captain Heinrich out."

The briefing ended, and the channel closed.

"Sorry about that," Zero said. "Captain Heinrich insisted. But like I said, your feeds are looking good."

Another chime on the comm, this time accompanied by a shuddering of the Cougar's chassis that suggested a particularly violent manoeuvre.

"You might want to quit your blabbing, trooper," said the pilot. "We've just made atmospheric entry. You're about to start earning your pay."

"I hear you," I said. Back to Zero: "Jackals out."

"Solid copy. Kill some fishes for me."

A range-finder that signalled the expected distance to the LZ appeared in the corner of my HUD.

"Eyes on the prize," I said. "We're coming up on the target. Here we go."

We were landing during what passed for morning on Vektah Minor. It was a planet swathed in jungle and primordial forests. Thick clouds cloyed the atmosphere, while the foliage beneath was cloaked by dense, choking marsh gas.

"Two klicks out from Nest Station Gamma," the co-pilot confirmed.

Nest Station Gamma: our objective. The largest Krell settlement on Vektah Minor.

"Christo and Gaia..." the pilot said. "You might want to get a look at this place before you get dirtside."

According to intel, the planet beneath us had once been a thriving Krell nest-world. The Krell liked things hot, wet, humid as all hell, and green. *Very* green, usually. But if that was how Vektah Minor had once appeared, it was now anything but. The Harbinger virus had come to Vektah and claimed its dues.

The Cougar screamed low over a brackish, dead swamp, and advanced on a forest. Or rather, the remains of one. The trees of the alien jungle had been replaced with black, crystalline forgeries, twisted effigies of what they had once been. Petrified like burnt wood. Further mountainous black structures tipped the skyline.

"What in the Core is that?" asked Reed.

His voice trailed off. The Cougar cut through the mists, gliding lower now, and the landscape changed again. Something rose out of the desiccated forest. Coralline and almost waspish; an ant-mound of epic proportions. The construction was honeycombed and studded with further living structures.

"That's our target," I said.

"It's infected, right?" Reed asked.

It was hard to argue with that. Most of the nest had turned black, and parts of the coral had died. Fluid wept from the open orifices, like blood from a wound, and veins of silver criss-crossed the nest's outer surface.

Lopez looked over at Reed. "All Krell tech is prone to

infection from the Harbinger virus. This is what happens on every infected planet."

"Firing countermeasures!" yelled the pilot, as the Cougar jinked sharply. "The locals are waking up."

"Looks like several weapons emplacements," Feng concluded.

Lopez nodded. "And more in the direction we're heading."

Bio-plasma boiled up from the jungle, tracing a bright blue arc across the sky.

The dropship banked starboard. The pilot had needle-sharp reactions, but despite his simulated senses, he wasn't fast enough. I heard the patter of small arms fire against the hull, saw the flash of the null-shield activating as it repelled energy-based weapons. The Cougar spat out flares and decoy drones, and fire chased us lower still.

"This is Angel One, this is Angel One," said the pilot. "We are encountering heavy resistance. All Cougars, be aware."

The Cougar launched missiles into the jungle. Krell bodies scattered, and the landscape was soon on fire. Other Cougars were dropping in behind us, clustered around the Sci-Div transports. They got the same welcome. In some cases, even worse.

"*Angel Three is hit!*" came a squawk. "*Angel Three going down!*"

"*Angel Four, taking heavy fire. Repeat, heavy fire.*"

"*Angel Seven has taken an impact. We've lost yaw control, and—*"

The voices bubbled from the Cougar's console. On my HUD, lights winked out: turning from green, which meant operational, to red, which meant extracted. A list of casualties began to scroll there, too. But even as I watched, some names were deleted from the list, and icons flashed green again. As each trooper died, they were being sent back into combat in a new body.

Our dropship's deck lurched as it fired volley after volley into the landscape. The gunfire against the hull intensified.

DISTANCE TO LZ: FIVE HUNDRED METRES...

"Kicking in the retro-thrusters," the co-pilot said.

"Do it," said the pilot. "We're dropping our cargo."

The Cougar's engine pitch changed. The dropship decelerated, and its VTOL engines activated. Those would allow the ship to hover for a limited period.

"Jackals, ready!" I yelled. "Get moving!"

The safety-harnesses retracted. Troopers grabbed weapons. We all carried plasma rifles, but other weapons—ranging from Widowmaker pistols to a variety of grenades—were strapped across armoured thighs and chests. It's fair to say that you can never have enough methods of killing the enemy on a simulant operation. For this mission, each of us also carried more esoteric, non-lethal equipment. Novak had a huge metal tube strapped to his pack, while the rest of us were equipped with shock-batons.

"Deploying rear ramp in three..."

"You ready, kid?" I asked Reed.

He nodded. "I think so."

"Two..."

"Stick with us," said Lopez, giving the kid an encouraging smile, "and you'll do fine."

I was excited. Damned excited. I'm ashamed to say that war has that effect on me.

"One!" the pilot completed.

"EVAMPS ready!" I commanded.

Each of us carried an EVAMP—an "extra-vehicular mobility pack". The EVAMP was a thruster unit that allowed for flight in zero-G, or limited "bounces" plan-etside.

The rear ramp yawned open, and hell waited for us below.

A volley of living ammunition peppered the inside of the Cougar. Flesh-ripper flechettes sparkled blue as they trailed bio-energy, and the Jackals hunkered down, their null-shields activating. Reed and his squad were torn apart by enemy fire. The Rippers' reactions were a second—a fraction of a second, maybe—too slow. Where the Krell were concerned, that was more than enough. The shredded bodies of all five troopers collapsed in the mouth of the cabin, tumbled down the ramp. Life-signs extinct.

"Reed's down!" Lopez yelled.

A primary-form—a member of the Krell warrior-worker caste—erupted from the jungle, and tore through the bodies.

"Yeah, Rippers is about right…" Feng said, without any hint of irony.

"Just make sure that we don't end up like them," I ordered. "Repressing fire."

"Who wants to live for ever, yes?" Novak roared, the words a battle-cry as he launched out of the dropship, his EVAMP flaring.

All I could hear was Novak's uproarious laughter, as though it was the funniest damn thing he had ever experienced.

CHAPTER TWO

NEST STATION GAMMA

We emerged from the dropship into a nightmare made real.

Enormous trees covered the area, but they were twisted, warped, blackened things that barely resembled their terrestrial counterpart. Beneath the canopy of black-green foliage, there was another world; hidden from the spy-eyes and orbital surveillance of the Alliance fleet. The terrain was swampy, dense, with more of the vaporous mist clinging to the ground. Without the benefit of a tactical-helmet, visibility would've been shot to shit. Mobility was similarly hampered. We were knee-deep in brackish water, if this really was water, and not some alien equivalent. Beneath my boots the ground was soft and squishy. I couldn't shake the feeling that the thick vines and roots lacing the forest floor were actually moving...

"Go, go!" the Cougar's pilot yelled, over the comms. "Covering fire, keep your heads down!"

"Copy that," I shouted back. "On the bounce, Jackals."

The Cougar hovered behind us. Its chin-gun—a forty-millimetre automatic cannon—swept the jungle.

Krell bodies disintegrated under the weight of fire. The Jackals advanced through the swamp, moving in tandem, using bio-scanners and sensor-suites to pinpoint targets. Shapes loomed out of the mist. I fired from the hip as I moved.

The Cougar's engines roared. Backwash from the VTOL unit flattened a ring of trees around our position.

"We're taking fire!" the co-pilot said.

He was right: the Cougar was attracting a *lot* of fire. The dropship's null-shields flared as it ablated heavier Krell weaponry. The Cougar was a big, slow target this close to the ground.

"Missiles out," the pilot said.

Missiles snaked across the landscape. The Jackals hustled and hunkered down as the warheads impacted. Clods of earth, tree, Krell and bone showered our location. Our null-shields took the worst of it, although some debris bounced off my armour.

"Push on towards the objective," I ordered.

"The bio-scanner is going wild," said Feng. "Multiple targets."

Krell spilt out of the nest. Using all six limbs, the aliens made rapid progress through and across the structure, or took up vantage points from which to snipe down at us. The Cougar made short work of them. Rounds pummelled the structure, and splinters of black coral rained down on us.

"*Angel Twelve is going down!*" someone declared over the joint comms.

Further down the line, barely visible, a fireball erupted in the sky. The wreckage spun for a second, then crashed somewhere in the jungle.

TSUNG'S FINEST EXTRACTED, my HUD said.

"Too bad," I declared. "Zero, do you copy?"

"Affirmative, ma'am," said Zero. "The Sci-Div shuttles are about to go dirtside."

"We see them," I said. I was shooting as I spoke, aware that I couldn't lose concentration for even a second.

A pair of Cougar dropships provided close protection to the Sci-Div transports. Those were converted Wildcat shuttles; slower than Cougars, but with a heavier lift capacity. Two of the three shuttles were hit by heavy bio-fire, and went down before they reached the landing zone. The third touched down in a clearing at the foot of the nest. The shuttle's rear ramp immediately deployed, and more simulant squads piled out. Rather than proper Army, these were Sci-Div security officers. They were armed with TT-5 trench sweeper plasma carbines—higher-powered weaponry, but with a shorter range. Immediately, weapons-fire flashed through the milky twilight.

"Fuckers are doing it," Lopez declared.

The Sci-Div away team was met by a hail of bio-fire, but this was a numbers game. Enough of the security force survived the landing, and the initial onslaught, to establish a perimeter. The troopers planted metal rods in the ground, and as each went in, it began to crackle with blue energy. The rods connected to make a domed null-shield that extended over the camp, holding off enemy fire.

BEACHHEAD SECURE, my HUD updated.

"Assisting fire inbound," Zero suggested.

A piercing whine split the air. Almost immediately, a half-dozen Tac-3 strike fighters appeared on the horizon—their swept-back wings instantly recognisable, engines blazing bright blue through the dense mist.

"Danger close!" I declared.

The fighters took a low pass over our location, strafing

the upper levels of Nest Base Gamma with their automatic cannons. The infected Krell leapt from their vantage points, tumbling around us. Some were caught by Cougars, as more dropships made planetfall, while others were picked off by simulant squads.

The tac fighters passed by, their strafing run complete. They were closely followed by a wing of Needler bio-fighters. Their hulls were sleek and seamless, and their prows bone-sharp: the Krell counterpart of Alliance technology. The Needlers chased off the tac fighters, plasma guns strobing.

"Sweet, sweet Christo!" Feng exclaimed, although he sounded more excited than frightened. "Now we really are in the shit!"

Lopez howled. "Take that, you infected fucks!"

ADVANCE, my HUD commanded. ADVANCE.

"That's our cue to hustle, troopers," I said.

Half my mind still focused on shooting, I identified an opening in the side of the nest. The portal yawned darkly; like the mouth of an organic cave, a possible refuge from the fighting. With a thought-command, I logged it on my battle-grid.

"Go, go," I said. "In there."

The world still burning around us, the Jackals stormed inside. The open orifice was the biological equivalent of a hatch, and it clamped shut behind us. The interior of the nest was shadowy and dank. My tactical-helmet immediately adapted, and the multi-sense package kicked in: painting the entry tunnel in lurid green light.

"Deploy drones," I said.

Each of the Jackals carried a half-dozen surveillance drones, nestled into our life-support packs. The drones disengaged and activated anti-gravity motors. Their purpose was to map the inside of the nest, to give us intel on the safest and quickest route into the bowels of the facility. As one, they disappeared into the shafts that branched off the main tunnel, their drives whirring softly as they went.

A sick wail filled the air, loud enough that it was audible over the chatter of weapons-fire from outside. Feng cocked his head, listening, and Lopez shivered. It felt as though the very nest base was crying out in pain: the noise coming from the walls, from the swamp-wet deck.

But before we could question the noise, Novak was up and firing his plasma rifle.

"We have the company!" he declared.

Dark shapes disengaged from the ribbed walls and dropped from the deckheads.

The Krell were on us.

There was a smooth action to the process, a sort of rhythm to our attack. It felt a lot like a training simulation.

Aim.

Fire.

Repeat.

Aim.

Fire.

Repeat.

Through the haphazard arrangement of tunnels and chambers we went, literally pushing against the tide of Krell. Wave after wave crashed against us.

The walls, floors and deckhead were covered in sinewy, muscle-like flesh. Everything in here was alive, and it was hard not to think of biological analogies everywhere I looked. Tunnels—*veins*—spread out into the distance. Smaller shafts—*capillaries*—branched off from them. We passed chambers filled with control consoles—*organs*— that churned and screamed. The structure hummed and throbbed and pulsed.

"Fire in the hold," Feng said, as he pumped a grenade

into a chamber. Krell grafted to living machinery disappeared in a wave of fire.

Military Intelligence and Science Division had estimated that there were likely to be several thousand Krell war-forms stationed at Nest Base Gamma. The planet itself, and therefore the nest, was irrevocably contaminated with the Harbinger virus. It had probably been infected in the earlier stages of the epidemic, perhaps one of the first outbreaks. That explained the black coral, and the tranches of infected jungle. It was Science Division's theory that such a critically colonised outpost would eventually enter terminal decline. Mili-Intel was therefore reasonably confident that Nest Base Gamma would be a weak target.

You see the problem there?

Phrases like "reasonably sure": they work on paper. They aren't so reassuring when you're looking down the business end of a Krell spiker. The Simulant Operations Programme was no stranger to audacity where mission execution was concerned—after all, when you go to war in a body that isn't coming back, you can afford to take risks—but this was something else. There's a thin line between courage and recklessness. Looking at the mission statistics, it seemed High Command had very firmly crossed it...

"Watch that corner!" I yelled.

Feng blasted apart a Krell thrall—original designation completely unknowable, from the twisted husk of a thing that remained after Harbinger had taken root—and two more took its place.

"Fucking fishes!" Novak lambasted, taking them out with a frenzied blast from his plasma rifle. He turned to Feng. "Thank me later, Chino."

Feng nodded, tossed a grenade back the way that we had come. The Krell were attempting to cut off our escape route, and more bio-signs coalesced behind us. The entire base bristled, its corrupted soul screaming at our intrusion.

My HUD continued to fill with data. The drones were now well inside the nest. They were flagging hostiles, painting possible targets for us, and the Jackals responded to that data.

"Push on," I ordered.

Sure, if it got too hot we could extract and just come back, but I didn't much savour the prospect of fighting our way back into the nest. The other simulant squads were getting the same welcome. My battle-net was a clusterfuck of distress signals, of bio-signs, of extraction and transition markers. The sound of conflict—from the pitched scream of exotic Krell bio-weaponry, through to the bass pulse of plasma weaponry firing—filled the tunnel. The structure shuddered with impacts, and I had no doubt that air support was still doing its thing, pouring fire on the defending forces.

We cleared enough hostiles to reach the next junction.

"Jesus, this place stinks," Lopez said, gasping for breath.

Nausea threatened to engulf me. It receded after a second or so, as my Pathfinder suit dumped a shitload of combat-drugs into my bloodstream. Got to love those sweet, sweet drugs. I checked the rest of my team's vitals. They, too, were feeling it, and I thought-commanded another dose of combat-drugs direct for each of them as well.

"Keep your atmo-filters running," Feng suggested.

"I am!"

"You get used to smell, yes?" Novak suggested, as he slammed the butt of his rifle into the face of another deformed thrall. "Is like Pariah's scent."

"P's smell is different," argued Lopez. "These infected bastards…I'll never get used to that."

The nest was foetid, rotten. The facility's living components were choked with floral blooms and infection-nodes. I switched on my shoulder-lamps—throwing bright beams of light across the tunnel walls—and saw motes of diseased matter drifting in the air, like pollen from an infected plant. New growths, composed of black, shiny material, sprouted from the deck, creating weird, asymmetrical shapes. A flash of activity overhead caught my attention. There were shafts along the ceiling, and a shape formed there, lining up with a hook-nosed bio-rifle.

"Check the ceilings!"

"I see it," Feng said, dropping to a knee and bringing up his rifle.

The Krell raked Feng with barb-rounds; flechettes formed of a compound as hard as any Alliance munition.

"Fuck!" Feng yelped.

His null-shield took the worst of it, but some rounds penetrated the field. An alert appeared on my HUD.

But I had no time to worry about that. A primary-form burst out of another shaft in the wall, and I opened fire. The Krell was a ragged mess of a thing, covered in lesions and sores. And not just the body itself; the alien's equipment—from its shredded bio-suit to the plethora of living artefacts grafted to its carcass—was equally riddled. I put two shots in the xeno's head.

Feng staggered, one hand to his chest.

The Krell sensed weakness. As one, they surged towards us. More bio-fire split the air, accompanied by the angry shrieks of the infected horde.

"Fall back to the last junction," I suggested.

Except, I realised, that wasn't an option either. Bio-signs were massing behind us. Krell thralls scuttled along the ceilings, clutching the ribbed walls with claw-tipped appendages. Novak turned, pumped another grenade.

"Fuck you all!" he roared, as bone-shards pattered against his armour.

I twisted about-face. A primary-form—big, armour-plated, with claws outstretched—loomed out of nowhere. It lurched towards me. Reflexively, I slammed my plasma rifle into the xeno's cranium. The force was enough to split the creature's skull. It spouted ichor.

The Krell were all around us.

"Just…wait…" I gasped.

A signal appeared on my HUD. Flickering in and out of existence, as though the entity responsible for it could somehow control its own bio-signature.

Something grazed the edge of my consciousness.

Burning bright and leaving a trail of fire, what could've been mistaken for a comet dropped from the heavens.

This, however, was no comet. It was a Krell Type 3 bio-pod. Aerodynamic, made for speed, but also armoured, covered in a shell-like carapace that protected its single occupant.

Although I couldn't see any of this, I could *experience* it: both as battle-net data through the neural-link of my combat-suit, and as something far more visceral, through my connection with the pod's user. Of course, "user" was hardly the correct word. The pod's sole passenger was snugly encased in living tissue, soft-wired into the actual transport.

"We are inbound," it intoned, over the general comms-net, updating Command.

Pariah—more commonly known to Jenkins' Jack-als as good ol' P—took a more direct route down to the surface than the rest of the squad. P was the product of an aborted covert operations programme, run out of North Star Station by Science Division. Courtesy of the Black Spiral, P was also one of a kind: the Spiral terrorist organisation had been responsible for taking down North Star, and terminating Pariah's creator.

Right now, P had an express ticket, straight down the pipe. It had been launched within seconds of our dropship, and penetrated the upper atmosphere at about the same time, but whereas the Alliance Army and Aerospace Force had attracted a lot of enemy attention, P—being a fish and all—had not. P's pod slid right through the Krell's defensive line. The xeno had selected a landing sight away from the main combat zone. That had slowed its arrival, although not by much.

P had never been to Nest Base Gamma before, or even Vektah Minor, but that was fine. The Krell's memory didn't work like that of a human. As the alien's clawed feet made contact with the corrupted hull of the nest base, it just knew what to do, where to go. Deepknowing filled the creature's mind. Six limbs spread, embracing the diseased carcass of the base. It found an aperture that had the uncomfortable architecture of a sphincter and breached the facility.

We are in, it said.

The words sort of penetrated my head, like unwelcome visitors. We were still too far apart to use conventional communications, and P was several klicks distant of my position, so this...*connection*, or whatever the fuck it was, was the best that we could do.

The alien's senses were both familiar and foreign to me. It smelt the air, tasting the rot. That atmosphere would be perilous to a native-strain Krell, but not to P. Possibly as a result of its detachment from the Krell Collective, P was immune to Harbinger.

The xeno used all sets of its claws to grab for handholds, quickly scuttling down the corridor. It followed a direction-sense that I couldn't even begin to understand. It knew, without any equipment at all, where we were located. P could even sense the electrical output of the other assault teams, although their positions were equally distant to ours.

Watch yourself in there, I said, sensing the dark around the alien coming to life. *We're encountering heavy resistance.*

We know, P answered me.

Pariah reached the first Krell. It had once been a tertiary-form, and although not as big as Pariah, its muscle mass was still significant, and I doubted whether *mano a mano* even a simulant in full Pathfinder armour would be capable of bringing the thing down. It bristled with spiked appendages and chitinous hide.

P stood its ground.

Don't take risks! I yelled.

We do not take risks.

The tertiary-form paused...

Then shrank back into shadow. The rest of the Collective did just the same; heads bowed, limbs clutched against dying bodies. Like a pack of dogs, cowed by the alpha.

What the hell just happened?

They are afraid, P said. *They know what we are here to do.*

CHAPTER THREE

STRANGE FISH

And then the mind-link cut.

I was getting better at understanding the connection, that was for sure. When P had started doing this strange psychic bullshit, I'd found it overwhelming, which is not exactly a good place to be when you're in the middle of a warzone. Now, it was more manageable. My bio-rhythms barely spiked as the link broke.

"Hold up!" I ordered. For the first time since we'd breached the nest, I could actually catch my breath.

A shadow separated from the rest.

Krell-shaped, but bigger. Different. More alien...

Pariah stomped down the corridor. Its enormous body almost filled the tunnel.

"Pariah-form reporting for duty," came a monotone voice over the comms-net.

P deployed both barb-guns from its forearms. The weapons were biological extensions; bulky, pistol-like armaments that the alien could conceal within its own body when necessary. It raised the weapons, threat crackling around it like an aura.

"What's happening?" Lopez asked, the shock apparent in her voice.

"I . . . I'm not sure," I answered.

Feng lifted his rifle to fire on the retreating thralls, but I held up a hand to stop him.

"Cease fire, Feng."

The Harbinger abandoned their assault. They slithered back into the walls, away from the path of our fire. We'd already taken down a lot of them—steaming piles of corpses were stacked up at each junction we'd passed—but that wasn't what had disrupted the attack.

That accolade went to P. It was solely down to Pariah, and nothing else.

"These *strigoi* do not like you so much, fish head," Novak said.

Strigoi: that was Novak's word for the Harbinger-infected Krell.

"The infected Kindred do not appreciate our presence," P said by way of explanation.

The alien had a crude augmentation grafted to its sternum; a battered metal voice-box that acted as an external speaker. In contrast to its physical appearance, P spoke in a flat robotic tone. The words were broadcast straight to our suits, over the general squad channel.

"Good to see you, P," I said. I kicked at the corpse of a primary-form. "Things were getting a little hairy there."

"We were delayed," P said. "There is conflict across this sector."

"We're aware."

The bank of bio-antennae that sprouted from P's backplate bristled, twisted with a life of their own.

Lopez lowered her weapon. "You okay there, P?"

"This station is frightened of us," said Pariah.

The alien had grown in stature and musculature

since we had first liberated it from North Star Station. A short but dangerous period of confinement in an Asiatic Directorate prison had awakened something inside the alien; something powerful and dark and terrifying. The Collective had every right to be afraid. Although P had physically grown, that was just the half of it. Its mental expansion was where its real threat lay, and that was made all the more impressive because no one in Sci-Div even pretended to know what it was really capable of.

"I'm just damned glad that you're a Jackal…" Lopez said.

"We are," said P, dipping its head. It pointed to a marking on its bio-suit helmet, where flesh and carapace became one. A crude Jackal-head symbol had been chemically burnt into the plate. "Novak-other assisted."

"Nice work," Feng said. "Now you really are one of us."

The Jackals advanced on P. It felt like we were falling within its protective aura.

"Will you look at that," Lopez said. She indicated the wall.

Novak grunted. "Is fascinating, Senator."

Lopez put a hand on her hip. "That's not even technically accurate any more, Russian. Daddy is Secretary of Defence, not a Senator…"

But what Lopez had seen *was* interesting. Where Pariah walked, the station infection receded. The nest was threaded with a silver tracery; a by-product of the plague that had claimed the Collective. In Pariah's shadow, the poison seemed to retreat. The alien held out a claw and watched as the stuff in the walls shifted, flowed.

"I didn't know that you could do that," I said.

"Neither did we," said P. "Our powers…mature. The objective is this way."

*   *   *

Deeper and deeper into the tunnels we went. There was no light here, and there was little activity around us. The sounds of conflict—of the wider strike-force's progress—were distant and muffled.

"Comms are down," Feng said. "We're out of range."

"Quit worrying about Zero, lover boy," Lopez said.

P was somehow able to understand the layout of the base. The drones hadn't penetrated this far, as though their limited machine intelligence was aware it was a bad idea. The Jackals, however, weren't so smart.

"We are approaching the main nesting chambers," said P. It took point, bounding from surface to surface, using the tunnel's ribbed walls as handholds. For something so big, it sure could move fast.

"Hold up," said Feng. "I . . . I think I see something."

The tunnel opened into a chamber, and the sound of active machinery carried on the air. Not human machinery, but Krell tech. That sound was far more organic; an angry, heartbeat-like pulse that made the atmosphere vibrate. My ears felt like they were on the verge of popping, as though the pressure was about to drop.

The Jackals slowed a little, filing into the chamber. Trepidation crept across my skin, and the squad gasped across the comms. I heard Lopez swallowing, and could taste bile at the back of my own throat.

Capsules grew from columns of gristle that linked the floor and the ceiling. Like grapes on a vine, except that these grapes were huge, throbbing, and filled with bodies. Some pods were illuminated, while others had turned an inky dark. Inside, bodies were suspended in amber fluid, straining at the semi-translucent membranes that held them in place. I involuntarily shivered as I recognised not just Krell in those pods, but other humanoid shapes.

"This is a communion chamber," intoned P.

"Just when I thought that this place couldn't get any grosser…" Lopez whispered.

"Every day is a school day," Feng added.

Pariah rolled its head back and forth, with obvious caution, evaluating. There were bio-signs everywhere on my scanner now, but I noticed that most were immobile.

"The things in these pods," I said, my fingers tightening around the stock of my rifle, "are alive."

"Correct," P said. "This chamber allows interface with the Deep."

"The more I hear about this 'Deep'," Feng said, "the less I like it."

"There is nothing to dislike or like," P argued. "The Deep *is*."

According to P, the Deep was a communication technology that allowed the Collective to transmit thoughts, emotions and directions. It represented the Krell's intelligence pool, the singular consciousness of an entire species—a concept beyond true human understanding.

One of P's barb-guns retracted into its wrist with an uncomfortable snap of bone. The xeno caressed the outer canopy of the nearest pod. The action was almost tender.

"The bio-capsules allow the others to…" P paused, considering the right word to use, "*swim* in the Deep."

"Drown, more like it," Feng commented.

Novak drew a mono-knife from a sheath across his chest. The blade instantly activated, glowing bright blue.

"Stay back, Novak!" I hissed. "We don't understand what we're dealing with here!"

Although he obviously didn't, he answered, "I know what am doing."

"Stand down, trooper."

I grabbed Novak's arm, but it was no use. He was bigger than me, in or out of a simulant, and his eyes had taken on a sort of manic gloss. He slit one of the fleshy pods. There was a wet *shucking* sound as the knife went in, and then the hiss of pressurised atmosphere escaping.

"Is for intelligence," Novak said, as though that was some kind of answer.

"What do you mean 'intelligence'?" Lopez said. "You'll summon more Krell here!"

Novak ignored Lopez's protest, and worked his knife down the pod, expertly slitting the organic membrane. A sickly amber fluid—vile afterbirth, tinged with chunks of flesh—gushed out. The pod's occupant slid free.

"Jesus Christo, Novak!" Lopez squealed.

Novak wasn't so squeamish, and he didn't show the slightest sign of revulsion. He caught the atrophied body with one hand. The thing was, or rather had been, human. Almost skeletal now, the figure was shrunken, having lost muscle mass. P cocked its head with something like curiosity. The alien didn't seem bothered by the fact that Novak was desecrating the communion chamber.

"This other was traitor," it said, referring to the man from the pod.

"He—*it*—is Black Spiral," I said.

Novak nodded, almost absently, as he inspected the body. The figure wore a survival suit; a Black Spiral badge sprayed across the torso panelling.

"Disciples," Feng muttered grimly. "That's what they call themselves."

Organic machinery had partially integrated with the agent's body, and living tendrils anchored his limbs and chest to the capsule. Novak held the body by the scruff of its suit, and inspected it.

"What are you looking for, Novak?" Lopez said, her voice jittery. "We don't have time for this."

I knew exactly what Novak was looking for: gang

tattoos, clan markings, anything that might indicate that the convert was a Russian ganger. Most specifically, Novak was looking for Major Mish Vasnev, or one of her followers.

But this Disciple was not what Novak was seeking. The man's skin was saggy, melted by the corrosive fluid that filled the machine, but carried no ganger markings.

"Never mind," Novak muttered. "Is not important. I just—"

The body came alive. It lurched forward, skeletal fingers grazing Novak's chest, doing nothing more than smear dark fluid across his armour plates. Mottled flesh sloughed off bone. Lopez let out a pitched scream, then managed to stifle it, embarrassed by her own reaction.

"Please, k-kill me!" the figure croaked. The sound of his voice was horrifying; the gush of air through a twisted larynx. His eyes—sightless, near pits—rolled back in his skull.

That sealed it for Novak. The accent wasn't identifiable, at least not to me, but he wasn't Russian.

"My pleasure," said Novak.

There was a wet crack as the man's neck broke. Novak dropped the corpse—left it hanging in the organic webbing—and moved on to the next capsule.

"Goddamn it, Novak!" Lopez said. "We're not here for this!"

"We are killing Spiral," Novak justified.

Novak set to it, slitting open the other pods, inspecting each of the occupants. Pariah watched the bizarre scene.

"The Spiral-others have been here for many years," P deduced. "They came here to spread the rot."

"How do you know any of this?" Feng asked, from his post near the chamber entrance. "You've been saying a lot of shit lately, P, which you don't have any right to know. Is this more of your Deep-knowing?"

"Not this time," P said. "We base this conclusion on available evidence."

P scraped a foot on the floor. That was spongy and flesh-lined, but something metallic was embedded into the deck beneath the nearest pod. A canister lay there, covered in gunk and webbing.

"The Spiral-others brought the rot here," P said. "They released the Harbinger virus, but they were captured. They were integrated into the Deep, but by then it was too late. Harbinger had reached the knowing-pool. It spread, infecting the planet. Eventually, the rest of the Red Claw Collective was also infected."

I crouched down, inspecting the canister. I wasn't quite sure why I was doing it, but I pulled it free. It was as long as my forearm, and heavy. The cap was missing.

"Shit. So it's that easy, huh?"

P nodded. "The Collective likely did not understand that they were infected until it was too late. By the time they had captured and integrated these specimens, the Deep was already contaminated."

"So someone pissed in their pool," I muttered. "Thus the hive falls. I wonder what Zero would make of this."

I ran my shoulder-lamps across the length of the canister. Something bothered me about it. Markings had been stencilled on the side, but those were now faded, the text illegible. Where had the Spiral got this tech from? The canister had been inside the nest for as long as the infected prisoners, and the metal was corroded. I popped a medical-probe from my wrist-comp and ran it over the canister's end. The readings were rough and ready, and subject to the usual caveats that came with any field analysis, but they were enough for my purposes. The canister was swarming with Harbinger cells, with "viral plaque assays". Yeah, I didn't know what that meant, either, but Zero used the phrase and it now flashed on my HUD. The viral load was very high.

Although the Spiral's plan to infect the Krell had been so simple that it was almost insulting, it had plainly worked. Scenes like this—infected prisoners, integrated with the Deep—had been reported throughout infection sites. None of those raids, however, had found actual hardware.

"Is finished," said Novak. "I am done."

Novak's voice pulled me out of my reverie. I stood and snapped the canister to my backpack. It was possible intelligence that we could investigate later, if there *was* a later.

"You're fucking gross, Novak," Lopez complained.

Novak sort of shrugged his shoulders, and the expression behind his face-plate was a mixture of anger and disappointment. His armour was stained with fluid now, and I saw that he had opened several pods. He had dragged bodies from inside each and murdered them with the same cold precision.

"Did you find what you were looking for?" I asked.

"No," said Novak.

Was Novak *ever* going to find what he was looking for? He wanted revenge. He wanted retribution. But those things depended on Novak discovering the whereabouts of his family's killer. The idea that he might find Mish Vasnev, or some evidence of her location, in the bowels of the nest base was almost fanciful. Sure, there was some intel that suggested the Sons—and Vasnev in particular—were working with the Spiral, but it wasn't verified. A Russian crime syndicate like that operated by Vasnev tended to be fluid as water: likely to run through your hands just as soon as you've grasped it.

"It is more than they deserve," Novak muttered. "This is not—"

"This way," P interrupted.

The xeno paused in front of a section of wall that looked different. With a swipe of its claw, the bulkhead collapsed—folded in on itself, receded into the wall.

"How'd you do that?" Lopez said.

"We are Kindred," P answered. "The nest is infected, but it is still of the Collective." P turned sharply to me, and said, "The objective is beyond this portal."

"Then let's get to it," I said.

I turned my shoulder-lamps deeper into the nest. A vast hold, with more skeletal ribbing lining the walls and deck. Pools of fluid pocked the floor; churning with dead Krell spawn. Pariah crushed several underfoot, making wet squelching sounds as the immature spawn burst.

"Do you have to do that?" Lopez protested, her voice a low whisper.

P didn't turn as it responded; instead, it remained focused on the deep dark at the centre of the chamber. "Kindred are infected, Lopez-other. These will not make maturity."

"Well, they won't now…" Feng added.

"The eggs are corrupted," Pariah explained. "They carry the infection."

Jelly-like egg clumps—demonic frog spawn—floated in some pools, but it was all wrong. The stuff leaked black and silver fluid, polluting the liquid. The entire place had the feel of a crypt; of a sepulchre, a graveyard for the Krell species.

"We are sealed in," Novak complained.

Back the way we had come, the hatch slicked shut: red-raw tissue covering the exit.

"We'll worry about that on the way out," I said.

The chamber was so big it was difficult to make out

the perimeter. At the edges of my vision, the dark positively rippled with activity. There were Krell out there. They did not communicate with us at all, but they didn't need to. Their intent was clear. They waited and watched. This felt like a Krell holy-place, and it represented not only the heart of the nest base but also a gateway to the Krell's central intelligence network...

P froze ahead of me, poised.

"We advise caution," it said.

"On the ready line, Jackals," I muttered. "Target acquired."

"Holy shit..." Feng whispered.

In the centre of the chamber sat a huge bio-pod, supported by a web of coral growths. Like machinery with a variable power supply, the pod glowed sporadically.

"On me," I said to the Jackals.

The squad fell in, silent now. I took a cautious step down into the pit of the chamber and craned my neck to look at the pod. Something vast and alien and very fucking ugly lay dormant inside.

"Is this it?" Lopez asked me.

"I think so," I said. Looked to P.

"This is the Krell warden-form," P confirmed. "This is our objective."

Graphics popped onto my HUD, superimposed over my vision. The warden-form was much, much bigger than any specimen we'd seen so far on Vektah Minor— two, maybe even three times the size of a simulant in combat-armour. Like all Krell, it was six-limbed, and covered in organic armour, with a distended head that was more cephalopod than fish. This was, so Science Division told us, some sort of warrior-caste off-shoot of the equally rare navigator-form. But whereas the navigators piloted the Krell ships through deep space, the warden-fish commanded the ground troops.

"Let's get this bad boy secured," I ordered.

"The Kindred are not gender-specific," P intoned. "Jenkins-other is factually inaccurate to refer to this specimen as 'boy'."

I kept my eyes pinned on the xeno, but shook my head. "Whatever, P. Novak, deploy the launcher."

Novak unshouldered what looked like an oversized missile launcher from his pack. This was a PT-5 netgun— non-lethal pacification technology, fresh out of R&D. No simulant team had done much more than train with it— because the device wasn't made to inflict lethal force, it was at odds with other Sim Ops-issue weaponry.

"Am almost ready," Novak said, checking over the enormous firing tube. The gun was so big that Novak was the only Jackal capable of properly carrying and firing it. "This is tax dollar at work."

"You don't pay taxes, lifer," Lopez said, but then nodded. "Just don't miss."

Pariah clambered up the structure at the foot of the pod, using the bone-like cabling as support. It stroked a claw across the warden's pod.

"Warden is in pain," P said.

"It's infected, right?" Lopez asked, without turning to look at P: keeping her eyes on the dark.

"I don't know what gave that away..." Feng muttered.

"Of course," said P.

"So why are you bothered about it?"

P paused. "We are still Kindred, Lopez-other. Even if we are Pariah."

"We'll need to open that pod, P," I said. "Can you do your thing and get it to work?"

P paused. "There will be no need."

Feng gave a strangled laugh. "Why's that, P?"

"Because," P said, its flat robotic tone matter-of-fact, "the warden-form is waking up."

CHAPTER FOUR

HAMMER AND ANVIL

The warden thrashed inside the pod, untangling itself from bio-cables. The capsule ruptured, and fluid gushed across the chamber floor.

Lopez had her rifle up, aimed at the warden's over-sized head.

"Don't fire!" I yelled, grabbing her shoulder. "We need this thing alive."

Of course, the Jackals already knew that. We'd been thoroughly briefed on the capture of a live specimen as the primary objective of the mission, but instinct is a powerful mistress, and I could quite understand Lopez's overwhelming need to shoot the xeno. The fish looked *seriously* pissed. Lopez didn't look much better.

"It's bigger than the briefing said," she said.

"A *lot* bigger," agreed Feng, as he fell back from the emerging xeno.

"Novak, fire the damned launcher!" I ordered.

"Am trying," protested Novak. "Need to wait until it gets out of pod!"

The Russian lined up a shot with the netgun. The

weapon's control panel lit, indicating that it was ready to fire.

With unreal speed, the warden pulled free of the pod. It rose up to full height.

But Novak still couldn't take the shot. His weapon's laser-sight danced across the alien's carapace, as it dodged sideways, out of range.

"Fucking shoot it!" Lopez complained.

The warden shrieked. I staggered backwards, away from the enormous son of a bitch. Without a word, the Jackals fell into a defensive perimeter around the creature.

"Use the batons," I said.

Although intuition screamed that this was a terrible, terrible idea, I shouldered my plasma rifle and drew my shock-baton. Standard-issue shock-batons were designed for use on soft targets, but this particular model had an increased power output for use against xenos. I racked it, and the baton extended to full length: almost as long as my plasma rifle. The heavy charge pack incorporated into the hilt generated an energy discharge that would be capable of killing a human. It would, Science Division's R&D department insisted, be more than enough to incapacitate an infected Krell warden-form.

Probably.

All of those thoughts ran through my head in the split-second I had to react as the warden swiped for me. Its claws scythed the air. I rolled sideways, barely avoiding the swing.

The warden-form was incandescent with anger. It stomped forward, and the very chamber seemed to shake with a combination of the warden's movements, and its sheer rage. It was huge; barely capable of supporting its own weight on the twisted arrangement of limbs. But while the alien was enough of a physical threat, it was also much more than that. The oversized head throbbed with infection, and waves of dread emanated from the thing.

"Bring it down!"

Another swipe, and the alien was now properly out of the pod. Gas and liquid vented from the remains of the bio-machinery.

I dove forward, beneath the creature's upper limbs. In the same motion, I slammed the shock-baton into its right leg, aiming for a dog-leg joint.

The baton impacted, and impacted hard. The noise was a little nauseating, even if my target was an infected fish. I'd hit one of the warden's lower limbs, and sparks shivered over the xeno's skin. The scent of ozone and of fried fish filled the air.

The warden roared, and the sound sent shivers through my body and mind. It turned about-face, directing every ounce of its physical might in my direction.

I racked the baton again.

TAKE EVASIVE ACTION, my HUD insisted. THREAT LEVEL CRITICAL.

I cracked the baton into another of the xeno's legs. It took the impact and drove a claw towards me. The light glanced off the xeno's black, serrated fingertips. Its hands were webbed, limbs finned.

I scrambled backwards. The ground underfoot was slick, wet with the pod's discharge. Compounded by the combat-suit's heavy armour, I slipped. Felt the ground give, and winced as I anticipated the incoming blow...

Except that it didn't come.

The warden pulled back, rearing up.

"We will assist," said P, leaping between the warden and me.

Then Pariah was on the xeno's back, holding on for

dear life. A cowboy riding the biggest bucking bronco in existence. The warden-form stumbled into more of the coral structures, causing part of the chamber to collapse. P was tossed aside—thrown hard against the chamber wall, and the Jackals scattered in the big xeno's wake.

Lopez activated her baton and launched forward. She struck the xeno on the torso, then dodged back, using her EVAMP to perform a limited jump. Feng saw what she was doing, and copied.

"Stay operational, troopers!" I yelled by way of encouragement. "Novak, use the damned launcher!"

"Am trying to get clean shot!" Novak said. He was tracking the fight with the launcher.

"Just shoot," Lopez said, as she danced around the warden, her EVAMP blazing.

"I don't know how long we can keep this up for," Feng echoed.

The warden swiped a claw at P, and the xeno impacted another wall. Again, P was up and at the warden without pause. Say what you will about that fish: it was one hell of a trooper.

The warden shook itself angrily. It was covered in spiked armour plates, and those showed evidence of the combat: striped with dark Krell blood, or marred by burn marks from baton discharge. Now though, the carapace sort of shifted, as though the alien inside was inflating. It looked like a puffer fish, expanding, spear-tips shimmering as they popped up all across its shelled body, or in the softer flesh between armour plates. I had no doubt that those would be poison-tipped, and that poison would be debilitatingly painful. The Krell were specialists at that shit.

"Am ready!" Novak roared.

Just as the warden-form was about to activate whatever bio-weapon it was equipped with, Novak fired the net-launcher. The weapon emitted an electric hiss as it activated.

"Get clear, P!" I shouted.

"We are trying," said P.

The net rapidly expanded as it launched. It instantly electrified.

P leapt free of the navigator, catching a pillar with outstretched claws, scurrying higher and out of harm's reach.

The warden turned, realising what was happening.

The net caught the alien, full-on. Direct hit.

It wrapped around the warden. Microdrones built into the grid ignited, seeking to hold the alien inside the mesh. The warden slashed at them with its clawed limbs, but they were too fast. The net closed, and its electric field fired again and again.

Like a porcupine's quills, the spines across the xeno's body flattened. It convulsed with the current running through the net, and the scent of burning flesh grew stronger. The xeno collapsed to the floor. My HUD confirmed that the alien was still alive, but that it was incapacitated. Exactly as we wanted it.

I let out a sigh of relief. "Novak, Feng," I shouted. "Secure that fish."

They fell in around the warden.

"Fish is very heavy," Novak protested.

Novak hauled the enormous warden along the deck, Feng at the other end. They looked like a bizarre parody of fishermen, except that the catch in their net was the size of a shark, and far more dangerous.

"Be thankful for the man-amps," Feng said. "I know that I am."

The combat-suits were equipped with manpower-amplifiers, which augmented the already impressive strength of a simulant body. Even those were being pressed to the limit by the warden's weight.

Krell advanced from shafts in the chamber walls, and erupted from pods.

"Quit griping and get moving," I ordered. "We'll hold them back."

P continued fending off the newcomers, and Lopez was doing the same now, glad to be firing her plasma rifle instead of relying on the shock-baton. She was far more comfortable with shooting shit than hitting it, which I could quite understand. I pumped my plasma rifle, launching grenades into the morass of targets.

"Just keep a grip on the fish," Lopez blasted. "We won't be able to hold these bastards off for ever."

"Lopez-other speaks objective truth," said P, as it fired a volley of barbs into an oncoming primary-form.

"Move on the exit, through the communion chamber."

The portal had closed, muscle-fibre around the door twitching in protest at the invasion.

"Clearing door," Lopez shouted.

She planted a demo-charge on the hatch. No time for a countdown or breaching discipline: we just needed to evac, and fast. The charge's activation panel flashed green, amber, red, and we all paused as it detonated. Bloody chunks of flesh showered the area.

"I fucking hate this place," Lopez whined, wiping gore from her visor.

"Then let's pick this up, and get the hell out of Dodge," I said. "Keep that body moving."

The tunnel outside brimmed with more xenos. They were whipped into a fury; this was the Krell—infected or otherwise—at their most dangerous. Leader-forms—ordinarily, the biggest and baddest field-level bio-forms—lurched from side-tunnels, directing artillery-forms onwards. Secondary-form thralls, equipped with esoteric living weaponry, fired on us, splitting the air with bone-shards. My null-shield flared violently, repelling most of the gunfire, but never enough. Rounds hit my suit all over.

"Move, move, move!"

A route through the maze of tunnels appeared on my HUD. This was collected battlefield intelligence, derived from every operational simulant team, as well as the drone network.

"This way," I directed.

Novak and Feng groaned as they took the weight of the xeno, and steered it around a corner.

"Easy at your end," Feng said.

"Is not easy at all!" Novak answered back.

As though reacting to something in a dream, the creature lazily lashed out with a claw. The blow almost caught Feng, who only just dodged it—

"Feng!" Novak shouted.

The alien body slipped out of Feng's gloves. It hit the deck, with a loud *thunk*.

The alien's eyes flared wide. Angrier than ever. One claw sliced at the net.

"It's getting free!" Feng said. "Novak, move up!"

"Secure that shit," I said.

"We're being overwhelmed," Lopez replied.

I couldn't even see where P was among the smoke, the debris, the mess. The fog of war had well and truly descended over the nest, and we were stuck right in the middle of it.

Only one thing for it. I thought-commanded my suit to open an all-channels comm-link.

"This is Jenkins' Jackals," I said. "Requesting immediate back-up. All squads! We have the objective. We have the objective!"

The warden continued to struggle. Lopez kept firing, repelling thralls with her plasma rifle. Novak had drawn his Widowmaker pistol, and was firing haphazardly into the oncoming horde. P was clutching the deckhead, firing away with its barb-guns. Such was their fervour, the Collective seemed to have lost their fear of Pariah.

"All squads!" I yelled. "All squads! Requesting assistance!"

There was a rumble through the deck.

Ahead, a hatch blew outwards. New bio-signs appeared on my scanner, and a chime sounded over my internal comms.

"You assholes call for back-up?" came a voice.

Captain Marcus Ving, also known as the Phoenixian, commanding officer of Phoenix Squad, stood braced in the doorway.

Ving was tall but somehow also squat; his body broad, overly muscled. That was the same in or out of his sim: indeed, his real skin and his simulants were infamously similar. His features were stoic, heroic, disdainful. Like Lopez, he was Proximan, but now his lip was curled in a disgruntled sneer. Behind him, the rest of his team were present: four troopers in full Pathfinder suits. I heard muttered tuts and groans over the comm-channel. Phoenix Squad were no friends of the Jackals, that was for sure.

"Affirmative, sir," I answered. I tried to avoid sounding patronising, but that wasn't easy. Ving was still a senior officer, even if I didn't like him very much…

Ving sucked his teeth. "We'll talk about this later, Lieutenant. For now, we need to get that fish off-world." He nodded to his team. "Fall in, Phoenix Squad. Let's bail the Jackals out, and get this job done."

Captain Marcus Ving was a poster boy for the Alliance Army's Simulant Operations Programme. He was one of those guys you see on the recruitment adverts—riding the thin line between arrogant and intrepid, both threatening and promising that, by joining up, you can be more than human. Over the last few years, his chiselled features had become *the* face of Sim Ops, with Phoenix Squad nothing short of minor celebrities. Ving was a glory hunter, and revelled in the publicity and kudos. He was a favourite of both Captain Heinrich, first captain of my company and my immediate senior officer, and General Draven, head of the Sim Ops Programme. Marcus Ving also held the current record for the most active transitions in Sim Ops. That struck a particularly personal note with me: my mentor—the legendary Conrad Harris—had held the record for a long time, and it felt all kinds of wrong that a trooper like Ving now claimed it as his own.

I didn't like Ving, and he didn't like me. That's life, I guess: not everyone is always going to get along. But the bad blood between Ving and I ran deeper than simple dislike.

All that said, this was one occasion when I was glad to see him and his band of shaved apes. New ambulatory bodies had to be a good thing, whoever was behind the controls.

Phoenix Squad fanned out into the corridor, adding their own plasma fire to ours. The Krell weren't exactly repelled—there were simply too many of them for that—but they were momentarily rebuffed. That was all the pause we needed.

"Feng, Novak! Get that specimen secured! Move on the beachhead!"

My troopers did as ordered. Ving waved on two of his squad as well; the names MORENTZ and RICHARDS printed on their torso plates. With the strength of their man-amps added to our own, the warden's stunned body was soon up and moving through the corridor network.

"That was close, Jenkins," said Ving, over our suit-to-suit comms. "Do you have any idea how important that specimen is?"

"Of course, sir. I'm not stupid."

"Really? Because it looks a lot like that to me."

"The asset is secure, and under control."

"Phoenix Squad should've been on point," he bickered. "*I* should've been in the warden's chamber."

I couldn't help myself as I answered, "Well, you weren't."

"Only because you have that damn fish on your squad," Ving muttered.

He talked as he worked, firing a jet of napalm from his flamethrower, creating a wall of fire beyond us. That was Ving's trademark weapon; in keeping with his public image as the Phoenixian. He and his squad worked fast and proficiently.

"P's a Jackal. Don't talk about it like that."

Ving shook his head, grimacing behind his face-plate. "I'll talk about it any way I like. It's a *fish*, Jenkins. A fucking *xeno*."

"We appreciate the save, sir," I said, sounding as though I really didn't appreciate it at all.

"Don't think for one minute this means I've forgotten about what happened at Darkwater."

"Goes without saying," I answered, picking off Krell ahead of us, clearing our path.

Darkwater Farm had been FUBAR. The Jackals had assaulted a simulant factory there—colloquially known in Sim Ops as a "farm"—and found Ving and Phoenix Squad running guard duty. We had raided the farm, put Phoenix Squad in evacuation-pods and fired them into deep space. Yeah, I could well see why Ving was still pissed with me. I wasn't proud of what had happened, of what we had done, but at the time it had been necessary. *A lot of bad shit happened at Darkwater*, I thought, and tried to repress those memories.

Ving tossed a glare behind us, in Lopez's direction. She was busily and obliviously fending off Krell from the side-tunnels, making sure that our makeshift convoy wouldn't face a flank attack.

"We all know why you're back on the force," Ving said, with real vitriol. "Don't forget that I'm watching you. Her *father* can't protect you for ever."

Of course, I hadn't asked Senator Lopez—now Secretary of Defence for the entire Alliance—to put his neck out for us. But he had done so, and I knew that it had helped. I also knew that the rest of Sim Ops felt we had been given preferential treatment. As far as I was concerned, that just meant we had to try all the harder, to prove to everyone that we could succeed.

"DZ coordinates coming up," I said. "The end's in sight, troopers."

I received new battle-net data with each footfall. The closer we got to the surface, the more assets I detected operating in the vicinity. The Jackals and Phoenix Squad were the only two units in their original simulants; all other squads had suffered extraction and fresh transition. Several teams had been deployed outside Nest Base Gamma.

"Get that specimen outside," Ving hollered, indiscriminately torching the walls of the nest as he moved. Smoke, thick and noxious, lingered in the air.

Ahead, part of the nest base's organic wall had opened up: a literal rent in the structure's outer flank. Light stabbed through, bright as day, then dark again. An explosion; that was what it was. The nest shook with the force of the impact, as a warhead struck the side of the structure.

"The tac fighters are still conducting strafing runs," Ving said. "It's the only thing that seems to keep the fishes in check."

Debris rained down from above, as something ruptured in the deckhead. Meanwhile, the sounds of conflict were increasing. We were close enough now that my suit had detected a recovery beacon: a broad-spectrum data transmission meant to guide any lost souls back to the pick-up point. Of course, that beacon could also be detected by the Krell and they were focusing their efforts on it. I might've thought that the Krell were giving it their best in the tunnels, but the fighting was just as intense here.

"Hustle it, Jackals," I said. "Not far to go."

"You heard the lady," Ving said, with emphasis on the last word. "By the numbers, cover our retreat to the DZ."

Neither squad needed much encouragement beyond that. Both teams fired their extra-vehicular mobility packs. EVAMP thrusters glowed bright blue as troopers vaulted down the tunnel, each soldier covering the other's movements. The tunnel rose upwards, and through the hole in the wall desiccated jungle was visible.

"Keep that fish protected," ordered Ving, as his team covered Novak and Feng, the slowest-moving members of the group.

The Krell were everywhere. They teemed up the sides of Nest Base Gamma; lurching out of the jungle, exploding from the swamp. They were an almost uniform mass of living ammunition, enveloping everything in their way.

"Threat level critical," Ving said.

"I think we can see that for ourselves," Lopez muttered.

"Then why are you still standing around here jawing?" Ving spat. "Get your asses outside and to the evac point!"

Graphics on my HUD told me that the beachhead was somewhere below us. The outer walls of the nest base rapidly inclined towards the swamps. That was where the fighting was at its thickest, and getting down there was the only way we were going to get the warden off this planet.

The beleaguered science team was composed of a dozen Sci-Div officers in hazmat suits. They worked beneath the blue umbrella of the null-shield, and although there were dead thralls piled around the perimeter, the team wasn't going to hold out much longer. The null-shield was on the verge of collapse, such was the volume of energy-fire it was absorbing. In the middle of the null-shield sat the Wildcat. The shuttle's Aerospace Force crew were already buttoned up, but the shuttle's rear cargo bay was open, waiting to receive the asset.

Around us, other simulant teams appeared from openings in the nest base's honeycombed walls. There were more explosions, and more warnings on my HUD. TAC-FIGHTER SUPPORT OFFLINE, my suit's AI told me. The nest base rumbled, and Needlers screamed by overhead. We bounced down the nest base, under heavy fire from every direction.

"Heads down!" yelled a trooper in a battered combat-suit.

I recognised Reed, and his Rippers, huddled behind a box of ammo crates. The corporal's eyes were wild, verging on panic, and he cycled the launcher on his battle-rifle: throwing grenades out into the swamp in lazy arcs. Although the backwash of the multiple detonations sent shrapnel across the landing site, it kept the Krell at bay.

"So you made it, green?" Lopez asked.

"Uh, yeah, ma'am," Reed muttered. "We made it."

Novak looked unconvinced. "How many times you die, soldier?"

"Six," said Reed, laying down plasma into another clutch of thralls. "Six times."

We'd only been on Vektah Minor for twenty minutes. Six extractions in that space of time was tough going for even a veteran sim operator. I could read the horror of it on the troopers' faces. They, along with the remainder of the Sci-Div security detail, were a disorganised rabble. The veneer of military discipline had been more or less completely eradicated by the magnitude of the Krell's response.

"Troopers, do you have the specimen?" asked a voice.

It came from a man with a shaved head, wearing a white non-combatant power suit that denoted his rank as a Sci-Div officer. Another officer—a woman, with the same air of anxious interest—appeared to evaluate the warden.

"What does it look like?" Ving spat back, as Feng, Novak and Phoenix Squad hauled ass under the null-shield.

"It is alive, yes?" enquired Science Woman.

"It should be," I said.

"It must be!" said Science Man. "That is crucial to this operation!"

"It is alive," intoned P. "It is in pain, but it is alive."

Both science officers wore sensor-visors over their upper faces. They paused, scanning the specimen; focused very intently on gathering intel, even if the rest of the operation was turning to shit around them.

"It is injured," said Science Man. "Is that a shock-baton burn?"

"Yes," agreed Science Woman. She pointed out blackened flesh on the warden's twitching leg. "Most regrettable. That injury could be serious."

"We did our best," I argued. "The recovery wasn't straightforward."

"It's imperative that the specimen is healthy if we are to—"

Science Man's head exploded in a shower of gore and brain matter; body crumpling. Bone-shards from a bio-weapon peppered the null-shield, penetrating it in places. The woman next to Science Man looked down at her armour—now streaked bright red—and started wailing. Of course, it didn't matter. The Sci-Div team were using next-gen skins; not combat-rated, but better than real death.

"I can't hold this much longer!" Feng yelled, struggling to handle the warden. The enormous fish had started to shift in the net again.

"Phoenix Squad, secure the specimen," Ving ordered. "Jackals, cover the retreat."

Ving turned his flamethrower on the Krell advance, and torched them all. The heat was so intense I could feel it through my combat-suit. Still-smoking warrior-forms threw themselves at us.

The science team flocked around Phoenix Squad, as they dragged the warden-form towards the shuttle. They set about the warden, securing it in place with archaic-looking metal clamps. The Wildcat's cargo bay was barebones and sterile; everything not essential to the operation had been removed.

The Krell redoubled their efforts at that point, realising that their revered warden was about to be captured. They threw themselves at the null-shield, shrieking, screaming, caterwauling.

"Fall back to the shuttle," I said. "There's nothing else that we can do here."

"That's a negative," Ving muttered. "Jackals, stay where you are. Get onto the ship, you damned fish head!"

This time Ving wasn't talking about the warden. He pointed his flamer at P.

"We are a Jackal," P said. "Our squad requires assistance."

"I don't want to give the order twice, fish," Ving snarled. "We're leaving, with or without you."

"Just go, P!" I ordered.

With marked reluctance, Pariah clambered onto the ship. It kept firing on the infected Krell, and I knew it didn't want to leave us.

"What are you doing, Ving?" Lopez asked, half turning towards the Wildcat. Final lift-prep was underway, and the Jackals weren't on the shuttle.

"Cover the retreat," Ving repeated, more firmly this time. "The warden-form is coming with us."

"But that's *our* asset!" Lopez protested.

"It's an Alliance asset," Ving countered. "Which Phoenix Squad has just successfully recovered." He smiled a perfect grin at me. "Pilot, we're cleared for evacuation. Get us out of here."

"If you're sure, sir . . ." the pilot queried.

The Wildcat's ramp shut. Its VTOL engines ignited, sending out a backwash of fire that roasted many of the advancing Krell. I put a hand to my face, watched as the ship gained altitude. The Krell had almost lost interest in the Jackals. They vaulted for the shuttle. Some grabbed the hull, and were thrown clear as it accelerated. Another wave of heat rolled over me, set off my armour's safety alerts.

"So that's it, huh?" Lopez said. Her voice was weary, tired. "Phoenix Squad gets the glory, and we get left behind?"

"Looks that way," Novak said.

The beachhead was in ruins. Bodies, both alien and simulant, were strewn everywhere. Some were still alive—badly injured, but not yet put out of their misery. The Krell, I noticed, were dragging some of the simulants back into the nest. Somewhere to my left, the remainder of the security detail were being torn apart. Reed and his Rippers went with them, consumed by the tide of Krell. The infected thralls were like rabid dogs, a mass of scything limbs and outstretched claws. Bio-fire sprayed the area, angry as all hell.

An uplink icon flashed on my HUD.

"We've got comms to the *Providence*," I said.

"A fat lot of good that will do us..." Lopez complained.

"Zero, do you read?" I said, into my communicator.

"We read, ma'am," came Zero's voice. "There aren't many Sim Ops teams still operational down there."

Feng shook his head. "First in, last out."

"Every time," Novak said.

"Asset is inbound, Zero," I said. "Mission accomplished."

The shuttle was gone. Before it had even made safe distance from the nest base, it hit hard burn. It left a smear of light across the sky as it went.

"The *Providence* has Angel Ten on the grid," said Zero, no doubt reading data directly from the ship's bridge. "Ready to receive the package."

"Good. Initiate code hammer fall."

"Copy that. Initiate hammer fall. Do you have anvil?"

"I am anvil," I said. "Fire everything you've got on my position."

This was a formality; requisite authorisation for the deployment of plasma warheads. Even as the words were spoken, I knew that somewhere up there in orbit—aboard the *Providence*—missile tubes were being loaded, and firing solutions locked.

"Confirm that you are senior officer in theatre," said Zero, her voice dropping into an officious tone.

"Confirm."

"Execute."

I thought briefly of those sorry bastards in the communion chamber; webbed and wired into the Deep. They had asked for it, sure, but no one—Spiral or otherwise—deserved that sort of an existence. *The canister.* The memory was dislodged by recall of the communion chamber.

"Z, stay on the line," I ordered. "Lopez, keep me covered."

"I'll try," said Lopez.

Lopez's plasma rifle was firing on full-automatic, spitting bright pulses all around. All of our energy weapons were smoking ominously, approaching the end of their operational life. A lot like the simulants, I guess.

I plucked the canister from my belt pouch. Turned it over in hands that were slick with Krell blood, fluid that probably swam with the Harbinger virus...

"You still reading me, Zero?"

"I copy."

"I'm sending you an image."

The camera mounted on the left side of my tactical-helmet snapped an image of the canister, and I thought-commanded a transmission back to the *Providence*. But not just to the *Providence*; directly to Zero's station, double-encrypted. Her eyes only.

"What is it?" she queried.

A counter appeared in the corner of my HUD.

HAMMER FALL PROTOCOL IN T MINUS 30 SECONDS...

"I don't know. Something we found in the communion chamber, inside Nest Base Gamma."

"Is that a serial code?" Zero queried.

"I think it might be. Run checks on it for me."

"Solid copy."

HAMMER FALL PROTOCOL IN T MINUS 20 SECONDS...

"Looks like we're out of time," I said. "*Sayonara, kemosabe.*"

"Zero out."

There was a single dot of light on the horizon, burning through the cloud cover. Feng whooped in delight as he realised what was happening. We were going down, but we were going to take out a good chunk of this continent with us. The Jackals had involuntarily gone back to back, a tight circle now.

"Good job, troopers," I said.

Then the hammer fell, and everything was obliterated in the force of the explosion.

CHAPTER FIVE

ALL GUTS, NO GLORY

EXTRACTION CONFIRMED.

The neural-link severed, and in an instant the simulation collapsed.

Nest Base Gamma was wiped from Vektah's surface by a plasma barrage, and the Jackals along with it. That triggered a rapid extraction event and sent the Jackals back to the simulator-tanks. It did just the same for every other trooper or Sci-Div operator trapped on the planet and ended the assault phase of the Vektah Minor operation.

I prised my eyes open and took in the Simulant Operations Centre. Although I'd served on numerous strikeships in my time as a simulant operator, what I saw was on a completely different scale. Everyone, and everything, on the operation had been expendable: there had been no real-skin casualties whatsoever. The *Providence*'s SOC contained twenty individual bays, each capable of holding a simulant squad. Some were vets, others were green. The away team had included personnel who weren't even properly designated for a simulant operation. Those included the Sci-Div crew, who were uniformly vomiting, shaking, and rocking as a result of the extraction. You can fit almost anyone—except for negatives—with data-ports, but that doesn't make them an operator: not everyone is made for Sim Ops.

I slammed the PURGE command on my simulator-tank. The gel-like fluid holding me in place swirled away, leaving me shivering with the sudden cold. The tank's canopy popped open, and I yanked at the cables connected to my data-ports. I clambered free, wearing nothing but my dog tags.

Zero appeared in front of my tank, data-slate in hand, blocking my path. She was small, slight and a little delicate-looking; her ginger hair escaping in loose strands from a ponytail, her freckled face showing signs of anxiety.

"Objective achieved," she said, with a tight grimace. "Command confirms that all Alliance forces are retreating out-system. That was a good result. Well done."

"You saw what happened, right?" I asked, without any preamble.

Of course Zero had seen what had happened. She'd been watching the vid-feeds from the ship, and her station was a nest of monitors, each showing a different angle of the conflict on Vektah. She knew every detail of what had occurred.

"I saw it," she confirmed. "Just let it go, ma'am."

"Don't 'ma'am' me, Zero," I argued. "Phoenix Squad stole our asset. That was the Jackals' objective!"

"The important thing is that we have the specimen," Zero said. "Look at this rationally."

"I just got left behind on the surface of an alien planet, and erased by a plasma barrage—so forgive me if I'm feeling a little cranky."

"Jenk, let it go!" Zero implored.

"Stand aside, Zero."

Angrily, I shook the liquid from my skin and pounded towards Phoenix Squad's ops bay. Lopez, Feng and Novak watched on, ready to provide support if I needed it. Zero seemed to freeze, glaring at her terminal screens: tense at the expectation of confrontation.

"You're a fucking asshole, Ving!" I exclaimed.

The warden-form had no doubt been handed over to the *Providence*'s waiting security team. Having completed their mission, Ving and Phoenix Squad were decamping from their own tanks. Every member of the unit looked surprisingly like their commanding officer: buff, broad, so heavily muscled that the operators themselves could be mistaken for simulants.

Ving turned his head sharply when he heard my voice. His real skin was filled with holo-tattoos, pictures of birds with tails of fire, of planets on which the squad had fought. When Ving moved, the tattoos followed the shift of his musculature; in particular, making the feathers of the phoenix on his chest animate. It was a cheap tri-D effect, but one that Ving was known for.

"Oh? It's you, huh?"

"What the hell was that?" I yelled, jabbing a finger into Ving's chest.

Ving raised an eyebrow and sipped at a green-coloured nutrient shake. "What did I tell you about using proper military address, Lieutenant?"

"We're supposed to be on the same side!"

"Yeah, well. Maybe that was a little payback for Darkwater."

"That was different!"

"Not from where we were sitting." Ving turned to his meathead squad mates. "How many days were we on that evac-pod, boys?"

"Enough," muttered one.

Ving continued: "Sixteen days. Sixteen fucking days

drifting in deep space. We were only picked up by chance. You hit an Alliance Sci-Div facility, and yet you're still wearing the uniform. How do you figure that?"

"We were doing what we thought was best."

Now Ving poked a finger at me. We were both stark naked, after the tanks, but that didn't matter. A crowd had gathered around the bay now, troopers taking both sides of the argument.

"You're a simulant operator, Jenkins!" Ving shouted back at me. "You follow orders, just like the rest of us."

"We had orders from Lazarus," I said.

But my voice dropped. I'd lost a little of my conviction. There were some repressed sniggers from Phoenix Squad, as well as other operators on Ving's side of the divide.

"Lazarus?" Ving said, shaking his head. "So you're relying on a dead man's name to defend yourself?"

"You saw him too."

The sneer grew across Ving's broad face. "I saw an old guy wearing a Directorate uniform," Ving muttered back. That caused some more murmuring from the gathered crowd. Eyes swivelled in Feng's direction. "And I'll testify to that. Get back to it, Lieutenant, and take the Directorate clone with you."

Feng's expression dropped. "You need some new material, Captain."

"You were activated, Chino. Activated! And yet you're still on the force." Ving turned his attention to Lopez now. "Of course, we all know how that happened. Senator's little girl and all that."

Lopez bared her teeth. "Go screw yourself, Ving. My father isn't—"

"Quiet!" Zero hissed.

The mood in the chamber suddenly changed. Hush

descended, and some of the sharper operators tried to look like they were doing something.

"*Officer on the deck!*"

Three figures, all wearing full Army uniform, cut through the crowd and made a beeline for Phoenix Squad's bay.

I recognised Captain Peter Heinrich, and my heart sank a little. Because he was the only non-operational member of the strike-force, he was in his real skin, and looked even shorter than usual, sandwiched as he was between two simulants. Those two officers looked equally out of place; you hardly ever saw sims wearing anything but combat-gear, and they looked wrong in formal uniform. With the *clip-clip* of boot soles against the deck, hands clasped firmly behind his back, Heinrich advanced on the bay.

The Jackals fell into an uneasy salute. His eyes still on me, Ving did the same.

"What's going on in here?" Heinrich scanned my face, then Ving's. "What's the meaning of all this noise?"

Technically, Ving and Heinrich were the same rank, but Heinrich was first captain of the strike-force. He had been promoted straight out of officer college, and from there he'd managed to skulk his way to the top. As first captain, he reported directly to Command. He'd never been a line trooper, and had never actually faced deployment. Although his blond hair and blue eyes were unusual for a Proximan, Heinrich had proper ancestry—like Lopez, his family had political roots back on Proxima Colony.

"We were having a disagreement of sorts, about the mission outcome," Ving said, curtly.

"In what way?" Heinrich asked.

"Lieutenant Jenkins was the subject of a late extraction," Ving said. "Due to, ah, an accident."

I sighed noisily. My jaw danced with pent-up aggression and anger.

"That was no accident," Lopez muttered, under her breath.

Captain Heinrich didn't hear her, which was probably for the best. "Is that so, Lieutenant?"

"Yes, sir," I said. "That's right."

"Well, it's no cause for disorderly behaviour. You know how I like to run this company—with or without your presence." Heinrich lifted an eyebrow in disapproval, looking me up and down. "Maybe the period of operating out of the chain of command has led to a lapse in regulation."

"Possibly, sir," I said, through teeth that were almost gritted.

"Fine," Heinrich said. He turned to Ving. "No doubt Captain Ving will fill out the necessary incident report."

"Of course, sir," said Ving.

Ving and Heinrich were in one another's pockets. I knew that if I pushed this, it would get me nowhere. Better to just agree, and get it over with.

"I'm sure that the lieutenant will endorse your version of events," Heinrich said, sealing the deal. "Isn't that right, Lieutenant Jenkins?"

"That's right, sir," I parroted back.

"Good. That's what I like to hear." Heinrich nodded to himself in approval. "You successfully initiated code hammer fall. I suspect that you took out a good many fishes as a result. Now, I wanted to come down here to congratulate you all. Thanks to the efforts of Captain Ving and Phoenix Squad, we successfully executed the mission objective."

That roused some applause and cheering from the deck. Ving raised a hand, nodding along with the clapping, basking in the attention.

"We have a living, breathing Krell warden-form in our custody," Heinrich said. "This is truly an unprecedented feat. It has never been attempted before, and I doubt that it will be attempted again."

"It was nothing," said Ving, with mock embarrassment. "We were only doing our duty."

Heinrich continued with his address. "This asset will allow us to explore the possibility of a cure for the Harbinger virus," he said, "in a way that has previously been impossible. Well done, Captain Ving and Phoenix Squad."

Heinrich flashed a glare in any direction as he said those words, as though he was almost daring me to speak out against him.

"We're currently heading to Sanctuary Base," Heinrich said to the deck at large, "where our intelligence will be digested by Science Division. You should all be aware that Secretary Lopez will be in attendance, so best behaviour all around, please. I don't think that you'll have to wait long for the next deployment."

"As you were," called one of the simulant officers accompanying Heinrich.

The atmosphere of oppression lifted as the trio left the deck, and the Jackals visibly relaxed. Zero tossed me some fatigues, and I retreated back into our dedicated bay. It felt safer here, surrounded by our own tanks. I towelled myself dry and got dressed.

"So we don't even get recognition for our hard work?" Lopez griped.

"Looks that way," I said.

Zero sat at her terminal. "You did the right thing back there, ma'am. By not hitting Ving, I mean."

Novak rumbled a laugh. "Hitting Ving is not good idea."

"You know that you've crossed the line when Novak is the voice of reason," Feng offered.

"What?" Novak said, shrugging his enormous tattooed shoulders. The ink was evidence that Novak had made more than his fair share of bad decisions. "I am most reasonable man on squad."

"Right, right," Lopez said.

"How do you feel about seeing your father again, Lopez?" Zero asked.

Lopez pouted. "Not great. Daddy can be difficult."

"And don't we know it," Feng suggested.

"I don't think that his interference is helping," Lopez said. "Maybe I should talk to him."

I buttoned up my fatigues. "Well, it stopped General Draven from throwing us in the clink, so I guess that has to be something."

"Daddy never does anything without a reason," Lopez said, shaking her wet hair. She was exceptionally pretty, although her time in the Army had made her leaner and harder.

"Not even for his little girl, huh?" Feng said. "That's cold."

Lopez just nodded. "That's Daddy."

"Catch some downtime until we reach Sanctuary," I suggested. "You're dismissed, Jackals."

"Where are you going, ma'am?" Feng asked me.

"I want to make sure that we all got back safely. I'm going to check on Pariah."

Despite its crucial role during the raid on Vektah Minor, P's liberty was restricted as soon as it boarded the *Providence*. Captain Heinrich had issued an edict that Pariah was to remain in confinement and under observation at all times while aboard the ship.

I found the entrance to the Science Deck guarded by two Military Police officers in full battledress.

"Here to see your fish again?" asked one of the MPs.

Shock-rifles were standard armament for shipboard security, but both guards were equipped with tactical shotguns. Bandoliers of alternative ammunition—from incendiaries through to frags—were strapped across their torsos. Heinrich's safety briefing insisted that in the event of a "containment failure", P was to be terminated with extreme prejudice. Captain Heinrich liked P almost about as much as he liked me…

"Same as ever," I answered.

The other nodded at me. "Doesn't it bother you, Lieutenant? Fraternising with one of *them*, I mean?"

"It's a member of my squad, trooper."

"But it…" said the MP. "It's a fish, ma'am."

"So?" I challenged. "You going to let me through, or what?"

The MPs didn't have much of an answer to that, and the bigger guard shrugged. "Have it your way," he said.

I passed through a security gate, and into the lab complex that made up Science Deck. P's fishy scent lingered on the air, overwhelming even the military grade atmo-scrubbers, and I just followed my nose to its cell. Whether Sci-Div wanted to admit it or not, that was what this chamber really was: a cell. P, tended by a couple of medtechs, was a prisoner behind an armour-glass wall. The single Science Division officer stationed outside the cell looked up as I approached.

"Good evening, Lieutenant," he said. He gave a warm smile that looked halfway genuine.

"How's my trooper doing?"

"It's doing well," the officer said. "Very well, in fact. I don't think that we've met. I'm Dr Wesley Saito." He tapped the name-tag dangling from his lapel. "I'm Chief Science Officer on this operation."

Although one science type looked the same as any other to me, I was pretty sure that I hadn't seen the guy around before. He was maybe forty Standard years old, with a small frame concealed beneath a plasticised smock, which was the closest thing that Sci-Div had to a uniform. Shorter than me, with shaved dark hair and Japanese features, Saito was handsome in a geeky sort of way. He clutched a data-slate that danced with tri-D images.

"I'm Jenkins. Keira."

"I'd guessed that already. You're something of a celebrity on the ship."

I shrugged. "Don't believe everything you hear," I said, not very keen to go back into the Jackals' various exploits.

"I just got transferred, out of Cristobal Complex."

"Cristobal?" I asked. "Didn't that get wasted?"

"Not completely," said Dr Saito. "Science Division moved all Priority Three staff off-world before the Spiral took control of the facility. I was lucky; I got out before they bombed it."

"Right. Good for you. Why's it so quiet in this sector?"

P's lab was usually crawling with personnel, eager to make observations and take readings. It felt unnaturally calm.

Dr Saito explained, "Most of the Sci-Div contingent is concerned with analysis of the warden-form. It's stirred up a lot of concern."

"I'll bet. So everyone's lost interest in P?"

That was Science Division for you, I guess. Always keen to move on to the next big thing, to work on the next quick fix to a particular problem.

"I wouldn't say that. It's just that... well, nothing like this has ever been done before. We didn't even know that warden-forms existed until relatively recently. The Krell..." Dr Saito clucked his tongue. "They are a species of infinite variation. We weren't expecting the warden-form to have those defensive bio-adaptations."

"Those spine things?" I queried. "Yeah, they came as a surprise to us, too."

"Six months ago, the very idea of bringing a senior Krell bio-form into custody would've been unthinkable."

"I guess so," I muttered.

Dr Saito smiled. "I know that there are some in Sim Ops, and in Sci-Div too, who bear you and your squad ill will. I'd just like you to know that I'm not one of them."

Dr Saito put the data-slate down on a medical trolley, and rolled up the sleeve of his smock. His forearms lacked data-ports—he obviously hadn't been one of the Sci-Div staff sent to Vektah—but his flesh was badly burnt there. The skin was warped, a virtual morass of scar tissue.

"My family are Japanese," he said. "I was a scientific advisor to the Directorate, during the Krell War. Born on Tianjin Prima." His eyes twinkled a little at that revelation, as though he was holding back tears. He went on: "Like your Private Feng, I was liberated from a Directorate prison camp."

"When did that happen?"

"Oh, don't worry," he said. "Tianjin Prima was one of the Alliance colonies invaded by the Directorate, during the hostilities. They took me prisoner. I'm not a clone. I was born and bred."

"So was Feng," I said, defensively.

"I'm not making any judgement. My point is, I'm not carrying anything like the private had in his head. I've read the debrief on him; I know what happened in the Kronstadt system."

"I'm not sure anyone really knows what happened to Feng," I said, with a spike of irritation in my voice.

"Probably not," Dr Saito said. "But I know the Directorate about as well as Private Feng does. I spent almost five years in a prison camp. No amount of hypnotherapy or drug treatment is going to make me forget what I saw there."

I noticed that the doctor had a serial code tattoo splashed across his wrist, where the scarring was worst.

"I was made to work for them, you know. Not everyone in the Directorate agreed with their policies, with what they tried to do." He looked up at me, sharply. "I'm grateful for what you did at Kronstadt," he said, his voice dropping so that there was a measure of intimacy to our conversation. "You dealt a mighty blow to the Directorate. Not everything has to be a battle, Lieutenant. Not everything is a threat."

"It is from where I'm standing."

"That's sad," Dr Saito muttered. "That's a terrible way to see life."

"And it's not true? Look at what the Directorate did to you."

"I forgave them for that."

I snorted a laugh. "Really?"

He shrugged. "I can forgive them and take pleasure in the fact that they are destroyed. Those things aren't mutually exclusive."

"You're too highbrow for me, Doc."

Dr Saito laughed. "I just wanted you to know that I'm just grateful for what you did."

"I wish everyone had that view."

"The rumour is that the Directorate will never really recover. They say that you've finished them."

Where had I heard that before? The Asiatic Directorate was like a hydra. Although you could cut off one head, there were always many more waiting to bite you. I wasn't sure at all that it was gone, no matter what the news-feeds and the Press Corps said.

"Well done. Thank you."

"Any time," I said. I meant that part if nothing else:

I was proud of what we had done to the Directorate, whether we had finished them properly or not. Small victories, and all that.

I nodded at P, beyond the glass. "It isn't right that P is locked up like this."

Dr Saito smiled, but the expression faltered. "You can thank Captain Heinrich for that. His orders, I'm afraid."

"So I hear, but it doesn't mean that I have to like it. Are the geeks going to be long with my trooper?"

Pariah was tethered to a medical monitor by a series of cables. Feeds ran into the gaps between the xeno's bio-armour, where the flesh was softest.

"They're finishing up now," Dr Saito answered. "I must say, the Pariah is an astounding specimen, and its attachment to the Jackals is an interesting development. But I doubt that you've come down here to talk about the finer points of Krell bio-adaptation." He picked up his data-slate again, and tapped at it. Put his thumb to the reader panel. "I think that my people are just about done in there."

The two scientists, carrying trays filled with blood samples and tissue cultures, filed out of the cell. The geeks were lost in their own discussions, almost ignorant of P.

Dr Saito reached over, gently touched my forearm with his hand. "It's immune, you know," he said. "Pariah is the only Krell bio-form—the only example of their technology—to develop a positive response to the Harbinger virus." But then Saito's sidelong look was gone, and he withdrew his hand. "Just go on through. I'll file it as a debrief session. Every trooper deserves that, right? Even Pariah."

The glass partition between P and the rest of the science lab darkened, became opaque at Dr Saito's command. Something like sympathy crossed behind the officer's dark eyes.

"Thanks."

"Go on."

I was blasted with anti-bacterial mist in a decontamination lock—some sort of quarantine between P and the rest of the ship—and then allowed access to the nest. The place stunk. The cell had started out as clinically pristine, but P's presence had already changed that. The weird resinous compound the Krell used to build their nests crept up the walls. P had retreated to a corner, its huge bulk semi-curled.

"Hey, P. How's things?"

Pariah glanced up at me, barbels drooping from either side of its fish-like mouth twitching. "Jenkins-other."

"Who else?" I said. I dropped to the floor beside P, and sat with my back against the wall. "Were you injured on Vektah?"

"Not sufficiently to inhibit our performance," P answered.

Pariah's armoured body was stitched with scars, some of which were old, others new. The latest injuries suffered on Vektah were already healing though. That was a consequence of P's enhanced metabolism; it had incredible regenerative abilities. Whatever had happened on Vektah Minor, it would be okay.

"Isn't this place a little bright for you?"

The lights were bright, and the room clinically cool.

"The others insist that the illumination remains at this level," P said, waving a claw at the glass wall to indicate the science staff. "They say it assists their observation."

"Maybe I'll speak to them, get the lights lowered or something."

"That would be preferable," P said. "And the temperature is not comfortable, either."

I nodded. "Got it. You want it hot and dark."

"A compartment at the aft of the craft would be more suitable. In Engineering, for instance."

"I don't think that Captain Heinrich is going to allow that."

"Understood." P paused, and I detected glumness. "It is objective truth that the habitation conditions were preferable when we were not working with designation Heinrich."

"I hear that."

In other words, P had been allowed to do its own thing before we were brought back into the Alliance fold. When we'd been working outside of the chain of command, decisions such as where Pariah nested weren't subject to the same level of micro-scrutiny.

"We sense that Jenkins-other does not like designation Heinrich either," P said.

"You don't need to be psychic to figure that one out, P."

"We do not understand 'psychic'."

"Neither do I. What's happening, between us?"

P turned its head and evaluated me with its alien eyes. I saw my own reflection in those black, fathomless orbs.

"Jenkins-other tasted the Deep. We are connected. We are able to sense."

"I...I can sometimes feel you in my head. I'm not sure that I like it."

"What is to like?" P intoned. "The connection simply is."

"Have you told the Science Division people about this?"

"Of course not. They would not understand. They have not tasted the Deep. Has Jenkins-other informed those that observe?"

"No," I said. "I haven't. But I'm not sure how long I can hide it from them."

Since our escape from Kronstadt, the Jackals had been

through numerous debriefing sessions. We'd undergone psychometric testing, loyalty evaluation, and hypno-training. Our accounts had been subject to analysis by Military Intelligence's most rigorous testing techniques. Pretty much everything we had seen and heard had been recorded, but this—the mind-link, as I'd taken to thinking of it—had remained secret.

"Jenkins-other is still disturbed by the others' rejection of the Jackals' account," P said.

"I am," I said. "No one believes that we found Lazarus."

"We saw the unit designate Lazarus. We believe."

"No one in Command accepts our account though, P. No one will even recognise the existence of the Watch."

That was the most troubling aspect of the story for Military Intelligence. Who, or what, was the Watch? Harris had given me the scantest of details about the agency—describing it as some sort of shadow agency, working in deep cover—but we had found no evidence of the Watch's existence. Since we'd returned from the Kronstadt mission, the Watch hadn't made contact with us in any way at all.

"We do not understand how the others' organisations work," P said. "It is alien to us."

"It feels alien to me, sometimes."

"Then we do not stand any chance of understanding it."

"Good point."

"What was the purpose of Jenkins-other's attendance?" P asked.

"I just wanted to say well done. We couldn't have executed the mission without you."

"Jenkins-other's thanks are unnecessary. We did what was required. We wish to stop the spread of the rot, and the capture of the warden-form was a necessary step in that process."

"You didn't have to help us though." I stared around the room, blinking at the intense light from the glow-globes overhead. "Especially considering the way that Heinrich is treating you."

"Heinrich-other does not understand us. The unit's reaction is to be expected."

"Can you feel the warden-form?" I asked.

"We can. It is in pain, but..." P paused for a moment, then said, "it will not remain so."

"Whatever, P. Whatever." I stood up and brushed my uniform down. I could've sworn that the fish-gunk that covered the walls had crept further up the bulkhead since I'd entered the room. "As long as you're keeping well."

"We are well enough."

"I'm not happy with how they're treating you in here. You aren't a prisoner."

At that, P rose above me. The fish loomed; at full height, easily eight feet tall now. It produced both barb-guns out of their hiding places in its forearms, bones snapping and skin folding so that the weapons popped into the alien's clawed hands.

"Make no mistake, Jenkins-other," it said, "we are not a prisoner on this craft. The Alliance requests our assistance, and we give it freely."

"It's a turn of phrase," I said. Despite P's menacing demeanour, I wasn't afraid. I knew that the alien's display of force wasn't meant for me. "Put away your toys. Don't forget that you're being watched."

P's guns retracted back into the alien's forearms with a wet slurp. "Understood."

"We're heading back to Sanctuary. There's talk of another mission. Lots of scuttlebutt."

I felt P projecting its thoughts directly into my head for an instant and winced as it made the connection.

<We have to find the Aeon,> it told me. <Is this to be the next deployment?>

"Maybe," I said. "Let's hope so."

<It has been months, objective, since we left Kronstadt.>

"I know. I know."

The Aeon: a fourth species, one of a pantheon of aliens that had once allied with the Krell against the Shard. The Jackals had secured key intelligence that could be used to locate the Aeon, during the Kronstadt operation. On our induction back into Alliance forces, however, that intelligence had been locked down. In some ways, the Vektah operation felt like a detour: a distraction from what really mattered.

<The Aeon is the key,> P replied. <We must stop the others from finding it first.>

"Just be ready," I told P.

<We are always ready,> P said.

I left the cell, and found Dr Saito waiting for me outside. He reactivated the observation window.

"Try to do something with the heating and those lights," I said. "P doesn't like them that bright, and it's too cold."

"I'll do what I can," Dr Saito replied.

CHAPTER SIX

SOME SANCTUARY

Under the power of her quantum-drive, the *Providence* took us back towards Alliance space. There was an alarm, a ten-second warning, then a Q-jump. Then another, and another. The journey took only two days subjective, but several months objective. Time-dilation did its thing and we all paid the debt. Of course, a Shard Gate would've solved the problem: the Gates compressed time and allowed for near-instantaneous travel. But the Shard Gates had long since fallen to the Black Spiral, and we had no choice but to rely on good ol'-fashioned Q-travel. Still, it beats walking.

The *Providence* was sufficiently large that many of the commissioned officers had their own quarters. That wasn't anything to write home about: my compartment was big enough to hold my property locker and a cot, all told. But it was private, and by the time we'd finished post-mission debrief, that was all I cared about. I was ready to collapse straight into bed, eager to get some shut-eye before we reached Sanctuary.

I slid open the door to my compartment. The chamber beyond was dark.

"Lights," I instructed.

The AI didn't respond, and I felt an immediate prickle down my spine.

No. Not here. Not now...

The fact that I could conduct mind-to-mind communication with Pariah wasn't the only secret I was hiding from Command. When I got back to my quarters, the other one was waiting for me.

"Lights!" I yelled. "That's an order!"

The computer didn't respond. The chamber viewport was open, the star field outside was bright, but there were plenty of shadows in the small room. A shape detached from the dark and became distinct. I recognised the ghost, because I'd seen it plenty of times before.

"So you think that this will help?" it asked.

The figure's bright, perfect teeth were visible in the low light. It grinned, reflecting the stars outside. The expression was positively malicious.

Corporal Daneb Riggs.

"You're not real," I said. Repeated, over and over: like a nursery rhyme to keep me safe from the bogeyman. "You're not real. You're not real..."

Riggs gave a tired sigh. "Quit the bullshit, Jenk."

"You're dead."

"We both know that isn't true. I escaped Darkwater Farm, and I'll keep escaping."

"You're not real..."

But the words were worthless, were useless. They wouldn't protect me here, or anywhere. Was there anything in the universe, I wondered, capable of stopping this son of a bitch?

"Of course I'm not real," said Riggs. "But does that actually matter?"

My sometime confidant, and former lover, stood in the corner of the room. He appeared to me as I'd known him. Tall, rugged and youthful; aged a decade or so younger than me. Riggs' upper body was well-muscled, and wore his Alliance Army uniform almost nonchalantly, as though it didn't really matter. Maybe that had been portentous: ultimately neither the uniform, nor the flag, had meant anything to Daneb Riggs. He had betrayed me and the Jackals and everything that we stood for.

Riggs detached from the dark. He ran a hand down his clean-shaven face, as though tired, and put another through his messy dark hair. Sat on the end of the bunk.

"Seeing you, here, like this," he said, staring down at the bed sheets. "It brings back real memories, you know?"

"Fuck you."

"Every chance we got; we used to steal the moment and make off to your quarters. Do you remember that? We had some good times."

"None of it mattered."

"You let me in, didn't you?" Riggs' voice dripped with lecherous glee. "You let me do this to you, the Alliance, the Jackals." He grinned now, and again the expression was tired. "How've you been, Jenk?"

"Fine," I said, taking a different approach to the hallucination. "I'm fine."

"I don't think you are," he said. "You might be back in the fold, so to speak, but everyone is waiting for you to step a foot wrong."

"That's not true."

"Who's going to fuck up first? Will it be Novak: lifer, prisoner, a man obsessed with finding his family's killer? Or maybe Feng. They took the metal out of his head, I hear."

"Feng's fine too," I said. "He's looking forward to seeing you again."

Riggs stood. He was physically imposing, but that didn't scare me. What really frightened me was the extent of my own hatred for the boy. I'd never hated something so much, so powerfully, as I hated Riggs.

"And still you haven't found the Aeon. Military Intelligence is sitting on your intel, right?"

"Don't concern yourself with it."

"The standard military mantra of 'hurry up and wait', I guess. Or maybe you don't have the ships to go after it."

"We've got plenty of ships. But it doesn't matter, because you aren't real."

"Dear ol' Dr Locke," Riggs said, affecting fake sympathy. "She died for nothing. That would make sense. Lots of people you come into contact with seem to die for no good reason. Take Harris, for instance."

"You killed Lazarus," I said. "You killed Elena. You destroyed the Watch."

"Did you ever stop to think that there is no Watch? That maybe it was Harris, a tired old man, doing things on his own, trying to make himself relevant in a universe that had forgotten all about him."

"I'm going to find you," I said, through bared teeth, "and I'm going to take you apart, piece by piece. I'm going to win this thing, Riggs. Mark my words."

Riggs advanced on me, crossing the room. "Maybe Lopez will be the one to break first. Perhaps her father will withdraw his support for you, take away his protection. You ever wonder how that would go down, if Lopez left the Jackals?"

"It's not going to happen."

Riggs took another step forward. For a ghost, he sure looked and felt awfully real. I could even smell his body odour, feel the warmth of his breath. He breathed out slowly, doing his best to intimidate me.

"Or perhaps Zero will fold. She's the softest, isn't she? How's she bearing up? This isn't what she signed up for."

"Leave Zero out of this!" I yelled, charging across the chamber, into the thing of shadow.

Except, suddenly, the lights came up. The room was empty.

"Everything okay, ma'am?"

Zero stood at the door, a look of concern plastered across her face, a cup of java in her hand. I turned around sharply, one hand balled into a fist, and Zero shrank back.

"I…" I started. Rage bubbled inside of me, unable to find a release. "I'm good."

"I was passing by," Zero said. "I heard shouting from your room."

"The lights weren't working," I said. "I…I lost my temper with the AI."

"Right," Zero replied. She didn't sound very convinced. "Okay."

"They…they seem to be working now though."

Zero gave a sympathetic smile. "The AI can be a little unreliable sometimes."

"Yeah. Tell me about it. What're you doing?"

"I was about to start running checks on that canister," Zero said.

"What canister?"

"The image that you sent me," Zero said, frowning. "From Nest Base Gamma, remember?"

I rubbed a hand over my face. "Right. Of course."

"I've isolated the data."

"Keep it that way."

I knew that Riggs hadn't been here. Not for real, anyway. Rationally, the hallucination had to be the product of my shattered emotional state. Even so, I still found myself checking around the room, looking for some sign of him. Where he had been sitting on the bed, there was nothing. The sheets were still in position, not even a crease to prove that Riggs had been real.

"You looking for something?" Zero said, no doubt reading my distraction. "Are you sure everything is okay?"

"It's just... well, we've made a lot of quantum-jumps in a short period of time. Q-space always messes with my head."

Zero lifted her eyebrows. "True. Ten, in the last eight hours. Only another three to go before we reach Sanctuary. Do you want some more downers?"

Downers were military-sedatives. Insomnia was a regular problem for many simulant operators.

"Can you get me some out of the infirmary without being noticed?" I retorted. "Don't get yourself into trouble on my account."

"I have my ways." Zero paused, as if unsure of herself. "Are you still having the dreams?"

"Are you?" I countered.

Zero sighed, and unconsciously her hand went to her temple. Her hair was loose there, covering the remains of the burn-mark, where the Directorate had attempted to remove intelligence from her head. That hadn't worked, but it had left her with some permanent scarring. I wasn't the only who was often awoken at night with bad dreams...

"*Touché,*" she said. "You know what I mean."

"Sorry. And yes, I'm still having them."

Zero was referring to another of the consequences of my connection with Pariah. I'd been having dreams; virulent, vibrant and horrible dreams. Worlds on fire. Kelp-beds reduced to diseased pools. Bio-ships trailing contagion across the void. I, on the other hand, had struck a low blow, and I knew it. Zero was the last survivor of Tau Manis; a French-American colony that had been her home, and that had been destroyed during the Krell War. She'd lost every member of her family through the conflict.

"Do you think that you should speak to someone about it?" Zero said, anxiously. "A psytech, maybe."

"What's the point? They'd lock me up, like P."

"Maybe they could help."

"Drugs can help. I need some proper rest, is all."

"Okay. I'm just saying." Zero gave a brittle, concerned smile. I knew that she meant well.

"Thanks. Even if I don't tell you as often as I should, you know that I appreciate it."

"Hey, we're friends, ma'am. I know you better than anyone else on the squad. I'll drop by those downers."

"I'll come to Medical with you now."

Zero sipped her coffee. "Okay. Whatever suits you."

She turned and walked out into the corridor, and I quickly followed her. I took one last look into the room, as the lights dimmed again.

There was no one there.

Sanctuary Base was located among the mining stations that populated the outer cordon of the Former Quarantine Zone, on the border of Alliance space. It represented the last best hope of the human resistance in this sector; a military outpost like no other. This was the third time since our rescue from the Kronstadt massacre that the Jackals had been recalled to Sanctuary, and the place never failed to impress.

Sanctuary Base was a hollowed-out asteroid, with thousands of kilometres of interior space converted into hangars, barracks and armouries. It even had its own simulant farm; a factory capable of producing sims for the ever-hungry war effort. There were several dry docks, and every berth was filled with a starship. All nationalities were present here, all territories of the Alliance united under one flag. There was a frisson on the air, a bristle among the gathered assets that not even the vacuum of space could dispel.

According to the scuttlebutt, Sanctuary had been built in secret somewhere in Proxima Centauri system, then quantum-jumped to its current location. The Jackals' original home station had been Unity Base, but that—like so many of the border posts—had been abandoned. Everything was concentrated on Sanctuary Base, all forces drawn together. There were hundreds of ships here, ranging from corvettes to battleships to dreadnoughts. The Alliance fleet was *mustering*, so the rumours went. The newscasts reported that battlegroups were being recalled, patrols reassigned. Something big was happening, and it was happening soon.

Along with a couple of hundred other sailors, techs and operators, the Jackals jostled for disembarkation orders. The umbilical tube that would allow us to board Sanctuary was hot and crowded, and the mood became impatient as clusters of ships drifted by.

"I hear that Sanctuary was made under contract from the Proximan government," Feng said, needling Lopez. "I'd wager that Secretary Lopez oversaw the construction personally."

"I don't think that Daddy would have the time for that," Lopez said, dismissing the idea.

"Senator is embarrassed, yes?" Novak suggested. "So while her daddy tries to cut Sim Ops budget, he is secretly building this base at home. Is Proximan station."

"It's an *Alliance* station," Lopez insisted.

Novak jabbed a meaty finger at the obs window. "Speak of the Senator, and he shall appear..."

Despite the huge range of starships docked at Sanctuary,

one craft stood out: a sleek, dark space yacht, almost militaristic in design, with an armoured prow and a delta wing-shape. The name DESTINY was printed in bold white letters on the ship's flank, together with the Alliance, Proximan and American flags. The yacht had appeared on hundreds of newscasts, been the subject of numerous press reports. It was known throughout the thirteen Alliance territories as the personal transport of Secretary of Defence Lopez.

"As Heinrich said, Daddy's here again," Lopez muttered. There was a disparity between her choice of description—"Daddy"—and the way that she spoke the words. To say that the relationship between Lopez and her father was complex would be an understatement.

"He seems to be on-station a lot recently," Feng commented. "Was he here last time we were recalled?"

"He was," Lopez said.

There was a chime over the ship's PA.

"All hands, all hands," came the AI's dulcet tones. "Prepare for disembarkation to Sanctuary Base."

"Finally!" Novak exclaimed.

The station's artificial gravity envelope took us, and the Sim Op teams all disembarked. We emerged into a hangar bay, which was alive with activity: technicians repairing fighter wings, sailors ready to take over watch of our ship, other Sim Ops teams returning to shore.

"Miss Lopez?" called a voice, cutting through the surrounding noise.

A man and woman approached the Jackals. Both wore dark suits, neckties and white shirts, which made them stand out from the crowd. I knew who these guys were before they even made the introductions—their presentation positively screamed Secret Service.

Lopez's shoulders sagged. "Great. I guess Daddy wants to see me."

The lead agent gave a precise nod of her head. "Welcome back."

Lopez pouted, turned to me. "I know these two. They've been Daddy's security since I was a kid."

The agents were both obvious Core Worlders, with broad faces and suits pulled taut over equally muscled bodies.

"Great," said Novak. "So you now have your own security guards, yes?"

Lopez sucked her teeth at the Russian. "Go fuck yourself," she said. "They're here to protect Daddy." She nodded at the agents. "Special Agents Megan Cambini and James Butler. These are the Jackals. They're assholes, but I love them."

Agent Cambini's face looked as though it had been reconstructed at least once—either as a result of an injury, or through the insertion of subdermal armour plates. Her dark hair was pulled back from her head in an all-business way. She looked less than impressed by the exchange.

"Well done on a successful mission, Jackals," Cambini said. "Your father sends his congratulations, Miss Lopez."

"Save it, Cambini," Lopez said. "What does he want this time?"

"Just the pleasure of your company," said Butler. "Can I take your bag?"

Butler was remarkably similar in appearance to Cambini, with a squared-off head and a blank expression.

"I can carry it myself," said Lopez.

"If you're sure," said Butler. The beginnings of a smile touched the edges of his lips.

"Good luck, Lopez," I said, with a mock salute. I turned to the Jackals. "Logistics will probably want to—"

"No, ma'am," said Agent Cambini. "We're here for

you too, Lieutenant Jenkins." Images flashed over the insides of their smart-glasses, no doubt providing confirmation of my identity. "Secretary Lopez requests your company as well. If you'd like to come with us."

"And if she does not?" Novak said, puffing up his chest, preparing for a fight.

Cambini shrugged, but Butler's right shoulder extended, just slightly. Enough that I could see the gunharness beneath his jacket. It wasn't a threat, exactly, but it could turn into one.

"It's okay," I sighed. "Who needs downtime, anyway?"

"This war won't fight itself," said Butler.

Lopez rolled her eyes. "You guys are the worst."

"We try," said Cambini. Her face hardly ever seemed to move, which I found disconcerting.

"This way," Butler suggested. "We have a transport waiting."

Captain Ving appeared from the bustle of personnel behind us. He looked incredulous and rather angry. Now that, I kind of liked.

"How come she gets facetime with the Secretary?" he said, exasperated. "Phoenix Squad captured the Christodamned warden-form!"

Before I could answer, there was a commotion from further down the deck. The crowd parted to make way for a large metal cube to be transferred from the *Providence* onto Sanctuary. The special cargo was surrounded by Sim Ops troopers in combat-suits, preceded by a security detail. The box was printed with numerous safety warnings, fitted to a grav-sled so that it hovered a half-metre off the deck. The security detail wasn't standard Army—their armour looked a different pattern. Maybe some sort of Spec Ops team. Even so, they looked spooked, as though they wanted to get this over and done with as soon as possible.

"That's the warden-form, I take it," Lopez said.

"I think so."

I felt a stab of anger, and disappointment, as another shape emerged in the warden's wake.

Pariah.

The xeno—*our* xeno—was paraded across the deck, flanked by four guards equipped with plasma carbines. P wore manacles at the wrists, and held its upper limbs out in front of its body as though demonstrating its captivity. Jeers and pointed words were directed at the captive alien. P rose above it all, and didn't react. I could feel the aura of calm radiating from the alien, could sense it lingering in the back of my head. P certainly had more patience than me.

"It's for show," Lopez said. "We all know that P could break out of those chains in a heartbeat."

"Faster, probably."

"Let's not keep the man waiting, huh?" Cambini said, to her colleague.

"I hear that," Butler muttered back.

CHAPTER SEVEN

JUST ANOTHER PROBLEM

The agents had arranged for one of the anti-G transport buggies that filled Sanctuary's every corridor, and the four of us piled in. Cambini drove across the station, while Butler swept a watchful eye over every corner and junction. The journey didn't take long.

"This way, troopers," said Cambini, as we reached *Destiny*'s private dock.

She showed us through to the umbilical. I couldn't help frowning as two remote sentry guns whirred into action, the big fifty cals tracking us as we walked by. One wrong move and those bad boys would shred even the most heavily armoured target. Lopez was less bothered. She gave a yawn, and even managed to look slightly sullen.

"What?" she queried, as I caught her eye.

"You're not bothered by the big-ass guns watching our every movement?"

She shrugged. "I guess not. I've grown up with this shit. You forget; Daddy was a big shot a long time before he made senator. Agents following you everywhere, remote safety systems that won't let you out of their sight: none of this is new to me."

"Follow me, please," said Agent Butler. "Secretary Lopez would like to meet with you in here."

We were shown through to a two-tiered chamber that was probably best described as a lounge. The *Destiny*'s interior was politely restrained opulence. Bulkheads were hung with paintings from famous Core System artists—all of which was far too highbrow for me to recognise, other than the general style—and the deck was covered in a plush cerise carpet. One wall had been tuned to show the view of Sanctuary, and the planet that the station orbited, but it wasn't clear whether that was a view-port, or the bulkhead itself was a monitor.

In the well of the chamber, sitting at a low coffee table, was the man himself: Secretary of Defence Rodrigo Lopez. He reclined with practised languor on a sofa of dark red velvet, one long leg crossed over the other. This Lopez was handsome, in an everyman sort of way; each strand of his dark hair perfectly composed, every line of his face there for a purpose. He was middle-aged, but only because he wanted to look that way. His features were vaguely Hispanic, like Lopez's, but generic enough that he appealed to the broadest demographic possible. He and his family had been the subject of the best gene-sculpts the Alliance had to offer.

Lopez's addresses on the war effort had been broadcast the length and breadth of the occupied universe, and had been the rallying cry to the military assets in this sector. He was a leader who preferred to lead from the front: as evidenced by his decision to come *here*—to Sanctuary Base. That had to fly in the face of his security team's advice, because there were plenty of other ways to conduct business that didn't involve physical attendance. Lopez could've sent a recorded address, beamed in via an FTL link, even used a simulant. But no; Secretary Lopez was here, simply because he wanted to be.

He was that sort of man and that was why the troops liked him.

Lopez was deep in conversation with another figure, focused on projections that sprang from the table, images that danced like ghosts between them. An opened bottle of Proximan whiskey sat beside the projector, and both men cradled glasses half filled with amber liquid.

All of this wealth and power in one place immediately made me feel uncomfortable, and I paused at the threshold of the chamber. I threw a crisp salute and waited for further instruction. Lopez had no such compunction. She sauntered into the chamber without pause, while Cambini and Butler took up positions either side of the hatch.

"Ah, my daughter, and her commanding officer," Secretary Lopez said, looking up from his discussion. He wore a bright white shirt, in the Old Earth fashion, open at the neck without a tie. "Excellent. Stand down, Lieutenant."

"Yes, sir."

"Really, there's no need for any of that around me," the Secretary said, pinching the legs of his expensive slacks as he stood from the couch. His dark leather shoes—real leather, not a synthetic substitute—reflected the chamber's muted illumination. "I don't bite." He grinned, exposing a set of just-right teeth to prove the point. "Haven't you explained, Gabby, that I'm not one for formalities?"

Lopez lifted her eyebrows and made a sound of disapproval at the back of her throat. "No one calls me Gabby any more, Daddy."

Secretary Lopez strode over to his daughter. "Well I do. My Gabby, my dear Gabby. I am so pleased to see you."

The Lopezes embraced. It was a little brittle, not

quite genuine, but more or less reflected the relationship that Lopez had with her father. Gabriella Lopez was cut from a very different cloth to the Secretary, but around her father she regressed.

"Patrico and Josef send their love," the Secretary said. "They often ask of you."

Lopez faltered a little. She'd spoken fondly of her brothers, and I knew that she missed them. She sort of smouldered, in a way that suggested a million unresolved family resentments.

"Really? They do?"

"Of course."

"Where are they now?"

"They're both on Proxima Colony. They want to know when you're coming home."

Lopez curled her lip, swinging into petulant teenager mode. "*You* want to know when I'm coming home."

"Don't be like that."

"I'm not being like anything," Lopez said. "You never wanted me to join Sim Ops, and you never wanted me to serve."

"I wanted—and still want—you to be safe."

"I *am* safe."

Secretary Lopez winced. "Don't forget who I am, Gabby. I've had access to your debrief material. I've seen what you've been through."

"I'm still here to tell the story," Lopez said. "You don't need to worry about me."

Secretary Lopez turned to me. "It is good to see you again, Lieutenant. I hear that the last operation was a resounding success."

"Yes, sir. The specimen was secured."

"That is excellent news. On behalf of the Alliance, I'm truly thankful for your efforts."

The Secretary smelt of expensive cologne, a scent that

reminded me of wealth and power and carried just a hint of intimidation. It was a heady mix, a bit intoxicating.

"It's fine, sir," I said. "Do you want me to take my boots off? This carpet looks awful expensive."

"Don't worry about that," Secretary Lopez said. "If you are a friend of my daughter, then my home is your home. *Mi casa es su casa.* I'm very proud of my daughter." He looked to Lopez, nodded. "Our relationship can be a little fraught, sometimes, but what relationship between father and daughter isn't?"

"True," I said.

"I know you've had your own difficulties," Secretary Lopez said. "Your father is Theodore Jenkins, isn't he? Theodore was something of a war hero, as I understand it."

"Back in his day," I said. "Now ma and pa are safe and sound, back home."

"As safe as anyone on Old Earth can be," he said. "I'm trying to get to know my officers. I feel I have a duty to do that; to understand what you people are giving up in defence of the Alliance."

"They say that you're going to be running for another office," I blurted, "soon enough."

Secretary Lopez paused. "Is that the 'scuttlebutt', as you call it?"

"That's the scuttlebutt," I repeated. "Is it true? Are you going to be running for Alliance Secretary General?"

Lopez shrugged. The motion struck me as very practised; as far too self-deprecating to be natural. "Perhaps. This war; people have lost a lot of faith in the old systems." As if to say *speaking of the old systems*, the Secretary turned to the other man at the table. "Have you met Yarric—ah, Director—Mendelsohn?"

"No," I said, "we haven't met, Director."

Chief Director Yarric Mendelsohn remained seated.

The Director wasn't known to me personally, but as head of Science Division, everyone knew who he was—in his own way, he was as recognisable as Secretary Lopez. Mendelsohn had appeared on numerous press briefings and news-feeds, and had become the public face of the Alliance's efforts to cure the Harbinger virus. He wore the ubiquitous Science Division smock, with rank-bars and service accolades prominent on his lapel.

Mendelsohn sat back in his chair, a frown creasing his forehead. He was in his autumn years, and his features were every shade of grey, from his silvered hair down to his tired-looking skin.

"Lieutenant," he said, earnestly. "I've read an awful lot about you."

"I'm fine with the 'lot' part, sir, but not so much the 'awful'."

I'd meant that as a joke, but Mendelsohn took it seriously. "It was a mixed review, shall we say."

"In the circumstances," Lopez chimed in, "we'll take that as a positive."

"Take a seat," Secretary Lopez said, indicating one of the plush leather chairs opposite the sofa.

"Thank you, sir," I said.

Lopez had already done the same. How Gabriella Lopez—*my* Lopez—was able to slide so effortlessly between the two personas of line trooper and politician's daughter was beyond me. This place—the *Destiny*—felt as though it had a different atmosphere, a mix of gases that wasn't breathable for a grunt like me.

"Help yourselves to the whiskey," Lopez said. An aide appeared from nowhere and produced two glass tumblers. "It's Proximan, a real taste of home. I might have American citizenship, but the Proxima Colony national creed is very different from that of any other planet in the Alliance. We have our own identity, and we like things our own way—whether that be our alcohol, or our politics."

"So I hear."

The Secretary shot a sideways glance at his daughter, as she slid a glass across the table in my direction. I took it, and sipped at the whiskey. It was good, likely expensive.

"The Director and I were just discussing the Kronstadt situation," said Secretary Lopez. "Your intelligence from the dying days of the star system has been invaluable in understanding what happened there."

"Several systems have fallen to the Harbinger virus," Mendelsohn said, "but we haven't had assets in-system at the time of their loss. Kronstadt was different. We've pored over the data-stacks from your ship, the *Firebird*."

"There wasn't much left of her," Lopez said. "I'd be surprised if you got anything."

"More than you might think," said Mendelsohn. "And every scrap of intelligence allows us to understand more about this threat, and what we're up against."

"There has been a…*development*," said Secretary Lopez. He leaned forward, into the light of the holo-projections, his glass held in his hands between his knees. His expression hardened. "We'd like your observations on something."

My gut tightened. This, I realised, was no social call.

Lopez nodded at Mendelsohn. Secretary to Director.

"Take a look at these pictures," said the Director.

I focused on the swirling tri-D projections from the smart-table. Images of planets in the clutch of the Harbinger virus. Of diseased Krell bio-ships in orbit, around moons. Scattered through an asteroid field. Black, spiralling matter that polluted the space between worlds…

"They were taken by a spy-asset in the Mu-98 system," explained Mendelsohn. "We sent probes back into

Kronstadt's space, using your course trajectory. The images show the system in its current condition. As you will note, it has undergone certain changes."

"I can see that," I said.

"We're especially interested in this material here," said Mendelsohn, pointing out a particular image. "Science Division is calling it 'shadow matter'. It is produced, we believe, by the virus."

"How?"

"Harbinger is consuming worlds," said Secretary Lopez. "Every time a Krell colony falls to the virus, it consumes biological material. It *refashions*—if that is the right word—this material, into something else."

"Kronstadt wasn't a Krell world."

"Correct," said Secretary Lopez. "But this is the catch."

"Harbinger is not really a virus at all," Mendelsohn said. "It's a highly effective and very complicated nanophage."

"What's that?"

"On a cellular level, Harbinger is composed of nano-machines. At a preliminary stage, these nanites behave like a regular virus. When a subject is infected, the virus attacks the central nervous system. It acts with a singular purpose, and usurps the patient's free will. The Krell thralls are the result."

"I've seen enough of those," I said.

"But that is only the first objective of the virus," Mendelsohn explained. "We believe that its real purpose is something else. You see, Harbinger's true threat is that it is capable of self-replication. With each new host it infects, it adapts. *Mutates*. The nanotech adopts certain patterns and changes behaviour. Once it reaches a certain level of mutation, the 'virus' breaks out. At that stage, it can consume *all* biological material."

"Not just Krell?" I queried.

"No," said Mendelsohn. "Although, because the Krell

are so reliant on bio-technology, their worlds are especially prone to infection and subsequent repurposing."

"Show her," Secretary Lopez said, sipping at his whiskey.

Another image popped into existence between us. The air instantly felt colder, and my spine stiffened.

"What the fuck is *that*?" Lopez whispered.

Black and angular and warped, I knew exactly what it was. The vessel seemed to absorb light, draining the stars around it, visible only as an absence. Empty planes, angles that were all wrong. It was a floating monstrosity, a slab of dark matter.

"It's a Shard starship," I said.

Director Mendelsohn gave a tight nod in what could've been approval. "That was what we suspected, but your confirmation is helpful. What else can you tell us about these ships?"

"Not much," I truthfully answered. "I've only ever seen one Shard starship, and that was one too many." I swallowed. "It destroyed a whole planet, or its technology did, during the Second Krell War."

"We've reviewed your account," Secretary Lopez said. "This was during your service with the Lazarus Legion, wasn't it?"

"That's right."

The Shard were a machine-species that had left behind artefacts of their technology after a war that had once ravaged the Milky Way. The Black Spiral were clearly intent on bringing them back, one way or another, but their connection to the Shard wasn't clear. The Shard were responsible for the Harbinger virus, and that was what had brought the Maelstrom to its knees.

"Experience of a single xeno ship of this type is more than most operators can boast," Mendelsohn said. "Very few have first-hand experience of operational Shard technology. Did you see anything like this on Kronstadt, during the Harbinger invasion?"

"No," I said, which was also the truth. "You've read my file, no doubt."

"Of course," said Secretary Lopez. "I've read yours, and my daughter's too. But sometimes things can be left out."

I pulled an unconvinced face. "I haven't heard of that happening before. A hypno-debrief is pretty extensive, usually."

Except that I knew my debrief hadn't been complete. I'd managed to somehow hide information from my handler; in particular, the mind-link with P. The Secretary and the Director regarded me coolly, and I suspected that they knew I was hiding something. But they obviously had no proof, and therefore Mendelsohn moved on.

"You'll notice that the ship appears incomplete." He highlighted aspects of one image, which appeared to show the bare bones of the vessel's hull, its underside open to the void. Every completed plane of the ship's frame was etched with glyphs; machine-text that shimmered uncomfortably. "This is the best-quality image we have, and we're almost certain that the ship is under construction."

"Those could be weapon-emplacements," I offered, pointing out spire-like eruptions. "But I'm not really sure."

"Do you have any idea what sort of weaponry a Shard ship might employ?" Mendelsohn probed.

I shrugged. "If it's anything like the rest of their technology, it'll be brutally effective."

"You're talking about the Shard Reapers, I take it?" Secretary Lopez suggested.

"That's right. It's about the only Shard weapons tech I've witnessed, up close."

Shard Reapers were constructs developed to act as

soldiers and guardians, sometimes posted on artefacts. Composed of millions of nanites acting together, Reapers were capable of adapting their shape and size as required, as well as forming bladed weaponry from their liquid metal skins. They could absorb plasma blasts, even at close range, reforming to repair damage. In combination, those abilities made them murder machines.

"The Reapers are nano-tech based too," Mendelsohn agreed. "Harbinger is an evolution of the technology. We hypothesise that most, if not all, Shard weaponry is based around a similar blueprint. Planetary invasions could be conducted by larger machines responsible for 'harvesting' bio-matter."

"The Reapers are bad enough," I said. "How is this shadow matter, and the ship construction, linked to the virus?"

Mendelsohn breathed in sharply. "The evolved version of the Harbinger virus breaks down biological matter, and reassembles it into shadow matter. The ships are the end result."

Ice trickled down my spine. "*Ships?*"

"That's correct," said Secretary Lopez. "This isn't an isolated event."

"There are ten of them," said Mendelsohn. "Ten Shard warships."

A further scattering of images sprang from the table. Vessels in various states of completion, each undeniably of Shard construction. Tendrils of shadow matter danced around some; material flitting like flies about the unfinished ships. They were stripping planets, assembling ships from the remains. The sites were in several star systems spread across the Maelstrom.

"As you can see, the ships aren't finished yet," said Secretary Lopez. "This process—automated construction— is fast by our standards, but still takes time."

"But by chance or design," said Mendelsohn, "the Black Spiral now hold every identified Shard Gate in the Maelstrom. If these Shard ships reach completion, they will have access to the entire Shard Network. The Spiral—with their Shard allies—will be able to launch raids on Alliance and Krell territories with utter impunity."

"Well, that's just great," said Lopez. She noisily gulped down her whiskey, and reached for the bottle to pour herself another. "So you're saying that we're screwed?"

Secretary Lopez gave a wilting glare in his daughter's direction. I could almost read his thoughts: *Shush, child. The grown-ups are speaking now.*

"The situation is not that bad," said Mendelsohn. "Not yet, at least. We don't know, for example, whether these ships are the actual Shard, or just some reconstruction of their technology."

"Does that make a difference?" I challenged.

"It might," Secretary Lopez countered.

"So what are we going to do about this?" I said. "It has to be stopped."

"General Draven is about to call a briefing," Secretary Lopez said. "I'm giving you advance warning of this development." He looked at me levelly. "I wanted to forewarn you that the Jackals are going to be given a mission of great importance to the Alliance."

"Can you tell us what it is?"

Secretary Lopez flashed an insincere smile. "I can't share that information yet."

"You could if you wanted to," said his daughter.

"No, I couldn't, Gabby." He looked back at me. "I just wanted to inform you. This is my gift. For bringing Gabby back from Kronstadt, back to safety."

My heart had started to beat faster. Either the drink, or the excitement, was making me heady.

A communicator chimed.

Secretary Lopez's face crumpled in irritation. "I'm sorry, Lieutenant. Duty rarely considers convenience. I'll just take this call—"

"It isn't you, sir," I said. "It's me."

My wrist-comp gave another urgent chime, and I glared down at it. I'd grown used to that particular tone, having set it up specifically, so that I was alerted when certain conditions were met. I stifled a sigh of annoyance as I read the text-only message that filled the screen. *He's doing it again*, it said.

"I'm very sorry, sir."

"Everything all right?" asked Secretary Lopez.

"Fine," I said. "But I'm afraid I have a situation to deal with." I downed the remainder of my whiskey, and placed the glass back on the table. "It can't wait, unfortunately."

"I understand," said Secretary Lopez. "No doubt you have important military business to attend to?"

"That's overstating it somewhat."

"My agents will show you out. Remember what I said: the briefing will be soon."

"Yes, sir. Thank you for the drink."

Lopez said her goodbyes to her father, and Cambini and Butler walked us up the umbilical, watched us leave the private dock. Lopez said nothing until we were out of hearing range of the Secret Service agents.

"You do know," she said, with an amused smirk on her face, "that you are probably the first person ever to cut short a meeting with Daddy?"

"Trust me; it wasn't intentional," I said, as we pushed through the crowded corridors.

My wrist-comp continued to chime, with increasing urgency.

"He'd have a fit if he really knew where you were going," Lopez said. She knew what the problem was.

"It's not like I have a choice," I said. "If I don't see to this, you know what'll happen."

Lopez nodded. "I get it."

Unfortunately, this wasn't the first time I'd had this particular alert.

It was fast becoming an itch that I couldn't scratch, and my sense of annoyance increased as I descended through Sanctuary Base's sub-levels. I headed straight for Declan's Drinking Hole.

Sanctuary had many compartments and hidden sectors, lots of places in which to get lost, or to go off-grid. The opportunity for profit dwelt in those darker nooks. And what better way to make money on the largest military space station ever built than to sell alcohol. Declan's Drinking Hole was neither licensed nor official, but it stayed in business because it fulfilled a need. You get enough soldiers and sailors in one location, a place like Declan's becomes necessary. There's only so much stress that a speedball court can relieve.

If Declan's had any chic about it at all, it was best described as "pseudo-industrial". The walls were bare rock, and repurposed cargo crates made up most of the furniture. An improvised bar was stocked with a variety of alcoholic drinks, while a couple of holo-monitors fixed overhead silently replayed speedball matches from the Core. Glow-globes in the ceiling were set to minimum illumination, in an effort to avoid drawing attention to the fungus that grew on the walls. The place wasn't busy, and most of the patrons didn't even look up as I entered.

I approached the bartender. We weren't known to each other, except through this mess.

"He's over there," he said, nodding to the back of the room.

"Thanks," I said. "I hope he wasn't too much trouble."

"Not to me. But I think he broke the other guy's jaw, and my data-terminal got caught in the middle of it."

"The other guy was lucky there were no knives around…" I muttered. I fished a universal credit chip out of my fatigue pocket and passed it to the tender. "Will that cover the damage and the inconvenience?"

"Same as ever," the tender said. "I won't call the MPs."

"That's decent of you."

"He needs help. He can't keep coming down here and doing this, Lieutenant."

"I know," I said. "I'll take it from here."

Leon Novak sat at the end of the bar. He wore a vest that strained at his huge, tattooed shoulders, and had a bottle of Russian vodka in front of him. He rubbed his left hand with his right, where the knuckles were swollen and raw.

I slipped onto the stool next to him. "What the fuck are you doing, Novak?"

Novak's eyes slid in my direction. "Oh. Is you."

"Yeah, it's me. Your friendly neighbourhood commanding officer."

"This is no neighbourhood. Not any more."

"You're drunk."

"No, I am not. It would be in breach of life-contract, yes?"

"You're damn right it would."

In theory, Novak's life-contract prohibited him from drinking alcohol. He was an indentured prisoner, on licence to the Alliance military. Breach of any one of his numerous conditions of release could result in recall to the gulag. Of course, that wasn't going to happen. The war needed people like him. One more body in prison was one less body on the front line.

"Tell me what happened."

"I got into fight. I punched other man. I win. Is

simple." Novak grabbed for the vodka bottle and swigged it noisily. "Is nothing else to say."

"Get rid of that bottle, trooper. I need you frosty."

"I'm tired. So tired."

"I know that you're tired. I also know what you've been doing."

"What do you mean?"

"It wasn't the fight that drew me down here," I said.

Novak paused, and something inside of him seemed to shift. He was most definitely drunk, but he either wasn't anywhere near as inebriated as he appeared, or my words had an abruptly sobering effect on him.

"I wasn't doing anything," he answered.

"You've got to stop this, Novak. You've got to let this go."

"What do you mean?" he muttered.

"Don't play dumb with me, you son of a bitch."

There was a public data-terminal in the corner of the bar, an old-fashioned computer that could be used to access the local network. Nothing complicated, but in the right circumstances it was capable of hacking intel-feeds. This machine's holo-screen was damaged, flickering erratically, and a bloody handprint marked the keyboard.

"You were searching for *her* again, weren't you?" I asked. "And I take it that's why you got into a fight."

Novak was morose and silent for a moment, but answered, "No."

"Fine. Then I'll ask the tender to tell me."

"Was only fight."

"Tell me what really happened."

More silence, and Novak seemed to sober up even more. Eventually, he said, "He tell me he can get into grid. I pay him money."

"You paid this guy money to search for her?"

"Yes. To search for *her*." Novak swallowed. "To search for Major Mish Vasnev."

And there was the truth. Where this name was concerned, I knew that Novak wouldn't—*couldn't*—lie. It meant too much to him.

"I paid tech to give me information," he explained, slowly. "This is something I cannot do on own, you understand, but something I need to know. He do search, say finds nothing. I am angry at this."

"You can't keep doing this," I said. "That name—that individual—is a known Black Spiral sympathiser, if not a full-blown accomplice." I looked over my shoulder again, without any conscious thought. "Military Intelligence, the Secret Service, whoever: they're looking for these people."

"So?"

"So I told Zero to keep an alert on that search-string," I explained. "And every time you do this, I get called down here—or wherever else you've dragged your sorry ass—and have to dig you out. If *I* know you're doing this, then Mili-Intel probably knows it as well."

"I need to find out everything about Major Vasnev," Novak said, as though that was some sort of explanation. He seemed desperate to make me understand this, to spell it out for me. "I hunt her, yes? I find her."

"No."

"We must find ship," he said. "We must find Vasnev, and I will kill her. There are refugees from Mu-98 still out there."

"We've been through this before." *Too many times*, I resisted adding. "Your duty is to the Alliance, Novak. You're an indentured, licensed prison operator, not a free agent."

Novak's features cycled through a variety of expressions as he struggled with the urge to argue with me.

"She was not real major, you know," he said, sourly. "Was never in Army."

"I kind of guessed that."

"Was very high-ranking *bratva*. Was godmother of whole city, of Norilsk. Did terrible things."

"I'll bet. But that isn't the point."

"She get name from killing real Army major. He go to Norilsk to finish gangs, to make city safe."

"Martial law?"

Novak nodded. "Yes. She find him, she kill him. Sons of Balash rise up, take back city. She cut this major's head. Plant on a stick in city square, to send message. She make everyone know this is her, that police, army—no one can stop her. Then, no one ever come again. Is bad place. Vasnev, she gets this name, this rank—'major'—and everyone understands that she is in charge."

"It's a long way for an Old Earth crime lord to come," I said. "I guess that Warlord is paying her well."

"Distance for Russians is nothing," Novak argued. "Where money calls, we go. Is way of life. All I know is her. When I sleep, she is there. In my head."

Novak had no way of knowing how much I understood that. The Russian took the vodka bottle, but continued waving his arms, trying to explain himself.

"I cannot think of anything except her," he said. "I must find her. I *must*."

This was eating Novak alive. Becoming an obsession. Killing him. It was all he was now. *Like finding Riggs is killing you, huh?* my conscience taunted me.

"I prefer the knife, the blade," Novak went on. "Because it is quiet, is silent. I know this. When I find Vasnev, I will be ready."

He swigged from the bottle again, but there was no pleasure in the action. The anger was building up in his shoulders, across his face.

"We've talked about this already," I said. "You need to park it, Novak. You need to turn this anger—this rage—and use it."

Novak grimaced. "I know," he muttered.

"We might never find her. This Vasnev is elusive, right?"

Novak shrugged, not understanding the word.

"She hides?" I said.

"Yes," he agreed. He waved at the data-terminal. "I search all database. No one know about her. Only small informations. Sighting on this planet, rumour on that moon."

"We may never find her," I repeated. "But you're a Jackal. I need you to be sharp. Can you do that for me?"

Novak slowly nodded. It wasn't a very persuasive response, but I knew that it was the best I was going to get out of him. A pep-talk from me wasn't going to stop Novak. Not permanently, anyway.

"Sharp as a knife," he muttered.

"This ends here. You aren't to do this any more. No more searching for Vasnev, no more obsessing about her. The research, the asking questions: it'll only get you into trouble." I sighed. "Or *more* trouble, at least."

Don't get me wrong: Novak was one ugly bastard. From his over-tattooed forehead, to his broken teeth, all the way down to the nerve-studs drilled into his temple, Novak wasn't anyone's conventional idea of a hero. But in that moment, as he sat there, in the dank and dirty bar, the look on his face was heartbreaking. His eyes were dark, eager. Sure, he wanted to find and kill someone, but he wanted to do it for a good reason. I could sympathise with that.

"You need to get cleaned up," I directed. "Something big is happening."

"Something involving Black Spiral?" Novak queried, hope rising in his voice.

"I can't talk about it here," I said. "But it's happening soon. Like hours away." I waved over the bartender with another credit chip. "We'll take a detox tab. Make it double-strength."

The meds would sober Novak up more or less immediately.

"I am not drunk," Novak protested.

I swiped the vodka bottle from him. I noticed that it was triple-K brewed: Kronstadt-quality alcohol. The smell of the open bottle alone made my eyes water. There was very little of the bottle left; Novak had drunk almost all of it.

"You most definitely are," I said. "And how can you drink this stuff?"

"It is Russian."

"It's shit."

I slid off the stool and pressed down my fatigues. Just being in the bar made me feel kind of dirty.

"If you don't quit this, and soon, Captain Heinrich will get wind of it. He'll assign you a surveillance drone again."

As part of his service contract, Novak had once been accompanied everywhere by a surveillance drone. However, Novak had used it as a makeshift weapon, and it had met a rather unfortunate end on North Star Station. Since our return from Kronstadt, no one had bothered to reimpose the restriction on his liberty.

"Understood," Novak snorted.

I glanced down at the thick network of self-harm scars on his forearm. The blade marks criss-crossed his tattoos, and were partly healed. There were so many scars there that I couldn't even count them. Novak marked himself every time we made a transition, as a reminder of the discount to his sentence.

"How many years do you have left on your sentence, Novak?"

Novak pursed his lips. "Do not worry about it. I am not going anywhere yet."

That sort of information—how long Novak had left on his sentence—was only available to senior Command. Heinrich probably knew, but I doubted that he would tell me.

"You don't get to kill as many people as me and walk away from it," Novak continued. "Not even if you join Sim Ops."

"You're good at what you do, and I need you on the squad. Just take those meds, and get sober."

"Yes, ma'am."

Novak took the two pills from the tender, and dry-swallowed them. His timing couldn't have been better. The bar seemed to freeze as a station-wide alert sounded. My wrist-computer chimed.

NEW ORDERS, said the screen. ATTEND BRIEFING ROOM 93 AT FOURTEEN HUNDRED HOURS, SHIP TIME. ALL SIMULANT OPERATIONS PERSONNEL GRADE 3 AND ABOVE. THIS IS NOT A DRILL.

Novak's wrist-comp lit with the same message. He grinned a vacant, slightly psychotic smile.

"Who wants to live for ever?" he asked.

"You've been saying that a lot lately," I replied. "Come on. We've got a place to be."

CHAPTER EIGHT

A PERFECT STORM

Briefing Room 93 was Sanctuary's largest auditorium, capable of seating hundreds of attendees. It was a horseshoe-shaped chamber, with a raised podium at the front of the room, which was backed by an enormous Alliance badge; the infamous stars and stripes of the thirteen territories.

The chamber was crammed with troopers and intelligence handlers, with admin staff struggling to get personnel seated. Everyone who was anyone was here: from Ving and Phoenix Squad, to the Executioners, to Walker's Dead—"Grade 3" personnel meant pretty much anyone with combat experience. The Jackals settled into a line of chairs a few tiers back from the front.

"It's a full house," Feng said. "P is down there."

"Hey, fish!" yelled Novak, with a wave.

Flanked by two Mili-Pol guards, P stood on the main podium. The xeno nodded up at us in recognition, and I felt its presence at the back of my head. Not much, but enough to tell me that P was doing okay. It looked in good shape, at least. Dr Saito also milled around the podium, trying to keep out of the way.

P was soon joined by several military officers. I recognised General Draven, wearing full military uniform, with his peaked cap, salted moustache and tired eyes. Alongside him was Director Mendelsohn, as well as Secretary Lopez. The Secret Service agents hung back, scanning the auditorium for threats, but unwilling to completely discount P as a potential either. Other faces filtered into the room. Every senior officer aboard Sanctuary was present, occupying the first tier of the auditorium's seating. They were a mix of nationalities and planetary allegiances, from a variety of limbs of military service: Navy, Army, Marines, Military Intelligence. Whatever was happening, it was clearly going to be a combined arms operation.

"Some of these guys look like they've been dragged out of retirement," Feng said, nudging Zero.

She gave a shrug. "That sounds about right. I read that Admiral Vester was reactivated last month."

"He isn't the only one," I said. "Anyone with command experience is being recalled."

"That's great," drawled Novak. "So now they put old men in charge?"

"I guess they know more about running a war than you do, Novak," Lopez said.

Captain Heinrich prowled the ranked troopers. "Simmer down, people! Simmer down! Let's get this briefing done, so you can get back to doing what you do: killing Spiral and catching fish!"

General Draven stood to address the auditorium, and the chamber fell quiet.

"Let me begin by welcoming Secretary of Defence Lopez to this briefing," Draven said, his voice low and gravelly. The exhaustion of running this war showed heavily on his expression, in the hang of his shoulders. "I'd like to thank him for his attendance on-station. As you will all have noticed, there are several—"

What followed obviously wasn't part of the plan, but Secretary Lopez couldn't contain himself. He stood in front of the Alliance seal, perfectly framed by it. A surveillance drone hovered in front of him, recording his message.

"Thank you for the introduction, General Draven," Lopez said. "I see many, many brave faces here. I see good faces. But mostly, I see Alliance faces."

He walked the length and breadth of the podium, nodding slightly as his gaze met that of every participant in the meeting. General Draven entertained the intrusion, but he didn't look particularly impressed by it.

Secretary Lopez continued. "I've travelled a lot during my time as Secretary of Defence. I've seen the refugee fleets. I've seen the survivors. It doesn't matter whether they're from the Outer Colonies, from Barnard's World, from Kei Tripoli. Each and every one of them, to a man, woman and child, is grateful for what you're doing out here. I want you all to know that.

"What you are about to hear is the product of months of planning. It represents the efforts of all the Alliance military forces. We are striking back, friends. We are taking the stars back from the Krell, and from the Black Spiral. It's happening now, because of you."

The mood in the room became almost jubilant. Cheering spread like wildfire. Some more senior officers had even joined in. I shot a sideways glance at Novak, who noisily slammed a hand against the seat in front of him.

"What?" he said. "Is contagious, yes?"

"Don't buy into it," said Lopez. She was the least persuaded of the Jackals; appearing almost embarrassed by her father's performance.

"What's up, Lopez?" I asked. "You don't believe him?"

"I've seen Daddy do his thing too many times before," she answered. She sort of squirmed in her chair, uncomfortable. "The subject is different, but the presentation is always the same."

Zero leaned into me. "He's quite the showman," she said.

"Isn't he just," I replied.

Secretary Lopez was riding a wave of approval, and loving it. The crowd eventually settled down, and he smiled broadly, turning to the wall behind him. He tapped a remote control in his hand, pointing it at the bulkhead as he addressed the audience again.

"We have custody of a live Krell warden-form. The boys down in R&D tell me that they have made a breakthrough, as a result of the operation on Vektah Minor. They've done what we once thought was impossible."

A hitch formed in my throat. Lopez bit her lip.

"We've done it, troopers. We've created a cure for the Harbinger virus."

That sent the audience into overdrive. Troopers stood, yelling, cheering. Officers clapped, although surely they must've known what was coming. The Secretary's words lit the fuse, and the bomb positively exploded.

To support the Secretary's claim, holographic projections winked into existence and filled the podium. A glowing representation of the Harbinger virus, warping and twisting Krell DNA. But on Secretary Lopez's command, another strand of *something*—the presentation wasn't specific—intervened, and neutralised the virus. The result, so the demonstration suggested, was a pristine cellular structure: good as new.

It was hard not to be influenced by the Secretary's enthusiasm, and Novak deliberately sat on his hands to avoid clapping. Lopez looked sullen. Zero was frowning, peering at the tri-D: no doubt trying to figure out how Science Division had done it. Feng was quiet, but I could tell that he was impressed.

"But all of this," Lopez said, waving a hand at the tri-D graphics, "doesn't mean anything. Results: that's what you really want to see, right?"

The bulkhead behind Secretary Lopez shifted, and heavy blast doors retracted, revealing a concealed chamber. It was a starkly lit cell, divided from the briefing room by an armourglass wall. Inside, three medtechs in full hazmat suits tended to a bulkier figure.

"It's the warden-form," Zero said.

The enormous xeno was strapped to a medical table, buckled in place with mag-locks. Despite that, its chest rose and fell as it breathed. None of the physical signs of Harbinger infection were visible. There was anger on its battered face—reminders that it had been forcibly extracted from a Krell nest—but nothing like that the infected carried with them. Any doubt I had that the alien was truly cured was dispelled by a glance in P's direction. I felt the alien's emotions, knew what it knew.

"Is this for real?" Feng said.

"It's real," I muttered. "They've done it."

Troopers rose to their feet, craning necks to get a view of the cell. Everyone wanted to see the show. Secretary Lopez prowled the deck, standing scant metres from the alien captive, like it was his trophy. Here was mankind, triumphant over the Krell, bringing the very Shard to heel. *Nothing can stop us*, said the expression on Secretary Lopez's face.

General Draven stepped forward, and his iron gaze quietened the crowd immediately. Lopez took his cue. He nodded at Draven, stepping back from the podium.

"If you've quite finished, Mr Secretary," General Draven said, "we should get on with the briefing."

"Yes, yes, of course," Secretary Lopez said. "My apologies for the intrusion, General." The grin on his face suggested that he wasn't sorry at all.

"We have a lot to get through," General Draven said.

"We do," Lopez agreed.

General Draven called up some graphics on the holo beside him. P. watched on, drinking in the data. From the other side of the glass wall, safely contained in the cell, the warden-form did the same.

"This is a briefing on Operation Perfect Storm," Draven commenced, pressing his hands into the podium's command lectern. "I can, without hesitation, say that this is going to be the largest-scale mission into the Maelstrom that we have ever attempted. Operation Perfect Storm will involve sixteen hundred starships. Thousands of sailors and simulant operators. Hundreds of engineers, scientists and other support assets. Our objective will be the eye of the Maelstrom."

General Draven wasn't one for theatre, and he wasn't one for dramatics, but *now* he had my attention. I sat up a little straighter, listening more intently. The shift was subtle, but everyone around me seemed to do the same.

"We will be deploying directly into the Reef Stars," he declared. "We have ascertained the location of several reliable quantum-space jump points, which will allow us to deliver the fleet into the heart of Krell territory."

A tangle of stars, maybe six closely linked systems, appeared on the podium. A particular system, and its ring of planets, was highlighted. One world was emphasised; all blues and greens and swathes of dusky cloud.

"This planet will be our target," Draven said. "It has been designated 'Ithaca Prime', and we believe it to be the physical home of the Krell High Council, the so-called Deep Ones."

The Krell homeworld. Back when we had first been at war with the Krell, when I'd started my career in Simulant Operations, men and women had spilt real blood trying to obtain the location of the Krell homeworld.

Over the years, many missions had been launched in an attempt to identify the planet. All had failed. Pariah had changed that situation: it had volunteered the information willingly. It hadn't always known the homeworld's location, but it had developed the knowledge. This was Deep-knowing, as P called it.

"'Ithaca Prime'..." I said, rolling the words around in my mouth, trying them out for size. It was like putting a name to a face; being able to identify a long-held adversary, only to find that it was no longer my enemy. "It has a certain ring to it, I suppose."

"The Deep Ones represent the controlling minds of all Krell Collectives," General Draven continued. "They have not been in direct communication with the Alliance, but we understand that they remain uninfected. Several Krell war-fleets have fallen back to this location. Military Intelligence believes these have been recalled to defend the Reef Stars, and specifically Ithaca Prime, against infection."

The image now changed to a long-distance view of Krell bio-ships, sailing through the cold of space. I couldn't identify the Collective to which they belonged, but there were several fleets, likely hundreds of vessels, and they appeared to be uninfected.

"Intelligence also suggests the movement of human assets within the Maelstrom," General Draven said. "Black Spiral ships have been observed in neighbouring star systems. They appear to be progressing towards the centre of the Maelstrom. These ships can move with relative freedom, as a result of the Spiral's control of the Shard Gates."

Riggs is probably on one of those ships, I thought to myself. *With the arch-bastard Warlord, moving closer to the Maelstrom's dying heart...*

Director Mendelsohn nodded along with Draven. He stirred from his seat. "Science Division is of the opinion that the Spiral is planning to contaminate the Deep Ones with Harbinger. Needless to say, if this occurs, the consequences will be catastrophic. Given how Harbinger spreads, the infection of the Krell's higher consciousness will trigger a mass-infection event."

Mendelsohn called up some more imagery on the tri-D. Krell homeworlds obliterated by rains of plasma. Pyres composed of stacked alien bodies. Then human colonies, slaughtered by the infected Krell. Finally, that weird black material that polluted every system that Harbinger claimed: spirals of shadow matter growing in deep space. My stomach churned as I remembered Mendelsohn's images aboard the *Destiny*. The Maelstrom would be turned in on itself, a breeding ground for Shard starships.

"This is the result of a Harbinger infection," General Draven said, quietly now. "Every planet, every system, that falls, is corrupted. Every Shard Gate we have lost is filled with these infected bastards, moths drawn to the flame. We still don't know why the Spiral are doing this, what they want to achieve. This operation will therefore fulfil a dual purpose. We will both inoculate the Deep Ones—by force, if necessary—and land a killing blow to the Spiral."

A ripple of applause spread through the chamber.

In the well of the briefing room, an officer stirred. She was a stern-looking woman with short red hair, shaved into a pseudo-buzzcut, wearing a Navy uniform of a type I didn't recognise. She had no rank insignia or medals. For some reason, her whole presentation screamed black operations. Hers was a face that had seen things— the jagged Z-shaped scar down her left cheek suggested a story in itself—and she wasn't afraid to ask questions.

"General Draven, how do we intend to dispense the Harbinger cure?" she asked.

"Good question," I muttered.

General Draven nodded, as though he had been expecting this challenge. "Thank you, Commander Dieter. This is an essential part of the mission. There will be two methods. First, Simulant Operations squads will be assigned to each battlegroup. All squads will be equipped with Pathfinder suits, in the expectation of a deployment via drop-capsule into enemy territory. Virtual testing of the cure suggests that even a single application, applied directly to a Krell nesting site, could be sufficient to neutralise the Harbinger virus.

"Second, each starship will be equipped with a limited number of anti-viral warheads. These munitions can be deployed directly from orbit, to the infected sites. Again, Science Division believes that a direct strike via this method will be sufficient to establish inoculation."

More graphics popped up around Draven. A table of organisation demonstrated the distribution of the various assets across the operation. The fleet had been organised into five main battlegroups, with each spearheaded by a dreadnought.

"The UAS *Defiant* will lead the charge," Draven said. "She will head up the 1st Battlegroup Division. The 2nd Battlegroup will fall under Admiral Tharsis's command, and will be led by the UAS *Titan's Dream*. The 3rd Battlegroup will be led by the UAS *Sweet Justice*, and Admiral Vester will assume command. That will be supported by the 4th and 5th Battlegroups, led respectively by Captains Abdullah and Kleinman."

Zero read from the table of organisation, and pointed out, "The Jackals haven't been attached to any of those battlegroups."

"Maybe they forget about us," suggested Novak.

"Just listen," I said.

"Some ships have been assigned secondary objectives,"

General Draven said. Names of ships, and the squads allocated to each, appeared on the holo. "These ships have specialist assignments, in support of the main fleet."

"It's okay," Feng said to Zero. "See, we've been assigned to the *Valkyrie*."

General Draven continued, oblivious to the Jackals' reaction. "The *Valkyrie* will be tasked with exploration of a potential lead on Special Asset X-93, also known as the Aeon. Jenkins' Jackals and the Executioners will be responsible for making contact with the Aeon, in an attempt to obtain their support. Other teams will have similar objectives. Those squads with such orders will receive individual briefings, given their specialised nature."

My wrist-comp pinged as it received a fresh data-inload.

"The Executioners?" Feng whispered to my left. "Have you ever worked with them, ma'am?"

"No," I said, "but I hear good things about them." I continued reading from my wrist-comp. "It's not them that I'm worried about."

"Shit," Novak drawled, as he did the same. "We go into Maelstrom under Captain Heinrich!"

"Looks that way," I said.

Secretary Lopez sat at the back of the podium, not making eye contact with me or his daughter. I couldn't help but feel betrayed. Why hadn't he mentioned this plan during the meeting on *Destiny*? Not the mission, but that we were going to be deployed under Captain Heinrich.

The briefing continued. General Draven handed the floor to a Navy admiral, and the specifics of squad deployment and ordnance distribution—none of which was relevant to the Jackals—were addressed. I began to tune out, and around me lots of other troopers did the same. Most squads were eager for deployment, now that they knew the plan.

"…throughout the Amartes sub-cluster," droned on the admiral, trying his best to keep the crowd's attention. "Although certain jump-routes have become unstable as a result of quantum interference, we believe that…"

Even the warden-form, safely harnessed in the cell behind the officer, looked bored. Lopez wanted to show it off, to demonstrate how successful his plan had been…

The tri-D graphic hovering beside the ageing admiral shivered with static. Goosebumps crawled over my skin. P's stance dropped. Its mind sharpened, grazing mine. I was awake. Air escaped my lungs in a sort of gasp. I hadn't meant to make any noise at all, and it pierced the quiet of the auditorium.

"Are you paying attention, Lieutenant?" Heinrich asked.

"Yes. Sorry, sir. I mean, ah, no."

"What?"

I stood up. "Something's wrong."

"Sit down, Lieutenant!" Captain Heinrich said, his voice rising in volume until it was a positive yell. "You're interrupting proceedings. Pay attention to the damned briefing!"

On the podium, the admiral's words caught in his mouth. He frowned, old face creasing, staring at the corrupted holographic projection beside him.

A figure formed in a burst of static.

It was Sergeant Clade Cooper, also known as the Warlord of the Drift.

CHAPTER NINE

DOMINION COME

Projected directly into the briefing room, Warlord was clad in his trademark exo-suit—the armour battered and worn, a Black Spiral insignia sprayed onto the chest-plate, tattered camo-cloak draped over his shoulders. That was of a type worn by Army Rangers, a reminder of what the man had once been. His helmet was locked in place, crude skull-motif stencilled over the visor plate. A forced silence spread through the room. Although almost everyone had watched Warlord's messages to the Alliance, very few had seen him for real.

"Get a tech up here," Secretary Lopez said, standing, waving a hand at the tri-D. "Close this channel down!"

"I have come to deliver a message," Warlord said. "This ends. *Now.*"

General Draven took a step towards the hologram. "Stand down," he said. "This is a protected channel. You will immediately desist—"

"You're a tired old man, Draven," Warlord said. His voice was a wet rasp. Sick: that was the word. He sounded worse than when I'd last heard him, which made me wonder if his "addresses" to the Alliance had perhaps been pre-recorded. "You, like the Alliance, are wasted. *Rotten*. I do not submit to your authority."

The technician that Secretary Lopez had been ragging on desperately tried to manipulate the controls of the holo-feed, to block the transmission, but to no avail. It was being broadcast on every channel—protected, encrypted or otherwise.

Secretary Lopez stood beside Draven, in a show of strength. "This will not—"

"Rodrigo Lopez?" Warlord asked. "Do you really still think that you can interfere in this?"

"It's not interference," Lopez said. "You will surrender yourself to Alliance law enforcement, on pain of death."

Warlord laughed. The noise made my skin crawl. "I'm not frightened of death."

The visor of his helmet shifted, became transparent, and Warlord showed his true face to the world. Terribly scarred, sewn back together by a barrage of operations. Less a man than a tapestry of atrocities, a reminder that just because Science Division *could* do something, it didn't mean that they *should*. I heard Zero's audible reaction beside me—a sharp intake of breath that she couldn't repress—and the same response rippled through the briefing room. Warlord was an artefact of the Deep. His chestnut eyes seethed through the morass of scar tissue that made up his face.

"But you, Secretary," he continued, "are more than afraid. I can smell your fear from light-years away. You reek of it. Your stink repulses me."

Lopez stood defiant. He had an audience, after all. "Why are you doing this, Cooper? What do you want?"

"Does there have to be a 'want' behind everything? Sometimes we just *are*. I'm living proof that the consequence of existence is enough. People like you made this mess. You let the Krell into our world. You let this happen. You made *me*."

Dark shadows danced around him; quicksilver flashes. Another ripple of surprise from the auditorium. These were Shard Reapers, coiled around Warlord like terrible but tamed snakes. Faces formed in their dark skeins, shifting in and out of reality. I had no doubt that everyone in the room saw people they had known, had loved, in those dark mirrors.

"I am going to bring about Dominion," Warlord promised. "I am going to bring the Shard here, to the Maelstrom. You cannot stop me. It is already too late. The Krell will be eradicated. I am salvation. All who stand against us—against me—will perish, for I am the Spiral, and I live for ever."

And with that, the image shivered and disappeared.

"What was the point of that?" Feng asked. "He's put the biggest cross in all of Alliance history on his head…"

"It was a message," I said. "We need to get the Secretary out of here." I grappled my way out of my seat. "Sound the retreat, Captain Heinrich."

No one was listening to me. Why was no one listening to me? Only P was bristling, shaking at the triple-reinforced mag-locks that bound it. The MPs were focused on the alien, carbines up and shouting orders to *stay calm, stop moving*. But they had it all wrong; P wasn't the threat. Dr Saito was still up there with them, gesticulating at the soldiers to put their weapons down.

A hatch at the back of the warden-form's cell slid open. P whirled around in response to the sudden movement. Two new figures, both wearing full hazmat suits, virtually indistinguishable from the other techs, entered. At first, I thought that they had realised what was happening in the briefing room. Maybe someone had triggered a security alert. That would've been the smart thing to do, but it wasn't that.

One of the new medtechs produced a pistol from the folds of his medical suit. The weapon was up in an instant.

"Get the brass to safety," I screamed. "P, get them moving! Away from the cell window!"

Behind me, another MP was slamming a palm to the hatch panel, trying to access the controls that would open the briefing room's exit.

"We're locked in," he said. "We're locked in!"

The tech in the cell opened fire, and a medic disappeared in a blaze of pistol shots. The body collapsed sideways, bleeding out. The second newcomer—dressed in the same hazmat suit as the other—approached the warden-form. He held a canister.

The xeno's eyes widened. Despite the gulf between our species, I could feel the horror dawning in the alien's mind. The imposter held the canister up. Twisted the lid. Something noxious and black—like living smoke—slid out...

"Oh fuck," said Feng.

...and into the warden's mouth.

The alien fought, thrashed.

Director Mendelsohn crouched in front of the window, watching with a rapt expression on his face. I could see the calculations going on in his head.

"It's been inoculated," he shouted, to no one in particular. Despite the certainty of his response, his voice faltered as though he had become unsure of himself. "The anti-virus will—"

Do fuck all.

The warden-form began to change. Silvered veins spread across its carapace, at a rate that was surely impossible. I'd never seen the virus take hold so quickly. Its body convulsed. The warden's deep, alien eyes flickered open, and it saw with new purpose. It scanned the chamber, then tested the mag-locks that bound its limbs.

"It's … that's a grav-table," said Mendelsohn. "There's no way that it can get loose."

"This guy likes being wrong," I said to Zero.

The alien wrenched its body free. The force required was immense, and self-destructive. Musculature strained, skeletal structure warping as the creature prised itself off the table. The mag-locks failed; popping open. Everything was soundless—the armourglass separating us from the warden was thick enough to hold back the noise—but I could imagine the tearing of muscle fibres, the cracking of bones. With a triumphant shake of its head, the xeno was up.

Around me, the briefing room was yelling, shouting, chaos.

The imposter medtech went to take a step back, away from the warden's infected body. Too slow. The alien slammed the Spiral agent aside. The corpse hit a wall, sliding down the clinically white tiles, leaving a trail of crimson.

A dozen thoughts ran through my head. How had the warden-form become reinfected so quickly? Had the Spiral somehow modified the Harbinger virus? I shunted all of that from my mind. In that instant, keeping the Secretary alive, protecting the officers, and then staying alive myself: those were my only objectives, and in that order.

"Will that view-port hold?" Feng yelled, above the din.

"We're not waiting around to find out," I answered.

I made a dash for the podium, pushing against the tide of troopers making for the exit. Agents Cambini and Butler were encouraging Secretary Lopez to get moving, but he was in a state of complete shock. Meanwhile, the

senior brass were stumbling around, failing to understand that they had to act now or die.

Another tech was thrown aside as the warden went
berserk. P was straining at its own bonds, the MPs trying
to hustle the alien away from the window. It begrudg-
ingly complied with the order.

"You need to leave now, Mr Secretary," I said, grabbing for Lopez's forearm.

"I'm…" he said, swallowing back alarm. "My agents—"

On the other side of the armourglass window, the
remaining imposter medtech let loose a volley from his
machine-pistol. Rounds hit the window, spiderwebbing
the surface. The warden stomped across the cell, and the
deck shook with each footfall. It tossed aside another
technician, slamming the body into the window.

Secretary Lopez's face was stained by fear and horror.

Feng got his answer, as the glass wall spectacularly
shattered.

Glass fragments showered the auditorium, as the tech's
body went through the window. It sailed over my head
and slammed into a senior officer with a sickening
crunch.

The remaining Spiral agent in the cell sprayed the
room with gunfire. Several officers were caught in the
volley, bodies blossoming red as they jerked and twisted
with impacts. Draven and Heinrich dodged aside, barely
managing to avoid being hit. I couldn't properly assess
the damage, but there were several cries as troopers or
officers were wantonly executed.

"I'm calling for back-up, sir," Agent Butler said to
Secretary Lopez. "We'll get the doors—"

His words were silenced by a round to the head, skull
rupturing in a glorious red starburst, spraying the Secretary and me with gore. Secretary Lopez's face dropped.

"Butler!" he yelped.

The warden-form twisted, further enraged by the gunfire. All six limbs deployed, its already huge form became truly massive. It lurched towards the Spiral agent with the pistol. In an instant, it tore the body apart, throwing the corpse across the cell. Then it turned to the shattered view-port. The xeno let out a cry that chilled me to the core, so shrill that it made the air vibrate.

Secretary Lopez just sort of stood there, as though he had been infected with a lack of activity. An alarm sounded in the distance—the pitched warble of a security siren. I could just make out the chatter of gunfire, although that could've been my imagination.

"Mr Secretary," I managed. "You need to get down, and stay down. We'll get you out of here. Jackals!"

The Jackals were about the only squad doing anything productive. They were scrambling to the prone officers. Feng had Draven, while Lopez was trying to shield Mendelsohn. Zero was at the back of the chamber, still trying to open the exit hatch. The doors weren't opening, which told its own story.

The auditorium wouldn't have looked out of place in a warzone. Bodies were strewn all over, snagged across chairs, slammed against furniture. The damage was catastrophic. I got to my feet, hauled Secretary Lopez along with me. He was very nearly a dead weight. I'd seen this in civilians too many times before. The Secretary was shell-shocked, approaching combat paralysis.

"We'll get that door open," said Cambini. Her smart-glasses were smashed, her security-issue pistol unholstered. "I've called for back-up, and the hatch will be released in a moment. It'll be fine."

"I hope so," Secretary Lopez said. "This is turning out to be a very bad day."

"Just one in a long line," I muttered back. "Stay low."

The warden-form's shape was a blur. It pounced from inside the cell, launched into the briefing room. Cambini turned her face, pistol up. The gun let out a harsh *snap-snap-snap* as she squeezed the trigger.

Her aim was good. Pretty damned exceptional, given how fast the warden moved. I guess that was Cambini's enhanced physique in action; inbuilt bio-modifications, courtesy of the Secret Service. All three rounds impacted the warden's skull, even as it propelled itself forward.

Still, it didn't stop the xeno.

Like a speeding freight train, it collided with Cambini. Slammed her straight off her feet. I was close enough that I heard the gush of air from her lungs as her ribcage shattered, as the look of shock and surprise broke across her face. Her body—lifeless—crashed into the deck.

"Go, go!" I ordered Secretary Lopez. I pulled him to his feet, put myself between him and the alien.

Gun.

Cambini's pistol clattered to the ground, dropping from dead fingers. I stooped for it, trying to keep pace as the beast behind me responded to the sudden flurry of motion. My fingers clasped around the plasteel grip of the weapon, and I had it up, firing. More rounds bounced off the alien's head.

"Hey, asshole!" Novak shouted. He'd torn a seat from its moorings, and hurled it at the warden.

The chair clattered off the alien's body. It did nothing more than further irritate the alien, but that didn't stop Novak. Without pause, he tore out another chair, and threw that one too. As tactics went, it wasn't effective, but it did succeed in slowing the alien down.

Maybe, I thought, *the hatch will open before the alien reaches us...*

Except that Secretary Lopez stumbled ahead of me.

He slipped on something wet and gross that had once been one of the commanding officers. I half turned, emptying the pistol's clip into the alien's body.

"It's going to fire the spines!" Zero yelled. "Get down!"

The warden snarled, exposing rows of shark-like teeth, and I was quite sure that this was over. Those spines would shred a real skin. The poison that they carried would be overkill; Secretary Lopez and I would be history. I threw the empty pistol away, and collapsed over Secretary Lopez's prone body.

A shadow passed over us.

"Stand back," came an electronic voice. "We will assist."

Pariah smacked the enemy xeno aside with a claw. The warden was bigger, most definitely more heavily armoured, but the strength of the blow knocked it off its feet. The body hit the far bulkhead so hard that the panelling deformed.

"Up, up," Novak insisted.

He had my shoulder now, and I let him drag me to my feet. Lopez was there too, grabbing her father under the arms, away from the conflict.

"Are you okay, ma'am?" she asked me.

"I'm alive," was all I could say.

P and the warden were having a throwdown like no other. The warden slashed at P. P lurched sideways, its barb-guns extended: firing volleys of living ammo. The warden screamed as it took bone-shards to the face—the ammo capable of piercing its armour—and stomped across the chamber.

P tried to evade a blow, but the warden's reach was long. The xeno smashed into a bulkhead with force. The watching troopers collectively gasped, wincing as alien blood smeared the walls.

But P was very far from out. It squirmed beneath the warden's bulk, and slashed at the alien's torso with its claws. Being of the same species, P knew exactly where there would be weaknesses in the creature's armour. The warden's body was opened up, ichor weeping from a dozen wounds. The enemy xeno roared, its spines rising up again.

"Down!" Zero warned.

I caught a flash of activity as P rose up with both barb-guns, twisting to dodge the incoming fire—

This time, it was too slow. Like a volley of arrows, dozens of spines launched from the alien's torso and extended head-crest. They filled the chamber. Embedded in the walls and the ceiling.

And caught P full-on.

"Pariah!" I yelled, unable to contain my reaction.

P stumbled back. Its own armour was pierced, bits of bio-plating hanging loose, exposing shredded flesh beneath.

The warden-form was up, taking advantage of the sudden lapse in P's attack. It rose over the smaller xeno—*our* xeno—and drew back a pair of claws.

The briefing room hatch hissed open. A tide of soldiers poured out, and more figures piled in. The warden-form twisted its head, eyes widening—enraged that its kill had been disturbed.

A Sim Ops containment team in full combat-suits were braced in the hatch. Plasma rifles up, covering P.

"Weapons free," the lead trooper ordered.

The warden-form almost disintegrated in the hail of plasma fire that followed. Its smoking corpse slumped against the deck with a dull thump.

"Are you hurt?" Feng asked the Secretary, roughly patting down his body to check for injuries. "Respond, sir."

"I'm not hurt," Secretary Lopez said. "But—but my

agents." He swallowed. "They served with me for years. *Years*."

"They're dead," said Lopez, bluntly.

Her father nodded. He turned to me. "And I'm not. Thank you, Lieutenant."

I didn't answer him. Novak and Zero were gathered around P's collapsed body. Their expressions were grim. Dr Saito fought his way through the crowd as well, shouting orders for an emergency medical team. Pariah lay still and bleeding on the deck, the broken ends of several spines protruding from its body.

"Forget about the fish," Captain Ving said. "It's the least of our worries."

"How can you say that?" Lopez protested, fire rising in her eyes.

But Ving's face was set, his expression chiselled from stone.

"Sanctuary wasn't the only place that got hit," he said. "The Spiral has attacked everywhere."

CHAPTER TEN

AFTERMATH

The assault on Sanctuary Base was one of several terrorist attacks across the length and breadth of the Alliance. There had been a single unifying feature of the Black Spiral's plan: each target, no matter how varied, had some strategic relevance to Operation Perfect Storm. Simulant farms, automated munition factories, monitoring outposts, dry docks: nowhere was safe. The Spiral overloaded the atmosphere-processing station at the Navy docks on Vega III, causing on best estimates upwards of a thousand deaths. On Pesca V, the life-support systems had been disabled, leaving the troopers there without heat, water or air. Not for them a fast death. Overnight, the base had become a tomb.

Every view-screen on Sanctuary Base had the newscasts on repeat. Harried broadcasters broke the news as it was received; updates carried through quantum-space at almost real-time speeds.

For the Jackals, the source of our grief was closer to home. From Briefing Room 93, P had been transported straight to the medical wing. A veritable army of sci-techs and medics had descended on the alien, doing everything they could to save it. Not because they particularly cared—Command had made it perfectly clear what it thought of P—but because P was a valued asset. There was still much to be learnt from the alien, and that could only be done with a live specimen.

Then there was the question of how to actually treat P. Science Division's understanding of the Krell had come on a long way in the last few years, but research had mostly been directed into killing the fishes, not saving them. There was a big difference. Dr Saito pioneered the efforts to save Pariah, but even his knowledge had limits.

So we waited outside the operating theatre, by turns raging against the universe, then falling into sullen quiet. The hurt ran deep. It didn't matter about the species; one of the Jackals had been cut down.

"This isn't real," Zero said, her head in her hands.

"You better believe it," I ordered. "Because if you don't, you can't put it right."

The medical wing was on high alert, filled with activity. Secretary Lopez hadn't been injured in the attack, which was something of a result, but several senior officers were among the dead. Bodies were rushed past us on grav-stretchers, into overworked emergency rooms. The walking wounded, expressions shocked, stumbled by. Black bodybags were stacked against one wall. Most of those casualties had come from the attack on Briefing Room 93, but there had been other attacks across Sanctuary as well.

"How did it come to this?" Feng asked.

"No one knows yet, Feng," said Lopez, parroting back the official line.

"They'll find exactly who did this, soon enough," Zero said.

"And make them pay," said Novak.

"That's not what I mean," said Feng. He threw his hands up in the air, exasperated. "The Black Spiral are everywhere. They're just fucking terrorists, right?"

I nodded, repeated, "Fucking terrorists."

"Then how have they found so many supporters out here? And what do these bastards want?"

I shrugged. "Maybe it's like Warlord said. They don't want anything, except to bring it all down."

Feng breathed out. Bit his lip. "But why?"

Lopez glared up at a view-screen set into the wall-panel. The viewer repeated what was known about the attacks. Words scrolled across the bottom of the holo: CULT OF THE SINGULARITY, IRON FIST, FRONTIER INDEPENDENCE FRONT—ALL DECLARE WAR ON ALLIANCE. Those names had been known before the Spiral's appearance on the galactic stage, but now they had a fresh purpose. A disparate collection of criminal organisations, of gangs, of insurgent bodies—all unified under a single banner.

"Isn't it obvious?" Lopez said. "The Spiral are sweeping up the disaffected, the underclass, anyone who has a problem with the Alliance. With Proximan control, with the universe in general. Veterans, washed up from the last Krell War." She laughed, and the noise was hollow, disappointed. "From where I'm sitting, there are more than enough assholes who fall into those categories. Warlord just has to offer them a new start."

"A new start that involves bringing the Shard back to our galaxy?" Feng challenged. "No one will benefit from that."

"These people don't care," said Lopez, still staring up at the viewer. "I doubt many of them even know what they're really fighting. They'll overthrow local government, burn it down. Get what they want, in the short term. The

Shard—Warlord's Dominion—will be an unfortunate consequence."

"Nice speech," I said, more caustically than I'd intended. "You'll make a good politician someday."

Lopez's lips formed into a tight smile. "It's in my blood. But what do these people have to live for? They don't have anything left. Not after the last Krell War. And every time an infected fleet crashes into the Alliance border, and brings down another planet, the cycle repeats. More disaffected, more dissidents. More anger, more hurt. Everyone's lost someone in this mess." Unconsciously, she glanced over at Zero. She'd probably lost more than all of us put together, in the last Krell War. "In another universe, some of us would've been on the other side of the line—fighting for Warlord, rather than against him."

Warlord had said as much to me when I'd first met him on North Star Station. At the time, his suggestion that we were the same had seemed absurd. But maybe there was more to it than I appreciated.

"Like Riggs…" Zero said, the words spoken under her breath.

Novak snorted, dismissing the point. Rubbed his big hands together. "I need something to break," he said. "I wish that Riggs was here right now."

Lopez formed a gun out of her index finger and thumb. "You and me both, Big Man."

The hatch at the end of the corridor whirred open, and, as one, the Jackals started. Dr Saito appeared there. His smock was torn at the chest, and a nasty laceration on his forehead was stapled shut. I jumped to my feet as he approached.

"What's the news, Doc?"

"P is doing fine," Dr Saito answered, not seeking to

draw out the report in any way. "It's... it's more resilient than we can truly understand."

Lopez breathed out in relief. Novak grunted.

"Thank Gaia that P made it," said Zero.

"P took three spines to the chest. We've removed them, and the prognosis is good. The specimen has unprecedented regenerative capabilities. It also has an excellent antibody response to toxins generated by other members of its species."

"So P's going to be okay?"

"I'm certain that it'll pull through," Dr Saito said.

That wasn't quite news to me. I had strongly felt—even if I hadn't known—that P had survived the attack, but something also didn't feel *right*. It was almost impossible to explain.

"When can we see P?" I asked.

Dr Saito went to answer, but he was cut off by the arrival of another figure. A Military Police officer, wearing full flak-suit and carrying an armed plasma carbine, rushed into the corridor.

"Jenkins' Jackals are required on the Command Deck," the officer said. "The Secretary and General Draven need to see you."

Dr Saito's expression was sympathetic. "I'll tend to the Pariah, and keep you posted."

The MP showed the Jackals to a compartment where several officers were crowded around a tactical-display. Army, Navy, Military Intelligence: this was the remainder of General Draven's war council. From splatters of gore across uniforms, to minor cuts, to medpacks taped over more serious wounds, they all bore scars from the attack.

Secretary Lopez was deep in discussion with General Draven. He looked up as we approached.

"Reporting as required, sir," I said.

The Jackals jumped to attention, and General Draven returned the salute. The MP escort took up a post behind the Secretary, his eyes scanning the Command Deck with brittle caution.

"That was quite something, in the briefing room," Draven said.

"It was incredible," Secretary Lopez added. Despite his words, he looked intensely agitated. Maybe he was riding the comedown of an adrenaline high. "I owe you my life."

"It's all part of the job. You should thank Pariah. It did most of the work."

"You have my sincere thanks, Lieutenant. Once again, you've surprised me."

"What's the situation?" I asked, pressing my hands on the edge of the display and looking over the data-feeds. The Jackals moved in around me, doing the same.

"As of now," Draven said with about as much solemnity as he could muster, "all thirteen Alliance territories are at DEFCON one. The Alliance is facing a terrorist threat of unparalleled scale."

"We've seen the broadcasts," Feng said.

General Draven exhaled slowly. "We can't allow Operation Perfect Storm to be derailed." There were general murmurs around the display. "We have to focus on the war effort, and the localised damage to Sanctuary Base."

"How did they get onto Sanctuary?" Zero asked.

"They used a starship: the *Svetlana*. She's a Russian warship, 1st Kronstadt battlegroup."

That revelation hit Novak like a bullet. "Kronstadt?"

Draven nodded. "That's right."

The holo showed a battered battle cruiser, war-weary and space-scarred from decades in the void. The ship was old, her armoured flanks grey and featureless save for Cyrillic text, and an identifier code in Standard. The Russian and Alliance flags on her prow were almost completely faded with age.

"*Svetlana*..." Novak whispered. His hands were shaking, his bruised face draining of colour.

General Draven continued. "She was using old military codes, part of the 5th expeditionary fleet from Shangri VI. She arrived two days ago, without incident, and docked here." Another image of the ship in dock. Completely unexceptional, nothing out of the ordinary. "Several unregistered personnel were allowed access to Sanctuary. How this was possible is currently unclear."

"I guess Mili-Pol has some questions to answer," Feng said.

General Draven stared at the display. "Base security seems to have let us down on this occasion. The same personnel infiltrated the warden-form's holding facility."

Images from security cameras and spy-eyes flickered across the display. None of the faces meant anything to me; they were anonymous. The last image was a vid-clip of the infiltrators moving through Sanctuary, firing plasma and assault rifles, their cover now blown.

"The uniforms were stolen," General Draven said. "Navy, Army, Science Division...This was very well planned." He magnified the faces on the screen, and Novak audibly gasped. "They weren't Spiral," Draven added. "They are members of a prohibited criminal organisation." His eyes bored into Novak. "The Sons of Balash."

An old woman's face filled the holo. Wizened, ancient-looking. Skin like leather, with a mane of plaited dirty silver hair over one shoulder of her exo-suit. Despite her age, the woman was agile, her aim true as she fired on advancing Alliance security troops. MAJOR MISH VASNEV, said the display.

Feng turned to Novak. "Hey, isn't that ... ?" he said.

Novak balled his hands into fists. "Where is she?"

General Draven sighed. "I wish we knew, son. I wish we knew. She, and her gang, managed to escape Sanctuary during the chaos. Once the warden was free, they retreated via the same route they entered the station, using the *Svetlana*."

"Where did ship go?" Novak said. His voice dripped with cold fury, the need for revenge crackling around him like an energy field.

"It broke dock," Draven said. "The ship, together with Vasnev, is gone."

"We must follow her," Novak insisted. "This has to be done!"

"There are bigger issues to worry about right now," said Secretary Lopez. "We need to move, and we need to move now. I've authorised acceleration of the Perfect Storm deployment schedule. We can't risk another security breach." He looked around the table, and none of the officers dared to meet his eye. "They tried to kill me. The Spiral and their allies had the audacity to make an attempt on my life."

"What about the anti-virus compound?" I asked. "We all saw how quickly the Spiral reinfected that warden-form. This cure is no good if that's all it takes."

Secretary Lopez glared over at Director Mendelsohn. The camaraderie that they had shared aboard the *Destiny* was gone, and the Director was now plainly frightened of the consequences of failure. His position was precarious; Secretary Lopez could've been injured or killed, on his watch.

"We're already working on another transmission model," Mendelsohn said. "It can be fixed. It'll take some time—one of the targets of this raid was our lab section, and we lost several replication vats—but examination of the deceased warden-form is proving informative. We'll improve the anti-virus, increase the antigen load. Build a new manufacturing plant."

"And that'll work?" I asked.

"I'm confident that it will," he said.

"I'm glad someone is…" Lopez muttered.

General Draven glanced at me. "Lieutenant, your mission has priority status. You have immediate disembarkation orders. Due to the situation aboard Sanctuary, Captain Heinrich will brief you en route. You've been assigned to the *Valkyrie*, under Commander Dieter." I recognised the name from the briefing; the officer who had asked questions. That was a good start. "I understand that Pariah has been provided with medical attention."

"That's right," I said. "Dr Saito says that it'll pull through."

"We'll see to it that the alien is transported to your ship," said General Draven. "You're dismissed."

The officers around the display saluted, and we did the same.

Secretary Lopez nodded at Lopez.

"My own daughter, so eager to enter the grist of war," the Secretary said. His tone was somewhere between complimentary and disapproving, and I wasn't sure how Lopez was supposed to take the comment. "Your mother would be proud of you."

Lopez nodded, curtly. "I'm just doing my duty."

"It's all I can ask of any citizen of the Alliance," said Secretary Lopez, regaining some of his politician's composure. "I hope to see you all when your mission is complete."

*   *   *

We left the Command Deck, and an MP escort was waiting for us.

"You guys expecting us to make a break for it?" I asked, with a grin.

"Not you, ma'am," said the sombre MP sergeant, as he loaded our away bags—I hadn't even bothered to unpack since the mission on Vektah Minor—onto the waiting buggy. He risked a glance in Novak's direction. "But I wouldn't put it past the lifer."

Novak lifted his lip in an impression of a snarl. "I go where am told."

That was probably a fair assessment of the facts. I had already made the decision to keep a close eye on Novak, after what we had just been told. His breathing was still ragged, and he continued to pump his fists. The rage inside of him was barely restrained.

The MP officer navigated the corridors cross-station, towards the docks. He was jittery, as though he expected more Black Spiral agents to jump out of the shadows at any moment. There were troopers and sailors everywhere, prepping for the collection of missions that made up Operation Perfect Storm.

We pulled into the main dock, the MP pushing through the crowd. The UAS *Valkyrie* sat in a docking armature, her profile visible through the hangar's viewport. The umbilical tube that led to the ship was open, crew and deckhands coming back and forth. The MP pulled up the buggy, and started unloading our gear. We made our way down the umbilical corridor, carried along by the flow of Navy crew.

"The *Valkyrie is* a Special Operations ship," Zero explained, reading from her wrist-comp. In the short period since leaving the Command Deck, she'd already downloaded the ship's specs. Standard Zero. "She's nominally under the command of the Alliance Navy, but otherwise functions outside of the usual chain of command. An assault-carrier, with a full range of Simulant Operations upgrades. She's got a high-spec Sim Ops Centre, a cryogenics storage vault to keep your skins on ice." She pointed to the ship's underbelly. "She's also got a Pathfinder-deployment bay."

"That's marvellous," I said.

"I wish I could find out more," Zero added. She shook her head. "Everything's happening so fast."

"I hear that," Feng replied.

It felt like everyone and everything on Sanctuary was under pressure to *move, move, move*.

"Permission to come aboard, *Valkyrie*," I said.

The duty officer gave a salute on our approach and nodded. "Approved."

"I'm glad to see that you made it out of that compartment," said another voice. "Welcome aboard the ship, Jackals. I'm Commander Vie Dieter."

I recognised Commander Dieter as the officer from the briefing fiasco. Vie Dieter was tall, lean-faced, and looked about as tired as I felt. She ran a hand through her short red hair. She might not have been physically hurt during the attack, but mentally it had surely taken its toll.

"It was a little closer than we would've liked," I said.

Dieter nodded. "Twenty-six casualties, so I hear. The Spiral are getting bolder every day."

"We'll have to see what we can do about changing that," I said.

"Your fish has already been boarded," Dieter informed me. "The security team is keeping the specimen under observation." She gave the slightest impression of a wince, and indicated over her shoulder. "I didn't give the order. It came from the top."

Another figure emerged from the docking staff, a voice cutting through the background noise.

"Double time it, sailors! Double time it!" Captain Heinrich yelled. "We've got a war to win!"

It was disappointing to hear that the captain's sense of micro-management hadn't diminished as a result of his brush with death. There was some immutable law that applied to officers like Heinrich: their ability to escape injury was about as universal as physics or general relativity. I was more surprised to see that Heinrich was accompanied by an all-too-familiar face. Captain Ving was at Heinrich's side, and the rest of Phoenix Squad marched behind Ving.

"What's *he* doing here?" Lopez hissed at me, as the ship's crew completed final checks.

"I have no idea," I said.

"The briefing said that we were working with the Executioners!" Lopez argued.

"Jackals, to attention please," Heinrich said. He smiled at me, through his moustache. "Any time today will do."

"Yes, sir," I said. My team dropped into a sullen series of salutes.

"Phoenix Squad are here at my request," Heinrich said, proudly. "You'll be deploying with them."

"There was no mention of Phoenix Squad in the briefing session," I protested.

"Hmmm? No, I suppose there wasn't. Well, that attack changed things. The Executioners suffered a fatality."

Despite Heinrich's news, Ving cracked a smile. He looked supremely smug. Phoenix Squad chortled around him. They really were buffoons.

"You don't think you could be trusted to do this alone, do you, Lieutenant?" Heinrich asked, signing something off on a Navy ensign's data-slate. "Put those crates over there, in the secondary hold. Yes, with the main weapons load." He looked up at me again, as though surprised I was still there. "The mission specified a second Simulant Operations team. I selected Phoenix Squad."

"There are plenty of other teams on Sanctuary," Feng complained.

Heinrich's eyes flared with anger. "*I* am mission commander," he said. "*I* will decide who is assigned to this mission, if you please. Now get your shit together, and start towing the company line, Jackals."

"You heard the man," Ving muttered.

"*All hands, prepare for disembarkation,*" came the ship's androgynous AI. "*All hands, prepare for disembarkation.*"

Captain Heinrich turned tail and marched across the bay.

Ving nodded at me, gave me a head tip with his fingers. "Look forward to working with you, Jenkins."

Lopez gave a sigh. "Is it too late to back out?"

"Probably," I said, watching Ving and his team go.

"Do you want to?" Zero said.

Lopez shook her head. "No. Not really, but I don't like the idea of spending another day in that bastard's company."

I grinned. "You mean Heinrich, or Ving?"

"Both," she spat.

"Stand clear!" an ensign called. "Docking bay door all close!"

"Wait!" someone yelled.

A figure scrambled up the umbilical, into the hold. It was Dr Saito, dressed in the usual Sci-Div uniform, clutching an away bag. The deck chief stationed at the door control frowned, blocking Saito's path.

"The crew manifest is full," the chief said. "You're on the wrong ship."

"I'm a late assignment," Dr Saito said, fumbling with his data-slate to prove his credentials. "Here. I have papers."

The deck chief glanced at Saito's authorisation. He scanned it with his wrist-comp, and was obviously satisfied with what he saw.

"Science Officer Ames has been taken ill," said Dr Saito. "I'm her replacement."

"All right, you're cleared. Get moving. We're already running behind schedule. All clear, all clear!"

The bay doors whined shut at both ends of the umbilical, severing the link to Sanctuary Base.

CHAPTER ELEVEN

VALKYRIE'S PATH

Several hours into the mission, the ship's PA chimed, sounding a general address.

"Now hear this, now hear this," said Captain Heinrich, his every word dripping with self-importance. "The UAS *Valkyrie* expects to make the first quantum-space jump within the hour."

Lopez lay on the bunk opposite me, her hands locked behind her head. She stared up at the deckhead.

"That was fast," she muttered. "Leaving Alliance space, I mean."

"This ship must have a decent drive on her," Feng remarked.

But Heinrich hadn't finished. He continued: "There will be a ship-wide briefing at twelve-hundred hours. All command and mission-essential staff are to attend. That is all."

As he finished speaking, my wrist-comp chimed. The rest of the Jackals got the same alert.

"Huh?" Novak said, looking down at his own comp. "So now I am mission-essential too, yes?"

"Essential to us as ever," I said, with a grin. I rolled

off my bunk. "Look alive, people. Get mustered for the briefing."

"Copy that," Feng said. He stretched his legs across the deck, and Zero nearly fell over him.

"This sharing a ship with another squad is going to take some getting used to," Zero said.

She had a point. The *Providence* had been a big strike-ship, one of the older class models. The *Valkyrie* was newer, built for speed, a proper Spec Ops ship. Luxuries like personal space weren't a consideration, especially when the ship was fully crewed. With more personnel came smaller quarters. Somewhat ironically, there was never enough space to go round on a starship.

The chamber hatch slid open. Ving stood there, a towel over his shoulder, exuding malice, testosterone and over-confidence. The phoenix tattoo rippled across his bare chest, and he smelt of fresh sweat. I assumed that he had been using the starship's gymnasium, and made a mental note that was an area of the ship I should avoid.

"Enjoying your new quarters, Dogs?" he asked.

Lopez sighed, but I glared at her, and she said nothing.

"Yes, Captain Ving, we are," I answered. "What's your malfunction?"

He sneered. "I came by to remind you not to be late. Major Heinrich; he doesn't take kindly to lateness."

"We heard the address, just like everyone else," I said.

"Yeah, well, I remember what you guys were like back on Unity Base."

"We've changed a lot since then," I said.

Ving glanced around the room, disdainfully. "Christo and Gaia, these are some small quarters."

"They work for us."

"I'll bet. You should see Phoenix Squad's quarters. Now, that's a barracks for a *proper* Sim Ops team."

"If you say so. Was there anything else, or are we just

about done? I ask because, as you've just reminded us, we have somewhere to be."

Ving bristled a little, but stood back. "Be seeing you," he said.

The hatch hummed shut behind him.

"Jesus, that guy is an asshole," Lopez said, as soon as we were on our own.

"We should watch him," Zero whispered.

The *Valkyrie*'s briefing room was filled with staff. Captain Heinrich had insisted on the attendance of most of the Naval command-element, as well as the Sim Ops crew and support staff, including Dr Saito. We were all seated around the tac-viewer.

"The flight plan will take us through the Former Quarantine Zone," said Commander Dieter, circling the display, "then towards the Van Diem Straits." She pointed out a system known only by a string of numbers. "We'll use the gravitational pull of this star here, to bring us into the Maelstrom proper."

Dieter reeled off technical data on the various pitfalls we could expect. There were more than enough of those: just because this was charted space, didn't mean it was safe. The danger increased as we sailed closer to the Maelstrom. There were black holes, stellar rifts, and Christo-only-knew what else along the way.

"A trip into the 'Strom never fails to surprise," I said.

"That's very true," said Dieter. She spoke with a clipped, Euro-Confed accent, and had a manner about her that settled somewhere between practised professionalism and cold detachment. I liked her. "Once we breach this system, we'll be in an unexplored sector of the Maelstrom."

"This would be a lot safer if we still had access to the Shard Gates," Zero said, with a dismayed sigh.

Commander Dieter nodded. "And faster, too."

"We must work with what we have," said Captain Heinrich. "Proceed, Commander."

"The first phase of the route will finish here," Commander Dieter concluded. "That jump will take us into the Drift. It will be crunch time; there are several stellar disturbances in the vicinity, and the Q-jump points are likely to be unstable. We'll then engage a series of manoeuvres deeper into the Drift, to reach our final objective." She called up more graphics, and things started to become interesting: Dieter's eyes flickering with passion. "The intelligence on this place is quite remarkable." She looked over at me. "Is it right, Lieutenant Jenkins, that this came from a *tattoo*?"

"That's correct," I said. "Dr Locke carried it with her."

Well, there was a bit more to the story than that, but I chose not to give an explanation. Dr Olivia Locke had copied a map, with supporting stellar data, onto and into her body: so that it had become part of her. She had carried that intel around with her, and gone into hiding on Kronstadt so that it wouldn't fall into the wrong hands. It was the only surviving copy of this information.

"Yes, the doctor," Heinrich muttered, disapprovingly. "The *rogue* doctor."

"According to Dr Locke's intelligence, our final destination will be the Ghost Maker Nebula," Commander Dieter said. "The Nebula itself is virtually unclassifiable. It contains several black holes, the remnants of at least a dozen stars. The entire sector is swathed in exotic energies." Dieter manipulated the viewer controls, zoomed in on a particular star system, then a specific planet. "The target is a planet in orbit around this neutron star. Command has designated the world 'Carcosa'."

"What are Carcosa's conditions?" Feng asked.

Commander Dieter shook her head. "Unknown.

Alliance probes haven't been able to penetrate the outer veil of the Ghost Maker Nebula. There's a lot of interference there, worse than most areas of the Drift and the Great Veil."

"But no enemy contacts?" I queried.

"Not so far. The region appears almost deserted."

Novak snorted. "So Krell do not like so much?"

"That seems to be the case," Commander Dieter said. "We'll obtain more data as we get nearer."

"The *Valkyrie* is equipped with a full drop-capsule bay," Captain Heinrich said. "We're going to do this the old-fashioned way, with boots on the ground. I want the bay prepped for launch by the time we reach the Ghost Maker Nebula. The strike-force will make planetfall via drop-capsule, and can be considered expendable. You're all Pathfinder drop-accredited, so this won't be a problem."

Lopez nodded. "We remember Kronstadt."

The Jackals had used drop-capsules to deploy from a strikeship in orbit around Kronstadt, during the Krell invasion. That had been the squad's first taste of the technology—essentially, a system that launched a user from orbit, directly to a planet's surface. It was crude, outdated and typically very dangerous for the user: a perfect deployment technique for the Sim Ops Programme.

"And I remember you used the *Firebird* to make the drop…" Captain Ving snarled.

The *Firebird* had been Phoenix Squad's ship. Ving wasn't going to let us forget that any time soon, but Heinrich didn't want to dwell on our rivalry.

"Dr Saito is now going to brief us on the Aeon," he said, before Ving could follow up. "If you will, please, Doctor."

"Thank you, Captain Heinrich," Dr Saito said. The injury to his head was still prominent, but he seemed to be working through it. He cleared his throat. "Although this is less a briefing, and more of a speculation session."

"Is what?" Novak blurted.

"A speculation session, Private."

"I think what Novak is trying to say is, what do you mean by that?" Lopez asked.

"Well, I mean that we know so little about the Aeon that to call this a briefing would be inappropriate," Dr Saito said. "There's little concrete evidence on which we can base an analysis."

Phoenix Squad gave the obligatory sighs of disapproval. There was much shaking of heads.

Captain Heinrich harrumphed as well. "That's not very helpful, Doctor. Just tell us what you know."

"Of course, Captain," Dr Saito said.

The viewer was filled with tri-D images of the Shard ruins on Tysis World; a wind-swept, barren rock of a planet, which had come up too many times for my liking. The Shard architecture was unmistakable. Angular, obsidian-like structures jutted from the deserts, huge outcroppings of dark crystal. Holos of Science Division officers exploring the facility appeared. Blackstone structures, half-toppled spires, dark twisting tunnels.

"First, we have written records from Tysis World," Dr Saito explained. "It was here that the Alliance initially uncovered proof of the Shard's existence. An entire facility was discovered in the desert, well preserved despite thousands of years under the sand. Dr Locke was the chief scientific advisor on this site. She made many significant findings that advanced our understanding of the Shard. The ruins on Tysis World have been analysed extensively. The Shard have a very complicated machine-language, and they were very specific about recording their activities."

Shots of tightly scripted symbols, lining corridors.

Walls, ceilings, floors. Even tech. The text had a machine-like precision.

"Why did the Shard record all of this?" Lopez queried. "If they were machines, what's the point?"

Dr Saito smiled. He obviously appreciated the Jackals' curiosity. "That description isn't quite accurate, Private. The Shard were non-biological entities, but the term 'machines' is something of an oversimplification."

"They were alive," Zero added. "Some speculate that they were conscious machines."

Dr Saito nodded along with that explanation. "That represents the limit of our understanding. The Shard were vastly intelligent, non-biological entities. Whether they began as some sort of mechanical construct—perhaps the result of another species' work—or they evolved into their current form is unknown. But we do know that the Shard have been around for a long, long time."

"Like millions of years," Zero said, proudly.

"That's even older than Jenkins," Ving said.

"In any case," said Dr Saito, eager to keep the presentation on track, "the Shard represent a super-intelligence, on a magnitude that the Alliance has never previously encountered. So, to answer your question, Private Lopez, the Shard employed other biological and technical species to work for them, as slave labour. During the Great War, they subverted the Krell to fight for them."

"Shit," said Lopez. "So that's what's happening now?"

"Maybe. It would explain the deep-space structures we've seen in those systems infected with Harbinger."

"Great," I said, flatly. "So how does all of this fit with the Aeon?"

"I'm getting to that," said Dr Saito. "The ruins on Tysis World included several references to what Dr Locke called 'the Great Destroyer'. The script found on

Tysis suggested that the Destroyer was an ancient enemy of the Shard; an ally species to which the Krell turned in their hour of greatest need."

"So what does Aeon look like?" Novak said, frowning as though the thought was difficult to process. "Is like fish, or man?"

"There is no visual record of the Aeon," Dr Saito said. "All we know, by inference, is that they were a member of the Pantheon—that is, the group of organic species allied against the Shard."

"What about their ships, their tech?" Ving asked.

"There have been a handful of confirmed encounters by Alliance Navy forces," Dr Saito said, "but none have resulted in actual contact."

He called up another collection of images; starships captured by long-range scopes. The ships demonstrated the same lineage; very different to Krell, Shard or human tech. These vessels were seed-shaped and sleek, with an eerily beautiful aesthetic. Their hulls were pitted and worn with age, made of a compound that was neither organic nor metallic.

Dr Saito said, "The Tysis World scriptures suggest they are an elder race—predating the Shard. Hence the name 'Aeon'. We believe that they originate from beyond the Milky Way Galaxy."

"So this is the first intergalactic species we've become aware of?" Zero asked with amazement. "That's quite something."

Dr Saito nodded, pleased with Zero's reaction. "It really is. There's so much that we could learn from their technology."

"They must have an ability to travel between galaxies," Zero said. "Just think of what they must've seen."

"How are we going to communicate with these xeno

assholes?" Ving said, his voice dripping with annoyance. His reaction was markedly different to Zero's sense of wonder.

"Pariah will act as our bridge," said Dr Saito. "The Krell and the Aeon are known to each other, and as such Pariah will be able to establish communication. Science Division has also imposed some specific parameters on first-contact scenarios, which you should read."

My wrist-comp chimed, as did everyone else's. Dr Saito had distributed a document titled *A Treatise on First Contact with a New Alien Race: Binding Directives*. Around me, most of the troopers were quick to hit the DELETE button. Dr Saito saw the reaction and seemed to deflate.

"Due to the extreme circumstances in which we find ourselves," Dr Saito said, "Command has directed that—on this occasion—first contact will be achieved via simulants."

"And a plasma rifle," someone from Phoenix Squad said.

"I hear that!" another added.

"If necessary," Captain Heinrich said. "But that's not to be our primary approach. Diplomacy first, troopers. Once we have boots on the ground, and we've opened a dialogue with the Aeon, Commander Dieter and I have authorisation to negotiate on behalf of the Alliance."

I could already see how this would play out. If things went well, Captain Ving and Phoenix Squad would get the glory, just like on Vektah Minor. Heinrich would mop up the planning accolades, probably get a promotion, and then retire to Proxima Colony. Ving's role as an Alliance war hero would be cemented: he would help recruit another generation of simulant operators into the programme, and all would be well with the universe.

If, on the other hand, things went badly, then we

could all be cut loose. Phoenix Squad would be sent off to a black ops project, out of the public eye. The story—if it ever got released—would be that Jenkins' Jackals had fucked up. I'd probably get the blame for the mission's failure, and Captain Heinrich would escape without demerit. It didn't surprise me at all that Sim Ops were being tasked with first contact with the Aeon.

"Well," said Heinrich, "that's enough for now." He stood from the table, pressed down his uniform. "Thank you, Commander Dieter, and Dr Saito. We'll review the intelligence as we approach our destination."

"I'll keep you updated, Captain," said Commander Dieter.

"Before we break, some ground rules are in order for the Sim Ops personnel," Heinrich said. "Just because we're on a starship, doesn't mean that discipline should lapse.

"I want all weapons and equipment primed and ready for deployment by phase one of the mission. I want full tactical database assimilation by oh-eight-hundred tomorrow. I want all suits marked up, rifles tested, systems activated." Heinrich clapped his hands together. "Right, now that's understood, we can all make some progress."

"Sounds like a plan," Ving said.

There was a rumble across the deck, and the briefing room lights fluctuated. Anxious murmurs spread through the room, but the lights came back up again and remained on.

"What just happened?" I asked.

"It's nothing to be concerned about," Commander Dieter reassured. "My executive officer is running some checks, but we think it's a faulty power relay."

"And *that's* nothing to be concerned about?" Lopez argued.

Dieter nodded. "These things happen. It's a secondary relay. We aren't going to drop out of space any time soon."

The Navy contingent responded with nervous laughter. Already some of Dieter's crew had broken away and were working on the problem, reporting to Engineering.

"That's enough discussion," Captain Heinrich said, sharply. "You all have your duty assignments. Make yourselves useful, troopers."

The briefing broke up, and each of us received our orders. My wrist-comp pinged with a duty rota, but I wasn't concerned about that.

"Hey, Doc," I called, after Dr Saito.

"Something I can help you with, Lieutenant?" he asked. His expression was amiable, friendly even.

"How's P doing?"

"Remarkably well," he said. "It asks after you."

"Yeah, about that. Can I see it?"

"Of course."

Two Navy security officers stood watch on the Science Deck entrance, but Dr Saito swiped his palm on the combination DNA and fingerprint scanner and they nodded him through.

"I have most of the facility to myself," Dr Saito commented. "Sergeant Campbell has the Simulant Operations Centre, at the aft of the deck, but the main lab is my domain. The facilities here will be essential once we make contact with the Aeon. I'm not sim-operational, but I'll be able to remotely assess the situation from the lab."

"You think that it's going to happen? That we will really make contact with the Aeon?"

"I don't doubt it for a second."

"Is your optimism contagious, Doc? I'd like a shot of it."

Dr Saito laughed. It was a deep and welcome sound. "Dr Locke's intelligence *will* see us through. I'm sure of it."

The main laboratory was partitioned into various chambers. The medical posts were equipped with powerful microscopes, specimen analysers, and other devices that I couldn't even name. The air smelt of fresh coffee and something far more familiar.

"P!" I exclaimed.

Pariah loped into view, between medical benches. Its sheer physicality was immediate; it looked as though the alien had grown some more since we had last spoken. That wasn't the only change. Its hide was stitched with scars now, flesh swollen against its carapace. The xeno tilted its head.

"Jenkins-other," the alien intoned. "We are grateful for your attendance."

Dr Saito closed the hatch, sealing us inside the lab. "I probably should've said: the pariah-form has been assisting me with my research."

"We prefer the designate 'P'," P said.

"Got it," said Dr Saito, with a grin. "P has agreed to stay within the lab complex." He shrugged. "Which, strictly speaking, doesn't contravene Captain Heinrich's directive."

"Confinement does not suit us," P added. "Regardless of what Heinrich-other insists. We must be ready to meet the Aeon, in the Ghost Maker Nebula."

"How do you know about our destination?" I asked.

"We were not at the briefing, but we have been reading the *Valkyrie*-unit's mainframe. We have accessed many systems since we came aboard this craft. We are absorbing the other-knowing as well, and our knowledge grows with each passing cycle. We are expanding, Jenkins-other."

It swiped a claw—deftly, too deftly for something so big—at the nearest terminal. The machine jumped to life. A review of P's research into the Ghost Maker Nebula, and the planet Carcosa, appeared on the tri-D.

"Did you teach it to do that?" I asked Dr Saito.

He shook his head. "The Pariah—sorry, I mean P—has been accessing the ship's computers itself. The rate at which it can assimilate information is incredible."

The XT was undergoing both physical and mental changes. Just as we studied it, it studied us. As we learnt from it, it learnt from us. *Will you like what you find?* I asked myself. Understanding human nature might not be a good thing.

"I'd suggest you keep that to yourself," I said. "I don't think Captain Heinrich will be very impressed by that new, ah, *ability*."

"Understood," said P. "Although we observe that little seems to impress Heinrich-other."

Dr Saito and I laughed. Pariah's face remained expressionless, flat, but I felt P's presence at the back of my mind.

"How are you doing now, P?" I asked. "I'm sorry that I couldn't speak to you before we left Sanctuary. I wanted to check on you."

"Jenkins-other knew that we were still functional," P said. "Our connection remained intact."

"I guess so," I said. "But I'm still struggling to understand what's happening between us. You're right: I knew that you hadn't died. Even so, since Sanctuary...*something* has felt different. How are those injuries doing?"

P glanced down at the brace of wounds across its torso. The flesh there was puckered, raw; stapled in places, but imprecisely.

"Dr Saito provided medical assistance," P said. "The wounds will close with time."

I found myself wincing in sympathy. "The medical report said that you took four spines to the chest, P. Did they get all of the fragments out? That wound under your arm—it doesn't look very healthy…"

P lifted an appendage, and I got a better look at the injury. The flesh around the wound had gone a mottled, greyish colour; still weeping ichor.

"The injuries do not cause us excessive pain," said P. "The warden-form's spines were removed. We are still functional."

"I'm monitoring P's health," Dr Saito said. "I'd be interested to hear more about this 'connection' you speak of. I've seen your debriefing, Lieutenant. There's no mention of it in the files."

"Yeah, maybe that's another thing we shouldn't talk about…" I said, turning to P.

P had no such compunction, however. "Jenkins-other has touched the Deep," it said. "Very few others have experienced this connection. We are able to access the mind-link."

"'Mind-link'?" Dr Saito queried. "How does that work?"

"All who swim in the Deep can access the knowing. Designate Warlord has also experienced this connection. Jenkins-other, and the Warlord, are connected by the quantum-tides. It is how the Collective communicates across space-time. It is why the Collective is so prone to infection from the Harbinger virus."

Dr Saito frowned, considering that. "We might be able to use that to our advantage."

"The connection is not always reliable," P noted. "It is variable, dependent on distance and location."

"Still, we could use your ability to track Warlord," Dr Saito said, keen to turn this talent to some tactical use. "In the right circumstances."

"Perhaps," P agreed. "Although, most importantly, it will allow us to communicate with the Aeon when the time comes." P raised a claw, tapped it against its crested head. "This is Deep-knowing. This knowledge is unpacking in our head, as we expand."

"Thanks, P," I said. "You're one hell of a fish."

"Can you tell us anything new about the Aeon?" Dr Saito asked. He'd picked up a data-slate, and was poised to record whatever P told him. "I've trawled the Sci-Div archives on the subject. I know almost everything that has been recorded on the aliens, but you're the primary source, P."

"The Aeon were chief among the Pantheon," P said. "They were responsible for organising resistance against the Shard, during the Great War. Their existence predates the Krell; some Collectives believe even the Shard."

"Which makes them ancient…" I whispered.

"Correct," said P. "The Aeon possess technology beyond our knowing. They can manipulate time-space. They are capable of great acts of creation, but also of destruction. The Aeon's age, however, brings other concerns. Some Kindred refer to them as the 'many mind', due to their sometimes erratic behaviour."

"Why is that?" Dr Saito queried.

"Advanced age, on the scale by which the Aeon are judged, can lead to deterioration of mental capability," said P. "They are subject to decay like any other organic species. To combat this, the Aeon collect in Enclaves to amplify their mental strength. They are Aeon colonies; the resting place of what remains of the species."

"This is very interesting," said Dr Saito. "You've never told anyone else about this, P."

"It's news to me," I said, with a shrug.

"This is new knowledge. As we draw closer to the Aeon's location, we expect to understand more about them. Our presence in the Maelstrom allows us to tap into the Deep-knowing."

"We're all grateful for your assistance, P," Dr Saito said, scribbling notes down on his data-slate. His excitement at these revelations was obvious. "I'd like to ask you some more questions. You've mentioned their use of quantum technologies. Can they actually change space-time, or merely manipulate perception of the continuum?"

"We will discuss this further in future," P abruptly said. "We must rest now."

The alien turned and stomped off to an open hatch at the back of the lab. That led to an observation cell, like the one P had used aboard the *Providence*, except that the lighting was low and the walls were freshly plastered with Krell-gunk. Dr Saito put down his slate, satisfied with what he had been told.

I waited until P was out of earshot, which was purely cosmetic, given our mental connection, then turned to Dr Saito.

"Keep an eye on my squad-mate, please," I said. "I'm worried about it."

"Of course," he said. "That's what I'm here to do. Do you have any specific concerns?"

"I'm not happy about those injuries," I said. "They don't look right. Every time P has been wounded, it's healed fast—*very* fast."

"It probably just needs more time," Dr Saito protested. "We removed spines almost as long as my hand from the alien's carapace. That it survived the attack at all ..."

"I know what a tough son of a bitch it is," I said, "but I've seen it hurt before, and this is different."

Dr Saito nodded. "I'll keep it under observation."

Doubt teased at the edge of my conscience. "Have you run a viral-scan on P's blood?" I asked.

"We did that back on Sanctuary. Pariah's blood sample was clean of Harbinger, if that's what you're worried about."

That was exactly what I was concerned about. Dr Saito's answer should've given me some assurance, but it didn't. I couldn't shake the idea that there was something wrong with P.

"Maybe you should do it again," I suggested. I felt awful for just saying the words, for even considering that it might be possible. "Just in case."

CHAPTER TWELVE

LONG WALK, SHORT PIER

Over the next few days, we Q-jumped.

And Q-jumped.

And Q-jumped.

Dozens of short, sharp jolts ran through the deck. Every time, no matter what I was doing, my heart skipped a beat. So much could go wrong, and we wouldn't even know about it until it was too late. After all these years in space, I should've got used to the sensation, but I still found it nerve-wracking. It had got a whole lot worse since Riggs' betrayal. After the mission into the Gyre, he had jumped our ship into Asiatic Directorate space and left us stranded. I wasn't going to forget that any time soon, and although rationally—*logically*—I knew that this was a very different situation, it was still hard to break the association.

I tried my best to stay out of Heinrich and Ving's paths, which was easier than it sounded. Ving and Phoenix Squad mainly occupied the gym—impressing each other with weight-lifting prowess, in and out of sims—and Heinrich was obsessed with micro-managing every aspect of the flight-path. Meanwhile, the Jackals did their thing, taking inventory of the supplies, checking the simulants, running tests on the combat-suits.

There was a communications-blister on the underside of the *Valkyrie*, and Zero claimed the space as her own. If I couldn't find her in the Simulant Operations Centre, I knew that she would be in the comms-blister. It was quiet, and there was a kind of serenity to watching space drift past the open ports between Q-jumps. I understood why she liked it.

"Have you found anything interesting today?" I asked.

Zero brushed her ginger hair from her face, and pulled it back in a ponytail. "As a matter of fact, I have, ma'am."

"Give me a sitrep."

"We are currently six days into the mission timeline," she grandly announced. "And exactly three months and two days have passed in real-time. All being well, the rest of the Alliance fleet will reach the mustering point about now. From there, they will begin the journey to the Reef Stars, and to Ithaca."

Every jump we made separated us from the rest of the Alliance fleet. That distance was physical, but also temporal, as time-dilation created a chasm between the *Valkyrie* and the universe's objective continuity.

I sighed. "So we're on the clock."

"When are we not?" Zero suggested. "We're also past the point of safe transmission. We've lost contact with Alliance Traffic Control."

That was expected: running this close to enemy territory, our comms mast was dampened, and to be used only in the case of extreme emergency. Standard operating procedure it might be, but that didn't mean I liked it. Running in the dark like this meant that we didn't know what was happening out there. Harbinger was everywhere, spreading like rot on a cadaver, and the Spiral were watching, waiting, planning.

"I'm still getting a lot of backwash from the war," Zero said, scrolling through transmissions. She'd captured several local comms. Some were audio only, whereas others were vid-feeds. "Mostly it's military traffic, but there's a lot of civilian stuff too. There are at least two refugee fleets out here, according to the last brief from Traffic Control."

We watched and listened to some of the messages. Every transmission told its own story. Colonists escaping from their homes. Military vessels that had become separated from their battlegroup. Prospectors, fleeing the Black Spiral's advance. The apparent loneliness of the void was a deception. Even out here, this far from the Alliance border, space was never quiet.

"These transmissions could be years old," I said. "You're listening to the past, Zero."

"I know."

"It's a bit morbid. The ships that made these transmissions are gone. The crew and passengers are already dead."

Zero didn't answer, but continued scrolling through the data. There were clips of parents pleading for the rescue of their children. Some offered money, others equipment. We'd seen fleets like this in the Mu-98 system, during the closing days of the Harbinger incursion and the loss of Kronstadt. This, however, was much worse. Every faction of the Alliance was represented in those vid-feeds.

As I watched them, I realised why Zero was doing this. A dozen worlds like Zero's, reduced to dust. Cities, colonies, planets. All gone. These people were kindred spirits to Zero.

"This probably isn't healthy," I said.

"You know what's worse?" Zero asked.

"Tell me."

"I want to hate the fishes. I want to hate the Krell, I really do."

"But?"

She sighed, and it was a fraught expression. "I know it's not their fault. This—the chaos, the death—*they* didn't mean it. Not, not like—when—"

"When they destroyed Mau Tanis?"

Zero looked at me. She didn't appear distressed, only tired. Tired of this shit, of the war, of what it stood for. I didn't blame her for feeling that way.

"Exactly," she said. "But all this? It's the Spiral that are driving it. It's the Spiral that are directing it. The fishes—the Krell—are just weapons, pieces on the game board."

"That's very big of you, Zero."

"How so?"

"To take the high ground like that. The Red Fin Collective took everything from you."

"Hey, I didn't say I forgave them. Only that they're not responsible for this war."

"I get you."

She balled her hands into fists. The skin of her knuckles was chipped, broken. Not the hands of a REMF, that was for sure. That wasn't Zero any more.

"The Spiral will pay for this," Zero said. "I'm going to make them."

"Get in line, Z," I said. "You can have a spot right after me. I have my own agenda."

"You mean Riggs, right?"

"Yeah, Riggs."

Mention of his name stirred the embers of hate in me. The list of reasons why he had to die seemed to be growing by the day. He had betrayed the Alliance, and his own squad. He'd had a hand in the deaths of both Captain Carmine and Conrad Harris. He'd wormed his way into my life, become closer to me than he had any right to be. But there had been a time when Riggs had actually meant something to me. The sense of self-loathing that memory caused made me even angrier.

Zero watched me with a peculiar expression on her face. Her eyes flitted to the hatch, making sure that it was still shut.

"I knew."

"Knew what?" I said, trying to play dumb.

"That you and Riggs were, well, *you know*," she said. "Into each other."

"I was never 'into' Riggs, Zero."

"You know what I mean."

I thought about continuing the lie, but didn't have the strength to keep it up. "Yeah. We were closer than friends, if that's what you're getting at. How long have you known?"

"Since Daktar."

"And the others? They know too, I take it."

"We do talk, you know." Zero turned back to her monitor. "Enough about Riggs. I wanted to show you this. You asked me to look into that canister you found on Vektah Minor."

"I remember."

"Well, I've found something interesting."

I frowned as Zero worked, pulling up files on the holo, accessing an encrypted portion of the ship's main-frame. The grainy image I'd broadcast just before our extraction from Vektah appeared on the tri-D.

"The canister is Science Division issue," Zero said. She pointed out a bar code and serial ID tag. The canister's solid metal construction appeared to be machined with military precision. "It was manufactured on Delta Primus, sixteen years ago."

"Sixteen years ago?"

Zero nodded. "Before the Harbinger outbreak."

"What's Delta Primus?"

"It's a proper black op. There are protocols in place to stop general Army from nosing around those files, but…" Zero patted the console, with affection. "Well, I have my methods."

"Methods which I hope can't be traced back to you."

"Of course not. I downloaded a sub-portion of the projects database before we left Sanctuary, and I've been running it behind a firewall on a virtual drive. The local mainframe doesn't even have a security register, and I'm using less than one per cent of the overall operating system, so it shouldn't—"

"All right, all right, I get the picture. Tell me about this facility."

Zero nodded, calling up some scant historical notes on the station. "Delta Primus was a Science Division facility specialising in bio-engineering, as part of a wider weapons programme."

"Sim Ops?"

"No. The general remit seems to have been contagious diseases."

"Oh shit."

"The outpost also housed a veteran's reclamation facility. Certain personnel were shipped there after recovery on Fortuna, for onward processing."

Fortuna was a name familiar to me. It was an Army holding; a paradise planet reserved for the rehabilitation of veteran troopers, and if that didn't work, then their retirement. Clade Cooper had been sent to Fortuna, after his recovery from Barain-11.

"This is big, Zero. Very big. If the canister came from Delta Primus *before* Harbinger was discovered by the Alliance…"

Ice slithered down my spine. For a brief second, I wished that I hadn't ordered Zero to go poking around in the mainframe. There were clearly some things that grunts like us weren't meant to know.

"I could probably—" Zero started.

Her words were swallowed by the sound of an explosion. Immense, forceful and close enough that the entire comms-blister shuddered.

"What the hell was that? Was it inside or out?"

Zero was already working, her fingers dancing across the terminal access.

"Detonation." She turned to me, grimaced. "Engineering. Inside the ship."

A siren wailed in the distance. The ship's bulkheads vibrated with the deployment of blast hatches, a precaution against atmosphere loss.

"*This is an emergency,*" the ship's AI declared. "*Fire on Deck C. All crew take immediate safety precautions. This is not a drill.*"

We're past the point of safe transmission, I screamed at myself. There wouldn't be any help for us out here.

"Where are the Jackals?" I asked.

It took Zero only a glance at her console to read their positions. "Lopez and Feng are in Medical. Novak is in the cargo hold. P is in the lab."

"Tell everyone to meet in the SOC."

"Already done," Zero said, rising from her chair.

"We're out of here," I ordered, moving off towards the hatch.

"What've we got?" Feng asked, as he and Lopez bundled into the Simulant Operations Centre.

They had reacted with speed, and arrived in the SOC at the same time as Zero and me. The route to the SOC was clear.

"Explosion," I said, talking fast. "Origin unknown."

Zero had already powered up the main console, and was working even before she slid into her post. Dr Saito and P had been only a couple of compartments from the SOC, and they rushed in too.

"It could be an electrical fault," Zero said. "Maybe that secondary power relay Commander Dieter mentioned."

Although that fitted the facts fine, no one bought the explanation. Lopez was the first to voice what we were all really concerned about.

"Is it another ship?" she asked. She left unsaid, *is it the Spiral?*

"I hope not," was all Zero could offer.

Novak was last into the chamber, and his fatigues were stained dark with soot. He nodded at the rest of the squad.

"Starship alert," he said. "Something bad happen."

"That's kind of stating the obvious," Lopez said.

"Engineering bay has been hit," he said, almost breathless. He'd raced to the SOC, but it wasn't just that: he had been closer to the explosion than any of us. "I saw damage. Whole sector is gone. Is fire down there. Everyone is running away."

The ship's AI intervened, continuing its bad news mantra: *"Fire controls offline on Decks C and D. Compartment D-15 is experiencing a high-temperature event."*

Dr Saito's face dropped. "Compartment D-15 is mission-vital."

"Why?" Lopez asked.

Zero flipped through screens on her console. "Because it's right next to the munitions store. The *Valkyrie*'s warheads are in the primary weapons bay. If those go up, we'll be history…"

"Get me a connection to the bridge."

"Affirmative."

The holo hazed with static, and Commander Dieter's image appeared on the console. She wasted no time with protocol, military or otherwise.

"Lieutenant? Are your people still alive down there?"

"The Jackals are in the SOC, Commander. What's happening?"

"We've suffered significant damage to compartment C-13," Dieter said. "An explosion occurred in Engineering, and that has caused a fire. The automated fire suppressant system is offline, and we don't know why."

"Can you open the compartment to vacuum, flush the fire?"

"If only it were that easy," Dieter said, rolling her head. Her face settled into a stony expression. "We do that, and warhead storage will be purged as well. I can't risk damage to the munitions, but we can't leave that sector burning, either. Our life support could be compromised."

"What can we do, Commander?"

"Someone needs to get down there and put that fire out manually. Captain Heinrich and Phoenix Squad are with me in the CIC." Across the SOC, Phoenix Squad's simulator-tanks sat empty and useless, without operators. "You're on your own down there, Lieutenant."

"I read you. We're on it."

"You'll need to manually activate the fire suppressant system. I will send you the electronic key."

"Real old school, huh?" I queried.

Commander Dieter's disembodied head nodded. "It's the only way. I would send one of the maintenance drones, but they aren't responding to my commands."

Zero looked up. "Another glitch?"

"Maybe," Commander Dieter said, although her expression suggested it could be more than that. "Boots on the deck is the only option at this time."

"Solid copy," I said.

"Report once you've executed those orders. CIC out."

The connection terminated.

"I think she will know if we fail…" Novak said, with a broad grin across his tattoo-covered face.

"Let's do this while we still can," I said. "Lopez, Feng: power up the simulator-tanks. Zero, get the sims prepped."

"Already done, ma'am," she said.

"Armoured too?" Lopez asked.

"Do you have to ask?" Zero replied.

"Ready for transition, people."

The simulator-tanks sat ready. Zero had already initiated the start-up protocol. My data-ports were almost on fire, hungering for the connection, and when the simulator's canopy hummed open, the scent of the fresh conducting fluid was sweet as liquor. I snapped the respirator over my lower face, and—naked now—clambered into my tank. The earbead in my ear synched to the rest of the squad.

"We will assist," P said, its voice-box linking to the comms-channel.

"The temperature levels down there are incredible," Zero said, with genuine concern in her voice. "Will you be safe?"

"We are not troubled by exposure to high temperature," P said.

I couldn't help noticing that the wounds across its torso were still puckered, weeping thin, pus-like fluid. P repositioned itself, a limb folded against its body, in what could've been an effort to hide the worst injury.

"I don't think that's a good idea, P," I said.

Dr Saito shook his head. "You won't be safe, Pariah."

"Stay here," I ordered. "You can provide assistance without going into the damaged sector."

P exuded a psychic wave of dissatisfaction, directed at me, but didn't argue. There was no time to discuss the situation any further.

"Zero, where are the simulants located?"

"In cryo-storage," she said. "You can make direct transition to those bodies. I'll plot you a course to the location of the fire."

Across the chamber, each of the Jackals was in position now. Our canopies whined shut, sealing us inside the tanks.

"The Jackals are prepped and ready for transition," said Zero. "All bio-readings are stable. On your order, ma'am."

"Solid copy. Good to go."

Feng, Lopez and Novak collectively hollered and whooped.

"Transition in three...two...one..."

I opened my eyes in my new skin, blinking away the vestiges of chemically induced sleep. Kickstarted by combat-drugs delivered directly from my combat-suit, the simulant came online immediately. I was wearing a tactical-helmet, and data flushed the HUD right in front of my face, and via my neural-link.

I took a split-second to orient myself in my new body and evaluate my surroundings. We were in the cryogenics vault, the storage area used to contain our entire stock of simulants. The hold was filled with capsules. These were stacked vertically against every bulkhead, and each held a new skin. Readouts on the base of the capsules flashed in the dark, indicating that the bodies were still on ice. Although most of them would take some warming up before they could be deployed, Zero had prepped several. I was very glad she had. A single copy of each skin had been armed and armoured, in case of emergency. This most definitely qualified.

"Transition successful, Zero," I declared.

I was already wearing a Class X Pathfinder suit. The armour was docked to the bulkhead behind me, attached to a charging cradle. I disengaged the external cabling and slid free.

"We're in zero-G," I realised. "Watch yourselves, troopers. Mag-locks on."

The Jackals went through the same routine, and unhooked themselves from the bulkhead. Mag-locks anchored each of us to the deck. Lopez switched on her suit-lamps. She panned the bright beams across the rows of slack-faced simulants.

"At least our skins are safe," she said, looking in awe at the number of bodies contained in the hold.

"What's happened to gravity in here, Zero?" I asked.

"The envelope has failed in that sector," Zero said, "but I'm not sure why. I'll run an analysis on the life-support systems, and see if—"

"This is Captain Heinrich," interrupted another voice, on the priority communications channel. "What's your status, Jackals?"

Lopez rolled her eyes at me, and I scowled back at her.

"We're in cryo-storage, sir," I said, my breath fogging the inside of my face-plate. "We're advancing on the damaged compartment."

"Well move faster," Heinrich said. "I'll send you the route."

"Received, sir," I said, as the data-packet uploaded to my suit. "We're on the move."

"All crew are accounted for—there shouldn't be anyone left down there. Not alive, anyway. Get that fire extinguished."

Glowing graphics appeared on the interior of my face-plate. Schematics showed the route we should take through the *Valkyrie*'s damaged interior.

"Understood, sir. Jenkins out."

"Move. Heinrich out."

The line closed.

I unlocked my mags. With a short burst from my EVAMP, I boosted towards a hatch that would take us into Deck C. The Jackals did the same.

"Zero, can you see to this door," I said.

"I should be able to open hatches as you go, direct from the SOC."

"Good work. Keep in touch."

"This is the place," said Lopez.

The words on the outer hatch read C-13. It was still sealed, but my suit-sensors detected a steady rise in temperature.

"These must be the fire extinguishers," Feng said.

Four heavy spray cannons were inside a unit on the wall. Feng opened the locker and distributed one to each of us. Although the extinguishers were heavy, the Pathfinder's man-amp made their weight manageable.

"These are halon sprayers," I said. "Point them, and deploy the gas."

"Nice and easy," Novak said. He hefted the cannon with one hand, aiming it.

"Do you read, Zero?" I asked.

"I copy."

"We're at the hatch to C-13."

"Here goes."

An amber warning strobe started overhead, and the

hatch began to grind open. Safety icons and black-and-yellow hazard stripes plastered the heavy blast doors. The words DO NOT ENTER stuck in my mind. The Jackals braced.

"Holy fucking Gaia…" Lopez said.

A wave of heat hit me like a fist. It was accompanied by a flash of light so blinding that my face-plate polarised to compensate. Worse yet, exotic energy—in levels that threatened to penetrate even my heavy armour—spilt out. Health warnings flashed across my HUD. *Yeah, yeah*, I thought. *I get it. But I'm going to die anyway, right?* Stepping foot inside the chamber just meant that it was going to happen a lot faster.

Feng put a hand to his face. It was a wasted gesture, but I could understand where he was coming from. Chemical fire raged across almost every surface. Baleful flames licked at the deck, the bulkheads; crept across the ceiling. The fire was like a living thing. Alien, unreal. It pulsed like a jellyfish, crawling, writhing…

"Inside," I ordered. "Sprayers up."

The lock behind us slammed shut, and the four of us advanced into the chamber. It took me a moment or so to get my bearings, to recognise our position. The map on my HUD flickered and flashed with energy discharge.

"I'm frying in this suit," Lopez said, panting hard. "Christo, this is unbearable."

"Stay mobile," I suggested. "Focus on the task."

We bounced through the module. Bodies—twisted, burnt, unrecognisable—spiralled by. We couldn't do anything for them; not even recover their remains. That sent a chill through me. These were not simulants. These were real bodies, real lives…

"Objective ahead," said Feng.

We fired the halon sprayers as one, and plumes of gas blanketed the bulkheads and deck. Fire twisted and turned in every direction. It was hypnotising, almost beautiful. Every surface glowed. That could've been down to the heat, the fire, or some more complex explanation. It was eerie.

"Advance on the next compartment," I said, spraying as I went.

TAKE EVASIVE ACTION, my suit suggested. TEMPERATURES REACHING CRITICAL LEVELS.

"I know, I know," I said. To Feng: "Open the hatch, trooper."

"Solid copy," Feng managed.

He reached for the crank wheel that activated the lock. Where his gloves made contact with the metal surface, smoke rose. He hissed, taking the increased heat, shoulder against the door. Lopez and I stood ready to deploy into the chamber . . .

"Fuck!" Feng shouted.

The hatch opened with a rush of escaping atmosphere. A backdraft of chemical fire washed over the four of us, with such intensity that it threw me backwards. I reached out, at the last moment, and caught a pipe on the wall. The mags in my gloves activated, and I anchored myself there.

Feng wasn't so fast. The hatch blew outwards. A metal panel slammed into him, sandwiched his simulant against the bulkhead. The force of the impact was strong enough to crack open his suit. His face-plate shattered immediately, blood squirting from the body inside.

PRIVATE FENG EXTRACTED, my armour told me.

"That intel is a little late," I countered.

Lopez spun by, thrown clear by the shockwave. Her fingers grazed my shoulder.

"Ma'am!" she yelled.

She disappeared into the raging inferno.

Novak's life-signs vanished from my HUD. Fire

consumed his body. The blaze seemed to rise in every direction.

Get a fucking grip! I screamed at myself.

My suit was on fire, and my halon sprayer was at my feet. I clutched it and dowsed myself with a burst of gas. The fires went out, although everything around me was still burning.

<You are not alone in there.>

"P? That you?"

The fish wasn't here, but I felt it in my head.

<Get up, Jenkins-other. Do this.>

I gasped. Used my mags to lock myself to the deck, and began the slow and inexorable walk towards the fire control console. My head had started to ache. In combination, the heat and radiation were certain to kill me.

Got to get this done. Then I can rest. Then I can sleep…

Everything was swimming, moving. It was like being drunk, but much worse. Something tangy and putrid seemed to fill the back of my throat. My vision had started to darken, and black spirals danced in front of my eyes…

<Input the key,> P told me.

"I'm trying, P."

"You've got to do this!" came Commander Dieter's voice. "I know that you can, girl."

"My comms aren't active," I said. "How are you speaking to me?"

Commander Dieter reminded me of Captain Carmine, in that moment. Dear old Carmine. I missed her a lot. I missed them all so damned much…

"Listen to me, girl!" yelled Carmine.

"I hear you," I said. My throat was so tight. Tight as Clade Cooper's throat, attached to the wall of the Krell nest…

"You've got a mission here, trooper," said Carmine. "Don't let me down. Activate fire control."

My sim seemed to take an age to respond. In slow motion, I started to input the code. My HUD was a scrambled mess of numbers, of transmissions, of garbage code. None of it made sense any more. The combat-suit must have suffered damage. The extreme radiation levels could've compromised the suit's AI. Any of that was possible.

<Enter the key. We will assist.>

My fingers jabbed at the keys. I made a couple of errors, and the small LED terminal flashed every time I got an entry wrong. But I went back, corrected the errors. Soon it was done.

The compartment's overhead lights flashed. I froze. Looked up. The fire control system activated, dowsing the chamber in white gas. Visibility dropped, and the temperature with it.

I frowned. "Something's not right," I said.

There was no answer, except for the chime of my bio-scanner. It was detecting a life-sign, somewhere in Engineering. There was someone still alive down here.

"Commander Dieter? Zero?"

No reply.

I stalked through a curtain of white mist towards the next compartment. There was a life-sign on the other side of the hatch. I cranked it open. An engineering sub-compartment was beyond, and it was dark inside. A sector that the fire hadn't reached. Why would someone be in here? Captain Heinrich said he had accounted for all bodies...

You could be imagining this, I thought. That seemed like a completely plausible solution.

"If anyone can hear me," I said, "I'm beyond the fire."

Carmine was gone now. Dieter was gone. I was pretty sure I was gone, too.

<We are still here,> came P's voice. <Be careful, Jenkins-other.>

A bank of steam enveloped the corner ahead, and I jumped back. Overcompensated in zero-G. I cursed myself for the reaction, but it was spooky as shit in there. Something moved through the steam. I unholstered my plasma pistol. Thankfully, Zero had prepped the armour for combat deployment.

A shadow broke from the rest. It pushed off from me, making the most of the zero-G conditions.

I followed. Fired my EVAMP to gain pace, grappled against the bulkhead with my free hand. Fresh combat-drugs flooded my skin, giving the dying sim a new lease of life. My bio-scanner throbbed with activity. The target was now confirmed.

"Hold it!" I shouted.

My voice echoed off the metal bulkheads, around the cavernous deck. Pistol up, I advanced on the next junction, passing through another steam-bank. The gravity did weird things to that, making the moisture coil and swirl.

A blow hit me full-on in the face, and my visor crunched with the impact, head snapping back. The sudden and abrupt violence stunned me, but didn't put me down. I recovered fast. Brought my pistol up. Aimed it at the shape.

"Stand down!"

"Make me," came the answer.

A blur of light slashed towards me. I recognised it as an active mono-knife, held up defensively in a warding pose. The shape paused. It had backed up into a dead end, with nowhere to go. My suit-lamps flashed on, catching the shadow in a pool of light.

Oh no no no no...

This couldn't be happening. Not here. Not now.

"You're not..."

"Real?"

I swallowed. Struggled to breathe. For a long second, we both just stood there, watching one another. The simulant felt like it was going to expire at any moment. At last I acted.

"Drop the weapon," I ordered, "and stay exactly where you are."

The attacker did as requested, then raised both hands. The mono-knife mag-locked to the deck, and I kept my eyes on it at all times. I thought-commanded a comm-link back to the SOC.

"Zero? Do you read me?"

"I copy, ma'am."

"Get a security team down here, immediately."

"What's the sitrep?"

"We have a stowaway. It's Riggs, Zero. Daneb Riggs is on the *Valkyrie*."

CHAPTER THIRTEEN

TRAITOR: RETURNED

"How in the Core did he get onto the ship?" Captain Heinrich asked.

An hour or so had passed since the incident in Engineering. The Jackals, with Ving and Heinrich, watched an image of the ship's brig on a security terminal. Daneb Riggs, the arch-traitor, sat on the other side of an energy barrier. Phoenix Squad had safely pacified the bastard after I'd called it in, and now he looked mighty sorry for himself.

"I can't say," said Commander Dieter. She prowled the *Valkyrie*'s Command Intelligence Centre. "But I'm confident that we'll be able to find out."

Since the attack, she hadn't been able to stop checking and rechecking every system of her ship. Dieter reviewed another camera feed, which showed the rest of Phoenix Squad searching the vessel. Real-time footage of their sweep was being broadcast to the CIC.

"Are we sure it's really him, and not a simulant?" Heinrich asked.

"That's what Dr Saito says," Ving answered. "He's run a scan."

"And the scan can't be fooled?"

"He has data-ports," I said. "That wouldn't be the case if Riggs was using a sim. And when I last saw Riggs... He didn't look like this."

"We should waste him," Ving said. "This guy is complete human trash."

"For once," I said, "I agree with Captain Ving."

I was back in my real body. My simulant had been totalled by the radiation levels, and Zero had ejected it into space. My head still spun, and I was involuntarily shaking. The Jackals weren't in much better shape, but they hadn't been exposed to the same radiation levels as me. Not that I had actually been exposed at all; it had been my simulant in danger. But that didn't stop my body's natural reactions from kicking in. The psychosomatic response was the same, simulated or otherwise.

Captain Heinrich swallowed, eyes still pinned to the camera feed. "Then it's a good job I'm in charge. I want questions answered before anyone 'wastes' the deserter."

"Deserter?" Lopez said, her voice dripping with anger. "That guy is a Black Spiral agent. He infiltrated Simulant Operations. This isn't about military protocol, Captain. He's a *traitor*."

Heinrich answered without looking up at Lopez. "Emotions are running high. I understand that. Don't forget, Private Lopez, that I'm Proximan too. We have a shared heritage. What the Black Spiral did—or tried to do, at least—to your father is bound to cause you great upset. But you've got to think with a level head."

"That's has nothing to do with it, sir," Lopez protested.

"He doesn't look like much," said Ving, sneering at the image. "Maybe I could go in there, soften him up." He cracked his knuckles.

"Do not trouble yourself, Captain," said Novak.

He loomed over Ving's shoulder, bigger still. Novak's breathing quickened, his body tensing in the expectation of violence. "If traitor is to hurt, I will do it. He was one of Jackals."

"He was hiding in the tunnels beyond the fire," I explained. "He came at me with a mono-knife."

Captain Heinrich shook his head. "Better tactical planning was required, Lieutenant Jenkins. You should've considered the possibility of an ambush."

"Yes, sir," I said, putting a cap on my anger.

"What's the ship's status, Commander Dieter?" Heinrich said. "Can we still sail?"

"We escaped any major structural damage," Dieter answered. She called up a holo of the ship and marked it with her finger to show the compromised compartments. "Available evidence suggests that the prisoner detonated an explosion in Compartment C-13. This was caused by a small blasting charge. Due to a pressure valve failure, the area became irradiated." Another glowing marker on the ship's outline. "It resulted in a chemical fire in this section. We suffered multiple casualties."

There were sighs around the chamber, some gaunt expressions from the Navy staff. The dead had been friends and colleagues of a tightly knit group.

"Is the *Valkyrie* still mission-capable?" Captain Heinrich persisted.

"The detonation wasn't powerful enough to hole the ship. Had the charge been placed on the outer hull, it might've been a different story." Dieter gnawed on her lower lip, but gave a determined nod. "We can repair the damage."

"What about the crew?" I asked.

"This is a next-generation strikeship, Lieutenant. We can fly with a minimal crew, if needs be. My people have operated under worse conditions."

That didn't lighten the mood much, but it at least meant that the mission could continue. Given how things could've turned out, it was a victory of sorts.

"Riggs was trying to cause chaos," said Feng. "Fucking typical."

"Well, Private," said Captain Heinrich, "in that respect, he certainly succeeded."

"He should've blasted cryo-storage," said Ving. "That would've been the smart thing to do—to take out our sims."

"Riggs is not so clever," said Novak.

"The blasting charge came from our inventory," Dieter continued. "He used our own equipment against us."

Captain Heinrich paced the CIC, his boots producing an annoying *clip-clip* as he walked. He rubbed his clean-shaven chin. "How do we know that?"

Zero scrolled through the equipment files. "The ship records the serial numbers from each charge." She looked around the CIC. Her face was paler than usual, the scars on her temple appearing especially prominent. "He stole three further charges."

"Phoenix Squad has identified a cache on Deck E," Commander Dieter said. "The prisoner likely intended to detonate these at some later time."

"At least the Jackals stopped him from doing that," Zero said.

"Barely," Captain Heinrich said, shaking his head. "Anyway, let's move on. Clear heads are what's required here. We'll have to file a report when we get back to Sanctuary."

"A report is the least of our worries…" Lopez muttered.

Captain Heinrich ignored her. "In the meantime, we're still some distance from the Ghost Maker Nebula. We're going to use that time to find out how, and why, Corporal Riggs got onto the *Valkyrie*. Someone's going to interrogate him. Phoenix Squad are already tasked with sweeping the ship. You have the duty, Lieutenant Jenkins."

I shook my head. "Sir, I don't think that's a good idea. I'm strongly in favour of Captain Ving's suggestion: that we terminate the prisoner."

"And I've already indicated that isn't going to happen," Heinrich said. "I want you to find out whatever you can from him."

My shoulders sagged. "Sir, Riggs is the worst sort of asshole. We won't gain anything from—"

"I don't want to hear it," Captain Heinrich said. "As I said, we will need to file a full report when we get back to Sanctuary. There's an opportunity for intelligence gathering here. The suspect will come to no harm. Understood?"

I couldn't bring myself to answer, but I nodded. If I didn't say it aloud, then it didn't count.

"Good," Heinrich said. "Then you have your duty. Dismissed, all of you."

Ving and I left the CIC together, neither of us happy with how that had gone.

"You want me to take this instead?" Ving offered. "The interrogation, I mean."

"I don't think that Captain Heinrich would allow it."

"Well, don't say I didn't offer," he muttered. "I want that fucker dead as much as you, Jenkins."

"You have a way with words, Captain."

Ving paused at the next hatch, hand on the control panel. "I have family on Proxima Colony."

I stayed quiet, because I wasn't sure how Ving expected or wanted me to react to that. I knew that he'd started as Proximan, although little of his muscle-bound body was original. He ricked his neck, rubbed a finger across his eyes.

"Ex-wife and kid. I never see them, but I write all the time. Kid's eleven, standard. Wife left me when I joined Sim Ops."

"That's nothing new. Relationships and Sim Ops don't exactly mix."

Ving managed a half-smile of agreement, despite himself. "Yeah. I get that. She refused to renew our marriage contract when I came back from the last tour. Said I wasn't myself any more. I got a million women out there, and probably just as many men, who want a piece of the Phoenixian. And this one woman who can't stand the sight of me."

"I like this woman already," I said, playfully.

Ving's smile kind of faltered. "After what happened on Sanctuary, I tried to call home. Tried to get an uplink with Alpha City." He exhaled. "Their processing grid got hit, see? But I couldn't get through to anyone. Not friends, not family."

Was Ving expecting me to give him a shoulder to cry on or something? I wasn't quite comfortable with that, but I was seeing Ving in a more sympathetic light. We'd never spoken about his background, or his life outside of the press promos and Psych Ops campaigns. To me, Ving was the Phoenixian, the thorn in my side. A constant reminder of what I could've been—what I should've been—after my time on the Lazarus Legion...

"I'm sure they're fine," I said, in my most reassuring tone of voice. "Proxima is likely the most secure territory in the whole Alliance. The Secretary is from there, for Gaia's sake. If the grid got hit, they'll repair it. You'll see."

Ving nodded. The expression of deep self-review on his brow didn't look natural, and made him appear a bit confused.

"I hope so, Jenkins. I hope so. Because if that useless fuck Riggs has hurt one hair on my kid's head, then I'm going to rain all hells down on him. You can promise him that, from me."

"I will, Ving."

Ving regained a little of his old cocksure attitude. "That's 'sir', to you, Jenkins."

"You're an asshole, sir."

"This doesn't mean we're friends or anything."

"I hope not."

"And you can tell that Chino trooper that he should stay away from me," Ving said, the armour of contempt rising again. "I catch him out in the tunnels by that comms-blister again, he's a dead clone."

"Not if he catches you first," I said.

We parted company, which was fine by me, and I made my way down to the brig.

The Jackals were waiting for me at the security station. All except for P, who was still restricted to the Medical Deck.

"What's Riggs' condition?" I asked Zero.

She strolled past the observation window, consulting a data-slate. "He's suffering from borderline malnutrition, consistent with surviving on scavenged rations. He's also indicating mild radiation sickness. He was probably hiding in restricted areas of the ship. I doubt Riggs knew that some of the crawlspaces aren't rad-shielded."

"My heart truly bleeds," Lopez muttered. Her words carried real venom, real animosity. "It's a shame he didn't get a lethal dose of something."

"Dr Saito pumped him with a dose of smart-meds," Zero said. "He won't be dying on us any time soon."

"Not from rad sickness, anyway," Feng added. He sat on an upturned crate in the corner of the brig.

"I don't need the rest of you here," I said. "Zero and I can take care of this."

"We're good," Feng said. "When he dropped the *Santa Fe* into Directorate space, he fucked us all."

"And let's not even get started on what he did at Darkwater…" Lopez said. "Think of us as back-up, in case Riggs gets out of hand."

Lopez had a Navy-issue sidearm on her lap, and was playing with the arming stud. The safety indicator intermittently turned from red to green, then back again. Armed, safe. Armed, safe. Armed.

"You want I should make him speak?" Novak asked. "I have knife. Now, if I go into stomach—with blade to bowel—this is not quick. This does not kill straight away, but is very painful…" He turned to the obs window. It was currently tuned so that we could see in, but Riggs couldn't see out. "Should I start interrogation off?"

Lopez and Zero looked away. They were no doubt remembering when Novak had last undertaken an "interrogation". That had resulted in a dead prisoner and a whole lot of unanswered questions.

"Not today," I said. "You heard what Captain Heinrich said. Riggs isn't to be harmed. Have you scanned him for covert tech, Zero?"

Zero continued to consult her slate, but nodded. "Yes, ma'am. He's had a full bio-scan. I took the liberty of comparing the results with his Alliance Army service record."

"And?"

"The only metal in him is his data-ports. Nothing new, nothing recently installed."

"Good work."

Zero's words—"the only metal in him"—poignantly reminded me of what had happened to Feng. The tech installed in his head had foiled Alliance detection methods, and resulted in Feng's deployment as an unwitting sleeper agent. Did the Black Spiral have more invasive techniques available than the Directorate?

"Riggs is to be kept under constant observation," I said. "All eyes: visual, biological, psychic. He so much as pisses, I want to hear about it."

"We get it," said Lopez.

I finally turned to look at the figure behind the observation-field. I'd dreamt of this moment, but I realised that I'd been doing everything possible to avoid actually seeing him. This was it. Not sim-on-sim. *Mano a mano. Tête-à-tête.* My skin prickled with anticipation. Through the obs-field, Riggs was caught in the spotlight glare of two glow-globes. Zero had turned the globes to maximum illumination: burning away any hint of deceit. They laid bare what Riggs had become.

We'd last met on Darkwater. Riggs had been using a simulant then, and it had made him look like the man I remembered. He'd been the old Riggs. Now, he was something else. Something darker. He was haggard and had lost muscle mass, as though the enormity of what he had done was a weight around his shoulders. Whiskers peppered his jaw, and his eyes were lined black, dark hair cut short. He looked like he hadn't slept for a long time. His youthful vigour was gone, replaced by something tired and bitter. He wore a dull tan jumpsuit, the word PRISONER written across the chest in bold white letters. Electro-shackles manacled his arms.

So what had Riggs become? Pathetic. Some small part of me felt sympathy for him. I hated myself for that reaction. It was weakness, pure and simple.

"Turn on the intercom," I ordered.

"Copy that."

"Can you hear me in there, Riggs?" I said.

Despite myself, my voice quivered. In the cell, Riggs'

ears pricked up. He looked around as though he had only just recognised where he was.

"Is that you Keira?" Riggs asked.

"It's Lieutenant Jenkins."

"Thank Christo you came," he said. "I—I hoped that they would send you."

"Why is that?"

Riggs pulled a face, shrugged. "You know me. You know what I'm really like."

"A treacherous, lying piece of shit? Yeah, I know you well enough."

Riggs jumped up and began pacing the cell.

"Don't be like that. I'd like to see you. Can you tune the field so that I can look out?"

"You just tried to kill me in Engineering. I think you saw me fine then."

"You can't treat me like this." He plucked at the tan-coloured jumpsuit. "I haven't been convicted of doing anything yet. I'm a POW—a prisoner of war." Riggs enunciated each of those words slowly, and pointedly, like they were weapons. "I'm still an Alliance citizen, and an American at that."

The room closed in around me. His sheer arrogance was blistering.

"Correction," I roared. "You're a terrorist combatant, not a POW. You have no entitlements, but let me tell you this: it wouldn't matter if you did. You, and the Spiral, have killed innocents. So don't you fucking dare talk to me about rights or citizenship."

"It's just collateral damage. We're fighting a war out here. It's nothing personal, Keira."

"Nothing personal? *Nothing personal?* What about when you dropped us into Directorate space and left us for dead? Was that personal?"

I slammed a fist into the hatch frame, where the invisible obs-field met the bulkhead. The sharp pain that spread through my knuckles was nothing compared to the agony in my heart.

Riggs shook his head. "It wasn't like that."

I turned to Zero. She had been inanimate during the exchange, listening but not reacting. Now she jumped, as though I frightened her.

"Turn off the field," I said.

"Are you sure about—"

"Turn off the damned field, Zero!"

She did as ordered, and the field dropped. Riggs grinned at me from inside the cell.

"Ah, that's better," he said. "Now I can see you properly." He glanced me up and down. "You're looking good, Keira. You're looking damned good."

"Fuck you," I spat.

"And you too, Lopez. I'm sorry about what happened at Sanctuary. How's your father?"

Lopez snarled from behind me. Her pistol went up, and the laser-dot targeting sight painted Riggs' chest.

"You're not supposed to have weapons in here," he said.

"I authorised it," I lied. "And believe me, Riggs: you put one foot out of place, I'll put the bullet in you myself. You're only here by the grace of Captain Heinrich. If I had my way, I'd leave you to Novak."

"I don't think you've got it in you," Riggs muttered. "But I wouldn't do anything to hurt you, Keira. What you and I had: it was something special."

My cheeks burnt. Not with embarrassment, but rage. The tactic was obvious. Riggs was trying to humiliate me in front of my squad. It wasn't going to work.

"The Jackals already know," I said, "so you can stop with the 'I'll reveal our secret' bullshit. How did you get onto this ship?"

Riggs paused. The response was almost theatrical.

"I confess that I was part of an operation on Sanctuary Base. Warlord employed some of Novak's buddies— the Sons of Balash—to do a job on the station. We used the *Svetlana* to get under your radar...Well, you know the rest."

"Where did Vasnev go?" Novak queried.

I didn't need a medi-suite to know that the Russian's vitals were spiking. He wasn't a complex man, that was for sure, and it was easy to push his buttons.

"I don't know where Vasnev and her gang went," said Riggs. "The Sons of Balash left me on Sanctuary, and I stowed away. I've been on the *Valkyrie* since the attack. Those Russians are crazy as all hell. This Vasnev; she frightens me. Warlord should never have asked for her help. She's insane."

Novak grunted, his eyes half hooded.

Lopez spoke next. "Was my father the target?" she said. There was a certain coldness to her voice, that seemed inconsistent with an accusation of murder of her own flesh and blood.

Riggs smiled. "Not everything is about your old man, Lopez."

"Then what was the target?"

"Warlord thinks that the Alliance has a cure for this virus. He wanted it neutralised."

"Figures," Zero whispered, unable to contain herself.

"I'm surprised Poindexter didn't figure that out for herself," Riggs said, looking at Zero. "Are you losing your edge, Sergeant?"

"Of course I'm not," Zero said. Her body language was tight, and I could tell that she wasn't comfortable with the field being lowered. Riggs was standing only a few feet away from her.

"Don't speak to Zero," I ordered. "Don't speak to any

of them. I'll ask the questions, and you'll answer me. What happened at Sanctuary?"

"The operation didn't go to plan. We failed to take out the source of the anti-virus."

"But you destroyed the labs," I said.

"That wasn't the source."

"Then what is?" Zero asked, despite my order that Riggs wasn't to speak to her.

I was the smart girl this time. "Pariah. P is the source, right?"

"Listen to yourself!" Riggs said, throwing his cuffed hands up in the air. "You're talking about that fish as though it's an actual person."

"It's a Jackal. You were too, once."

"It was the target." Riggs breathed out slowly, dark clouds passing behind his eyes. He had started to rub the data-ports in his arms now, through his prison suit. "Warlord paid the Sons of Balash to do a job, but they're hired guns and all they care about is the money. They're not believers. I never agreed with Warlord's policy on that. That Major Vasnev is as tough as nails, right, Novak?"

Novak said nothing. He seethed, and glared very intently at Riggs.

"Well, I'm sure the lifer agrees with me," Riggs said. "I was supposed to infiltrate your ship. That was my job."

"How did you know that the *Valkyrie* was assigned to this mission?" Zero asked. "To the Jackals?"

"The Spiral has people everywhere, Zero," Riggs said. "We have manifests, tables of organisation. The whole deal." He grinned, like this was all a big game. "My objective was to sabotage the mission. I almost did it, too. I would've killed the fish, but the Medical Deck has guards. The easiest way to stop you was to hole the ship."

"It didn't work," Feng said. "The mission continues. We'll find the Aeon."

"Warlord will make sure that doesn't happen," Riggs said. "He's a great man."

"Seriously?" Lopez questioned.

Riggs became more animated and waved his hands around. "Warlord has a plan. He has a vision. He has visions." The fervour I'd seen in his eyes during our past confrontations had returned, and burnt bright now. "He's seen the Great Dark. He's seen the Dominion. This virus is only the start. The fish heads are going to burn. He's bringing the Shard back to this galaxy, and they'll finish everything."

"That's no kind of a goal."

"It is for someone who has nothing," Riggs said. "You know what that feels like, don't you, Zero?"

Zero avoided eye contact and looked at the deck.

"I lost everything when my father didn't return," he said. "Warlord and the Spiral: they were there for me. Warlord is more of a father than my real one ever was. You might think that you know about Warlord, but he likes to keep some things secret. There's a lot more to learn."

"You're deluded," I said.

"Warlord has seen the Deep," Riggs said. He was talking louder, waving his hands around again. His electro-cuffs clattered. "He knows what the fishes know. He can sense their movements. He's taking this to where it'll end. The Reef Worlds will be his greatest victory. Nothing and no one can stop him."

He was shouting now. Lopez had her gun up.

"Raise the field," I ordered Zero.

"Wait!" Riggs said. "I want to talk to you about Warlord. You're connected with him! You crossed into the Deep in the Gyre. You saw the Great Dark too!"

The field popped back into existence; a blue glow between the prisoner and us.

"Activate the silencer."

"Solid copy."

The brig fell silent, Riggs' voice gone. Zero sighed. Lopez lowered her gun. I was physically exhausted, and I could tell that the Jackals were too.

"He's lost it," Lopez concluded.

Zero nodded. "Full Section Eight." She looked over at Novak. "But it was easier than we thought. See, Novak, we got answers, and not a knife in sight. All we needed to do was be polite."

"It was too easy," I decided. "Why did he tell us that?"

Novak pulled a face. "He did not want me to cut him."

"Why would he care about that?" I countered. "He was on a suicide mission to blow up this ship." I watched Riggs move behind the energy field. He paced like a caged animal. "He was only telling us what he wanted us to hear. I need to discuss this with P. It isn't…"

The words dropped from my mouth, and I staggered. A yawning, gaping chasm had just opened inside my head.

"Ma'am?" Novak asked, steadying me with a hand to my waist. "Something is wrong?"

The blackness was almost enough to floor me. I shook my head, grasping for the edge of consciousness.

The *Valkyrie*'s warning alarm sounded at that moment.

"*Lieutenant Jenkins is required on the Medical Deck,*" said the electronic voice. "*Attendance is urgent.*"

"Something's happened to P," I managed. "I can't feel our connection any more. P's not in my head."

Riggs stood on the other side of the obs-field, grinning like a fucking maniac.

CHAPTER FOURTEEN

THEY BROUGHT IT BACK

We rushed to Medical as fast as we could. Feng, Lopez and Zero were with me, leaving only Novak to guard the brig.

With each passing breath, the dark in my head seemed to subside a little, fraction by fraction. Whatever had happened, it wasn't going to kill me. But it wasn't me I was worried about.

Dr Saito was waiting at the hatch, wringing his hands, anxiety large across his face.

"Where is it?" I asked, breathless. "What's happened?"

"Is P okay?" Lopez said.

"I . . . I don't know," he answered. He shook his head, moving to the area of the lab where P nested. "I've sealed it in. This is beyond me."

Dr Saito opened the cell hatch, and the smell almost floored me. It was P's scent, magnified. The Jackals gagged and choked on the noxious smell. I peered into the cell, Feng behind me.

"Holy shit," he said. "I . . . I think that it's beyond anyone's capabilities."

"Anyone human, at least," said Lopez.

P's resinous gunk plastered the bulkheads, caking the lighting system and the air-vents. Strands of webbing hung from the deckhead, haphazardly criss-crossing the cell. Pockets held P's self-produced equipment and ammunition.

"What the hell is that?" Lopez asked.

A cocoon dangled in the centre of the mess.

"Hand me a bio-scanner, Doc," I said.

Dr Saito produced a handheld scanner. I tuned the device and panned it over the room. Most of the cell was alive in one way or another, and I got readings from the fibrous bundles of tissue lining the walls.

"P is in there," I confirmed. "And it's alive, although barely." I approached the cocoon. Experimentally tapped a knuckle against it. "It's hard. Solid. More like carapace, or shell, than flesh. P did this to itself."

"It was injured, during the attack on Sanctuary," Zero said. "Maybe . . . maybe it's trying to heal. I mean certain creatures—animals—can enter a suspended state. Catatonic immobility, it's called."

"And P can do this 'immobility' thing?" Lopez asked.

"I haven't heard of the Krell doing so," Dr Saito replied, "but I suppose it's possible. That, or some sort of further maturation. This could be another stage in the alien's development. It could be a chrysalis."

In which case, I thought to myself, *what is P becoming?*

"Did P explain any of this to you, Doc?" I asked.

Dr Saito shook his head. "Nothing. We've talked, at length, but it gave me no reason to believe this would happen."

The cocoon was a huge, swollen sac of a thing. It dangled there, oozing fluid, straining against the webbing. The surface shimmered. I ran a hand over the outer shell.

"P? You in there? Can you hear me?"

For the first time in a very long time, I couldn't sense

Pariah. The xeno wasn't communicating with me, and I couldn't even sense it in the back of my head. That was a strange feeling; something only appreciated in its absence. I'd reprimanded P for invading my head before. Now I desperately wanted to re-establish the link, to somehow know that it was all right.

"We'd like to know that you're still with us, P."

The cocoon gave nothing away. I retreated out of the cell and wiped my hands across my fatigues.

"There is one other possibility," Dr Saito said.

"Go on."

"The warden-form that attacked Pariah carried Harbinger," Dr Saito said. "This...this could be an immune response to the infection."

"You mean the virus?" Feng said. "Not likely. Our fish is resistant."

"But P tested negative for infection," I said. "We talked about this."

"We did," Dr Saito said, nodding. "And I ran a further virology test. That came back negative as well, like the first."

"Then what has this," Lopez said, pointing into the cell, "got to do with the virus?"

"The Black Spiral released a mutated Harbinger strain on Sanctuary," he said. "It was faster-acting and more aggressive than anything we've seen before. This could be a reaction to exposure."

There was a drawn-out pause around the room, as that information sank in. The Jackals' spirits dropped.

"Could P be infected with Harbinger?" Lopez asked, somewhat reluctantly.

Dr Saito rubbed his chin. "I don't know. This is new territory, and Pariah's genetic-sequence is so complicated."

Zero swallowed. "Captain Heinrich will need to know about this. If P is infected..."

I completed her sentence: "Then it's a liability, on a ship already carrying enough of those."

"I'll keep the compartment under surveillance," Dr Saito said. "Anything significant happens, we'll know about it."

"We can't let P die," Zero said.

Dr Saito gave a smile and nodded. "I've become quite attached to the subject myself."

"Fucking Riggs," Lopez spat. "Another life that bastard has to answer for."

As much as I didn't want to, I knew that I had no choice but to report to Captain Heinrich. He had an office amidships, one of the compartments that hadn't been hit. A trooper from Phoenix Squad was stationed at the hatch. He was skinned and armoured, with a plasma rifle over his chest. I recognised his name as Morentz.

"State your name and business," he said as I approached.

"I think you know perfectly well who I am."

"Identify name and business," Morentz said.

"Fine. Lieutenant Jenkins, reporting to Captain Heinrich."

I buzzed the hatch, and Heinrich answered.

"Enter," he said.

I entered the room and saluted. Captain Heinrich's office wasn't big, but it was larger than the cramped barracks the Jackals had been assigned.

Captain Heinrich sat behind his smart-desk. Commander Dieter sat opposite, and they both looked very tired. Tumblers of amber-coloured liquid—something alcoholic—sat on the table.

"At ease," Captain Heinrich said, waving a hand. "Take a seat, Lieutenant."

That wasn't expected. I took a chair on the same side of the desk as Commander Dieter.

"Drink?" Heinrich asked.

"Ah ... yes, sir," I said. "It's been that kind of day."

"That it has," Commander Dieter agreed, sipping at her glass.

Captain Heinrich reclined in his chair. His uniform was unkempt, open at the neck, and his eyes were bloodshot. Whatever I thought of Heinrich, I knew that he was under some intense pressure now.

"This," said Captain Heinrich, swilling the liquid around in his glass, "is ten-year-aged Proximan whiskey. Venusian filtered."

"That so?"

"I doubt that you've ever tasted anything so refined before."

"I have, actually. Aboard Secretary Lopez's yacht, on Sanctuary."

Captain Heinrich smiled self-assuredly. "Of course. But you're not the only one to have a connection with the Secretary, Lieutenant."

My eye focused on a picture behind Heinrich; a tri-D image of Heinrich in formal blues, shaking hands with the Secretary, both grinning at the camera. It looked like an Alliance function of some kind, and had probably been deliberately placed over Heinrich's shoulder, forcing anyone addressing him to look at it.

Captain Heinrich saw where I was looking. "That was taken at the official opening of the Alpha Settlement atmosphere grid," he said. "The Secretary and I have some history."

"Proximans do tend to stick together," I said.

"Proxima Colony is the closest thing the Alliance has to a seat of government," Captain Heinrich said. "You'd do well to remember that. You're an Old Earther, as I recall?"

"Californian, born and bred."

"Ah, yes. I remember. That must be where you get your callsign from."

"That's correct, sir."

"The old political powers are waning," Commander Dieter chimed in. She'd been quiet throughout the exchange, possibly because she wasn't Proximan.

"The universe is changing," said Captain Heinrich. "The Black Spiral will be defeated at Ithaca, and we will enter a new era of progress. Men like Secretary Lopez will see to it."

I stared down at the half-empty glass of whiskey. I didn't really feel like finishing it. Was this what we had become? Pawns for Secretary Lopez and his cronies in government? It felt that way. I wanted the Spiral decimated more than anyone. But, as ever, it's the "what comes after" that really defines whether a war is worth it…

"I take it that you've come to give me your report?" Captain Heinrich said, making clear that our discussion was at an end.

"Yes, sir."

"Then proceed."

I gave him a truncated version of Riggs' interrogation. Heinrich listened in without interruption, occasionally sipping at his whiskey. Then I gave my report on P's condition.

"So," Heinrich muttered, slightly reclining in his chair, "you're telling me that the xeno asset is no longer reliable?"

"It's more than unreliable. P is out of the game."

"Goddamn it."

Captain Heinrich searched the room for something, or someone, to take his frustration out on. When he couldn't find an immediate target, other than me, he launched into a diatribe.

"The Pariah Project has been a waste of resources

from start to finish," he exclaimed. "I told Command that it wasn't a good bet. And now, when we need the fish most of all, it isn't even available to us! When will it come out of this cocoon?"

"Dr Saito is observing the subject. I don't think he— or I—can give an estimate."

"Has it done this before?"

"No, sir. It hasn't."

"Well, isn't that great?" Captain Heinrich asked rhetorically. "Another Alliance project turned against us."

I narrowed my eyes at that. "What do you mean, sir: 'another Alliance project'?"

"Nothing, Jenkins. Nothing."

"What other assets have turned? Other xeno assets?"

That sense of creeping doom occurred to me again. It was a feeling that I had recently been experiencing far too frequently. Zero's discovery—that the canister on Vektah Minor had originated from a Sci-Div bioweapons facility—jumped to mind.

"You do know something, right?" I asked. "There are…rumours that the Alliance had a hand in the creation of Harbinger."

Heinrich exhaled through his nose and stared at his desk, where data-streams jumped across the tri-D monitor.

"The idea that the Alliance created the virus is an old spacefarer's myth," Dieter said. "But I can assure you that there is no truth in it at all."

"There's no point in holding back on this any more," Heinrich said.

"Then enlighten me, sir."

"The Alliance had nothing to do with the creation of the Harbinger virus. The nano-tech involved here is so far advanced, beyond anything we are currently capable of developing."

Commander Dieter placed her glass on the edge of the desk, and Heinrich refilled it. She looked at me coolly, framed by the view-port behind her. That showed a cluster of stars.

"I've been running Spec Ops missions for decades, Lieutenant," she said. "I was deployed with the Alliance Army Rangers for a long time."

Clade Cooper—Warlord—had been a former Army Ranger. More pieces fell into place, and I wasn't sure that I liked where this was going.

"Did you know Clade Cooper?" I asked.

She nodded, sullenly. There was no pride in her revelation of the relationship.

"Yes. I knew him, before he became Warlord. He was a decent man, someone who would do anything for those that relied on him. His squad was like blood." She smiled, and it was a weak and exhausted expression. "The Jackals remind me of them, in a way. The squad were called the Iron Knights."

"What has any of this got to do with the Harbinger virus?"

"I'll get to that," Commander Dieter said. "As I'm sure you're aware, this isn't my first command. My virgin Special Operations command was when I was aged just thirty-two standard."

Dieter pulled back the sleeve of her uniform. She was now pushing the ceiling of middle-age, but despite the years, the holo-tattoo on her arm was still active. It sparkled across her tanned skin.

I recognised the name.

UAS *Iron Knight*.

I looked at the tattoo, then back at Dieter.

"That...that was Clade Cooper's starship," I said. "You were captain of his squad's ship?"

Something inside of me said that I needed a gun, a

weapon, and I needed it right now. A voice screamed that this woman could be Black Spiral. But the words didn't seem to cause any reaction at all in Heinrich. He already knew about Dieter's background, I realised, and he still trusted her. Dieter was no threat to me. Her eyes looked glassy, as though she were fighting to hold back emotion. She nodded.

"I was captain of the ship sent to Barain-11, to extract Sergeant Cooper's squad. We had worked together on several deployments by then, and he trusted me. He used to say that I was the best captain he'd ever worked with. By the time I came up through the ranks, Cooper had worked with several other crews, but we had a special bond."

Dieter didn't elaborate on that any further, and I decided not to ask questions. Something in her expression suggested—but no more—that this could've been more than platonic. According to his files, Cooper had been a family man. He'd faithfully renewed his marriage contract, dutifully supported his wife and children despite the distance caused by his constant deployments...But Cooper wouldn't be the first to pay lip service to a contract, while he got his rocks off elsewhere.

"The operation should've been routine," Commander Dieter said. She laughed, and the noise came out hollow and bitter. "What bullshit that turned out to be. Mili-Intel fed us bad intelligence. There were Krell everywhere, and I couldn't reach the extraction point. Cooper was left behind. He—and his squad—were taken prisoner. He was a POW for two years."

Two years. The period seemed impossibly long. Made all the worst because the Iron Knights hadn't been simulant-rated. The Army Rangers recon teams didn't utilise simulants. They were expected to do their work in real skins. Cooper and his Knights had paid the price for that operational decision.

"Riggs' father was there as well," I added. "What was their mission? Why were they on Barain-11?"

There was a long pause before Dieter answered that question. Heinrich stared at his glass, like it held all the answers.

"You've got to remember that this was at the peak of the Krell War," she said. "When things were at their worst, when the Alliance would've done anything to end the stalemate." Dieter swallowed, dispelling a bad taste. "Sergeant Cooper and the Iron Knights were sent to Barain-11 in search of a weapon that could be used against the Krell. They found the Harbinger virus in the ruins of a Shard facility, on the moon's surface."

"And they brought it back with them…?" I said, my words trailing off, dying in my mouth.

"Yes," Dieter admitted. "The Iron Knights' mission was successful, despite what had happened to Cooper. He survived his squad, and delivered the Harbinger virus into Alliance hands."

"We didn't use it, though," Captain Heinrich quickly added. "Command thought that it was too powerful, too unstable." He gave a strangled chortle. "That was one thing that we got right, I suppose."

All of this made a certain, terrible sense. Clade Cooper's mission on Barain-11 had been to acquire the Harbinger virus, but he had lost *everything* to achieve that objective, only for the Alliance to make peace with the Krell, and abandon him. His homeworld had been invaded by the Krell, by the Red Fin Collective, and his wife and children had been killed during the evacuation. If that wasn't an event significant enough to cause a life-long grudge, then I don't know what is.

"The Jackals found a canister inside the nest station on Vektah Minor," I said. "I ordered Sergeant Campbell—Zero—to research the markings. She traced them back to a Science Division facility on Delta Primus. A bio-weapons facility."

"Figures," said Captain Heinrich. He was almost certainly drunk now, and poured himself another tall measure of whiskey. "When Clade Cooper left Alliance custody, after his rehabilitation, he stole certain restricted materials. Those included samples of the Harbinger virus. Early attempts at understanding the virus."

Heinrich propped his feet on the corner of his desk, resting his glass on his stomach.

"It goes without saying that this is all classified," he added, after the fact.

"Understood," I replied. "Although, if we don't come back from the Ghost Maker Nebula, I'm not sure that it will matter much."

Commander Dieter gave a tight smile, making the scar on her face curl around her eye. She popped a brightly coloured detoxifier pill from her fatigue pocket and slipped it into her mouth. The pill had an immediate sobering effect, and Commander Dieter primly straightened her uniform, pushing some stray hairs across her brow.

"Can I interest either of you in a detox tab?" she offered.

I knocked back my drink in a way that whiskey-drinking aficionados would seriously take issue with, and shook my head. I didn't want to be fully sober, not with that new knowledge knocking around in my head.

"I'm fine," Captain Heinrich said, his eyes half-lidded. "I like the feeling of being on the edge. It reminds me of home."

Commander Dieter nodded. She was back to business, her guard up again. "Just make sure that you're ready for deployment, Captain. We still have a mission."

"Don't I know it," he answered. "How long until we reach the Ghost Maker Nebula?"

"Thirty hours, subjective," Dieter said.

The fact that we were now measuring the journey time in hours rather than days brought home the immediacy of our situation. Dieter seemed to repress a slight shiver, and I knew exactly how she felt. My data-ports had started to ache, yearning to make connection with a simulant again.

A chronograph holo popped into existence on Heinrich's desk, displaying time zones and quantum-stream fluctuations. This was the universal clock by which the entire Alliance, and specifically its military assets, was coordinated.

"Very soon," Captain Heinrich said, "the Alliance fleet will be converging on Ithaca." He paused, flaring his nostrils. "I hope that we don't disappoint them with what we find out here."

Then Heinrich was back to himself as well. He snapped his boots off the table, and hurriedly buttoned his fatigues. Ran a hand through his hair.

"There's still a lot to be done before we reach the objective," he said, his tone terse, very much like the old Captain Heinrich that I knew and despised. "Dr Saito will be giving a briefing on the next stage of the operation at oh-nine-hundred tomorrow, ship's time. Be ready."

"Yes, sir," I said. "We will be. I'd advise that we keep Pariah under constant observation, and that we space Daneb Riggs."

Okay, I wasn't exactly expecting Heinrich to agree with that, but it was worth a try. He frowned at me and gave a curt shake of his head.

"Absolutely not. More like space the fish and observe Riggs, Lieutenant."

"Pariah is a vital asset. You said so yourself."

Heinrich thought on that for a fraction of a second,

before answering, "Fine. But if that fish so much as demonstrates a single sign of hostility…"

"Understood. What about Riggs?"

"The former corporal remains a potential intelligence source," Captain Heinrich said. "I can't order his execution here; not yet."

"I think that we've exhausted all avenues of investigation with him," I said, although I plainly knew that wasn't true. "There's nothing more he can tell us. He's been scanned; no covert tech except for his data-ports."

Dieter clucked her tongue. "We could always arrange for those to be taken out."

"That's an idea…" I agreed.

Heinrich wasn't buying it. "We don't have the necessary facilities to do that here."

That was true, although I was quite okay with extracting Riggs' data-ports using a rusty scalpel.

"All right," Heinrich said, standing now and circling the desk. "That will be all. You're both dismissed."

Dieter and I saluted the captain and left the chamber.

When I awoke, I was woven into the wall.

Without thought, I knew where I was. The Krell nest on Barain-11. Where this had all started, and where—for some—it had ended.

The place was moist and dark, and the air so thick with fish-stink that it was barely breathable. My body was woven into the nest. When I tried to move my limbs, I realised that they were broken. That was a technique used by the Krell. Not to torture, but to incapacitate. They wanted Clade Cooper alive.

There were others around me. Faces that meant nothing to me, but the universe to Cooper, peered from the incessant gloom. These were the Iron Knights, Cooper's Army Ranger squad. They were in a prison, but nothing like that the Alliance, or any human faction, would ever know.

How could anyone have survived for two years in this horror? I asked, in that twilight between my existence and Cooper's memories. *Was it any wonder that Cooper went insane?*

"You okay, Coop?" came a dry rasp of a voice.

"Now there's a question," I found myself answering. I was reliving someone else's memories; a mind trapped in a body while someone else was at the controls. "How about you, Riggs?"

Marbec Riggs, Daneb's father, was woven into the wall beside Cooper.

When the fishes had brought Cooper and Riggs into this place—whatever the fuck it was—they had brought the remainder of the Iron Knights with them. Singh, Boswell, Carpenter…The others, Cooper hoped, had died in the ambush, but he couldn't be sure. He had heard Singh praying. Heard Carpenter pleading to her husband, back home in Tau Ceti. A week or so into their captivity, Boswell—the squad's comms-man—had stopped talking. Cooper hoped beyond hope that Boswell was dead. He was just a kid, twenty standard. He fucking deserved better than this.

Cooper and Marbec outlived them all. Together, they had watched as each of the Knights had been claimed by the Red Fin Collective. Listened as shouts and cries devolved into requests for mercy. The squad's bravado only lasted so long. Cooper heard their voices become hoarse, then diminish to wheezes as vocal cords gave out. Finally, all that remained were harsh whimpers in the dark.

When had Cooper finally lost his sanity? It was impossible to tell. Had he dreamt of his children, of his wife, and their reunion, during those hot, warm months of confinement? *This wasn't how things were supposed to happen. This wasn't how things were supposed to go.* Sergeant Clade Cooper kept telling himself that, and it became a refrain. A mantra. A safety net. Because, if he told himself that enough, if he actually believed it, then the horror wasn't real.

Cooper was a career Special Operations man. He was supposed to do one of two things.

Option One: get old, get fat. In other words, get out. There were plenty of agencies out there, in the Alliance, that would want an ageing ex-Ranger on their payroll. Military Intelligence, the Core Intelligence Agency, the Secret Service… Any of them would do. It wasn't Cooper's preferred choice, but it was okay. It was an honourable, decent way to go.

Option Two: die in combat, go down a hero. The Army Rangers didn't have the luxury of simulant technology. Cooper would be remembered for what he'd achieved, and his family would be compensated for his loss. Another honourable end. *Fuck. Oh fuck.* A wave of melancholy and regret poured over him. He always got this way, when he thought of Option Two, because that meant thinking of Jandra.

Was this a divine punishment, a sentence for his sins? Cooper often wondered that, in the brief moments of clarity that dwelt between ages of madness. Commander Vie Dieter. She had been nothing but a fast lay, a dirty secret. Cooper was sometimes taunted, and haunted, by flashes of their trysts aboard the *Iron Knight*. Her tight, muscled body—so different to Jandra's—coiled like a spring beneath him. Their bodies rutting in rhythm. His hands through her short red hair, over the curve of her buttocks…

"Easy, Sarge," came a rusty voice to Cooper's left.

"I…I'm sorry," Cooper replied.

"Don't be so harsh on yourself."

It was Corporal Marbec Riggs. Cooper made out his shape. Marbec was webbed to the wall beside Cooper, his body so close that Cooper could almost touch him. Like Cooper's, Riggs' body was twisted, limbs contorted unnaturally. He'd suffered broken bones, for sure, but that was the least of Riggs' problems.

"How…how long, Riggs?" Cooper managed. His own voice-box was tight, dry, and he didn't recognise it as his own.

"How long we been here?" Riggs questioned. His eyes were bright stars in the dark, the curve of his face illuminated by bio-luminescent fungi that crawled across the cavern wall. "Too long, Coop. Too fucking long."

Riggs' lean, chiselled face was sprinkled with days'— weeks'?—worth of facial hair. He always went into the field clean-shaven. That was Riggs' thing, one of his rituals.

"That…that wasn't what I meant…" Cooper managed. Jesus, it hurt to talk.

"Then what, Coop?" Riggs asked.

"How…how long until they kill us?" Cooper replied.

Riggs let out a harsh, pained laugh. It was the laugh of a madman, of a dead man walking.

"Long time, Coop. Long, long time…" he said. "*Aeons.*"

The chamber walls were formed of organic matter, and Cooper and Riggs weren't the only captives in there. Mostly human, but other, unspecified things too: creatures that Cooper didn't recognise. The captives generated a background noise, a hubbub of cries, squawks and gibbering.

"This wasn't supposed to happen," Cooper said in response. "We did what they told us."

"You're telling me, bud. You're telling me. I got a kid. I got to get home."

"I know, Riggs. I promised you. I promised you all I'd get you home."

"It wasn't your fault, Coop," Riggs insisted. "You got to believe that. You got to know that."

"I ... I was squad leader ..." Cooper said.

He wanted to say so much more—that he should've checked the mission intelligence, that he should've argued with Command, that he shouldn't have been sleeping with Commander Dieter ... But it was too much, and he couldn't muster the energy.

"Military Intelligence did this to us," Riggs rasped.

"We succeeded," said Cooper.

And in that, he was right. The Iron Knights had penetrated the Shard ruins and had executed their orders. They had discovered the ... artefact. Where Cooper's flesh had touched the xenotech, it had become blackened. Corrupted. A darkness crawled under his skin, in his veins. He could barely make out the infection, as it crept through his limbs, into his torso. But he could feel it, well enough.

Clade Cooper was becoming something else.

"I'm ... s–sorry!" he shouted.

The noise stirred up the prisoners. More cries, shouts: other sounds that could've been alien, or were perhaps the product of tortured human vocals cords. It was difficult to really say.

"You get out without me," said Riggs, "I want you to promise me something."

"Anything ..." Cooper managed.

"You make someone pay for this," said Riggs. "You make them understand what happened here. Don't let them forget."

"I won't."

"And you look after my kid. You make sure he knows who I am, and that I cared."

The Krell hardly ever attended the prisoners any more. As the months dragged on, they saw fewer and fewer of the alien guards. At first, Cooper had thought that was his imagination. Perhaps, he reasoned, he was choosing not to see them. Or maybe, as his eyesight failed, he was missing them as they moved through the dark.

Except…except that wasn't right. If Cooper contorted his head just so, he could see other bodies on the floor of the cell. Those weren't prisoners. They were Krell. Partly decomposed primary-forms. Their skin was black, but silver strands danced beneath the flesh…

"The Krell are dying," Cooper said.

Marbec Riggs growled a laugh. "That won't help us, Cooper. It's too late for us."

From the corner of his eye, Cooper caught another flash of light. Silver tendrils, creeping under his own skin. Like living mercury, a thinking poison that claimed everything it touched…He'd seen this stuff—or something like it—before. This was Shard technology.

"We brought something back with us," said Cooper. His voice faltered. He could feel the infection inside of him, leeching his life-force, but renewing him as well. "The ruins…The Shard."

"That was our objective, Coop," said Riggs. "We did what we were told."

But not all of the Krell were dead. A fish appeared in front of Cooper. Upside down, using the organic vines and surface details to scurry down the chamber wall. Another clambered over a body that was webbed in place. A third clutched living pipework that sprayed mist into the chamber, and descended spider-like into the well of the prison. All three of the aliens were desiccated, dying. Their carapaces were blotched with black, filigreed with silver veins. They were infected.

"They're keeping us alive, Coop," Riggs ranted, his voice rising in volume. "They want to understand us."

Riggs started to spit insults at the xenos, but the aliens ignored him. The guards focused on Cooper. They peered at him with their deep, dark eyes.

"What... what do you want?" Cooper groaned. His throat was sandpaper: so dry, despite the intensely humid atmosphere that filled the chamber.

The XTs didn't answer. Instead, they forced living machinery into Cooper's body, using open wounds at his forearms, his chest, his legs. This had happened several times already, but that made it no easier to suffer. Pain coursed through his body. The blackness inside of him was soon out. It eagerly polluted the Krell nest.

Jandra's face was all that kept him going. Jandra and the kids—Tom and Rae—playing in the garden. Drinking a nice, cold American beer, with Marbec Riggs at his shoulder. The smell of barbecued meat in the air...

What was Marbec's kid called again?

Daneb. Daneb Riggs. That was it.

Cooper gave in to the dark now, because that was easier. That was all he could do.

CHAPTER FIFTEEN

LONG AEONS, EVEN
DEATH MAY DIE

The dark greeted me, and I sat bolt upright in my bunk. Nearly hit my head on the underside of the cot above, where Feng slept. *Christo, Christo, Christo.* My brain hurt like I'd just made the worst possible extraction.

That wasn't my memory, I told myself. *I wasn't there. None of it was real.* It was the Deep: the shared connection P. had described to me. I had been reliving Clade Cooper's memory, as though it were my own.

"You okay, ma'am?" Zero asked, her eyes visible as white dots in the shadow.

Like Marbec Riggs, woven into the wall on Barain-11...

I shook away the thought. Cancelled it. That wasn't easy: the images, thoughts, emotions were needle-sharp. If only P were around to explain this to me. The mind-link to the alien was still dead air. I pulled back the sheets. Breathed deep, and tasted the processed air. So much better than what Clade Cooper and Marbec Riggs had been breathing in the fish-nest...

"Are you all right?" Zero repeated.

"I . . . I'm good," I said, hesitatingly.

The Jackals' quarters were as they should be. Lopez and Feng in their own bunks, sleeping soundly. Zero across the room.

"Sorry if I woke you," I said to Zero.

"It's okay. I couldn't sleep anyway. Not with that son of a bitch still on the ship."

"Try not to let Riggs bother you. He'll be gone, soon enough."

"Were you dreaming?"

"Something like that."

"You were saying a name. You kept saying Marbec."

"Forget about it, Zero," I whispered. "Go back to sleep."

My wrist-comp chimed. MEDICAL ALERT, it said. I sighed and felt a sinking feeling in my gut. This was hardly unexpected, but that didn't make it any easier. I rolled out of the bunk, pulled on my fatigues.

"What are you doing?" Zero said, sitting up now. "It's late into the night-cycle. We have a briefing tomorrow."

"I'm going to check on Novak."

"Do you want me to come with you?"

"No. Get some sleep. As you said, we have a big day tomorrow."

I took a detour to the armoury first. Signed out a sidearm—a Navy-issue shock-pistol—and made sure it was armed. Hoped that I wouldn't need it, but it never hurts to be sure. Then I took the *Valkyrie*'s main elevator down to the brig. As the elevator descended the decks, I tried to pull up the surveillance feed of Riggs' cell on my wrist-comp. The image was being blocked. *You stupid fuck, Novak*, I thought to myself. MEDICAL ALERT, popped up on my comp again, confirming my suspicions.

The brig's main hatch was unmanned. A noise—an impact with wet meat—shattered the quiet. A groan, then gruff male voices.

"...need to find her," said Novak, his Russian accent instantly recognisable.

"It's not that simple," said Riggs. "She finds you, see? You know how difficult these—"

I tightened my grip on my pistol, pretty sure what I was going to find.

The observation-field was lowered, and Novak was inside the cell, looming over Riggs. The traitor's electro-shackles had been removed, and he was on his knees in front of the big man. Novak had the collar of Riggs' prison jumpsuit clutched in one paw-like hand, while the other was drawn back in a fist, ready to land another blow to Riggs' face.

"Put him down, Novak!" I roared, weapon up, aimed at the Russian.

Novak instantly released Riggs, and he backed away, hands up and open. Riggs slid to the floor. Crumpled, gasping in relief.

"Thank Gaia you got here in time," said Riggs. His words came out all slurred and imprecise, like he'd been drinking. "I thought he was going to kill me."

"What the fuck are you doing, Novak?" I almost screamed.

"He slip, hit head on bunk," said Novak. "I go in to help."

"You were hitting him!" I said. "And you blocked the surveillance feed. I set the cell to remotely monitor his bio-signs."

"Really?" said Novak, a look of genuine surprise on his face. "I did not know you could do that."

"Well, you can!" I yelled back. "If certain medical

safety parameters are breached," I said, tapping my wrist-comp while still holding the pistol, "then the ship sends me an alert."

"Ah," said Novak. He pursed his lips. "Then is good you come here. Riggs fell. Could've been serious."

"He did not fall," I said.

Novak shot a glance at Riggs. He'd staggered to his feet, and was rubbing a hand over his jaw. Already, bruising was beginning to show across his face. He wiggled his jaw around, checking that nothing was broken.

"Tell her," Novak said.

"I ... I fell," Riggs managed to say.

"You can shut the fuck up, Riggs," I said, waving my pistol in his direction. "My trigger finger is getting seriously itchy. Stand away from the field, and sit on your bunk. *Now!*"

Riggs shrank back. The observation-field jumped up again, sealing Riggs in the cell. I jabbed a finger into Novak's shoulder. He, too, wilted a little beneath by glare. I was pissed off.

"I told you not to have physical contact with the prisoner!" I said. "Your orders were that no harm was to come to him."

"I did nothing!" he argued.

"And you were talking to him! I specifically told you not to speak with him!"

"Is harmless," Novak protested. "Is nothing bad."

"Let me guess what you asked him about: Vasnev."

Novak swallowed, winced. "Yes," he said. "He knows about her. I ask him about where to find her."

"What was the point of that? He's a traitor! Do you think what comes out of this asshole is going to be anything but bullshit?"

"Is best source I have, yes?" Novak argued.

"And we've been through this a million times," I said. "Why don't you get it, trooper? You're a Jackal. We're on the eve of war."

"I do get it," Novak said. "I need to know where—"

I rolled my head at him. "Ah, ah, Novak. You need to know what I tell you."

Novak fell silent. I could detect Riggs' glowering sense of triumph from the other side of the obs-field; so pleased that he had driven a wedge between Novak and me.

"The prisoner is a proven manipulator," I said, eyes narrowing: glaring at Riggs now. "I know that more than anyone."

"What are you going to do with me?" Novak said, meekly.

"What can I do?" I said. "I can't send you back. I can't report you to Heinrich. But I can't have you standing watch on Riggs any longer."

Nothing from Novak.

"I'm confining you to quarters," I said, "with immediate effect. Feng will take over the watch."

I tapped my wrist-comp, and urgently requested Feng's attendance. He wouldn't thank me for waking him at this hour, but needs must. "You're dismissed," I said to Novak.

He grunted at me and left the brig. I shook with anger.

That only got worse when I turned to look at Riggs' smug face. *How did you ever care for this bastard?* I asked myself.

Riggs smirked. The expression was no doubt designed to make me feel uncomfortable, but it did nothing more than annoy me. Just being in his presence set me on edge. The only consolation was that his face was already swelling. I toyed with the data-ports on my arms. The flesh there was well healed, and the metalwork a little scuffed. The pistol in my hand trembled.

"You're shivering, Jenk," he said. "Getting the transition shakes?"

"Fuck you, Riggs," I snarled. "Don't ever speak to me, or my squad, again."

Riggs sat back on the bunk, his fingers interlocked behind his head. He stared up at the ceiling. "I remember the feeling," he said. "That urge to make transition is a tough one to master, isn't it?"

"You aren't ever going to make transition again. I'll make sure of it."

"That doesn't matter," Riggs said, with practised insouciance.

Still, his words were at odds with his actions. Riggs had pulled up the sleeves of his overall, exposing the data-ports on both arms. I felt a sliver of glee as I saw that both ports had turned bad. The one on his left forearm looked especially irritated; the skin around the plug inflamed.

"You want to get those ports looked at," I said, with fake sympathy. "Wouldn't want them to become infected, after all."

Riggs picked at one with a dirty fingernail, pulling a disdainful face. "I'll be fine. Don't be hard on Novak. He only wanted information."

"It doesn't matter what you told him," I said. "Because you can't use your position any more, Riggs."

"I don't know about that," he said. "I think I'm doing okay, considering that I'm in a prison cell. For instance, I know that your pet fish is currently out of action. Novak told me that, in exchange for a titbit on Vasnev. I also know that we're almost at Carcosa."

Riggs was successfully getting under my skin. I tried to hide my reaction, but I knew that I'd probably failed.

He continued to scratch at his data-ports, inspecting his bloodied fingernails.

"And how exactly would you know that?"

"I can hear the AI's announcements in here," he said. "And the *Valkyrie* hasn't jumped in hours. That, together with your obvious need to make transition, leads me to believe that we're almost there."

"You're a fucking genius," I said, clapping my hands together. "But none of this will get you anywhere. After tomorrow, this will all be over."

Riggs yawned. "If you say so."

I drew up a chair and sat down in front of the observation-field. I was, now, just killing time before Feng got down here, but I wanted to make Riggs suffer. I wanted to push his buttons, as he had mine.

"I keep having dreams," I said. "More like nightmares, really."

"Is that so?" said Riggs.

"These nightmares are about Cooper, and about his time on Barain-11. He was confined in a Krell nest base for two years, with your father."

The shift in Riggs' presentation was only small—his breathing becoming slightly shallower, his shoulders hunching—but I read it well enough. This was Riggs' motivation for getting involved in this mess, and that made it his weakness.

"So?" he challenged.

"You like to pretend that this doesn't matter to you," I said, "but I know that it does."

"Warlord told me all about it."

"I've got access to Warlord's memories. I know what really happened in that nest. Your father's name was Marbec Riggs. He was good friends with Cooper. They served together in the same outfit."

"He suffered," said Riggs. "But I'm going to make it right."

"What do you mean by that?" I asked.

"I plead the fifth. I don't have to explain myself to you."

"I know what happened to your father."

"Believe what you want," Riggs said. In an obvious attempt to change the subject, he said, "Warlord and the Spiral took me in after my father left. They showed me the true way."

"Fine," I said, shrugging. "If you're not interested in what I've got to say, we can leave it there…"

That was too much for Riggs, and he couldn't resist. He broke almost instantly.

"What happened to my father?" he asked. He'd undergone a transformation in the last few seconds, and the desperate look in his eyes was almost frightening. "I need the details, Keira. I *need* to know where he is now. He's still alive, isn't he?"

Alive? Was that what Riggs really thought? Was this why he had fallen to the Black Spiral, become part of their organisation? I'd accessed Riggs' military service record, read everything I could about him. He'd been turned at some point after Clade Cooper's return from Barain-11, as a result of his association with a Gaia Cult on Tau Ceti. I'd always assumed that Riggs accepted his father was truly dead. Now I wasn't so sure. Riggs' sudden and dogmatic insistence that his father was still alive was disarming, and my mask almost dropped.

"I thought that your father didn't matter any more," I said, regaining some of my composure. Pathetic or otherwise, Riggs was still a dangerous man.

"Warlord knows where he is," Riggs said. "If you know anything else, you have to tell me!"

"You don't have any right to know the rest," I taunted. "When the time comes, Riggs, I'll be sure to give you a quick death."

Feng arrived at the hatch, a sidearm holstered across his body. He looked from me to Riggs and back again.

"Sorry to wake you, Feng," I said. He was still rubbing the sleep from his eyes, but his senses sharpened as he took in Riggs' injuries. "He slipped, hit his head on the bunk," I said.

"Right…" Feng said. "That could've happened, I guess."

"No questions asked," I said. "Keep your eyes on the prisoner at all times, and don't let Novak in here."

"Yes, ma'am," Feng said, all formal now.

"Anything weird goes down, call for back-up."

"Copy that."

I stepped back towards the hatch. Holstered my own pistol. Riggs watched me go.

"Keira, I think—" he said.

I nodded at Feng. "Turn off the audio. Nothing he says means anything."

Riggs' final words were lost as the audio dampener activated.

I left the brig.

"Novak did *what*?" Zero asked, incredulous.

I went straight from the brig to the barracks, where I tore a strip off Novak. He had simply stood there, head hanging, and listened to my rebuke. Then he'd apologised, promised that he had not done anything else, and once again tried to explain about Major Vasnev. I'd cut him short—I was done with listening to his excuses, and Novak understood that—and confined him to quarters until we reached Carcosa. Then I'd headed to Medical, where Dr Saito was monitoring P. If Riggs had achieved nothing else, he had woken the squad and prevented us from having a decent night's sleep. It was still the early hours of the morning by the ship's wake cycle, but with all the commotion Zero was properly awake now, and had followed me down.

She was working at a terminal, Dr Saito examining some cell samples at one of the microscope workbenches. He paused, listening to our conversation.

"He hit him," I explained. "Several times, in fact." I paced the lab in a futile attempt to work out some of my anger. "I can't believe we're going through this all over again. When will Novak learn?"

"He doesn't think he has a problem, by the sound of it," Dr Saito said.

Zero pulled a face and sighed. "Well, from what I can see, Novak managed to deactivate the surveillance programme. I'm surprised that he did that by himself, but it wasn't a very sophisticated fix."

"Can you make sure it doesn't happen again?"

"Sure. I'll add a security key, so that only senior personnel can deactivate the system."

"Can you trust this trooper?" Dr Saito said. "I'm sorry—I don't know the full story, but he seems a little … unstable."

I threw my hands up in the air. "Unstable is about the size of it. Novak is a good trooper, but he's easily led. He is obsessed with this Vasnev character."

"Should you report the incident to Captain Heinrich?" Dr Saito said.

"I'm not going to do that," I said. "The Jackals take care of their own. Once we get to Carcosa, Novak won't have any further contact with Riggs. Then, when we re-join the main fleet in the Reef Stars, Riggs can become someone else's problem."

"Can't come soon enough," Zero said, smiling wanly. "There. The surveillance system is working properly."

"Thanks, Zero. What's the latest on mission prep?"

"Also done. All sims are armed and armoured, and have been thawed for imminent deployment."

"Good job. What about P, Dr Saito? Any news on the cocoon?"

Dr Saito grimaced and looked up from his work. "*Chrysalis*, Lieutenant, not cocoon."

"There's a difference?'

"A cocoon is like a nest. This is a chrysalis; made from super-hardened protein strands. 'Chrysalis' is used to describe the development of a terrestrial life-form from pupal stage to maturity."

"P's not terrestrial," I said, my eyes glossing over. "But whatever it is, has it changed?"

"Not significantly. It's enlarged and seems to be drawing in moisture from the surrounding atmosphere. I'm not sure what the pariah-form is using for nutrients."

"Have you tried—I don't know—cutting the pod open?"

Zero cringed at my use of the word "cut". "I don't think that would be a good idea. We don't know what's happening inside the chrysalis."

"Correct," Saito agreed. "P may be in a vulnerable state inside. If its immune system is actively fighting off the Harbinger nano-virus, we might interrupt the healing process. Plus, I've tried to use a laser scalpel on the chrysalis's outer coating. That stuff is very tough."

"That'd be P," I said. "Made of stone."

I bit my lip as I saw that Dr Saito had a dozen security eyes focused on P's lair. The chrysalis was swollen, shiny-wet with resinous gunk. The cell resembled less a compartment of an Alliance starship, and more the hold of a Krell bio-ship.

"I've increased the ambient temperature," said Dr Saito. "P seemed to like that. I wondered whether a temperature differential might prompt the chrysalis to…" He shrugged. "Hatch?"

I reached out to P with my mind. Tried to establish that link.

We need you, P. Now more than ever. I need you.

But there was nothing. Nothing at all.

Dr Saito sighed. "We'll watch. We can't do any more."

CHAPTER SIXTEEN

CARCOSA, IN YELLOW

The *Valkyrie* made final approach to Carcosa, and Captain Heinrich called a briefing in the CIC.

"These scanner results are very messy, Commander," Heinrich said. "Can't you do something to clean up the visuals?"

"Negative, Captain," Dieter said. She was plugged to her station by data-ports in her forearms, a sensory-deprivation helm over the upper part of her head. "There's a lot of hydrogen, interstellar debris, and other trace elements in the Nebula. This is as good as we're going to get."

Space here was twisted, all screwed up. Streams of purple and yellow drifted by, visible both on the ship's tactical-display, and also with the naked eye. Smears of light against the blackness.

"The disturbance is likely caused by ionisation of the Nebula's gas cloud," Zero explained. "Or the by-product of radiation bands in the sector."

"Whatever it is," said Commander Dieter, "it's playing havoc with the *Valkyrie*'s sensor array."

"Are we sure this is a natural occurrence and not some sort of deliberate stealth-tech?" I asked. Something didn't sit right with me. "It's all too convenient."

"I can't think of a better place for the remnants of an alien civilisation to hide," Dr Saito suggested.

"It has to be natural," said Commander Dieter. "I seriously doubt that any alien species has technology capable of shrouding an area of space this big."

"Not even the Aeon?" I queried.

"We don't know what the Aeon are capable of," offered Dr Saito. He was continually checking his wrist-comp—doubtless monitoring P's condition—but he still sounded excited. "We should remain alive to any possibility."

"This place isn't all bad," Feng said, trying to make light of the situation. "It's managed to shut up Phoenix Squad."

The Jackals stood on one side of the display, Phoenix Squad on the other. Ving's team seemed to fill the space with their over-muscled bodies, and there was a renewed air of hostility between them and us, the return to old rivalries. Soon, we were going to be getting into the tanks and doing what we did best. Each squad wanted to be the one to take the prize of first contact.

"I haven't forgotten about Vektah," Lopez said, glancing at her counterpoint across the display.

"We can have a rematch, if the Jackals want to lose again," said a particularly giant meathead from Phoenix Squad.

"Any time," Novak said.

Riggs was someone else's problem for a while. Commander Dieter's security team had been tasked with guarding him while we were away, under strict instructions not to have any contact.

"We've found your planet," Commander Dieter said,

leaning back in her command throne. "Dr Locke's intelligence has taken us this far, at least."

Carcosa filled the tactical-display.

The planet was diamond bright, reflecting light back out into space. It was almost jarring against the other colours of the Nebula. It moved in a tight orbit around the neutron star at the system's core.

The *Valkyrie*'s remote sensor-suite went into overdrive as it began to relay data. A band of black debris resolved on the scanner, and a series of alerts sounded across the CIC.

"Situation report!" Captain Heinrich demanded.

"I have fresh scanner-returns," said a crewman.

"Krell?" I queried.

"No..." came the officer's confused response. "The results are inconsistent with a Krell bio-ship."

"Send them to the tactical-display," Dieter requested.

"Aye, ma'am."

The tactical-display filled with scanner data. The image rapidly resolved, giving us a clearer picture of our surroundings. A tight ring of chaff surrounded Carcosa.

Commander Dieter manipulated the feeds, magnifying certain images. "Those...those are starships."

"How can that be?" Captain Heinrich said. "This region is unexplored!"

An ancient black hull—spinning endlessly in the void, warped by the heat of an unknown weapon— drifted across the *Valkyrie*'s path. Other starships followed, tumbling by in a haphazard formation.

Feng sucked his teeth. "They don't look like any ship design I've seen before."

Even Novak managed a sharp intake of breath.

"They're not human..." Zero muttered. "That looks

like a Shard warship." She turned to me, expectantly. "Is it?"

I nodded. "I think so." I felt my gut tightening, my data-ports tingling. The safety of the simulator-tank was calling out to me. "But these ships: they all look different."

All of the ships were ancient, and appeared long-abandoned, but they were of different designs. They were wrecks, reminders of a war that had been fought millennia ago. Some were torn open, trailing their entrails across space. Others were silent and dark, their structures tombs for whatever alien species had once crewed them. Ship designs varied from the obviously machined—such as the Shard warships—through to others that were pseudo-organic. Some had been rendered down to little more than individual modules, while others were bigger than the *Valkyrie*.

"It's a starship graveyard," Lopez offered.

"We do this in Norilsk," Novak growled. "We kill a ganger, then hang up his body. We gut him, maybe cut him some." Despite the subject matter, Novak's manner was very matter-of-fact. "We put this man on edge of gang territory. Leave to bleed out. Is warning to visitor, not to come here."

"That's not very helpful, Private," Heinrich rebuked. "I hardly think we can judge the actions of the Aeon—an ancient alien intelligence—against those of a petty street gang. It's not a useful comparison."

Novak shrugged. "Is not meant to be useful, Captain. Is fact. Aeon are here, hidden in this place. Are you sure they want to have visitor?"

"It doesn't matter what they want," Captain Heinrich said, dismissing Novak's concerns. "I want eyes on that planet, and as much intelligence as you can gather."

Commander Dieter nodded. "We have a full complement of surveillance probes."

"Then dispatch them," Heinrich said.

"Probes away," Commander Dieter replied.

"Aye, ma'am," said the operations officer. "Probes launched."

The *Valkyrie*'s probes were equipped with miniature jump drives, and we watched as they picked their way through the tangle of debris, then made hard burn towards the planet. They began to broadcast their findings immediately.

The probes could do no more than explore a fraction of Carcosa's surface, but they had been programmed to make planetfall at specific points, to give a wide overview of the world's condition. No matter where they had dropped, they sent back more or less the same data. Cold, high pressure, trace atmospherics, featureless ice-plains. The entire world presented a face of chilling indifference.

"Is that surface ice?" asked Zero. She was nervous, and I could tell. When she got nervous, she talked. A lot. "That means water! How is there water down there? Being that close to a neutron star should make that place completely uninhabitable. Did you know that neutron stars have about the same mass as Sol? Within a package that small? I'd expect Carcosa to be a pulsar-class planet. That would mean intense surface pressure, and, well..."

She looked around the table, hopefully, although no one else seemed to share her enthusiasm.

"This could be some sort of planetary engineering," suggested Dr Saito. "Perhaps the Aeon have manufactured this location. Deliberately cloaked it, somehow, then xenoformed it according to their own requirements..."

"It looks like one big snowball," said Ving. "So where are the damned Aeon?"

"Are you detecting any communications data?" Captain Heinrich asked. "Radio waves, tight beam, anything that would suggest a technical civilisation?"

Commander Dieter shook her head. "I'm not reading *anything.*"

"Maybe we're too late," Lopez said. "Maybe the Aeon are long gone."

More images scrolled by. Empty ice-plains that seemed to roll on for ever, beneath a still, cloud-filled sky…

A chime sounded across the CIC. One of the probes had dropped into a basin. That was shallow, but had a radius of several kilometres. A series of white pylons rose up around the edges of the depression. Those were barely visible against the consistent white of the surrounding terrain, but the probe's sensors picked them out. Thirteen structures, each almost a kilometre tall, arranged in a rough circle. Thinner at the tip, and much wider at the base, the pylons appeared to be half buried in the ice.

"Concentrate the probes on that location," Captain Heinrich said.

All probes in the vicinity focused on the site. It was eerily still, abandoned.

"P would probably know what this is," Zero said.

"Your fish can't help us now," Ving groaned.

Captain Heinrich made a sound at the back of his throat, like an anxious child. He circled the holo, taking in the view from every angle.

"Still no radio or comms data," Commander Dieter said. "No readings at all from those structures."

"We should investigate, sir," I suggested.

Captain Heinrich paused. Breathed in and out several times, no doubt seeking to repress the burgeoning sense of failure.

"All right," Heinrich said. "Commander, order the probes to set a landing beacon. All simulant squads, ready for immediate deployment. Prepare for drop-capsule insertion."

"Transition confirmed," I said. "Jackals, sound off."

The Jackals variously called in, voices bright and clear over the comm-network. Phoenix Squad did the same. My Pathfinder combat-suit booted up, and I opened my eyes to the waiting darkness. The insides of the drop-capsule were cramped, hot and claustrophobic. My arms were crossed over my chest, equipment strapped across my body. Still, it felt damned good to be back in a simulant.

"*Hoo-ah!*" yelled Ving, over the comm-link. "Come get some, people!"

Phoenix Squad echoed the Army war-cry—*hoo-ah!*—and my suit compensated by dampening the volume. Lopez's vitals spiked in annoyance.

"Do we have to take the same drop as them?" she asked.

"I don't think we have a choice," said Feng.

Novak snorted. "Every elevator goes down, yes?"

Zero's voice popped into my earbead. "That's a positive transition on all operators. Readings are in the green."

"Copy that," I said. "Command, we are ready to drop."

"Confirm that," said Commander Dieter.

My helmet was buckled into place—essential for use of the drop-capsule—and graphics popped up on the HUD. Processed atmosphere filled my suit, and I felt the prickle of apprehension run over my skin. The safety harness holding me inside the capsule automatically tightened.

"Permission to launch," said Captain Heinrich. Obviously, it had to be him to authorise the drop.

A slight pause, then a voice from the CIC: "Launching in three...two...one..."

In unison, nine drop-capsules fired from the *Valkyrie*'s drop-bay, and we launched towards Carcosa.

* * *

Each capsule was equipped with a thruster unit and acted as a one-man spacecraft, with a networked AI whose sole function was to safely get us to the surface. All flight was undertaken by the onboard navigation systems, and we just held tight until we hit the ground. The capsules dropped into the planet's gravity-well, then punctured the swirling mauve clouds of Carcosa's upper atmo. We took a drop straight down the pipe. It was almost textbook.

My capsule captured new intelligence as I fell, and fed that back to me via my HUD and my suit's neural-link. I focused on what mattered—satisfying myself that there were no local threats—and sent the rest up the chain to the SOC.

"Do you read me, Zero?" I asked.

"I copy, Jenk," she replied.

"Nothing new?"

"Nothing significant," Zero confirmed. "Your capsule's sensors confirm the results from the probes."

Feng sighed over the joint comm-network. "Damn."

"All this way for nothing, huh?" Ving asked.

"Keep the channel clear," Heinrich rebuked. "I want to ensure we aren't contaminating the theatre."

"What is to contaminate?" Novak bickered. "There is nothing out here."

It was tough to argue with the Russian's assessment. Carcosa was a bleak, bleak planet. Plains of ice spread in every direction, lit by the planet's dead star. Everything was a bizarre white, and the landscape almost glowed. The clouds were grey-purple, reflecting the light generated by the planet beneath.

"This just keeps getting better," Ving said. Phoenix Squad muttered in agreement. "I knew this was a bad idea. I fucking knew it."

Atmospheric readings scrolled across my HUD. I was

no scientist, but even I could tell that nothing was going to breathe the mix of methane, exotic gases and complex carbons that filled Carcoca's atmosphere.

"If the suits breach on the surface," Zero said, "even in a sim, you'll likely asphyxiate within seconds."

"All troopers are to remain buttoned up throughout the deployment," Captain Heinrich ordered.

"We'd have been better reinforcing the fleet," said a trooper from Phoenix Squad.

"Fuck yeah," said another. "Phoenix Squad, on the force. At least then we'd get to kill us some fish heads…"

Ving sucked his teeth noisily. "The Phoenixian loves to kill some fishes, that's for sure."

"Is it normal to speak about yourself in the third person, Captain?" Lopez said.

"The Phoenixian loves himself some ass, as well," said Ving. I sensed his leer even over the link. "Of the political variety, especially."

"I've got a fix on the ruins," I said. "Prep for landing."

The chronometer at the corner of my HUD—displaying the mission timeline—had started to twitch. It appeared to be jumping back and forth in time, sporadically, unevenly.

"Anyone else experiencing system fluctuations?" I asked.

There were words of agreement across the link, from both squads.

"Your systems are drifting out of synch with the *Valkyrie*'s," Zero said. "It…it seems to be getting worse the closer you're getting to the surface."

"Any idea what's happening?" I asked, suspecting that Zero would have at least a theory.

She didn't disappoint. "This could be a time-fractal," she said.

"What the hell is a 'time-fractal'?" Lopez queried. "And why are you only raising it now, Zero?"

"It's very interesting, really," Zero said. "Science Division hasn't actually observed the effect, not directly, but the neutron star could account for the spatial disturbance."

"Then why's it getting worse the closer we are to Carcosa?" Feng asked.

"All of this is hypothetical," said Zero. "We're talking quark displacement, which might interfere with the space-time quantum flow..."

"You had me at 'hypothetical'," I said. "Fill us in when we extract, Z."

"Will do."

Unless this was a deliberate response to our presence. Maybe it was an effect caused by the Aeon. P had suggested that the xenos had access to such a technology, but I hadn't been able to ask further questions. I reached out with my mind, searching for the connection with P, but got no answer. Once again, I sincerely wished that P was with us.

The *Valkyrie*'s probe had planted among the ruins. Half buried in the snow, the visual beacon glowed cherry red, contrasting with the crisp white of the surrounding landscape. With no other transmissions to foul the broadcast, it would've been detectable across most of the continent. Guided by the probe, the drop-capsules fired thrusters, and started to shed their outer layers. Pieces of friction-burnt debris broke away, and I felt the pod slowing down. The retro-thrusters kicked in as we closed on the landing site.

"It's started to snow," said Feng.

"Great," said Lopez. "Now we can't see shit."

A bright chemical drizzle fell from the violet clouds, throwing everything into a bright light. Visibility hadn't been great to start with, but decreased to almost nil in the backwash of the landing. For what it was worth, the "snow" did contain some water, but was also composed of a dozen other trace materials that would almost certainly kill a simulant, and would definitely be fatal to an unaugmented human.

The inner layer of the drop-capsule came free. Pieces of smoking metal showered the landing zone. Then the safety harness unlocked, and my EVAMP kicked in. I took control of my own descent, guided my armour down to the surface. The others did the same. We were somewhere in the centre of the basin, surrounded by the pylons.

"We have a successful landing," I said. "Adopt defensive formation, Jackals."

"Phoenix Squad too," Ving echoed.

By the numbers, Phoenix Squad and Jenkins' Jackals deployed back to back. Plasma rifles up, targeting software live. Ready to confront whatever was waiting for us.

"Run a bio-scan, full amplification."

"No returns on the scanner," Feng confirmed.

"Same here," said Lopez.

"Nothing," grunted Novak.

I gazed up at the pylons. Despite the developing storm—which seemed to have come from nowhere—the structures were still visible. Someone, or *something*, had made those things. Dr Locke's intelligence had been right. The landscape felt alive, in a way that I couldn't explain. Call it a sixth sense, soldier instinct, whatever: there was an echo of something out here. I swallowed back uneasiness. Carcosa's bizarre surface was constantly changing. Shapes seemed to shift in the blizzard, forming and reforming. I tried to dismiss the effect as just a trick of the mind, something caused by the unusual conditions. But that wasn't so easy. My skin had started to prickle, my heart throbbing a little faster.

"That's a negative on targets," said Ving. "The area is secure."

"I'm not so sure about that," I muttered back.

"Something...doesn't feel right," Lopez said.

"Still no life-signs," Feng said.

"Spread out," ordered Ving. "Phoenix Squad, left flank. Jackals, go right. Move on the structures."

I activated my EVAMP. The thruster pack fired, and I managed a short bounce. My boots left deep imprints in the snow when I landed. After a series of controlled jumps, I was at the base of a pylon. Around me, the rest of the strike team did the same—the brilliant blue flares of EVAMPs barely visible through the thickening snowstorm.

I got a better look at the pylons. They were enormous—stretching into the sky—and composed of a white, almost crystalline material. That seemed to take on an iridescent glow, reflecting the light of Carcosa's star.

"Zero, I'm getting a power reading off this structure," I said.

There was no answer, but I started an analysis through my neural-link anyway. Even that action felt sluggish, weirdly delayed. The chronometer on my HUD shifted erratically.

"Sound off, Jackals!" I called.

"We're here," said Lopez.

"What's happening?" Feng asked, voice brittle with anxiety. Novak followed him, his hard eyes scanning the white for something to kill.

"Jackals, form up on me," I ordered. "Ving, do you read?"

Through the squall, Phoenix Squad was now invisible,

and there was no response over the comm. I tried another channel.

Above me, the pylon rippled with light.

"...everywhere!" came Ving's voice, so panicked that it was barely recognisable. "Weapons free! Fire on... Fishes, here..."

Static punctuated his communication. I thought that I saw a flare of plasma—accompanied by a distant, atmospherically warped *whump, whump*—somewhere on my left flank. Screams started over the comm-link, but the noise sounded all wrong. It was the echo of ghosts.

"Could this be Zero's time-fractal shit?" Lopez said, her rifle up to her face-plate now.

"Whatever it is," Feng said, "here they come!"

A phantom emerged from the storm, and suddenly took shape as a Krell primary-form. I caught a flash of an ornate bio-suit, the blur of taloned limbs, as the xeno sprinted towards me. There was barely time to respond as the creature closed the distance. I brought up my rifle, fired once. The body exploded, sailed past me.

"There are more!" Feng yelled.

Another Krell appeared. This was a secondary-form, equipped with a boomer bio-cannon. The xeno's mouth was open in a pitched cry, and its carapace was layered with ice. The Krell didn't like the cold, the snow, and this creature looked as though it had been on Carcosa for a long, long time.

I swung my rifle around, squeezed the trigger again. The xeno vanished beneath a hail of plasma bolts.

"Jesus Christo!" Lopez gasped. "There are hundreds of them! How did we miss them?"

More Krell. Running, screaming, dying. My scanner was filled with targets, brimming with hostiles as they emerged from the snow. We'd landed in the centre of the basin, and there had been no life-signs at all.

Yet here they were, en masse, a virtual horde of bodies. The world was suddenly and inexplicably full of threat. Shapes danced through the storm.

"Fall back!" I ordered. "Regroup at the base of the pylon!"

Plasma rifles rippled to my left, to my right. Phoenix Squad were firing grenades at monstrous things that lurched through the snow.

"Lieutenant Jenkins is gone!" Ving screamed, over the comm.

"I'm still here," I said, as I laid down covering fire with my plasma rifle. I think I hit something, but as the plasma pulse made contact the target just disappeared.

"Extracting, extracting..." someone else added.

The combat-suit's battlefield intelligence package was filled with contradictory results. Lopez was dead, extracted. Then her vitals were blazing bright, as though she was in the midst of a firefight.

It was at this point I realised something.

The Krell weren't attacking. They weren't directing any fire at us at all.

"Cease fire!" I shouted. "All troopers, hold fire!"

A Krell primary scrambled and raced past. It was so close that I caught my reflection on the thing's deep, dead eyes. I read something there. *Panic.* The Krell were not just frightened, but terrified. They swarmed past, almost through us. Racing away from something emerging from the storm. Some stumbled on all six limbs, leaping, caterwauling. They bounded over one another in their singular focus to escape...

They aren't infected. That thought occurred to me, and lodged in my mind. It seemed impossible, improbable. The Krell had speckled red and green carapaces. *Red Fin Collective.* The Collective that had killed Zero's family, obliterated Mau Tanis Colony, and taken Clade

Cooper's future. But Red Fin had fallen to Harbinger. There was nothing left of them.

A Krell tertiary-form stumbled through the wall of white. It was eviscerated, its trailing innards steaming as they were exposed to the frozen atmosphere. A black metal lance caught the fleeing Krell squarely in the back, and pierced the fish's armour. The body recoiled, back in the direction from which it had come. Lifted off the ground, like a puppet on a string. My gorge rose as I saw more bodies disappearing in the same way. They were being dragged back into the storm.

Something huge and dark advanced through the snow squall.

Holy shit.

It absorbed light with its liquid metal body. Pseudo-pods fired in every direction, pulling more and more xeno bodies into the dark. Actually consuming them with the black tide.

"Please," I said, "someone else confirm that they're seeing this?"

"I wish that I wasn't," Lopez said.

"Me too," said Feng.

Novak just grunted. "Is big motherfucker, yes?"

A Shard construct—bigger than anything I'd ever seen before—coalesced from the white. It was a rippling mass of black quicksilver. Dark lances of energy speared some bodies. Others were cast aside, rejected by the living machine. But those that were caught were consumed. Taken into the nano-tech's suffocating embrace, to be broken down and used as nutrients to grow more of the machine...*Harvester.* That name popped into my head. The harvesting of corpses; just another reflection of the Shard's machine technology.

"Zero!" I yelled. "We have an active Shard construct down here!"

"...Copy...on the...ship!" came the garbled reply. "Everywhere!"

Overhead, shapes became distinct. Needlers—Krell bio-fighters—descended through the clouds, in precise formation. They dropped living Seeker missiles from their stubby wings, and more explosions rippled across the basin.

The Jackals were struck by the resulting shockwave, and hit the snow hard. The entire ice shelf shuddered. Warheads detonated on impact with the surface, creating miniature mushroom-heads. Every ripple threw up debris into the atmosphere, made it harder to see what was happening around us. The Shard Harvester reared up, on fire now.

With a sound like ripping fabric, more fighters broke the horizon. Needlers, but bio-ships too. Breacher-pods punched through the clouds, slammed into the ground. Larger Krell bio-ships hovered in low orbit, bio-plasma batteries illuminating as they engaged in combat with unseen enemies.

"Whoah!" Lopez screamed, struggling to remain standing.

The ground quaked, shook.

Somewhere in the space between the pylons, the ice sheets simply ruptured. More debris was thrown up, and pressurised atmosphere vented in a column.

"Don't fall under the ice!" I yelled. "Fire your EVAMPs, get clear of that break!"

Lopez tumbled along the ice, inevitably drawn to the breach. Novak and Feng went with her, trying to activate their EVAMPs, but failing. The theatre was utter chaos.

At its centre, the Shard Harvester was a thing of utter destruction. It speared bodies in every direction, absorbing more bio-mass. Krell weapons-fire was everywhere, with more vessels on the horizon now.

I barely took any notice of that, though, because I too was falling towards the fissure. I managed to keep hold of my plasma rifle in one hand, while clutching for the ice with the other, but it was hopeless. The snow and ice gave no purchase, and the shelf on which we'd been standing had nearly capsized. It was almost at a right angle now.

Together, the Jackals hit the water. My suit streamed errors and critical warnings, alerting me to the extreme temperature. Breath fogged the inside of my visor, and my medi-suite dumped a huge dose of combat-drugs into my bloodstream.

As soon as we hit the water, we were sinking. There was darkness all around. The shaft of light above me— the fracture that led back to the surface—faded. There was still a battle going on up there—the detonations that rippled across the underside of the ice were testament to that—but none of it made sense. I sank deeper and deeper, the light becoming more and more distant. Dwindling, dwindling. Until it was nothing more than a star.

Something pulled me down. I wriggled, squirming against the flow of the water. The fact that I was wearing almost a ton of military combat-armour didn't help. My fingers were deathly cold, and the pressure of the frozen ocean around me was insurmountable. Warnings blurted across my HUD, the thought-connection becoming thick with new alerts.

The Jackals were with me. Like dead weights, they sank too. Arms outstretched, bodies limp.

Another light dawned—throbbed—beneath us. Calling, drawing in. *We were so, so wrong about these guys*, I decided, as I desperately fought against the vortex. My stomach rolled like I was entering a gravity field and a wave of vertigo hit me. In the dark, I couldn't differentiate up and down any more. The rational, obvious thing to do would be to simply extract. I'd wake up in the simulator, back on the *Valkyrie*, and could explain to Captain Heinrich what a disaster first contact had been.

But I wasn't going to do that. Failure wasn't an option. No fear, no regrets.

The Aeon waited.

CHAPTER SEVENTEEN

FIRST CONTACT PROTOCOLS

I blinked away the darkness. The simulant rebooted instantly, and my thought-connection told me that I was still in armour. Except that this wasn't the suit that I'd been wearing when I'd fallen under the ice.

"You're all right," someone said. "Just breathe deeply. In and out."

It took me a moment to recognise the voice. The accent was cultured, foreign to me. British. The only person I knew who spoke like that was…

Dr Skinner.

He crouched beside me. His pock-marked face was folded in a grin, those creepy dark-moon glasses reflecting the outline of my heavy armour. I could see my own surprised expression there; the smoke marks wiped across my face. I didn't have my helmet, although I couldn't remember when I'd taken it off.

"You're dead," I whispered.

"And you're a fine one to talk!" Dr Klaus Skinner replied.

I shook off the vestiges of whatever had just happened

to me, and got to my feet. I wore a HURT—"heavy utility response team"—suit. This was the armour that I'd worn during the mission aboard North Star Station. I was in Dr Skinner's lab. The chamber was filled with workbenches, cluttered with scientific equipment. Cryogenics pods lined the walls, everything kept in a state of semi-darkness. Dr Skinner had conducted his research into Pariah here.

"This isn't possible," I insisted. "North Star Station is gone." Panic hit me. "Where are the Jackals? They went under the ice with me..."

Dr Skinner nodded. "They're fine. You'll see them soon enough."

The doctor's smock was badly stained with dark substances, adding to his macabre aura. He'd been known to Major Sergkov and Military Intelligence by the codename "Skinsmith", I remembered.

"This isn't real," I said.

"It's real enough to you, though," Dr Skinner said, "which is what matters. You're on North Star, during the last few minutes of the recovery mission." Skinner's smile became strained. "Which, as you will probably recall, didn't turn out so well."

"I remember."

"I'm a reconstruction of your memory." Dr Skinner grinned, exposing a line of nicotine and coffee-stained teeth. Scientific genius he might be, but personal hygiene hadn't been a priority. "This is one of our many abilities, Lieutenant."

"I'm not sure I like the sound of that."

"We are the Aeon," Dr Skinner said. "You are not like us. We understand that." The Skinsmith adjusted his glasses. "Your thoughts are easy for us to read. We have existed for a long, long time. And in that time, we have learnt a lot about how best to make contact with lesser races. Accessing memory is just one tool in our armoury. So, you sent soldiers to make contact with us, eh? That's telling."

"We came here for your help. We're fighting a war."

Something lingered at the edge of my vision. The Skinner-construct saw it, too, and half turned to inspect the phantom. It was Pariah. The alien's outline was ephemeral, wavering.

"Our war is over," said Dr Skinner. "You saw what happened on the surface."

"So none of that was real?"

"It happened millennia ago, during the Great War. The Shard destroyed many of our number. In this sector of the galaxy, we are all that is left."

"Is this your home?"

Dr Skinner laughed. "Oh, dear child, no. It is our tomb. We were once many, but now we are few. The Shard destroyed our Enclaves. Turned our allies—the Krell—against us." Dr Skinner sighed, thoughtfully. "Many members of the Pantheon were lost. Entire species, decimated. The Dominion almost won the Great War."

"The Shard are coming back," I said. "We've been looking for you for a long time."

"We understand this," said a voice.

But it wasn't Dr Skinner speaking any more.

The scene changed. I was on Darkwater Farm, in the simulant storage chamber.

I hurt all over. I wore a Directorate-issue Ikarus suit, but of far more immediate concern was the pair of hands that were locked around my throat. My neck was agony. I struggled to breathe.

"*Get back!*" roared a wet-gravel voice.

Lazarus. Lieutenant-Colonel Conrad Harris.

The hands around my neck shifted. Oxygen rushed into my lungs.

Daneb Riggs stood over me. He was using a freshly hatched simulant, wearing only a neoprene undersuit.

"You're not supposed to be here," Riggs said, to Harris, true to memory. "You're dead."

"You'd be surprised how often I hear that," Harris snarled in his gruff Detroit accent. "I'm Lazarus."

"But—"

"Enough talk."

The machine-pistol in his hands barked, and a volley of rounds hit Riggs across the torso. The sim collapsed, spilling crimson onto the sterile floor. Harris paused momentarily, eyeing the body as if to make sure that it was really dead.

"You okay?" he asked me.

I nodded. Rubbed my neck. "I'm fine. Why did you bring me here? This is a memory I'd rather forget."

"It's another construct," said Harris.

"Can you bring the real Harris back? Change events in the past?"

"No," Harris said, shaking his head. "That's beyond even us. What's done is done."

"That's a shame."

I stood. For a memory, the pain across my body felt surprisingly realistic. Harris steadied me on my feet.

"Why can't you show yourselves?"

Harris gave a half-shrug. Like me, he was wearing a Directorate Ikarus suit. The armour whined softly as he moved.

"It's complicated, Jenkins. We've been in seclusion—a sort of self-imposed exile—for a long time. This planet, Carcosa, isn't our home, but there are only a few of us left here. If we do this, join your conflict, we'll be exposing our species to the war all over again."

Before I could argue with him, Harris activated a hatch. Beyond, there was a corridor drenched with emergency lighting: an area of Darkwater that had been labelled the "dark sector". The bulkheads on each side of the corridor were filled with containment cells. Inside the small chambers, swirling black shapes turned and twisted and throbbed. *Shard Reapers.* Just being around them made my skin crawl, my very bones ache. The Harvester that we'd seen on Carcosa's surface was a larger example of the same technology.

"You've come out of exile before," I said. "Science Division has seen your ships, from a distance."

"That was a long time ago," said Harris.

"So? You've shown yourselves. You can do it again."

Harris paused in front of one of the containment cells. The black matter inside drifted in and out of reality. In the blink of an eye, it went from ethereal, barely visible, to completely solid. In reality, the Shard Reapers were colonies of billions of nanites, working together in perfect union. They were almost impervious to energy weapons, and damn near impossible to kill.

"The Harbinger virus, the Reapers, the shadow matter," Harris said, "are all the same thing. All aspects of Shard technology. This is the Dominion."

"It's what we're trying to stop," I said, becoming increasingly frustrated with the Aeon's riddles. "Are you going to help us, or not?"

"This is all your fault, though," said Harris. "Your people brought the Harbinger virus back to life, on Barain-11. Sergeant Cooper carried it into the Krell nest base. Then they made the mistake of trying to harness the virus, through Cooper. He became Warlord, and now seeks to bring about the Dominion."

"We're not all the same!" I argued.

But when I looked back to where Harris had been standing, he was gone.

Back into a simulant. The scent of smoke in my nose, despite the atmo-filters of my combat-suit.

Another death scene. Another person I'd let down.

Kronstadt. During the final phases of the operation in Svoboda.

I was in the cramped confines of a Turing MBT-900 automated battle tank. The crew cabin was on the slant, because the vehicle had crashed. The tank's control panel was filled with error messages.

Feng's comatose body sat beside me. This was when he had been corrupted by the Directorate Special Operations team, when the so-called Mother of Clones had come for him.

"Why are you only accessing my shit memories, Aeon?" I protested.

"You'd prefer not to relive this particular event?"

"I have plenty of good ones, too."

"Don't lie to us, Lieutenant."

Dr Olivia Locke was hunched in the passenger seat beside me, wearing a destroyed survival suit. Her face was stitched with minor lacerations, covered with red burn marks where she had been exposed to Kronstadt's acid rain. The doctor studied me with light eyes.

"Do you have a name?" I asked.

"We are Dr Locke," said the construct.

"That's not your real name."

There was an impact outside the tank. I heard gunfire, the pitched whine of plasma weaponry firing. That would be Lopez and Novak, fighting off the Directorate. Meanwhile, the Krell were also pouring into Svoboda, and would soon overwhelm not just the city, but the planet.

"The Krell came to Kronstadt with a purpose," Dr Locke said. "They were being directed."

"By the Spiral."

She nodded. "Yes. The Warlord has mastery over them."

"How can he do that?"

"Warlord *is* Harbinger. He and the virus are one and the same. The Harbinger virus, the technology used to create Warlord, all of it came from the same place. Warlord is able to manipulate the quantum-streams, and also access the Deep. He is the perfect conjunction of Shard and Krell technology."

"Perfect" seemed like something of an exaggeration, but I decided not to argue.

"We need your help," I insisted. "We can't do this on our own. The Black Spiral are massing a fleet in the Reef Stars. They are going to overwhelm the Krell, and infect the Deep Ones."

"This is concerning, we admit."

"Show yourselves to us," I said.

"Are you sure that you want to see our true form?"

"I'm sure."

Dr Locke looked at me with a fixed expression. "Do you still have that grenade?"

I reached for the frag grenade. The tank's cabin thundered with enemy fire, as every enemy on Kronstadt seemed to focus its attention on us.

"Then take care of it."

There was a milky, diffuse light somewhere beneath me, and I swam for it. Both hands scything through the freezing liquid that made up Carcosa's hidden sea. Although I'd been sucked downward I now felt like I was swimming up. I had the feeling that I was deep underwater, but my sense of direction was completely lost. Nausea and disorientation crashed around inside my head, suggesting that I had passed through multiple gravity envelopes. I kept swimming until, eventually, I reached the light, and felt something solid underfoot. I'd lost my rifle during the chaos, but I was quite confident that it didn't matter. No weapon was going to help me here. My HUD flickered with new data, and the Jackals' bio-signs appeared. Their shapes emerged from the water.

"Everyone alive?" I asked.

"Yes," Novak said, repressing what could've been a sob. "That was not good. Did—did you see things?"

"Memories," Lopez blurted. "Mostly bad ones."

It was no reassurance that the rest of the squad had suffered the same experience as me. Each of us had been trapped in our private hell; reliving the past.

"Was any of it real?" Lopez said.

"I don't think so," said Feng. "The chronometer says no time has passed. Where in the Core are we?"

"It's some sort of…vault," I decided. "We haven't made extraction, so I guess that we're still somewhere on Carcosa."

"It feels like we're underground," said Lopez. She turned back to look at the liquid, lapping around our ankles now. "We were dragged down here, but we just swam towards the light."

The chamber was large, with curved walls made from a substance that glowed with pale light. They were etched with geometric symbols that intermittently flashed, suggesting activity.

"Do you read, Zero?" Feng said, over the comm. "*Valkyrie?* Christo, I hope they're okay."

The hail was answered by a wail of static. Echoes,

repeated over and over. The noise grew in volume until it became too painful to listen to.

"Give it a rest, Feng," Lopez suggested. "We're making first contact with an alien race, and you're worried about your girlfriend—"

"Hold," I said. "I see movement ahead."

Several tunnels branched from the main chamber. There were jagged shadows inside each tunnel-mouth. Things lurked there, unwilling to reveal themselves. I swallowed back apprehension. *Here goes.*

"We've come a long way to find you," I said. "Can you show yourselves?"

The shadows quivered.

The floor gently inclined downwards, towards a pit in the centre of the cavern. Liquid ran in the grooves of the floor, through the channels etched into the deck, and a pool had formed in front of me. I cautiously approached it, watching as the surface shifted and rippled.

"Show yourselves!" I said, louder still.

This time, I got a reaction.

"Holy Gaia and Christo…" Lopez murmured.

The Jackals held firm, but I defensively put up a hand to my face. Droplets of liquid showered me, hit the walls of the chamber.

The Aeon rose from its cryo-pool.

The xeno was maybe three metres tall, although the creature's hunched posture suggested an even greater height if it stood upright. Centipede-like, with several pairs of limbs running along a slender body that was encased in a brilliant white exo-suit, made of a crystalline-metallic compound that reminded me of the pylons on the surface. The suit was wired into the pool, although as I watched, some of the bio-cabling withdrew and slithered away. The Aeon's head poked from the collar, and what skin was visible was pale white, almost translucent. A collection of tubes ran between the creature's mouth and the torso unit. Whisker-like proboscises shivered over its wrinkled head, as though tasting the air.

None of the details really made sense, and I couldn't seem to focus on the xeno's features. Everything about it was fuzzy, like it didn't want to be seen.

The Aeon ponderously advanced out of the pool. Its upper limbs unfolded, clicking and whirling, and the alien towered over me. Three pairs of unfocused black eyes sprouted from a nearly arachnid face, in stark contrast to the frozen white of the xeno's flesh. Those eyes blinked, out of conjunction, and scanned me blindly.

Despite its size, the creature didn't look like much of a fighter. On the contrary, my military instinct had already identified a dozen weak points in the exo-suit's joints, and the noise the creature made as it took a step from the pool suggested it was struggling to even breathe. A tide of smaller crystal spiders crept from the cryo-pool. No bigger than my hand, some of the scuttling things tended to their master's suit, while others formed a defensive line between us and the alien.

<I am Aeon,> it boomed.

The creature spoke in my head. I flinched at the sudden mental intrusion. Beside me, the Jackals did the same, and I knew that we were all receiving the same message.

<We are Aeon,> came a softer response.

<They is Aeon,> another voice.

From other pools around the room, other Aeon rose. Perhaps a dozen of the xenos, almost indistinguishable from the first. An army of Scuttlers appeared in support, seeping from the tunnel mouths.

<I am the many mind,> said the Aeon.

<We are of many minds.>

<They is many of minds.>

Every time it spoke, its voice was different in some way, and other speech patterns followed its words. Sometimes the whisper of rubbing spider legs, other times the distant cry of whale song. Were those other alien languages? That was my best guess. The effect was discomfiting.

<You have awoken our slumber,> said the lead Aeon.

"Ah, hi," I said. "My name is Lieutenant Keira Jenkins. You've just scanned my memory, and brought up the worst bits. I'm an emissary from the Alliance. I suppose you know that already."

The atmosphere around the lead alien's body seemed to vibrate and shimmer, rearrange at the Aeon's will. The creature was angry.

"We've come a long way to find you," I said. "Tell me your name; your designation. That's the least you can do, after the whole mind-scan thing."

<You are a warrior.>

<She is a fighter.>

<They is killers.>

I shook my head, trying to dispel some of the voices.

"Can you speak to me one at a time?" I said. "We are not a Collective."

There was a minute pause before a response came. Were the many minds communicating, I wondered?

<We are the Enclave of Torex Var Tor,> said the lead Aeon. The creature was haggard and almost skeletal inside its suit. It reminded me of a wraith, and that label stuck in my head: Wraith.

"I have come here with my squad, my people. Jenkins' Jackals."

<Soldiers all,> came the singular reply.

"That is us," said Novak.

<There is war,> said the Aeon.

A ripple of voices spread through the chamber, as though the concept of war disturbed the whole Enclave.

"The Krell are in great peril. They are being ravaged by a virus, which has been unleashed on the Maelstrom."

As one, all of the Aeon shivered, and their Scuttler army did the same.

<We know of this. The Krell know of us, and we have tasted the Deep.>

The walls around me shifted to show star fields, planets, the great stellar abyss at the edge of the Milky Way.

<We have fought alongside the Krell before.>

Worlds ignited around us. I involuntarily flinched as planets were burnt to a cinder by Aeon ships. Watched as stars were sent supernova by the arcane technologies of the Aeon.

"This is what we need," I said. "Your weapons, your ships. Please, help us."

The words didn't really matter, because I knew that the Aeon was accessing my mind, reading my thought-patterns. But what were we to something so advanced, so beyond the limits of our capabilities? There was a gulf in our communication.

<This was when we were many. Now, we are few.>

<The Machines do not die,> said another voice, out of synch with the first.

<But the many mind does,> said the third.

<Our curse,> added another voice. <We fear the darkness beyond.>

"You're frightened of dying?" I queried.

<This is so,> said the lead Aeon. <This world is our resting place. Too many like it have been lost.>

<Lost to the Great War,> said another xeno. <To us, it never finished. It will go on for ever. This is the eternity war.>

Now I saw dozens of other ships, of different designs

and patterns, flowing through the Maelstrom. Some were organic, obviously the result of advanced bio-engineering. Others were machined. Opposing fleets met, and battle was joined. The Dominion against the Pantheon.

<This is not here,> said the Aeon.

<This is everywhere,> said another.

<The Great War goes on,> said the final. <In the dark, beyond the Maelstrom.>

"Unless we stop it, an enemy faction will bring the war to the Maelstrom," I said. "They will see this whole sector of space—this galaxy—consumed by the Machines. Your crypt—or whatever this place is—will be destroyed."

<This is not our world,> said the Aeon.

<This is merely a place to hide.>

<This was our last stand.>

The images around me shifted, then darkened. Disappeared.

<The enemy is you,> the Aeon probed. <The ones you call "Black Spiral" are of your species. They collude with the Shard.>

A hum started to build up around the chamber. The atmosphere oscillated, molecules agitating. Slowly, the Aeon began to retreat back into their cryo-pools.

"You can't let this happen," I insisted. "You aren't above this, Torex Var Tor!"

<We have withdrawn from your affairs,> said the Aeon.

<We are not here to help.>

<We can only do what is required.>

"What the hell does that even mean?" Lopez yelled.

<Your species is in conflict,> said the Aeon, as it submerged its body into the dark waters. <You must finish that first.>

<It has already started.>

\<They are dead.\>

To my left, Novak dropped. Just like that.

To my right, Lopez did the same.

I stared at Feng. There was panic in his eyes.

"What's happening?" he managed, as he too collapsed.

The neural-link is being cut, I thought.

Then I pitched forward into the water, too.

I made extraction.

CHAPTER EIGHTEEN

YOUR WAR

I was back on the *Valkyrie*, in my tank, in the Simulant Operations Centre. Rapidly, I collected my thoughts and decided what had happened. I'd made extraction; from the frozen atmosphere of Carcosa, into the warm liquid that filled my simulator-tank. But there had been no emergency recall, no warning, nothing that justified immediate extraction.

As I processed those thoughts, a figure came into view outside my tank. Braced a hand on the tank's outer canopy, on the handle that would activate the simulator's emergency release.

"You promised me a fast death, Jenkins," said a voice, piped into the bead in my ear. "It's a shame that I can't do the same for you."

Lockdown! I ordered. *Do not release tank canopy.* Until my data-ports were disconnected, I still had limited thought-connection with the simulator, and I used that to initiate the command.

CONFIRMED, said the tank.

"Is all anyone ever ask for," said another voice, heavily accented, but with a mocking tone.

"It's all that she's ever wanted, I think."

Wearing his prison overall, a laconic smile plastered over his face, Riggs stood outside my tank. He must've seen my expression—which I couldn't hide—and the grin grew. Both hands on the release handle, ready to drag me out of the simulator.

There were other voices in my head, too.

"*...on ship! Repeat, vessel is comprom—*"

"*Defend the CIC!*"

Think. Think fast.

Sims. Vault. Storage. Zero prepared them for deployment—

I reached for the control panel on the interior of the simulator. The system was designed so that an operator could make immediate transition, could operate the tank from inside without a handler or technical support.

"Jackals!" I yelled, into the respirator clasped over my face. It had a built-in communicator, and unless something had gone drastically wrong—or *more* drastically wrong— I'd be in instant comms with the rest of the squad. "Riggs is free!"

"Ah, no, no," said Riggs. He pressed his forehead against the canopy so that I could see him better. He had a communicator at his neck, allowing him to speak with me. "Don't do that."

One sleeve of his overall was pulled back, and I saw the bright splash of blood from the data-port on his arm. I couldn't make out anything behind or around Riggs. Couldn't see what had happened to the rest of the squad, or to Zero. Or Dr Saito, or Captain Heinrich, or Commander Dieter...Someone would surely realise what was happening.

"It won't do you any—" Riggs started.

But his words were lost to me, as I slammed my palm
into the EMERGENCY TRANSITION button, and
the control panel lit.

I made transition and left the SOC.

In the instant that it took to make the jump into the waiting simulant, a deluge of thoughts flowed through my
mind.

How did Riggs get free?

The answer came in flashes, in the split-second it took
me to make transition into the new simulant.

"Have you scanned him for covert tech, Zero?"

"The only metal in him is his data-ports."

Riggs in his cell: scratching his ports.

Riggs had something in the connections. That was
why he kept scratching them, and that was why they
looked infected.

Next question: *is Riggs working alone, or is there another traitor on the* Valkyrie?

I was in the storage vault. Detecting movement in the
bay, an overhead glow-globe flickered on, dowsing the compartment in bright light. Racked bodies lined the walls—
copies of the Jackals and Phoenix Squad, all ready for
immediate deployment, just as we had left them. That
was good; I didn't need to waste any time with breaking out of a cryogenic capsule. Zero was true to her
word—she'd decanted our entire supply of simulants,
and every available sim was armed and armoured. The
combat-suit was attached to a charging station, plugged
into the bulkhead. My helmet was already locked, almost
as though Zero had predicted we'd find ourselves in this
mess. The face-plate HUD flashed with WELCOME,
OPERATOR: LIEUTENANT KEIRA JENKINS—
DISCONNECT POWER SUPPLY TO—

Boot all systems, immediately, I ordered.

PROCEED.

I snapped an arm free of the charging station, and the cables disconnected. I had a matter of seconds before Riggs dragged my ass out of the tank, and I lost connection with my sim. I registered that none of the Jackals' skins were moving, which probably meant they hadn't reacted as fast as me, or that Riggs had somehow incapacitated them.

Got to act now.

I had to get to Medical, and stop Riggs. Not just stop him: kill him. If that made me an assassin or a blood-thirsty bitch, I had to be honest with myself. Nothing short of obliterating Riggs was going to stop this.

I hit the ground at a pace, legs cycling. Each footfall thundered through the deck, and my M125 plasma rifle was in my hands. Zero had equipped each of the suits with a full combat loadout; another very serendipitous move. I reached the exit hatch. Slammed a fist into the release control. The door slipped open…

The hostile on the other side wore a full survival suit, including a respirator mask and goggles. The suit was covered with iconography: tight white script that was obviously supposed to be a reproduction of Shard machine-text. Gender, age and other personal details unclear to me, the tango looked a little surprised at my sudden appearance. Maybe they hadn't expected me to make transition so quickly. He or she brought up a machine-pistol, finger squeezed on the firing stud.

Well, I'm a girl full of surprises.

The muzzle of my plasma rifle was in the tango's face before he or she had even drawn a bead. My sim-senses, augmented by the combat-suit, were superior to those of the untrained fanatic in every way. I blasted the piece of shit into the great beyond. The body collapsed back-wards, and I charged on through into the corridor on the other side.

Go! Go!

I stole a glance at my bio-scanner. It was running on passive mode, results imposed onto the upper corner of my HUD. What I saw was almost enough to make me stop dead in my tracks. Bio-signs crawled all over the ship. Moving above and below me. Far more signals than there had been surviving crew, which could only mean one thing…

A siren cut the air, wailing mournfully in protest.

"This ship is experiencing a boarding event…" said the AI. *"All hands, prepare to repel invaders."*

There was a deep groan through the *Valkyrie*'s frame. Metal on metal: one ship's hull grinding against another. That was possible, and consistent with a hostile boarding action. An enemy ship, locked on one of our external airlocks? The Ghost Maker was one big sensor-blind, and we hadn't detected the wrecks in orbit around Carcosa until the last moment. Perhaps that had aided the attackers' approach on the *Valkyrie*. Commander Dieter and Captain Heinrich wouldn't have seen them coming until it was too late…

I ran into another Spiral agent. This tango was dressed differently to the first. He wore a tactical harness over a suit of space armour; nothing so advanced as a combat-suit, but military-issue equipment. The target was also devoid of any of the usual Spiral markings, which struck me as odd. No time to question that further. This bastard managed to loose a volley from his assault rifle as I hurtled around the corner.

My null-shield reacted, ablating the kinetic energy, but not quite fast enough. Gunfire bounced off my right shoulder-plate, producing a startling report in the closed corridor. I snarled, charged onwards.

This tango held his ground. Kept shooting.

A spherical energy shield popped into existence around

the hostile. He was using a null-shield generator, like that incorporated into my suit. Another piece of restricted military tech.

"I don't have time for—" I started.

A hail of heavy gunfire came from the direction in which I'd just come.

Medical alerts flooded my HUD. Of course, I didn't really need to see those to understand that I'd been ghosted. The rounds punched through my null-shield, then my combat-suit, and finally my simulant.

The shooter didn't take any chances. From behind me, the roar of the heavy cannon—a weapon most definitely not designed for use in a pressurised environment like a starship—continued. My simulant collapsed, faltered, and then toppled to the deck.

Fifteen seconds after I'd made transition into the new sim, I extracted.

Back to the SOC.

Riggs was joined by more shapes outside the tank. Black armoured bodies, watery outlines visible through the simulator's conducting fluid. Hostiles flooded the SOC.

Riggs came in and out of focus. With each shift, a ringing impact shook the simulator.

"As I was saying, Keira," Riggs said, "it won't do you any good."

Another impact. The head of a power wrench became visible as it made contact with the protective canopy. Riggs swung it underarm, like a baseball bat, with all the force he could muster.

"This is over now, for good."

Another impact. The wrench's powered element sparked, sending energy discharge across the canopy. That was made of armourglass, and wouldn't yield willingly.

"It's time you gave up."

But yield it would, eventually. A small fracture had already breached the glass.

DAMAGE DETECTED, protested the tank. INITIATE SIMULATOR EVACUATION?

Do not *evacuate tank!* I answered.

"The Aeon won't help. There's no point in fighting any more."

I keyed the EMERGENCY TRANSITION button, echoing the same order in my head, and left the SOC just as Riggs landed another blow on the tank.

New eyes opened, and I yanked my arms free from the charging station. This skin was in exactly the same condition as the last: ready for immediate activation.

But I realised that something was different this time.

A heavy pistol was aimed directly at my face, the muzzle locked against my face-plate. The owner of the gun was a woman, but I barely got to see her before I made extraction.

"Surprise," she said, as she fired the pistol.

"Fuck y—"

At that range, I didn't stand a chance. The kinetic shattered the face-plate and hit me squarely in the forehead. Right through the skull, and the braincase. Then probably out the other side, along with the insides of my head.

Another dead skin.

I extracted into my real body, almost simultaneous to Riggs breaching the simulator. He hurled the power wrench at the tank, and the canopy finally shattered. The tank's liquid insides poured out across the SOC's deck, and fragments of glass showered my naked body. I grasped for the emergency control again.

"This is your problem, Keira," said Riggs. "You think that everything can be solved by making the next transition."

The wrench slammed into my temple, so hard that I fought to stay conscious. I scrambled around inside the simulator, and broken glass lacerated my arms and legs. You're naked when you go into the tanks, and you're naked when you come out: this place was supposed to be a place of sanctuary, of safety, for an operator. Now, it was anything but.

Riggs got purchase on me, and my data-ports popped in sequence as the force was enough to disconnect me from the tank. I kicked out with both legs, into Riggs' body.

"Will you please just give it up!" Riggs shouted, grabbing a leg with one hand.

The last thing I saw was Riggs' face, contorted in a mask of fury, teeth bared in an animal snarl that would've done Novak proud. Not for the first time, I found myself asking what I had ever seen in him. *You'll be the death of me*, I thought.

I was vaguely aware in that sort of *I'm about to lose consciousness* way that the Jackals were out of their tanks and that things were happening around me. Clipped shouts. Gunfire somewhere nearby. Screams from the corridor outside. Other naked bodies, dark coloured shapes in the SOC.

Help me, P! Please! Help us! I projected the thought. Desperately searched for the mental link between us.

I tasted blood in my mouth. I hurt. A lot.

The power wrench landed in my face, one last time, and there was nothing at all.

Drip.
   Drip.
   Drip.

"Time to wake up, you lazy bitch."

Dark. Cold. Water in my face. No, not water. The pain in my head was so powerful that I felt sick, but it slowly receded, just enough for me to stay standing. There was something damp on my temple, and my vision blurred. Everything was sort of red-tinged; I had blood in my eyes. The air smelt of oil. *I'm in Engineering. One of the* Valkyrie's *work bays.*

Someone was crying nearby, in choked sobs. It sounded like Zero.

"You hurt her badly," came another harshly accented voice. "This is not good. We need her to talk."

"Yeah, well," said Riggs, pacing the deck in front of me. "She's been a real problem for me, you know?"

"She can die, but not yet."

Riggs wasn't in his real skin any more. The bruises that Novak had given him were gone, and the face that looked back at me was freshly decanted. He wore a combat-suit without a helmet, a Widowmaker pistol strapped to his thigh. That he was skinned meant his real body was somewhere either in the *Valkyrie's* SOC or aboard a nearby ship. The idea that the bastard was using our own technology against us repulsed me. His combat-suit definitely wasn't from our armoury, because it was blank and unbadged.

I tried to turn. Found that my arms were pulled over my head, and I was chained by the wrists, attached to a cargo rail or gantry. The chain had enough give that I could stand, but not that I could do anything else. My limbs were already numb, and the restraints bit into my wrists. That pain, however, was nothing compared to the storm inside my skull. Around me, the Jackals were in a similar situation. All five of us, now dressed in ship-board fatigues.

Phoenix Squad were lined up on the other side of the

bay. Ving's face was downcast, but he managed a flicker of his eyes in my direction. In the dim light, I made out that everyone had taken a beating. Bodies were bloodied, bruised, injured. One of Phoenix Squad—a trooper I'd never even known the name of—looked as though he might already be dead; hanging limp from a chain.

Light filled the bay, so intense that it burnt my eyes. The figure held an emergency flare in one gloved hand, and it fizzed, under-lighting an old woman's face.

"She has spirit!" she said. Her voice was dry and parched, like the crushing of old bones. "That is to be applauded. We are same, you and me, *da*? My foot soldiers are my family. I care for them. They are my sons."

"Who the fuck are you?" I asked, even though I already recognised the face. It was the woman from the vid-feed of the attack on Sanctuary...

"I am Major Mish Vasnev."

Novak's reaction was nothing short of nuclear. He roared. It was the sound of a possessed animal, a man gone completely feral. *Has he ever been this close to the woman responsible for killing his wife and child?* I wondered. The animosity and hate and frustration seemed to explode out of him in a wave that enveloped the compartment. He frothed at the mouth, eyes bulging. He'd been beaten like the rest of us, but no amount of punishment was going to stop him.

Novak lashed out with his legs, the only parts of his body that were free. He struck one of the captors—a figure dressed in heavy space armour—directly in the chest. The rail overhead creaked as it took Novak's weight, and the tango sprawled backwards.

"I kill you!" Novak screamed, flecks of spit escaping his lips.

A dozen figures in full hard-suits, covered with Russian military tags and gang markings, appeared from the shadows. These were the Sons of Balash, and they were Vasnev's kill team. They dripped with weaponry, from holstered handguns to multiple assault rifles strapped across their backs, and now they surrounded Novak, waving improvised melee weapons. If any of these assholes recognised Novak from his gang days, they weren't showing it.

Although Novak was bigger than Vasnev by a significant degree, the old woman stood her ground. Caught by the jittering light of the emergency flare, her face was impassive and unimpressed.

"Are you finished, my son?" she asked.

"I am not son! I am Jackal!"

Vasnev broke into a poisoned smile. "Ah, but you will always be a Son of Balash. That is your role in life, Leon Novak. What has happened to you?"

"I leave that behind," Novak said. "And you pay me by killing my Anwar and Vali!"

"Who are they?" Vasnev asked. Some of the other figures around her laughed, and it was a dark, mocking sound. "So many names. I am an old woman. I cannot be expected to remember everyone."

"You know who they are. You order them dead!"

"It was you who killed them," Vasnev said, "when you turned your back on *bratva*. I had no choice but to order redress. Their blood is on your ledger, Leon Novak."

A stream of Russian expletives spilt from Novak's mouth. He lashed out again, but after the first casualty, the other gangers were more careful. They stood in a wide circle around Novak.

Vasnev paced between the lines of captured troopers, looking us up and down. She wore an exo-suit that covered most of her body. Like its wearer, the armour was grizzled and battered, but it was more advanced than the suits worn by the rest of the gang. Only Vasnev's head was exposed, and her skin was so sun-baked that it looked positively ancient: the tone and texture of old leather. Cyrillic script was tattooed across her cheekbones and forehead, dark reflections of Novak's gang markings. Her hair, plaited down to the small of her back, was the colour of faded platinum. There was a patch on her shoulder; words in Russian, with a flag.

Riggs followed Vasnev. His face twitched, and he trailed the power wrench across the deck, producing a tail of blue sparks.

"This is the Major's private army," said Riggs, his arms open to encompass the occupants of the cargo bay. "The Sons of Balash. They've been extremely helpful in planning this whole operation."

Vasnev's face remained neutral. Her hand still rested on the stock of a carbine, which was slung across her shoulder. Old as she was, the years had done nothing to diminish her threatening aura. I could imagine this woman clawing her way up the greasy pole of the criminal underworld—every death, every atrocity, only adding to her reputation.

"Fuck that," a prisoner said. "We're Phoenix Squad, and—"

Vasnev's carbine was up. It aimed at the speaker, and barked once. The body sagged, dead. Together with the guy who was already dead, that put Phoenix Squad two men down. Only three bodies left.

Ving gasped. "No, no, no!" he shouted.

Adrenaline and panic and horror mixed into a debilitating concoction, and my blood froze.

Vasnev shrugged. "Next time, it will be one of your team-mates, Leon Novak. You are all going to behave, and give me the information that I require."

Novak shuddered, the rage clattering around behind his eyes. He had a big cut to his temple, and blood down one side of his face. There was still defiance there, but Novak was no fool. He waited, silently.

"A demonstration is in order," Vasnev said.

She waved the flare towards the end of the bay, at an auxiliary airlock. Commander Dieter's face appeared at the inner lock. She was slamming her fists against the interior view-port, in a desperate attempt to escape. A ganger had taken up a post beside the airlock controls. The implication was clear: they were going to space Dieter.

"The Warlord was very specific about this one," Vasnev said. "She is called Dieter. She and he have history, *da*? They were together on Barain-11. She could have saved him."

Riggs bowed his head in perverted respect at mention of Warlord's name.

"Are you really going to let her do this?" I asked.

"No, I'm not," he said. "Because one of you can stop it."

Vasnev nodded, with a wave of the flare. The aged hydraulics in the limbs of her suit whined as she moved. "Daneb Riggs speaks truth. You can change this. We have come for the alien. Tell us where it is."

"What alien?"

"Do not try to be smart," Vasnev said. She circled me, coming closer. She smelt of burnt wood and sweat, even over the chemical odour of the bay. "We seek the pariah-form."

You haven't found P? I thought. Hope detonated inside me like a grenade. I hadn't realised it until now—and I scanned the chamber, looking for them—but Dr Saito and Captain Heinrich weren't here, either.

"We don't know what you're talking about," said Lopez.

Vasnev exhaled slowly. "Ligachev, open the comms-channel into the airlock. Let us hear the commander speak."

The ganger did as ordered and Commander Dieter's panicked voice filled the bay.

"*...I didn't do this! I went back for him. I was on Barain, but I tried to save him! You have to believe me! I thought I loved him, but I thought he felt the same way—*"

"Enough," said Riggs. "She's a liar. Warlord never loved her."

The ganger didn't act on Riggs' command, but waited until Vasnev gave her assent. She nodded once and the comm-unit crackled. Dieter was silenced.

"Where is the alien?" Vasnev levelly repeated.

"I'm pretty sure that you should tell the old woman," said Riggs. "I meant it when I said these guys were crazy. She'll do this."

Lopez and Zero were beside me, and they rattled their chains. There were cries of anguish, and of protestation, but it was all wasted energy.

"We can't let this happen!" Zero said, half turning to me, using all the leeway the chains would give her.

"Would you rather that one of your squad was executed?" Vasnev said, swivelling the carbine in our direction.

"Do it!" demanded Riggs. "Ghost these useless fucks."

Vasnev's gun settled on Feng, the muzzle against his forehead. He valiantly—or foolishly, depending on how you look at it—stared Vasnev down.

"I'm not telling you anything," Feng said.

"You won't when you're dead," said Vasnev. Her finger was tight against the trigger.

"Don't kill him!" Zero blurted. "P was in Medical."

"That is not true," said Vasnev. "We have searched the Medical Deck. It is absent. Tell me where it has gone."

Vasnev dropped the gun down to her side again and nodded at her subordinate, beside the airlock. Dieter's face still filled the port. Her eyes grew wide, and although she wouldn't be able to hear what was being said, it was clear that she realised what was happening.

"It was in some sort of chrysalis," said Zero, babbling now, talking faster and faster. "We thought that it had become infected on Sanctuary. I'm telling the truth, I promise!"

Vasnev narrowed her eyes. "We find this chrysalis, but no alien. One last chance, *da*? Where is it?"

"It died, in the cocoon," I said. "We don't know why. Riggs could've told you that. The data is all on the mainframe."

"My access codes are locked out," complained Riggs. He looked like he wasn't sure whether he believed me or not. "I can't verify it."

"It was infected with Harbinger," Lopez said, developing the lie. "The Spiral did something on Sanctuary."

Riggs bit his lip. Vasnev was poised.

"It went into a…a chrysalis," Zero repeated. "The viral strain was weaponised. We…we tried to do everything we could to save it, but we didn't have the equipment here."

"So this may have been a wasted trip," Vasnev concluded. "When did this happen?"

"Novak and Riggs had a confrontation," I said. "It happened after that. Some time last night."

Riggs' expression brightened. "It looks like we didn't fail on Sanctuary after all. So the fish really was infected with Harbinger?"

I nodded as grimly as I could. "Yes. Pariah was infected. We had no choice but to space it."

Vasnev regarded me with deep green eyes that must've been augmented. They unnaturally contrasted with her near-gold skin tone. She made a decision.

Vasnev nodded at the airlock hatch. The ganger keyed the activation control. The airlock's warning lamp flashed red. Dieter's mouth opened wide in a perpetual scream, and she was gone. The airlock opened to vacuum. Dieter vanished. Around me, the bay degenerated into shouts and cries.

"What are you doing?" Lopez shouted. "Put me down!"

The gangers had unchained Lopez. Three of them pulled her into the centre of the bay. Vasnev barked orders in Russian, and the gangers dragged Lopez out of the chamber. She clawed at the hatch frame as she went, but the resistance was token.

"We've already told you what happened to P!" I shouted.

"And I believe you," Vasnev said. "We have searched ship, and there is no sign at all. We know that some of your crew are still here, but there is no alien. It does not matter, really. We will destroy ship, with you on it."

Novak had resumed his berserk thrashing. His muscles strained against the chains, in a concerted attempt to get free. Two, three, four gangers descended on him, deploying shock-batons. He roared like a wounded bear, slamming feet into everyone that came near, taking the pain.

"You can't take her!" I yelled.

The Jackals and the remains of Phoenix Squad were joined in protest, screaming at Vasnev and Riggs.

"I am sorry that your story could not have happier ending, my son," Vasnev said to Novak. She'd opened the hatch to the engineering bay, and was poised there, surrounded by a cadre of gangers. "But sometimes, this life is unfair. Kill them."

"Let me do it," said Riggs, drawing his pistol. "I want to make this mean something."

"Very well," said Vasnev. "We go to our ship now."

"You can go without me," said Riggs. He glared at me and smiled. So Riggs' real body was on Vasnev's ship. "I'll extract when you leave the system."

Vasnev tossed the emergency flare onto the deck. It was burnt to the nub, throwing off jittering shadows and juddering red light. The engineering bay door whined shut.

Alone with us now, Riggs prowled between the rows of dying simulant operators. He had the power wrench in one hand, his Widowmaker in the other. The pistol was armed, and Riggs held it up. It reflected the flare's twitchy illumination.

Riggs paused in front of me. "This could've turned out so differently, Keira," he said.

"Don't ever call me Keira."

"The Aeon are gone. No power readings from the surface. Maybe you're right, and the Pariah is dead. Maybe it escaped in an evacuation-pod. Like Vasnev says, it doesn't really matter any more."

I spat at Riggs. There was more blood than spittle in the gobbet of liquid that landed on his cheek, but it felt good nonetheless. Riggs wiped his face.

"Goodbye, Keira," said Riggs. He reached out to touch my cheek with his hand, and I wriggled away. "I'm going to find my father in the Maelstrom. I'm going to find him, and rescue him. Dominion come, thy will be done."

"He died on Barain," I growled. "He was the last to go, and it was painful, and the nest absorbed him like the rest of the Iron Knights!"

Riggs shook his head, cancelling my truth.

"The Jackals always had a problem with Phoenix Squad," he said, pausing in front of one of Ving's team. "It must've been a real blow when you found out you were working with them."

"Don't even think—" Ving started.

Riggs snapped his pistol up and executed one of Phoenix Squad. Blood spattered the bulkhead, and the body hung there. Ving's face contorted in panic and horror. There were no words for what had happened.

Riggs didn't stop. He moved on to the next body. The trooper tried to squirm, but there was nowhere to go. Gun up. Bang. Another dead soldier. He slung the power wrench over his shoulder, and strolled along the line of troopers.

"Problem solved," said Riggs.

The flare's light finally gave out, and the background hissing was silenced. Carcosa's glowing face was visible through the view-port set into the airlock hatch. It threw a pale illumination across the bay, catching Riggs' features very precisely.

"So, Jackals, who wants to go first?"

<We will.>

CHAPTER NINETEEN

GAME CHANGER

Riggs' face showed obvious signs of confusion as the voice touched his mind.

The effect didn't last long. He whirled around, his pistol up, and fired off a round without even taking proper aim.

P lurched out of the shadows.

The shot would've been true, had it not been for P's even faster reflexes. The xeno coiled, flinging a clawed hand at Riggs in response. The swipe had enough force that it punched through the combat-armour at Riggs' shoulder. Riggs yelped, but didn't go down. He whirled the powered wrench in his left hand, the element glowing bright blue, sparking as it charged up. He smashed the tool into P's carapace, momentarily illuminating the xeno's outline.

The look of horror and realisation that dawned on Riggs' face was precious.

"Christo and Gaia..." Feng whispered.

P had changed again. It was a Krell on steroids, big as a warden-form, evolved. Its body was covered in pleated bio-armour, and an enhanced musculature rippled beneath. Not even scar tissue remained of the injuries that P had suffered on Sanctuary. This creature barely resembled what had gone into the chrysalis, but I knew it was the same alien. P's presence was in my head again, anchored in place as though it were a natural state of being.

The alien absorbed the kinetic impact from the wrench head. In reply, P tossed Riggs against the bulkhead. His armour produced a startling crunch as he hit the metal panelling beside the airlock hatch. The collision wasn't yet enough to end him though and he slid to the deck, still fumbling with his pistol and the wrench.

"Go, P!" Zero yelled.

Riggs scrambled backwards against the wall. He aimed his gun, and fired off a volley of hard rounds. P's carapace sparked as bullets bounced off. When that didn't work, Riggs turned the pistol towards the nearest prisoner: Novak, still dangling from his chain.

"Fuck you, fish!" Riggs yelled. "They're not leaving here alive, either."

<Never threaten our squad, traitor,> P broadcast.

The xeno's armoured crest had grown, and blazed into its skull-plate was a chemical burn pattern. *A Jackal-head badge.* Novak's handiwork, before we dropped to Vektah Minor. When P spoke, the words formed in my head as clearly as any data-transmission, and from the expressions on the faces of my squad, I knew that they could hear it too. P's communication abilities had changed and the mind-link we had shared was no longer exclusive.

Riggs fired, but P intervened. It slammed a claw into Riggs' arm, disrupting his aim, and the round harmlessly ricocheted somewhere in the deckhead.

Then P punched into Riggs' torso unit, into the weak spot between armoured plates. Riggs gasped impotently.

Dark blood welled in his mouth—he'd suffered some critical internal injury—but the simulant technology was durable, and he wasn't out. Never one to give up, he grappled with his wrench again. Swung it in a wide arc against P's head.

The wrench made contact with skull-shattering force, but P wasn't troubled by the blow. It summarily batted aside the wrench with enough strength that Riggs' arm made a sickening crack. The alien then turned a clawed foot on Riggs' other hand, and stamped down on it. His Widowmaker pistol clattered to the ground.

"Waste him!" yelled Ving, coming out of his shellshock. "He killed my squad!"

<Not before Riggs-other sees this,> P said.

One clawed hand still planted into Riggs' stomach, the xeno bodily hauled him to the view-port. The white orb of Carcosa was visible beyond. Riggs tried to speak, but he was silenced with a mind-communication.

<Take this back to your masters.>

P smashed Riggs' head into the hatch so hard that I thought the armourglass might break. He probably died after the first impact, but he was certainly dead after the fifth. There was no question he was extracted. P tossed the battered corpse aside, and I tried not to look at the remains.

"We're sorry that we were late," said a familiar voice.

Two figures emerged from the service hatch at the back of the bay. Captain Heinrich and Dr Saito. Both looked worse for wear, but alive. In the circumstances, I called that a victory.

I swallowed in relief. "Cut us down, P."

<Of course.>

"What happened to you?"

<We have evolved,> P said.

"Your voice-box..."

<Is no longer necessary.>

Where the crude voice-modulator had once been grafted to P's thorax, there was now only hardened carapace. P glanced at me, reading my bewilderment.

<Do not be afraid, Jenkins. We are your ally.>

"They killed Dieter," I said.

"The commander is gone?" asked Heinrich, in disbelief.

"Spaced," I said. "They've taken Lopez, too. We have to hurry."

The *Valkyrie* had been comprehensively trashed. There were bodies everywhere. Some compartments had been ransacked, others opened to vacuum. The boarders had done a proper job on the ship.

There had been many casualties during the attack. Some had put up a fight, and there were sailors slumped in the corridors. Elsewhere, techs were draped over their consoles, murdered where they worked. But the attackers hadn't killed everyone. Dr Saito and Captain Heinrich put out an all-hands call across the decks, searching for survivors, and a pitiful few emerged from hiding. They had evaded capture by using crawlspaces and emergency air-shelters. Some had got lucky.

Dr Saito led the charge into the Command Centre, a sidearm clutched in both hands. I wasn't even armed— I just followed in P's wake, confident that nothing was going to stand in the fish's way. Soon, we were a reasonable-sized group of personnel, large enough to get the *Valkyrie* moving at least.

The CIC was abandoned. Whether they were properly trained to man them or not, the remaining Navy crew took up posts. It spoke of their discipline that none of them questioned why P had been let out of its cell.

"Seal us in, Captain Ving," Dr Saito said, waving his pistol at the hatch.

"Affirmative," Ving said, locking the CIC down. "Do we still have boarders on the *Valkyrie*?"

"No," said an officer. "I've run a bio-sensor sweep. We're the only survivors."

"Fucking shame," Ving snorted. "I'd like to get my hands on one of them."

Ving's eyes were red-rimmed and sore, and he stalked the CIC like a wounded animal, hands constantly rubbing the back of his thick neck. The loss of his team weighed heavily on his shoulders, and I tried not to think how close the Jackals had come to the same fate. War could be cruel, but what had happened to Phoenix Squad *wasn't* war. It was execution.

"Weapons hot," I ordered. "Null-shields charged."

"Aye, ma'am," voices chorused back.

"Where's their ship?" I asked.

An officer read from her console: "The hostiles engaged the portside airlock using an emergency override code, then disengaged five minutes ago. I have ID on the ship: the RFS *Svetlana*."

"That's the same ship that duped us at Sanctuary," Feng hissed.

"We need to find that ship, and fast," I said. "We can't let them take Lopez."

"They won't kill her," said Novak, anguish rippling through him. "They will do much worse."

<We share your concern,> said P.

P's hide was still flecked with brain matter from Riggs' busted head, and it impassively watched the CIC's open view-ports. The *Valkyrie*'s orbital path was decaying, and Carcosa now filled the view-ports. Something had changed down there…

The ice-shelves that covered the surface were no

longer uniform. The plains were rupturing, creating wide fissures in the planet's surface. Vast fractures soon formed. What couldn't be seen with the naked eye was relayed back by the *Valkyrie*'s surviving probes, and data scrolled across the tactical-display. Starships—like those Dr Saito had shown us, during the briefing—rose from the ice.

Aeon ships.

Six vessels broke the planet's crust. Liquid dripped from their frozen flanks, and huge chunks of snow and ice fell from their hulls. The ships left breaches in the planet's outer ice shell that resembled the impact of warheads; a symbolic reminder that the Aeon had abandoned the safety of their hiding place.

<The Aeon's long sleep has ended,> explained P.

The game had changed. A stunned silence spread across the CIC for a moment. The Aeon ships pivoted in unison, falling into formation, and then broke the atmosphere. Their lethargy thrown off, they moved with impressive speed. The ships' thrusters glowed a muted blue as they went, leaving streaks across the pale sky. Soon, the fleet was in orbit around Carcosa.

"Truly incredible..." voiced Dr Saito. He slapped his pistol down on the terminal next to him, his eyes pinned to the view-port. "We've done it. We've awoken the Aeon."

P nodded. <They will commit their vault-ships to the war effort.>

Captain Heinrich sighed. "Mission accomplished."

"Not until we get back my trooper, it isn't," I said.

Captain Heinrich looked like he might argue with me for a moment, but then shrank back into his seat. A taste of combat—up close and personal—had obviously cowed him.

There was a chime across the CIC.

"Incoming transmission," said an officer.

"Alien?" asked Captain Heinrich.

"No, sir." The officer grimaced. "It's coming from the *Svetlana*."

"Get a trace on that broadcast," I ordered, "and put it on the display."

A tri-D of Major Vasnev's face sprang to life on the main console. The image was crippled with distortion, rapidly shifting in and out of focus, but clear enough for our purposes. Vasnev was on the bridge of her stolen ship, and she looked angry.

"You lied to me, Lieutenant," she said.

"I want my trooper back. No harm comes to Lopez."

Vasnev's lips curled into a weary snarl. "Disciple Riggs says that the pariah-form lives."

Of course, as soon as Riggs had extracted, he would've informed the Sons of Balash of what had happened.

"I'm glad he figured that out. Ask him about his headache. Hand over Private Lopez, immediately."

"Why would I do that?"

"This is an Alliance Navy strikeship," I said. "Our weapons systems are locked onto your position."

I looked sidelong at the weapons station, hopeful that was at least partially true. The female officer manning the post nodded, sending her results to the main display. Rail guns, missile launchers and point defence lasers were all online. The mystery of the *Svetlana*'s location was solved by Zero. She motioned to the scanner-returns, and the weathered outline of a freighter, projected in computer-reproduced tri-D, appeared there. The RFS *Svetlana* had never been a beautiful ship. There was no grace in her blunt features, and her boxy shape told of a design purely for travel through the deeps of space, where friction and form were irrelevant. The ship was nestled among the debris surrounding Carcosa, running so dark that her outline was almost indistinguishable from those of the wreckage.

"You must think me very reckless," Vasnev drawled, "communicating with you like this. I take it that you have traced this transmission, back to source, in order to find me? All that firepower, trained on this one ship."

"That, and the Aeon fleet," I declared triumphantly.

All six vault-ships closed on the *Svetlana*'s position. The *Valkyrie* registered energy readings consistent with weapons charging up. What abilities the awakened aliens might possess—given what they had done on Carcosa's surface, during their hibernation—remained to be seen.

"You misunderstand me," Vasnev said. "Why would I give up the Secretary's daughter, when she is my only gambling chip?" The ghost of a smile twitched at her lips. "We both know that you will do anything to kill Daneb Riggs. We both know that Leon Novak would do anything to kill me."

A heartbeat passed, and the smile grew. Inside, my resolve faltered.

"And we all know that you would not endanger the Secretary's daughter. This, of course, will happen, unless my ship is allowed to leave here untouched."

"Do not listen to her!" yelled Novak. "We go, and we chase this ship!"

My anger was so intense that I shook with the heat of it. What could we do? If we took out the *Svetlana*, then Lopez would be in mortal danger. Vasnev or Riggs would kill her, and even if they were bluffing, there was no guarantee she would survive the conflict between the *Svetlana* and the *Valkyrie*...

"No, Novak," I said. "We can't do that."

"We must go to her," Novak said. "She cannot get away with Lopez!"

Ving's brow contorted in a tortured expression. "I agree with the lifer. We waste that bitch."

"Call off your allies," Vasnev's tri-D image ordered.

P glanced at me, and we made a private mental connection. <It is done.>

The Aeon ships clustered together at a safe distance from the *Svetlana*. We were still registering their weapon signatures, but for now they watched and waited.

"You are going to allow us to pull out of this debris-field," Vasnev said. "Then you will allow us to leave the Ghost Maker Nebula. Do not follow."

Novak went to say something but the words died in his mouth. He sat back in his seat, his anger simmering but not yet dissipated.

I sighed. "I'm going to find you, Vasnev. And when I do, I'm going to rip you limb from fucking limb."

Vasnev clucked her tongue as if in amusement. "I doubt that very much, Lieutenant. Greater women than you have tried."

The transmission ended.

The RFS *Svetlana* retreated through the ring of wreckage, her own weapon systems tracking us, her null-shields activated. She rapidly headed to the system's edge, moving at full thrust, then activated her Q-drive.

"I expect she'll jump to the next Shard Gate," Zero said. "The Spiral have full control of those. Her tachyon trail will become almost untraceable."

"We have to give chase," Feng insisted. "We...we can't leave Lopez with *them*."

<Lopez-other is a Jackal,> P said. <We will recover her. Alive, if possible.>

"We still have a mission," Captain Heinrich piped up.

The captain sat, pale-faced and withdrawn, next to Commander Dieter's vacant command terminal. I'd almost forgotten that Heinrich was nominally in charge of this operation.

Dr Saito nodded. "The captain is right. We've made contact with the Aeon, but now we have to bring them to the Alliance fleet."

"The ship will need repairs before we go anywhere," a senior Navy officer said. "She suffered a significant impact to the ventral thrust unit during boarding. Several compartments have been breached; we're open to vacuum on the lower decks."

"That will need to be rectified as quickly as possible," Captain Heinrich said, regaining a modicum of his former self. He repositioned his cap, straightened his uniform. "Get to it immediately."

The Navy officer nodded. "I'll organise a work crew and make a start now."

<The Aeon have offered to assist,> P said.

"You're in direct communication with them now?" asked Zero, excitedly.

<Affirmative,> P said. <We are a bridge. We can feel the Aeon's group mind. We were in contact with them before we reached Carcosa. Their representatives will shortly board the ship.>

I let out a long wavering exhalation of air. "The Aeon seemed pretty crazy when we were on the surface. Can we trust them?"

<We can. They pursue the same objective as us, Jenkins-other.>

An alert spilt across the Command Centre's main terminal, and we gathered around to see what had happened. To my surprise, I realised that we weren't being threatened, or blown up, or shot at. New electrical signatures registered inside and outside the ship.

"*Anomaly detected*," came the *Valkyrie*'s synthesised voice. "*Await update.*"

<Aeon constructs are coming aboard the ship,> P explained. <They will assist with the repairs.>

"Will they know what needs to be done?" Zero asked.

<They will,> said P. <We have given them the relevant information.>

"The Jackals need some medical attention as well," Dr Saito said. "You should get those injuries treated."

I knew Dr Saito was right. I'd been trying to ignore the pulsing throb in my head, as well as the patch of dried blood I could feel beneath my hairline.

"Hold up, hold up," I said. "Before we get there, I want to know what happened on the *Valkyrie*. How did you survive, P? And you too, Dr Saito? Vasnev's gang searched the ship. They surely wouldn't have missed you."

"It's complicated," Dr Saito said. There was something different about his presentation; he seemed very far from the mild-mannered science geek that had initially been assigned to the *Valkyrie*.

"Try me," I replied. "Complicated, I can deal with."

The more I studied Dr Saito, and the more time I spent around him, the less he looked like a Science Officer. There was a hard edge to the guy that was at odds with his professional front.

"When the boarders breached the ship, I moved P's chrysalis into hiding. We used an air-shaft. The pod suppressed P's life-signs."

<That is correct,> P volunteered.

"Right," I said, frowning, "but that doesn't explain how Dr Saito and Captain Heinrich managed to hide as well."

"I had some help," Dr Saito said. "I used this."

He produced a band from around his neck. It was a heavy choker, made of solid metal, with a control box on the side. A light on the box was currently flashing red, maybe indicating that the device was deactivated.

"What's that supposed to be?"

"It's a stealth band," he said. "It cloaks life-signs. This made us effectively invisible to the boarding party."

Looking over at Captain Heinrich, I saw that he had an identical band around his neck, except that Heinrich's control box flashed green. A quick assessment of the ship's bio-scanner demonstrated that Dr Saito was telling the truth. Heinrich's vitals weren't being detected.

"Where did you get those, Doctor?" Zero chimed in, coming to investigate. "Stealth bands are restricted tech, aren't they? We didn't have any on *Valkyrie*'s equipment manifest."

"I brought them aboard," Dr Saito said, licking his lips. Was that a defensive tell?

I stared from P to Dr Saito. The xeno wasn't phased by Dr Saito at all; I hoped that one of P's upgrades was a bullshit detector. I certainly wasn't buying what Saito was selling.

"Along with that gun, I take it?" I challenged.

"The weapon is a personal possession," said Dr Saito.

The pistol was an older-pattern kinetic; a semi-auto Army-issue model. Not something I would expect a Science Officer to be carrying around as personal property.

"Don't be impudent, Lieutenant," Captain Heinrich said. "Dr Saito assisted me during the boarding, and I'm very grateful for his help. Had it not been for him, well…"

I gave Dr Saito a glance that made clear we weren't done—that I wanted some real answers—but we had to focus on what mattered.

"All right," I said. "Jackals, let's get cleaned up."

"I'm going to take stock of the armoury and cryo-storage," Ving declared. He cracked his knuckles. There was a little more fire behind his eyes now. "When we find Riggs, I want to be ready."

I got patched up in Medical, and swallowed down some painkillers. A med-pack to the head and a session in the auto-doc, and I was good to roll. The Jackals had bruises and minor injuries, but other than Novak, they weren't in bad shape. Novak waved off any medical attention, just because he was Novak. The Sons of Balash had beaten him with shock-batons, causing nasty burns across his torso, but Novak wore those injuries like badges of honour.

Less than an hour after the Aeon had initiated their repair function, the *Valkyrie* was ready to fly. Although she wasn't going to win any beauty contests—half of her portside outer hull was covered in gossamer-like strands of glowing crystal—she was space-worthy. All primary systems were online and the main thrusters were running hot. Even the Q-drive was operational.

A tide of Aeon Scuttlers worked both inside, and outside, the ship. These were the "constructs" P had spoken of. They had the appearance of terrestrial spiders, and were equipped with some sort of tool where a true arachnid's head would be. Impervious to vacuum and heat, the Scuttlers phased in and out of reality as necessary. Whether they were fully automated, or guided by some remote intelligence on the Aeon vault-ships, was unclear. Whatever the truth, they were effective, and worked fast.

All that was left to do was clean up the ship. The Jackals pitched in, and we scoured the decks for bodies. In silence, we trawled dozens of corpses back to one of the storage bays, setting them down in neat rows.

Novak looked out across the improvised graveyard. Each body was draped with a bunk sheet, which made all of this easier to deal with. These people had families, had lives, meant something. Now, they were just bodies under sheets. Phoenix Squad was the worst. I'd never liked them, but what had happened to them was all kinds of wrong. We logged the details of each fatality. The bodies would be repatriated, if we ever got home.

Captain Ving met us outside the holding bay. I nodded at him.

"We've secured the bodies, sir," I explained.

"Thanks," he said. "This…this was a day I never thought I'd have to face."

"I hear that, sir."

"We're Sim Ops," he said. "We're not supposed to be in *real* danger." His eyes drifted to Novak, who stood beside me, and seemed to fix on the mass of bruises that covered the Russian's face. "I guess that's not so true."

"You can pay final respects," Novak suggested.

"They were my brothers," Ving said. He froze in front of the bay hatch. "I'm going to tell their families, personally."

"I think they'd appreciate that," I said.

"Maybe I've been too hard on the Jackals," Ving said. "Maybe I've been too tough on the fish, too."

"We can take it," said Novak.

"I'm sure that you can," Ving agreed, hand on the hatch controls. "But that's not the point. I just thought maybe you should know."

"Noted, sir," I said.

We left Ving to his private grief, and wandered the decks back towards Medical.

"We have to save Lopez," Novak said.

"We will," I said. I shook my head. "It's all I can think about right now."

An Aeon Scuttler crept across the deck in front of me, phasing through the bulkhead. Some would argue that we had succeeded. We had done the impossible: made contact with another alien species, a race that had only been recorded in myth and legend. Potentially, we could turn the tide of this war and end the Harbinger threat. But none of that mattered, I realised. Not unless I had my squad. Lopez's loss dominated my thoughts.

"We'll get her," I said. "I promise. The Spiral won't harm her."

"Not Spiral," Novak muttered. "She is with Vasnev. With Sons of Balash."

Novak's hand went to his forehead, almost unconsciously, and he traced the nerve-staples in his temple. His real skin was bruised and the flesh of his face still sore-looking. It might've just been the light, but his eyes looked watery.

"Take that hate, and use it. That's an order."

Novak saluted. It wasn't much of a salute, but it was heartfelt. I guess that was what mattered most. The big guy's Adam's apple bobbed, the emotion wrought on his face.

"I lose Vali and Anwar. They are gone for ever. Whatever happens to Major Vasnev, that will be the case."

"It's taken you long enough to figure that one out, Novak."

"They were my family. I thought for longest time that I have no one left, but I am wrong. I have Jackals. They are family now, and I fight for them."

I tried to laugh the words away, but Novak's vulnerability in that moment was disarming. He was deathly serious.

"Even Lopez?" I asked. "You've always said that she is a pain in the ass."

"Especially Lopez," said Novak. "And yes, she is a pain in my ass, but a good pain. The Jackals are the only family that matters. So I will do what is needed, when time comes."

"You're dismissed, trooper."

Novak nodded, and disappeared into the ship. A Scuttler—glowing, almost ephemeral—followed him.

I almost ran into Dr Saito as I entered Medical.

"Ah, Lieutenant," he said. "How is the med-pack holding up?"

"Well enough, Doc."

Dr Saito looked uncomfortable. He toyed with the hem of his uniform. "I was just monitoring the progress of these Scuttlers. They are remarkable creations. They seem to almost ignore the crew." He grinned. "I'd like to catch one for study, although I'm not sure our new allies would appreciate that."

"So, Doc," I said, "what's really going on?"

"What do you mean?"

I noticed that Dr Saito's pistol sat on the bench next to him, within easy reach.

"I think we both know what I mean. Who are you? Because I'm damned sure that Dr Wesley Saito isn't a Chief Science Officer."

Saito tried to repress a swallow.

"I *am* Wesley Saito," he insisted. "And I am a Science Officer. I haven't lied to you—or anyone else—about my identity."

"But there's more to you, Saito. You were a late assignment to this mission. Someone wanted you on this ship, and it wasn't Command."

"I'm not Black Spiral, if that's what you're suggesting," Saito said. He seemed very eager to demonstrate that point. "Surely you can see that. I protected P. I made sure that Major Vasnev's death squad didn't find him."

"I didn't use the rank 'Major' when we were in the CIC," I said. "Where did you hear that?"

"One of the crew might've mentioned it..."

"I don't think they did. I've never accused you of being Spiral, but we both know there's more to this war than just the Spiral and the Alliance. Who are you really working for, and why are you on this ship?"

Wesley Saito chewed on a thought for a long moment. "I'm with the Watch."

I laughed. "You're lying. There is no Watch."

Saito licked his lips, slowly. Indecision was painted across his face. "And who told you that, Lieutenant?"

"There is no Watch," I repeated. "It was Lazarus, and his partner, and a bunch of people who believed his crap. That was all."

"The Watch is deep intelligence," Saito said. "*That's* the truth. It might not be the most prolific of organisations, but it is the most effective. We are a new weapon, to counter the Black Spiral. An organisation that can be anywhere, when required—"

"Then why does Command deny you even exist?" I asked, very much aware that my voice was rising in timbre and pitch. I was angry, and struggling to repress it. "When we came back from Kronstadt, everyone was keen to tell us that the Watch wasn't real. That it was just Harris and his crew. Military Intelligence told me as much!"

"Which is what they believe," Dr Saito said. "Which is what we *want* them to believe."

"Why would the Watch possibly want that?"

"Because Mili-Intel is compromised. It has been since the Spiral first appeared as a threat."

"If you really are the Watch, then all you've succeeded in doing is standing by while four simulant operators were executed, and a ship full of loyal sailors was slaughtered."

"I'm the only Watch operative on this ship. I protected P, and hid Captain Heinrich. It was all I could do."

"Command Dieter was executed."

Dr Saito grimaced. "I sincerely wish that could've been avoided."

"And now, suddenly, you think that you can tell me this, and it's all going to be fine?"

Phoenix Squad's tanks sat empty—monuments to what had been lost. Lopez's tank yawned, the data-cables dangling limp from the main control unit.

"No," Dr Saito said. "I never believed for one minute that this would be fine, but I wouldn't be doing this unless I thought it was right. The Watch is a collection of individual operatives, spread far and wide. Dr Locke was an affiliate; a source of information. I'm the same. An agent, if you will. And I've achieved my objective."

"Which was?"

"To protect Pariah, and to ensure that communication was made with the Aeon," Dr Saito said. "That is what was required of me."

"So I take it that the Watch is going to just disappear again, now that this is done?" I asked, with a level of sarcasm that would've suited Lopez.

"Not quite," Dr Saito said. "There are other, deeper agents within the Alliance fleet. When the time comes, they will be activated too."

"How does that help?"

"They have orders," Saito said. "Just like me, they will execute them to the best of their ability. They'll do whatever it takes to end this war, and destroy the Spiral."

I bit my lip. That was a habit I'd shed as a teenager.

"Does Captain Heinrich know about the Watch?"

"No," Dr Saito said, shaking his head. He may as well have added *of course not*, but instead said, "Captain

Heinrich is a Proximan, and a loyal one at that. He thinks that Command knows what's best. He's wrong. We can keep this from him."

"Agreed," I found myself saying, without even thinking on it.

"General Draven doesn't know, either."

"And Ving?"

"Same. He's a poster boy for the Sim Ops Programme."

I nodded. Swallowed. "So now you've told me: what comes after?"

"We head for Ithaca. That's where Warlord, and Major Vasnev, will be. We use the Aeon to end this war."

"My priority is recovering Lopez," I said.

"Understood," said Dr Saito.

"Tell me one thing."

"Go on."

"If you really are Watch, then you're privy to restricted intel."

"It's highly compartmentalised. All on a need to know basis."

"I want to know something personal. I lost a friend on Darkwater Farm. He meant a lot to Zero, and he meant even more to me."

Dr Saito didn't reply. He really was going to make me ask the question.

"How is Lazarus doing?"

His expression told me everything I needed to know.

An alarm sounded across the deck, before I could get a proper answer.

"What is it now?" I asked, storming into the CIC.

"You're going to love this," said Zero, as she perched at one of the vacant terminals. The Navy crew were all focused on addressing the new threat. P loomed over the main display.

"What in Gaia's name is this ... ?" Dr Saito remarked, as he took in the latest development.

The Aeon fleet had assembled around Carcosa, in the same orbit as the *Valkyrie*, a short distance from our position.

"We're detecting a massive space-time anomaly," said an officer. "Directly ahead."

The officer looked to P, who was about the only entity within light-years that seemed to have any idea of what was going on any more.

<This is the Aeon's method of travel,> it said. <The Aeon's speciality is the manipulation of space-time. Their mastery of this technique is flawless.>

"The readings that thing is putting out..." Zero said, following up the comment with a long whistle. "They're amazing."

A white smear of light rapidly coalesced in deep space. It was a slit in the fabric of reality, spilling out exotic energies in every direction. But despite the anomaly's alien appearance, the *Valkyrie*'s AI detected something familiar about it.

"That's a Shard Gate, right?" I asked.

P stared at the terminal. <It is an Aeon Gate, but the principle is the same. It will allow us to access the Shard Network.>

"They can create jump-gates at will!" Zero said, thrilled, almost forgetting that only a few hours ago she was facing certain death. "Not even the Shard can do that."

"How do they know where to meet with the Alliance fleet?" Captain Heinrich asked. "We have specific orders to rendezvous with General Draven."

<We have provided the destination,> said P. <This Gate will take us directly to the Reef Stars, and to the Ithaca system.>

"Tell our new buddies we say thank you," I said. "I think."

"Can we make contact with them?" Captain Heinrich asked. "I'd like to meet with one of their, ah, leaders."

<The Aeon will initiate a plan when we reach the destination,> said P.

Captain Heinrich nodded. "Very well."

"Initiate thrust, sir?" asked a Navy officer.

"Immediately," ordered Heinrich.

The Aeon followed us through the breach in time-space, as silent as they had been since their appearance.

CHAPTER TWENTY

BATTLE LINES DRAWN

"That's a positive on realspace translation," said Zero, reading from the *Valkyrie*'s navigation console. "We are through the Gate."

"Can someone confirm our location?" Captain Heinrich said.

"I can do better than that," said a Navy crewman. "The *Valkyrie* is receiving tight beam IFF codes from several sources."

"I'm verifying," another officer said, amazement in his voice. "We've found the Alliance fleet."

"Looks as though your friends have dropped us right on the edge of the conflict," I said, to P.

<We provided the navigational coordinates,> the xeno answered.

By now, Novak and Dr Saito had also converged on the CIC.

"The Aeon are following," Dr Saito said, reading from a vacant console. "All of their ships made transition through the Gate."

Zero uploaded new data to the tactical-display. A tri-D reproduction of surrounding space appeared.

"I present Ithaca Star..." she said.

Everyone paused to take in what we were seeing. Ithaca was a main sequence star, the heart of a busy system that supported several planets. It was the primary Reef Star, and these were the Reef Worlds; the Krell's inner sanctum. In other circumstances, this would've been a big moment. Before the war, no human had set eyes on this star—its location had been unknown, during both the Krell War and the stalemate that followed. The Krell regarded their ancestral home as nothing short of a sacred place. From here, the Krell Collective had spread across the stars, and become fractured in the process. But despite those divisions, the rise of the individual Collectives, the Krell were still a unified species. At least, they had been—until the coming of the Harbinger virus.

<This is the birth system of the Deep Ones,> the xeno broadcast.

"The Krell High Council?" Zero probed.

<Correct,> said P. <Ithaca Prime is the third planet from the system's star. There are other worlds within this system, all of which harbour ancient Kindred holdings. The Kindred originated here, among the Reef Worlds.>

P had once told me—a very long time ago, it felt—that it had never been to the Krell's home planet. It had been created on North Star Station, from an existing bio-form. It hadn't known the cradle of Krell civilisation like some Collectives.

<We have knowledge of this place,> P explained, <and these worlds, through the Deep-knowing. This place is secret, and Ithaca Prime too. It is vulnerable, representing the easiest route by which to contaminate the Kindred's Collective mind.>

Since I had made connection with a navigator-form

in the Gyre—during one of the Jackals' early missions— I'd been having visions of this place.

"Huh," Ving said, staring back at the holo. "Well, it isn't secret any more."

The *Valkyrie*'s scanner was soon populated with energy signatures consistent with human starships. The outer orbits of the system were choked with vessels. This was Battlegroup Perfect Storm, assembled and ready to move on Ithaca.

"The war's started without us," Feng said.

"Then we had better deploy our secret weapon," Captain Heinrich said. He strolled towards the open viewports, looking out at the alien fleet. "We have the Aeon."

I nodded. "That's the idea, sir."

"Fly us into friendly skies," Captain Heinrich ordered, "and make contact with the fleet."

"Yes, sir," said an officer. "Running identification pattern check." She paused. "I've found the UAS *Defiant*, flagship of the fleet."

"The *Defiant*?" Heinrich said. "Good choice. She's a damned fine ship."

The UAS *Defiant* was as big as a space station, a true symbol of Alliance supremacy among the stars. Her hull bore the identifiers of the Alliance Navy, the flag of the United Americas, and the badge of assignment to the 1st Battleship Division. She was screened by dozens of other Navy assets, surrounded by a cloud of Hornet space fighters and remote drone craft.

Feng pointed out another feature of the titanic warship, as we came in to dock. "We're not the only visitors," he said. "Secretary Lopez is riding with the fleet."

The unmistakable outline of Secretary Rodrigo Lopez's space yacht, the *Destiny*, came into view. The ship was attached to one of the *Defiant*'s docks. The yacht somehow reminded me of a parasite, attached to a much larger animal, draining blood from its unwitting host…

"That's where General Draven and his command staff will be," Captain Heinrich said, nodding brusquely. "It's where we should be, too. Send a transmission declaring our arrival in the theatre, and request an audience with General Draven."

"Aye, sir."

I turned to P. "You'd better tell our new allies to hold fire until we've made contact with Command."

<Affirmative,> P said.

On the system's outer edge, the Carcosa Gate blinked out of existence, as though it had never even been there.

We went through the rituals that came with boarding any major military vessel and embarked onto the *Defiant*. The ship on a war-footing through and through. Her multiple hangars were loaded with gunships and shuttles, dozens of craft sitting ready for deployment. Soldiers in tight drill formation marched by. Army Sim Ops teams wearing full combat-gear received pep-talks in hangar bays. Pallets loaded with cryogenic capsules—filled with simulants—were shuttled from one end of the ship to the other.

A welcome party made up of a couple of very strungout looking Military Police officers greeted us at the dock. I was expecting some awkward questions about P, but these guys must've been briefed, because they ignored the xeno altogether. It was just another trooper now.

"Jackals," said the lead officer. "Please accompany me to the war-room. General Draven wishes to be updated immediately."

"Good, good," said Heinrich. "I'm eager to report as well."

"No, sir, not you. I've arranged an escort for you, Captains. You can get checked out, and fed."

Ving started to grumble, but the idea of food settled his complaint. Heinrich wasn't so easily placated.

"I really do think that it should be me who reports," he said. "I mean, General Draven is my direct superior. I shouldn't be—"

The officer waved a hand. "The general specifically requested the attendance of Lieutenant Jenkins, her Jackals, and Dr Saito. I'm sure he will see you personally in due course."

"Fine. Just let the general know that I survived."

With that, the Mili-Pol officers marched us through the ship to General Draven's war-room.

The chamber was filled with staff, with a dozen consoles processing data from the front. Officers of various rank, organisation and role were collected around a large tactical-display unit, which was currently set up to show the progress of the war. The lights were dimmed, and intensely detailed tri-D images filled the air.

No matter what limb of military service they had been drawn from, Draven's officer cadre were uniformly exhausted. All wore body-armour and carried sidearms, as though they expected the war to come for them at any moment. Even General Draven wore an armoured jacket, his desk-jockey physique straining against the solid flak plating across his stomach. Draven had been in mid-address, but he broke off sharply as we entered. The officer cadre around the table looked up. They parted to admit us to the display.

General Draven looked me up and down. "When I got the message that the *Valkyrie* had arrived on our scanners…" He shook his head. "I couldn't quite believe it. Great Gaia, it's good to see you."

"And you, sir," I said.

We saluted the general. Dr Saito and P looked over the schematics on the display, evaluating the development of the war effort.

Director Mendelsohn, looking as grey and worn as he'd been the last time I'd seen him, stood at General Draven's flank.

"What happened to the asset?" he said. "The pariah-form has changed..."

"For the better," Feng said, patting P on the carapace-clad shoulder.

<We agree with that assessment,> P broadcast.

"Did you all hear that?" asked an older officer wearing Marine fatigues. "Did the fish just speak...in my head?"

"Where is the asset's voice-transmission unit?" Director Mendelsohn queried, leaning across the display to get a better look.

<We no longer require such technology to communicate,> P answered. <We have evolved past that stage.> There was much frowning and consternation at the xeno's uninvited intrusion into some of the officers' heads, but that didn't stop P. <We are able to communicate mind-to-mind.>

"And the musculoskeletal enhancements..." Mendelsohn continued. "This is truly remarkable."

General Draven picked up on what he was really interested in. "I was informed that you bring news from the Ghost Maker Nebula. From the unusual scanner readings, I take it that these are alien ships."

"That's correct," I confirmed. "We have a lot to tell you, sir."

Director Mendelsohn stirred from his position at the display. "I'm especially interested to know about your contact with the Aeon." He indicated Dr Saito. "I want your debrief as soon as possible, Doctor."

"Of course, Director."

"We should commence negotiations with the Aeon," Director Mendelsohn said, unable to stop his eyes from glancing down at the display. "Their assistance will be invaluable in breaking through the—"

There was a sudden commotion from the war-room entrance. Every officer in the compartment reached for sidearms, turning to face the noise.

"Why wasn't I summoned immediately? I left strict instructions that I wanted to know as soon as we had a report!"

"Sir, the war-room is in session—"

"This is my fleet! I'll go where I damned well please."

Draven lifted an eyebrow at me, as Secretary Lopez and his security entourage bowled into the compartment. Tellingly, the aura of anxiety seemed to escalate, rather than relax, as the group made their appearance. The officer cadre saluted the Secretary smartly, but Lopez didn't make eye contact with a single one of them. He didn't even acknowledge General Draven. Instead, his dark, intense eyes were focused on the Jackals, and specifically me.

"Mr Secretary, sir," I said.

"At ease, at ease," he replied, waving a hand to stand down the meeting, his face scrunching in annoyance. "I've told you more than once that I'm not interested in protocol."

"Sir, you shouldn't be here," said a Mili-Pol officer, stirring at the Secretary's shoulder. "We have security in place at the *Destiny*'s docking berth—"

"What do you have for me?" Secretary Lopez said, speaking over the other man. "I want to know everything."

"The Jackals have made contact with the Aeon, sir," General Draven answered. "Lieutenant Jenkins was just about to give me her report. She'll need a formal debrief, under hypno, and then we can begin the process of making contact—"

"There isn't time for that," Secretary Lopez said. He spread his hands to the holo-display, which showed the imminent joining of battle. "Are these aliens going to help us or not?"

<The Aeon will assist,> P broadcast.

Secretary Lopez looked around the chamber in surprise at the sudden noise in his head. His reaction reminded me of when Riggs had first heard the mind-voice.

"What…?" he managed, inspecting P from across the table.

<We have evolved,> P said. <That is all.>

"The pariah-form's communication abilities have been upgraded," Dr Saito said, in the briefest explanation I'd ever heard a Sci-Div officer give.

"Right, right," said Secretary Lopez. He turned his attention back to the tactical-display, a frown still wrinkling his brow. "Your report, Lieutenant Jenkins?"

"We made contact with the Aeon. They have sent six ships in support."

"Excellent," said Secretary Lopez. He clapped his hands together, rubbing them in anticipation. "Then we need to shift up our assault."

"We have some other news," I muttered. "Private Lopez has been captured by the Black Spiral."

Lopez scanned the Jackals, as though—for the very first time—he was realising that there were fewer of us present. The reaction was a little delayed, but his face dropped.

"My Gabriella?" he said.

"I'm sorry, sir. We can explain."

He shook his head, as though he was trying to shake away the news, displace it somehow.

"Our mission was sabotaged by a traitor," I started. "The *Valkyrie* suffered significant damage. We were boarded by a group affiliated with the Black Spiral."

"That…that is terrible news. Really, it is. I'll give Gabriella's recovery some thought."

"Thought?" Novak grunted. "She must be rescued."

Feng was just as disturbed by the Secretary's response. "We can't leave her with them…"

"It has to be our priority, sir," I said.

The Secretary shivered out a sigh. "Of course," he said, very noncommittally. Staring down at the display again now, his mind was obviously moving in a different direction. "My daughter means the universe to me. But right now, the universe is at stake. We have a war to win. There's no time to waste."

<The Black Spiral are moving on Ithaca Star,> P said.

General Draven paused. "How do you know that, Pariah?"

<We can read the Deep, General Draven,> P said. <We are aware of the Spiral's movements within the Reef Stars. They have jumped in-system, ahead of your forces.>

General Draven gave a slow nod. "The Spiral were more or less waiting for us when we arrived in the Reef Stars," said General Draven. There was obvious disdain in his voice. "They have an entire fleet of ships."

Secretary Lopez breathed out through his nose. "And apparently there are more inbound from the Core Systems, if reports from Military Intelligence are accurate."

"They're using the Shard Gates to out-manoeuvre our forces," said General Draven. "Wherever they appear, the Spiral spreads the Harbinger virus."

"Has the anti-viral solution been effective?" I asked.

"It has," Director Mendelsohn said, "but we aren't yet in a position to implement a targeted application."

"The Black Spiral have launched counter-offensives across the Reef Stars," Draven said. "Although these planets are currently being supported by Krell war-fleets from the Silver Talon, the Blue Claw and the Nova Prima Collectives, losses have been extensive on all sides."

<The Spiral will burn up their fleet in this process,> P assessed, <but with each planet that falls, bio-mass will be added to the shadow matter.>

All forces were converging on Ithaca Star, the heart of the Maelstrom. This was where the war would be won. The system was surrounded by hostiles. The Krell forces that had dropped back to defend this sector were fighting Harbinger and the Black Spiral. Ithaca was cut off, under siege.

"This is civil war," I said. "The Krell are turning on each other. The infected against the uninfected."

<Correct,> said P. <But if the Spiral forces reach Ithaca Prime, then all will be lost.>

I sensed the wave of emotion that sheeted off Pariah. Rage, anger, loss. Images flashed through my mind: by now familiar scenes of Krell homeworlds dying. Vast seabeds, once the swamp-like ancestral homes of the Krell, reduced to dry wastes. Biological cities, collapsing under the weight of Harbinger's rot. Living starships, eating themselves from the inside out. And everywhere, everywhere, the spiralling shadow matter—coalescing, ephemeral, reso-nating the Shard's call to arms through corrupted space.

"Are you all right, ma'am?" Novak asked.

"I'm good," I lied.

I might be the only one who had been affected by P's visions, but the others had certainly felt something. Som-bre faces met mine across the display.

"What are *those*?" Feng exclaimed, pointing to the display: at a sector marked with flashing threat icons.

General Draven's face grew especially dark, his grey moustache the only colour on his ageing face.

"The Alliance isn't the only faction to have a new ally in this war, son," he said. "The Shard have arrived, and they're just as dangerous as we feared."

"We need to commence negotiations with the Aeon immediately," said Secretary Lopez. "And we can only hope that our guns are bigger than the enemy's."

"What about the other special operations?" I asked. "The *Valkyrie* wasn't the only ship to have covert orders. Have any of those missions returned results?"

"No," said Director Mendelsohn. "Only the Jackals have returned."

"So it's all down to the Aeon..." whispered Zero.

<We will request their attendance immediately,> said P.

Before the thought had even left my head, a security alarm chimed across the war-room. An anxious-looking officer called up scanner-returns on the display.

"Shuttle of unknown origin is requesting permission to dock, sir," he said, focusing on General Draven.

"Then let's meet our new allies," said Secretary Lopez.

A security detail—headed by none other than Captain Ving—was hastily arranged to receive the Aeon's shuttle, and within a very short period of time the aliens were aboard the *Defiant*.

Despite the war effort, every soldier and sailor on the ship wanted to witness the arrival of the aliens. Anxiety and anticipation crackled in the air like electricity. Troopers lined the corridors to catch a glimpse of the new arrivals, while surveillance drones and newsbots recorded the event for posterity. The images of the alien creatures moving through *Defiant*'s corridors, accompanied by a tide of Scuttlers, would be featured on Alliance newscasts for many years to come. This was the first contact with an intelligent alien race that the Alliance had yearned for.

The meeting took place in the *Defiant*'s war-room, and the Jackals were required to attend. The officer cadre stood replete in their finest dress uniforms, ready to receive the aliens.

"This is a truly historic moment," said Secretary Lopez, pressing down his suit, his eyes flickering over the Jackals. "I'm glad that you're here to see it, Lieutenant. That was some excellent work, in making contact with the Aeon."

"Yes, sir," I said. "Really, it was all P's doing."

P stood beside me, statue-still, but I could sense the alien's mind was elsewhere. It was remotely communicating with the Aeon.

The war-room hatch parted, and the Aeon entered the chamber.

"Welcome aboard the UAS *Defiant*," General Draven began, addressing the three alien visitors. P echoed the words via mind-link.

In the light of the war-room, the Aeon looked even stranger. Although they barely fitted in the corridors and compartments of the human-scaled ship, all three of the aliens were afflicted with an arthritic stoop that robbed them of their true height. The sense of age I'd felt when we first met was here in triplicate now that the aliens were out of their cryo-pools. All three wore bulky helmets, which occasionally emitted plumes of mist from valves built into the collar units. They were accompanied by an aura of pervasive cold, frost creeping across the deck as the aliens took up positions beside the tactical-display.

I saw Zero inspecting them with particular interest.

She hadn't seen the aliens on Carcosa's surface, and the away team's vid-feeds hadn't been broadcasting. With child-like glee, she peered at the crystalline exo-suits the aliens wore. Those shimmered in the war-room's low lights, throwing back reflections. The Scuttlers continued their tending process, always tinkering with some aspect of their masters' suits. I got the impression that they were maintaining the exo-units, perhaps keeping them at optimum performance.

Captain Ving was at the rear of the entourage. He nodded at me as he entered the chamber, and I nodded back. Waving off the surveillance drones and news-cams, he sealed the compartment. I felt better knowing that he was here, for some reason.

One alien took the lead, while the other two held back. The leader's mirrored helmet became transparent, exposing its face. That strange, almost arachnid visage appeared, and the sightless orbs of the alien's eyes peered at me.

<Your atmosphere is incompatible with our physiology,> the alien said. All three discordantly wheezed and hissed, as though verging on suffocation. <We will remain in our protective units for this reason.>

<It is hostile to us,> said the second alien.

<It will be our final breath,> said the third.

Director Mendelsohn started jotting something on his data-slate, nodding to himself. He could hardly contain his excitement.

"We understand," said General Draven. "We wish to extend the hand of friendship, on behalf of the Alliance, and the human race."

The lead Aeon nodded. <Received.>

<Rejected,> said the second.

<At this time,> said the third, <it is unclear whether you are truly ally or enemy.>

Secretary Lopez jostled in front of the alien. "I am Secretary of Defence for the Alliance. My name is Rodrigo Lopez."

The Aeon's leader paused. Its blind eyes narrowed. <Understood.>

"I have authority to speak on behalf of the Alliance," Secretary Lopez said. "We are in great need of your abilities."

<This, we already know,> said the lead Aeon. <The Kindred have told us the facts.>

<We are able to communicate with the Aeon at a speed faster than your methods allow,> said P. <We have appraised the many mind of the situation.>

There was little point in withholding intelligence from a hyper-advanced alien race such as the Aeon. As well as the frost aura that accompanied the xenos, I noticed that the tactical-display jumped and jittered in their presence. P had described reading the mainframe, accessing its data without permission. It was inevitable that the Aeon were able to do the same thing, and I had no doubt that they were leaching information from our systems. But these were desperate times and we had to trust them.

"By what name can I address you?" Secretary Lopez asked.

<We are the Enclave of Torex Var Tor,> said the leader. The alien stirred in my direction, and my skin chilled. <But Soldier calls us by another name. Soldier calls us Wraith. That is the name by which we will go.>

General Draven frowned at me, and I felt my cheeks burning.

"I never actually called the, ah, alien by this name to its face," I explained. "It was just something that came into my head..."

<The name will suffice,> said Wraith. Back to Secretary Lopez, the alien said, <You are responsible for bringing the Shard back.>

"Not us," said Secretary Lopez. "An organisation called the Black Spiral."

<You,> said Wraith. It raised a hand and pointed a lean digit at Secretary Lopez specifically.

He seemed affronted at that suggestion. "If the pariah-form has told you what it knows," he argued, "then you will understand that it is Warlord, leader of the Black Spiral, who is responsible. He has brought the Shard back to the Maelstrom."

<We will speak with the one that matters,> said the Aeon leader. <This is not you.>

"It is me," Lopez argued. "I am responsible for the military forces within this theatre—"

<We know what the pariah-form knows,> said Wraith. <And we will converse with the entity responsible for our awakening.>

It hooked a long finger in my direction.

A cloud of abject disappointment settled over Secretary Lopez's face. I caught a slight smile on Captain Ving's lips from the corner of my eye, and saw that even General Draven looked amused.

I shook my head. "I'm a soldier. I was following orders."

<They know who you are,> said P. <The Aeon also know *what* you are.>

"Then tell them that I'm not who they should be speaking to," I protested.

<We are satisfied that Soldier is the conduit,> said the Aeon, as one. <Soldier gave us a name. We will discuss plans with Soldier.>

A murmur spread through the gathered spectators.

Lopez pressed down his suit again, his agitation passing into frustration.

"Right," he said. "Well, if they want to speak with you, Lieutenant, then that will have to do."

"Are you sure, sir?"

"I said so, didn't I?"

The Aeon dignitaries watched the exchange without comment, wheezing and hissing as they breathed whatever product they called atmosphere. The Scuttlers had settled around their feet.

<Tell us your plans,> said Wraith.

"This is our current force disposition," I explained, pointing out the Alliance fleet at the edge of the Ithaca system, moving on a collision course with the Black Spiral's armada. "The uninfected Krell war-fleets are falling back here, in support of our ships. We have developed an anti-viral to counter the Harbinger virus." Icons on the tactical grid demonstrated distribution of the anti-viral. "We intend to fly the anti-viral into Ithaca Star, to administer this cure to the Krell High Council on Ithaca Prime."

The map lit with the label "Devil's Maw". That wasn't any official kind of name, but the advance fleet had labelled many features of the Ithaca system. Other choice descriptions included Ithaca Minor, the Jagged Moons, and the Ring of Thorns. Wraith evaluated the display without seeing it, dead eyes unblinking.

"This is our approach," said General Draven, displaying the five battlegroups on their flight to Ithaca. "We estimate, at this velocity, we will reach the outer planets of the Ithaca system within six hours."

<We will assist in breaking the advance to Ithaca Prime,> said the Aeon leader. <Your forces can deliver the anti-viral to these worlds, on the edge of the Ithaca system.>

More images in my head. Life-bearing planets, now

infected with Harbinger, but not yet lost. There was still hope for those worlds and the Krell that called them home. On the tac-display, icons illuminated. I looked to Secretary Lopez and Draven, both of whom nodded in agreement with that plan.

<This will be your new approach,> said Wraith.

The battle lines were instantly redrawn, revised into a spearhead formation that was aimed directly at Ithaca Prime. This plan made use of new Q-calculations and gravimetric assessments. The *Defiant*'s AI had not predicted this route, but rapidly verified it as viable.

<The quantum-tides are unstable in this region,> the Aeon said. <But we will calm them to allow your ships safe passage. Your forces will collect here, in support of our vault-ships. We carry the starfyre. It is a tool capable of unravelling the quantum. If necessary, we can unleash the full potential of our technology. It will render worlds lifeless, lost to all.>

<It is a terrible price to pay,> said the second.

<But sometimes a necessary one,> completed the third.

"Let's hope that it doesn't come to that," said Feng.

<It has been done before,> said P.

A flurry of images danced across my mind's eye. The Maelstrom's various interstellar anomalies made a terrible kind of sense, knowing what we did now. The Aeon had been responsible for them. They were ancient monuments to the war between the Dominion and the Pantheon; reminders of what the Aeon had done to repel the Shard when this war had first been fought. I felt physically and psychically weakened by the connection. It was more than just what I saw; also what I felt. The depth and wealth of emotion was overburdening, exhausting.

<We cannot allow Ithaca Star, and her worlds, to suffer this fate,> said Wraith.

<We must destroy this Spiral—and their machine allies—before they can reach the homeworld,> said the second Aeon.

<It may already be too late,> said the third.

<Inoculation of the Deep Ones may not be enough,> said Wraith, describing the High Council in the same way as P. <This virus must be destroyed at source.>

"How do we do that?" Secretary Lopez interjected.

<The Harbinger virus has a focus,> Wraith explained. <As we told Soldier, Warlord is the virus. If he is allowed to reach Ithaca Prime, to contaminate the Deep Ones, then the Kindred will be lost.>

A murmur of agreement rippled through the other Aeon. The Scuttlers became agitated, as though reading the disapproval of the masters.

P stepped up. Its huge bulk was comparable to the Aeon, and they regarded the alien with respect. <We can find the enemy leader.> It turned to me. <*I* can find him.>

<This one reads the Deep,> said Wraith. <When the time comes, it will be able to detect Warlord's presence. The Pariah will be able to sense Warlord's location.>

<And,> said the second Aeon, <if all else fails, it will be our final bulwark against the Harbinger and Dominion.>

"What do you mean by that?" I queried. Something in P's aura shifted, some indescribable change in its presentation.

<If this becomes necessary,> P said.

<It may yet,> said the third Aeon.

What were the Aeon suggesting? P was deliberately hiding something from me. It was only fleeting, but that was what I detected as I witnessed the exchange. But then the moment was over, as Secretary Lopez interjected again.

"We should ready our forces for the assault," he said. "There isn't long to prepare."

<We are ready,> said Wraith. <We have waited many centuries, millennia, for this time to come. Know that we are not warriors, not like Soldier. Every death we experience; it is one fewer of our dying race.>

"We appreciate the risks you are taking," I said.

<We sense loss here too,> said Wraith. <Many have fallen in this war.>

<Many remain to fall,> echoed the second alien.

<You have lost someone,> said Wraith.

"I have," Secretary Lopez replied. "My daughter has been taken prisoner by the Black Spiral. She was—"

<No,> Wraith said. <Soldier has suffered this loss. The Pariah showed us.>

I pursed my lips. "They took one of my troopers, while we were in orbit around your planet. She...she must be returned to us."

Wraith paused. Its alien face contorted in an expression of mourning. <We know of similar losses. We lost many during the Great War. Our mate was one such casualty. We understand, Soldier.>

I felt the aliens accessing locked memories of Lopez. Her loss was still raw, and it wasn't a pleasant experience. The brief contact reminded me of what the Aeon had done when we first landed on Carcosa, and how they had manipulated the Jackals' minds. I wondered what the limits of their powers were now they were fully awakened...

"Yes, well," said Secretary Lopez, "we must use the time to reorganise our forces, in accordance with your plan."

<We will return to our vault-ships,> Wraith said.

As one, the Aeon's face-plates re-polarised. They

plodded off towards the exit hatch, accompanied by the tide of Scuttlers.

"I don't think he likes the Secretary much…" Feng said, watching them go.

<We are *she*,> said Wraith, as it left the room.

Then the trio of alien ambassadors was gone. The temperature in the compartment rose sharply.

Dr Saito approached me. I hadn't even realised that he had been present at the briefing. He grinned widely. "Well, that was utterly exhilarating," he said. "I don't think that could've gone better."

I sighed. "I wasn't very comfortable being the focus of discussions, Doc."

"They trust you," Dr Saito said. "That's an important first step."

"When P finds Warlord's location, we should be ready to deploy," I said, both to Dr Saito and the Jackals.

Zero nodded. "There are more than enough Simulant Operations bays on this ship. I'll prep some simulator-tanks, and commandeer some drop-capsules."

Secretary Lopez overheard part of our discussion. "*If* the Pariah discovers Warlord's location," he said, churlishly. "To be honest, I wasn't very impressed with the Aeon. They offer much, but whether they can deliver remains to be seen."

CHAPTER TWENTY-ONE

THE WAR FOR ITHACA

"Whatever happens here," Zero said, as we watched the final assault prep from the *Defiant*'s Command Centre, "this war will go down in history. We'll be able to say that we were here, that we saw this event happen. Kind of exciting, right?"

"Depends," said Novak.

"On what?" asked Feng.

"Whether is good or bad history," said Novak.

Zero pulled a face. "That's sort of the point, Novak. We won't know whether it's good or bad history until after the war is done."

Novak snorted. "Then I will know whether I am excited afterwards."

The five battlegroups had been reorganised according to the Aeon's suggestion. That had taken surprisingly little time, largely because the quantum-tides had been in our favour. In the wake of the Aeon's six ships, jump points became useable again, and travel time seemed to be cut in half. Whatever Secretary Lopez thought, the Aeon seemed to have proved themselves prior to the first shot being fired.

"All ships are in formation," declared a senior Navy officer, from the workpit of the CIC. "I have confirmation from all battlegroups."

The entire remaining fleet was committed to breaking through the Black Spiral cordon, heading on a course that would take us directly to Ithaca Prime. Sixteen hundred ships, representing every one of the Alliance's thirteen territories, participated in a colossal show of force.

The CIC was crowded with personnel, all hyped to watch the initial stages of the assault. Multiple veteran Sim Ops teams milled around the tactical-display, trying their best not to get in the way of the Navy crew. Several Aerospace Force officers and Off-World Marine commanders had been appointed consoles in the well of the centre, alongside high-ranking tacticians.

Captain Heinrich had a new post; overseeing the Sim Ops ground assaults. He caught my eye as he coordinated the various squad rosters across starships, preparing to deploy them in whatever way was necessary.

"Save something for the Jackals, sir," I said.

"You'll know when we need you," he replied, a smile touching the corners of his eyes. "The Jackals won't be redundant in this war."

A siren cut the air. The CIC's lights automatically dimmed, her view-ports unshuttering. The huge tri-D display in the centre of the chamber lit with targets, showing the initial approach to the Ithaca system, focusing on the Devil's Maw. As we watched, new targets appeared across the horizon: the ragged line of starships that made up the Black Spiral's fleet.

Director Mendelsohn and Secretary Lopez watched on from the sidelines. The Secretary barked directly at General Draven, Captain Heinrich, and any officer who got too close.

"I don't think that Secretary Lopez appreciated the Aeon choosing to speak with you," Zero said.

"What gave you that idea?" I said, sarcastically.

"The Secretary doesn't like it much when people get in his way," Feng muttered.

"Lopez herself said something similar, a little while ago," I commented. I bit my lip, reminding myself that she was still out there, somewhere. "We should be looking for her."

"I agree," Novak grunted. "But is politics." He turned his gaze in Secretary Lopez's direction, fixing his eyes on the man. "This Lopez; he wants to win the war no matter what. He needs it."

"Don't we all?" I countered.

"Not like him," Novak said. "We have saying in Norilsk: 'politics is shit'."

Zero tried to repress a laugh, but couldn't stop herself. Novak remained deadly serious.

"That's... that's great, Novak," Zero said, recovering her composure.

The Alliance fleet pierced the outer cordon of Spiral ships like a spear. Simultaneously, a murmur spread through the CIC. Something was happening.

"This is it," Zero said. "Here we go..."

"First contact," reported an ensign. "Battlegroup alpha is meeting resistance."

I felt the bristle around us, as fresh intelligence flooded into the tactical-display. The Alliance fleet used real-time tachyon arrays and FTL uplinks to remain in contact. The battlefront spread across the outer planets of the Ithaca star system.

<Alliance forces have reached the outer cordon around Ithaca Star,> P broadcast. It stood at the edge of the CIC. One of the many benefits of its mind-link

ability was that it could be selective: could communicate with only those it wanted to hear, such as the Jackals. <The Aeon fleet is moving into position.>

The War for Ithaca was fought largely in space, but also in the air and on the ground. Several warships deployed drop-capsules, or gunships, to the Krell outer planets. This war had its own pace, its own rhythm. Ithaca Star had a dozen planets, but many times that in moons, and the Krell had colonised extensively. All of those settlements were prone to infection by Harbinger, and all of them had to be inoculated against the contagion.

"*Deploying anti-viral warhead alpha…*" came the first report, from the *Wings of Proxima*.

A minor cheer spread through the CIC, but there was still too much at stake for any real celebration.

"Do you have confirmation that the anti-viral has taken root?" asked Director Mendelsohn, back to wringing his hands with nervous energy.

A long pause filled the CIC with silence.

"*That's a confirm,*" came an officer from the *Proxima*. "*You can thank our Aeon allies for holding off the Spiral.*"

"I think we might actually do this," Feng said, optimistically.

Over the next few hours, as the fleet punched onwards—led by the Aeon—stories of valour and bravery were everywhere. The Navy clashed with Harbinger-infected bio-ships over the moons of Cybaris; scuttling a corrupted war-fleet. In the Pavonis Straits, squadron after squadron of Hornet space fighters met with Krell Needlers, destroying over a hundred enemy ships. The Krell orbital shipyards in the Ikarian Belt were found to be rampant with Harbinger virus, with every living ship a potential carrier of the pathogen. The Navy was forced to destroy those facilities rather than deploy the anti-viral warheads, such was the level of resistance.

And everywhere, *everywhere*, was the Black Spiral.

The Spiral had been planning this event since their inception, since they had first appeared as a threat on the galactic stage. Ships of every design and origin were present in the theatre. The Spiral had numbers on their side, and they were driven by a determination that verged on fanaticism. Every body united under the Black Spiral's banner was here—from the Frontier Independence Front, to the Cult of the Singularity, to the variety of religious and terrorist groups that called themselves the Spiral's allies. The Spiral thought nothing of throwing forces against a superior opponent, and the data-feeds were filled with accounts of Black Spiral warships self-detonating in the face of defeat, or sacrificing themselves to pollute opposing Krell bio-ships. They used guerrilla tactics, demonstrating knowledge of the territory, and putting their skills as spacefarers to full effect.

There was news of incredible acts of coordination between the Krell and the Alliance. Those elements of the Krell Collective that had not been infected by Harbinger acted in concert with Alliance forces whenever and wherever possible. Bio-pods blazed the skies of dying kelp-worlds. The Reef Worlds were defended by a mixture of human and Krell allies, fighting back to back. Blood was spilt, lives were lost. This was true allegiance.

The Aeon played their part too. The six ships were almost silent, sharing their intelligence only with Pariah, but their abilities were unerringly precise when called into action. The Aeon deployed their gate-technology to shuttle ships back and forth across the region, out-manoeuvring the slower human vessels, and lancing the Harbinger virus as they encountered it. Energy weapons arced across the dead of space, from distances of thousands of kilometres. Quantum-missiles skipped in and out of existence, destroying Spiral freighters before they had even realised that they were being targeted. Still, I had the feeling that they were holding back. The Aeon were here for a purpose, and this was not it. That, I knew, was still to come.

Simulant Operations was, as ever, front and foremost in the conflict. No one knew how many personnel had been committed to the conflict, but I'd hazard a guess that there wasn't anyone left at home. Farm-ships, whose sole function was to store and produce simulants, deployed fresh skins to frontline vessels. The cost in resources was huge, but there was no alternative. This was it: pure and simple. Victory or death. Every hangar in the *Defiant* was filled with skinned-up operators, ready to drop. When the logistics of taking the fight deeper into the Reef Worlds meant that operators had to be deployed directly into the theatre, Sim Ops went without challenge, without complaint. Such was duty. Every planet captured was hard fought until the very end, and success was measured in blood.

For a time, it looked like Feng might be right. The Black Spiral and their infected allies were being pushed back towards Ithaca Prime, and were caught between the Krell forces and the advancing Alliance fleet.

"I... I'm detecting a significant energy disruption around Cybaris," said a Navy officer. "Are these results verified?"

Another officer grimaced. "Affirmative."

Zero braced over the edge of the main display, her face painted green by the tri-D graphics that appeared. P tensed up in anticipation.

"*I'm reading something big... really big, on our scanners...*" reported one ship. "*Is anyone else seeing this?*"

"We're detecting the same," said an officer from the UAS *Valiant,* sister ship to the *Defiant.* *"Can Command verify?"*

"Command verifies," said a comms officer.

"Firing on the newcomer," declared another ship.

A pregnant pause filled the CIC.

The *Ceti Dream* was on the edge of the battlegroup, anchored around Cybaris. She was a dreadnought-class warship, and had opened up with everything she had. Plasma cannons, rail guns and missiles filled the display; a blizzard of munitions and energy weapons.

"No effect," said the same ship. *"We're reporting no response."*

A Shard warship filled the display, and it was untouched by the barrage. Most of the weapons-fire was intercepted by a grid of dark matter that protected the machine-ship. Munitions detonated against the defensive network, illuminating the deep of space.

"Wings of Proxima, advance in support," one of the *Defiant's* officers ordered. "Bring all null-shields to portside amplification. *Valiant* is breaking away to provide additional firepower."

"They're firing back—" started the *Sweet Justice's* comms officer.

The Shard warship opened fire.

Dark lances of energy whipped from a jagged spire on the ship's flank. The energy beams punctured the *Justice's* null-shield with ease. They did much the same to the ship's triple-reinforced hull.

To the amazement of the *Defiant,* and the rest of the Alliance fleet, the *Justice* broke in two. Less than a second later, a ball of shadow matter—exactly what wasn't clear, as the ship's sensors were now blinded—impacted the *Justice's* energy core.

"We're hit!" yelled the vessel's captain. *"Advise that we have suffered—"*

The UAS *Justice*'s energy core erupted. The space the ship had once occupied was now just superheated plasma. The *Sweet Justice*, and her two thousand crew, had become a white smear of light against the horizon.

"By Gaia..." someone said.

"There are more of them incoming," I said.

Other Shard warships made their presence known. At first, they were no more than sensor-blinds. Dark patches, where scopes could not penetrate. Then came the squall of exotic energies, and the disturbance in the quantum. Shadow tendrils polluted realspace as the ships jumped in-system, throwing off ripples of darkness as they made transition.

"How many?" asked Secretary Lopez, numbly, although he already knew the answer.

"Ten," said the *Defiant*'s sensor operator. "Ten ships, all in the Ithaca star system."

"There may as well be a hundred..." Captain Ving muttered, with real bitterness.

I looked to Director Mendelsohn and remembered the conversation we'd had aboard the *Destiny*, before Operation Perfect Storm had launched. There, he had told me that there were ten Shard warships. His intelligence had been reliable.

Dark tides threatened Ithaca in every direction. The Alliance's fragile, crude technology was barely able to comprehend the new arrivals. Sensor-errors and scanner anomalies filled several consoles, as the Shard warships deployed countermeasures. The atmosphere in the CIC soured and morale immediately plummeted.

Rather than appearing as a combined fleet, the Shard were spread across the Ithaca system. But when they attacked, they did so as one mind. Their assault was cripplingly precise.

UAS *Valiant*, sister ship to the *Defiant*, went down with all hands, in a repeat of the *Justice*'s demise.

"The *Wings of Proxima* has taken a critical hit," said a tactical watch officer.

The *Defiant*'s captain—a dour-faced Euro-Cornfed officer—waved a hand to the reporter. "Silence those comms," he said.

"Aye, sir."

The bubble of cries for assistance, of panicked screams, that signalled the *Proxima*'s demise, fell quiet. But there was plenty more where that had come from. Warning chimes sounded across the CIC, and officers began to call in more results.

"The UAS *Triton's Heart* is requesting permission to fall back."

"*Queen of Ganymede* is no longer broadcasting."

"...*Centaur* and *Hudson* have gone down..."

"...*Intrepid* is launching her evac-pods..."

The tactical-display illuminated with emergency distress beacons. A wash of mayday broadcasts suddenly filled near-space, and the ignition of energy cores and Q-drives was marked by bright blooms of light in the void. General Draven's face grew paler and paler as losses were called in, and the reality of the situation hit him.

"This...this isn't going to plan," Secretary Lopez murmured. He sounded lost, a little broken.

<The enemy is present in great numbers,> said P. <Machine and Spiral.>

"Silence all mayday broadcasts," said the *Defiant*'s captain.

"Are you sure, sir?" responded an officer. "We may be able to save some of the crew. The *Arcturus*, for instance, is within jump distance of those pods from the *Triton's Heart*—"

"Silence the beacons!" yelled Secretary Lopez. "You heard the damned captain!"

The young officer pursed her lips and nodded.

"Until further notice," said General Draven, a hand to the officer's shoulder as though that was some sort of reassurance.

"If we lose here, there will be no point in saving anyone," said Secretary Lopez, eyes still on the tactical-display. "What are the Spiral doing around the Jagged Moons?"

More enemy ships entered the orbit of the Jagged Moons, a ring of planetoids that harboured many Krell emplacements.

"The Spiral are deploying an orbital drop," read an officer. "They...they appear to be launching warheads to the surface."

<They are re-infecting these locations,> said P. <They are using the weaponised Harbinger virus to undo the fleet's work.>

One of the Aeon vault-ships was close enough that it fired off a beam weapon at the Black Spiral's stolen freighter. White light raked the flank of the converted transport, and the vessel was easily destroyed by the superior firepower of the alien ship. At the same time, the vault-ship fired another weapon towards the unnamed moon. Something like a falling star—its energies too complex for the *Defiant*'s sensor-suite to properly compute—impacted the moon's surface.

<They have initiated the starfyre,> said P. Its mind-voice sounded mournful.

"They...they're scouring that moon," said a sensor-officer, reading the *Defiant*'s scopes. "Christo; the Aeon just cauterised it."

In one action, the planetoid had been purged of any possible Harbinger taint. It had also been reduced to a smouldering husk. A wave of colour spread from the starfyre impact site, and the planetoid's surface shifted from a verdant green, through to a dead brown.

"This was why the Shard called the Aeon the 'Great Destroyer'," said Zero. "They have weapons that can cleanse worlds."

<This is correct,> said P. <But these weapons are not to be used lightly.>

The victory—pyrrhic or otherwise—was short lived. In response, the nearest Shard warship fired another of the dark-matter spheres. The weapon snaked through space, breaching the quantum, and found the Aeon vault-ship. The Aeon vessel had no energy shielding, and the Shard weapon was remarkably effective. It punched a hole right through the hull of the other vessel. The Aeon ship faltered for a long moment, pouring liquid or debris from a hole in its hull, then broke into two. Like the surface of the moon it had purged, the xeno vessel's hull changed colour, marking the ship's death.

"They die just as easily as us…" Feng said.

"That was the first casualty they've suffered," Zero said. She sounded distressed. "They're not so invincible after all."

The Aeon vault-ship didn't explode or collapse in on itself or do anything else spectacular. It floated there, debris scattering from the open halves of the ship's hull. Perhaps those were cryo-capsules, other Aeon in deep-stasis. We'd dragged them from their hiding place, and brought them back into this war…I hoped that Wraith wasn't on the dead ship.

"Where are the rest of the Aeon?" Secretary Lopez asked. He positively raged, his face flushed, spittle flying from his lips as he spoke. "Why are they dying so easily? Tell me that, fish head?"

P's eyes glowed within its crested head but it did not answer.

The CIC fell eerily quiet, as the miasma of voices and cries—the soundtrack to the Alliance fleet's demise, to the death of the Maelstrom itself—was silenced. Secretary Lopez descended into the well of the chamber, rubbing a hand through his hair. That was slick with sweat, and his tie hung around his neck awkwardly, his whole demeanour telling of a man on the edge.

The quiet was broken by a chime from the *Defiant*'s AI.

"We're receiving an incoming transmission," said the ship's comms officer. She was almost reluctant to speak, concerned that to do so might attract Lopez's ire. "It... it's an encrypted vid-feed. From the Black Spiral fleet."

General Draven looked to Lopez. That made perfectly clear to me who was really in control of this war now, and it surely wasn't the general. Lopez nodded. The comms officer opened the vid-feed.

A holographic figure formed on the tac-display.

The Warlord of the Drift, dressed in his exo-suit and camouflage-cloak. The skull-motif of his helmet grinning back at us; a reminder of imminent death. He reached up, and activated the polarisation controls on his face-plate, exposing the scarred and rictus face beneath.

The CIC waited in silence, collective breath baited.

"Cease all hostilities now, Clade Cooper," Secretary Lopez started, stepping up to the tac-display, so that he could be seen on the other end of the communication. "We can talk a pardon, possible terms of surrender. Some of your lieutenants could be spared execution, maybe even given prison terms as an alternative..."

"Is this guy serious?" Feng asked me, his voice barely a whisper.

"I hope not."

Around the CIC, other veteran teams had the same

reaction. Sighs and expressions of incredulity filled the chamber.

"Does he even have authority to offer terms like that?" Zero said.

"He is Secretary of Defence," Novak groaned. "He does whatever he wants. As I said, politics is shit."

Warlord was utterly still, calm, as the Secretary spoke. Then a crooked, warped smile crept across his face as Lopez finished his diatribe.

Finally, Warlord spoke. "You are pathetic."

Lopez's eyes widened. "This is your final chance, Sergeant Cooper—"

"Is using that name supposed to remind me of my former life?" Warlord asked. "Do you expect me to suddenly remember duty, sacrifice and what it meant to fight on your side? It isn't working." Warlord coughed, and the sound raked the CIC: caused a tightening in my chest. Dark snakes of nano-tech—Shard Reapers—crawled across his skin, both protecting and imprisoning him. "And who are you to make demands of me? I am exactly where I want to be."

"I will order every asset in this star system, human and alien, to decimate your fleet," Lopez said. "I have the Aeon."

Warlord's smile broadened. "I have your daughter, Secretary Lopez."

Words caught in Lopez's throat. His mouth cycled, but nothing came out. My own blood froze, and I could sense the Jackals felt exactly the same way.

"Call off your attack," Warlord said. "Or this necropolis will be monument to not only the Krell, but to Gabriella Lopez too. More than anyone, Secretary, *you* know what I am capable of."

Secretary Lopez shook. "Leave her out of this, Cooper."

"What is one more life, when so many have already

been lost? I am going to bring about Dominion. I have brought the Shard here, to the Maelstrom."

"I do not negotiate with terrorists," Lopez started.

Which is exactly what you were just trying to do, I thought to myself. Maybe Novak had the right idea about politics after all.

Warlord waved a hand dismissively. "Do not follow me. Call off your attack." He bowed his head. "Dominion come, thy will be done."

The transmission ended. The CIC was filled with noise, as the gathered officers discussed what had just occurred. Secretary Lopez glared at the space where Warlord had been. Almost imperceptibly, his shoulders were shaking.

"Cease fire," General Draven said. "Order all ships to await further orders."

"Aye, sir," came a reply.

"This wasn't how it was supposed to be," Secretary Lopez said, sounding distant.

More detonations filtered across the tac-display. The fleet's numbers were dwindling at such a rate that none of this felt real. Dark splashes of shadow advanced through the void, throwing lance-beams at enemy vessels. Only the *Defiant*, as flagship of the fleet, had received Warlord's transmission, but the consequences of the communication were everywhere. Other ships were querying orders, requesting confirmation, or asking why their firing solutions had been locked out. The assault was effectively frozen.

Very gingerly, the *Defiant*'s captain cleared his throat.

"What are your orders, sir?" he asked of General Draven, although his eyes flitted to Secretary Lopez. He appeared unsure of where the true power laid. "Do we proceed with the attack, or should…should I issue the abort code?"

"We proceed," the Secretary answered, definitively.

"Even if it costs Lopez's life?" Zero said. The words spilt out of her mouth, and as she said them, I could tell that she regretted speaking.

"I said that the attack is to *proceed*," Secretary Lopez said. He ground the words out, with real anger. "If we don't get that anti-viral to Ithaca Prime then nothing will matter. Gabriella will be lost, like the rest of the universe."

"You sound like this Warlord," Novak said.

"And I'm supposed to take advice from a lifer now?" Secretary Lopez roared.

Zero made a little noise at the back of her throat, surprised by the sudden causticity of the response.

"Perhaps Sergeant Campbell has a point, sir," I said. "We could consider another approach. Perhaps an exfiltration mission could be arranged."

"Are you questioning my orders?" Lopez said.

Of course I was. Rodrigo Lopez was consigning his own daughter to a death sentence. I detected the shift in Novak's posture beside me, the change that suggested he would attack if given the order. A glance around the CIC told me that although there were many here who agreed with me, there were just as many who still supported the Secretary. Sim Ops or not, this would be the wrong kind of suicide.

Secretary Lopez snarled, "We're in this very position because you allowed my daughter to be captured, Lieutenant."

"We can put it right," I said.

"*I* should never have been put into this position," said Secretary Lopez. "Get out of here. Get all of them out of here."

"He can give orders now?" Novak said, under his breath.

No, Lopez couldn't. Or at least, he shouldn't—not if the chain of command still meant something.

"I'll see to it, sir," said Captain Ving.

"Of course, it would have to be you—" Feng said.

"Shut up, Directorate," said Ving.

He jostled me with the muzzle of his shock-rifle.

"Just go with him," said General Draven. "Captain Heinrich, take the pariah-form to the Science Deck."

There was a momentary pause before Captain Heinrich responded, his blond moustache quivering.

"Captain Heinrich?" Lopez said.

Heinrich saluted. "Yes, sir. Understood, sir."

<Go with them,> P told me, privately. No one else was privy to our mind-to-mind conversation. <We will be in contact.>

The xeno followed Captain Heinrich out of the Command Centre without complaint.

"Look," Captain Ving said, "we can do this the hard way, or the easy way." He sucked his teeth. "Which is it going to be?"

"We'll come with you."

Secretary Lopez settled into one of the command consoles, looking down at the display. "On my order, all ships are to advance towards Ithaca Prime. Regardless of loss, regardless of damage, I want the Black Spiral's fleet neutralised."

We left the Secretary to his war.

CHAPTER TWENTY-TWO

RENEGADE

The greatest war in history, and we were being benched. That was the truth of it.

Captain Ving was all business as he led us out of the CIC, a shock-rifle poised at my back. His squad of rookies fell in step beside us, eyes on Novak in particular. Anyone with even the slightest combat instinct could tell that he was eager for a fight. The Secretary's words had bruised him. Zero had that same aura about her.

"I really hope that Lopez is okay," Zero said. She shook.

"I'll bet that you're happy about this," I said to Ving, as we marched across the ship. "Finally, you get to see the end of the Jackals."

"Not at all, actually," he said. "Truth be told, Lieutenant, I think that you're all right."

"Then let us go and do something useful," Feng said.

"I like you," Ving said, "but not that much. Secretary Lopez is in charge now."

"Since when?" Zero chided. "This is a military operation, sir. General Draven is the commanding officer."

"Lopez is Secretary of Defence, Zero. He's got the power."

"So you're going to stand by while he signs his own daughter's death warrant?"

"It's not like that."

"Whatever lets you sleep at night, Ving."

"Just play along, and shut the fuck up, okay?" he hissed at me.

Captain Ving turned to his own makeshift squad. They all jumped in line, daunted by the Phoenixian's reputation.

"I'll take it from here," he said.

"The Secretary's orders, sir, were to—"

"Listen, kid," Ving muttered, swinging the shock-rifle around in the direction of the extremely youthful-looking corporal, "I got this. I've been doing this since before you were born, and I can handle these guys on my own."

The boy's face dropped. "Yes, sir. Got it, sir."

"Get down to the armoury. Run a weapons drill, in case Captain Heinrich decides to deploy us."

That cheered the squad up. They disappeared into the corridor network, and out of sight.

"What are you doing, Ving?" I asked.

We'd stopped outside the ship's main elevator shaft. Ving keyed in a destination.

"As I said, I think you're all right," he said.

The elevator doors opened, and Dr Saito stood alone in the car. He had his Army pistol in both hands, making plain that he intended to use force if necessary.

"They're coming with me," said Dr Saito.

"Are we?" Zero queried, surprised.

Instead of protesting, Captain Ving just set his jaw and nodded. "Come on. We have somewhere to be."

We piled into the elevator. "Where are we going?" Zero challenged.

"Medical Deck," said Dr Saito, locking us inside the car, and keying the appropriate location. "We need to get you to the Sim Ops Centre."

"What's going on, Ving?" I asked.

The stupid bastard lowered his weapon and grinned at me. "You're not the only one that the fish can talk to privately."

The lift descended through the decks, and my dataports started to throb.

"Will Secretary Lopez come looking for us?" Zero asked.

"Quit with the worrying," Ving said. "There's a war going on. No one will notice that you're missing until it's too late. And, anyway, I'm as bound up in this as the rest of you. No one will question the Phoenixian."

"Still," said Dr Saito, "it never hurts to be sure."

Saito racked the slide on his pistol, readying it for use, then rearranged his white smock, like an impersonator checking on his disguise. That was very much how I was coming to think of Wesley Saito...

"You're unbelievable," I said. "Do you even know how to shoot that thing?"

"I thought that you'd be in a better mood, what with the fact that we've just sprung you from Alliance detention."

"Oh, we're grateful," Feng said. "That's for sure."

"But we weren't detained," said Zero. "Not technically, anyway."

"No one gets you out of thing like that without reason," Novak completed. "And I would like to know reason. Now."

Dr Saito ignored Novak's implied threat, and said,

"I'll tell you, as soon as we reach the SOC. Captain Heinrich and Pariah are meeting us down there. I told you that I had a mission, Lieutenant."

"Is this more Watch crap, Doctor?" I asked.

"Hold on," Zero said, to Saito. "So you're working for the Watch?"

"Get over it, Zero," I replied. "Dr Saito told me after the Sons of Balash attacked the *Valkyrie*."

"And you didn't think to tell us?" Feng said.

"What was there to tell? I'm not sure that I really believed it, at the time. Have you made contact with any of your assets, Dr Saito?"

"There are none immediately available," Dr Saito said.

I shook my head. "See? How convenient."

The elevator car chimed, and the doors peeled open. The deck was busy with operators hustling to and from their tanks. The familiar scent of amniotic and body odour hit me, and the tang of anticipation grew stronger at the back of my throat. True to promise, Captain Heinrich and P were waiting outside the elevator.

"Come along, troopers," said Heinrich, playing the part as well. "You've got a mission to undertake."

No one challenged him, and no one paid us any attention. He approached the deck manager—the officer responsible for allocating Sim Ops bays to individual squads—and started arguing with him. What with so many squads being deployed simultaneously, bays were in high demand, and the ops officer wasn't allocating one easily. Meanwhile, P used the mind-link to speak with the Jackals.

<We will explain,> it said. <Warlord is part of the Deep. We are also of the Deep. There are advantages to being connected in this way. We were able to trace the

Warlord's location. Lopez-other and Warlord may be on the same ship. We must act on this information.>

"Fuck yes," said Novak, unable to contain himself.

"That's the best news I've heard all day," Feng said, also out loud. Neither of them really had the hang of this mind-communications thing…

Captain Heinrich had finished negotiating with the ops manager, and hustled us along to a vacant bay. I noticed that he, too, had a pistol holstered at his thigh. It seemed like no one was taking chances any more.

"Can you seal us into this bay?" Dr Saito asked.

"Yes," said Captain Heinrich. He activated the hatch controls, and I noticed that his hands trembled a little. "I take it that Pariah has updated you on the position?"

"Yes, sir," I said. "I'm still not quite sure why you'd want to help us…"

"I'm not helping you," said Captain Heinrich. "Or at least, I'm not helping just you. I'm not happy about doing this, but your trooper can't die out there. Not like that. Not after what we did in the Ghost Maker Nebula. If it comes to it, I'll burn each and every one of you, but as things stand…I'm not sure that Secretary Lopez is the right man to be in command of this operation."

Captain Heinrich was right: Secretary Lopez was becoming increasingly unhinged. Heinrich was tight with General Draven, but that relationship wouldn't save him any more.

"Is that a very long way of saying you disagree with his orders?" I queried.

"I suppose it is," Heinrich replied.

"We'll make a renegade out of you yet…" Zero said.

"It's going to be okay, sir," I said.

Captain Heinrich scowled at me. "I wish I shared

your optimism, Lieutenant. This is all new to me. I'm not used to countermanding orders."

I shrugged. "It gets easier the more you do it."

"You're trouble."

"It's been said before."

There was a violent shudder through the deck and some shouting from the corridor outside.

<We are taking fire,> explained P. <Already, the Black Spiral forces are resisting the advance.>

Zero powered up the main operations console. She pulled her seat close to the monitors, and adjusted the various vid-screens so that they were to her liking.

"Then what's the mission plan?" she asked.

<Warlord approaches Ithaca Prime,> said P, <on a vector that will take his ship through the Kalliper Belt, into the Ring of Thorns.>

A flight-path illuminated on the main display. P had already plotted a route, through the Ring of Thorns, inbound to Ithaca Prime itself. There were questions here—like how the hell did P manage to do this at such short notice?—but they weren't for now. P's abilities had developed to such a level that none of this really surprised me any more.

Dr Saito sat in a chair next to Zero, looking at the tri-D imagery. "We haven't shared this intelligence with Secretary Lopez, or anyone else in the fleet. I hope the reasons for that are obvious."

The simulator-tanks started to hum as they powered up, and filled with conducting fluid. I stripped out of my uniform.

"How are we going to get to Warlord's location?" I asked.

"Drop-capsule," Captain Heinrich answered. "I've authorised the launch."

"P and I will stay on the *Defiant*," said Dr Saito.

"Can the Aeon help us?" asked Zero.

P paused. <The Aeon are preparing for the next stage of this operation. We have been in communication with Wraith.>

"They are currently engaging the Shard warships, in orbit around several inner planets," Dr Saito explained. "We can't bank on them doing much more at this stage."

"I'll cover the SOC while you're operational," Captain Ving promised.

I was inside my tank now, clasping the respirator to my face, putting my earbead in place.

"So," I said, testing the comms, "all we need to do is find Warlord, save Lopez, and wait for the rest of the fleet to mop things up. The anti-virus gets delivered to Ithaca Prime, and the war is over."

"This sounds too easy…" Feng said, also inside his tank.

"I'm sure that it won't be," I muttered.

"Is better than sitting in cell," said Novak, snapping himself inside his tank as well.

In turn, I attached each of the data-cables to my ports, feeling the buzz of the transition beginning to overwhelm me.

"If we approach Warlord's ship with drop-capsules," I said, "won't he see us coming?"

Dr Saito tapped his neck. "Remember those stealth bands? Well, they can be adapted for use with drop-capsules as well."

"You fucking Watch guys and your toys…"

Another shudder through the ship's spaceframe reminded me that we were on the clock.

"I'm ready when you are," declared Zero, poised over her console. "The capsules are loaded, and the launch coordinates are fixed."

<The Spiral will likely attempt to board this ship, when the time comes,> said P. <We will be their target.>

"I'll take care of that," said Ving, checking that his rifle was armed.

"Just make sure that Dr Saito doesn't kill himself with that pea-shooter," I said. "Zero, send us in."

Captain Heinrich saluted. "Don't disappoint me, Jackals."

"Good luck," Zero said.

I laughed. "Fuck luck, Z. Fuck luck."

Zero turned to her console. "Transition in three... two... one..."

Snap.

Eyes open. Breathe deep. Keep breathing.

Oxygen. Atmosphere.

Another new skin.

The dark of a drop-capsules interior. Cold, but not the freeze of space. That came later...

The armourglass shield of a face-plate was directly in front of me. I was wearing a combat-suit, tactical-helmet and all. The armour's intelligence systems booted immediately, and made uplink to the Alliance battle-net. I thought-commanded maximum encryption. A new icon appeared on my HUD, flashing intermittently. Dr Saito's stealth device was operational.

"Transition confirmed," I said.

"Copy that," said Feng.

"And here," said Novak.

Another shudder through the *Defiant*'s spaceframe, this time more aggressive.

"Are we still taking hits?" I asked.

"Affirmative," said Zero. No time to waste, she asked, "Are you ready to drop?"

"Born ready, Z. Born ready."

"And will die ready, too," said Novak.

"Who wants to live for ever, right?" I asked.

Novak's raucous laughter was swallowed by white noise, as the drop-capsules launched from the *Defiant*.

The trio of drop-capsules launched into space.

As we powered onwards towards our destination, my Pathfinder suit's AI built up a picture of the surrounding sector. Real-time updates on the war flooded my HUD, providing me with an overview of the fleet's progress. The *Defiant* was taking fire. Her point defence systems were working overtime, targeting incoming munitions and warheads. There were a series of blistering explosions at the perimeter of the *Defiant*'s null-shield, as energy weapons were ablated. In the vacuum of space, everything played out in a disconnected silence.

"Whoah!" Feng yelled, his breathing ragged and shallow over the comms.

Somewhere among the tangle of debris and dying ships that was the War for Ithaca, space seemed to warp. Searing white light licked the dark, and the battle-net flickered erratically.

"What was that?" Novak asked. Drops, and anything to do with zero-G in general, had never been Novak's thing; he sounded on the verge of being sick.

"Ah, I'm not sure," came Zero's clipped voice. "The conflict is progressing rapidly."

<It is the Aeon,> came a sudden intrusion into my head.

"That you, P?"

<No. It is the Governor of Proxima Colony. Who else would it be?>

Whereas Zero's voice was hazed with static, P's mind-link was crystal clear.

"So this hyper-evolution bullshit has given you a sense of humour as well?"

<Wraith has engaged, and successfully terminated, one of the Shard warships.>

"Tell her to do that again."

<She is attempting to out-manoeuvre another vessel,> P said. <The odds of success are limited.>

"Have the Aeon suffered any more casualties?"

<Not yet. We are in regular contact with Wraith and her Enclave.>

"Keep it that way."

The drop-capsules initiated second-stage thrust, and I felt the tug of acceleration across my body.

"Almost there," I said.

"Good," replied Novak.

"Aren't you glad that you didn't eat breakfast now, Big Man?" Feng asked.

Novak snarled. "Have not eaten in days. Am very hungry, in fact."

"Eating can wait," I said. "While Lopez is out there with the Spiral, at least."

Soon, we were behind enemy lines: inside the Black Spiral's cordon. The Kalliper Belt stretched out before us. It looked, for all intents, very much like the Drift; that ring of dangerous debris that surrounded the Maelstrom. The Ring of Thorns—the moon-sized asteroids that orbited Ithaca Prime—appeared behind the debris-field of the Belt. The field was dense here, and had obviously not been caused by the current conflict, but something more ancient. Maybe this was a remnant of the first war, of the last time that the Shard walked this area of the Milky Way. The press of history, of the ages, was everywhere. Ithaca Prime was visible through the band of rubble, her ocean's surface reflecting the light of the local star. The planet was distant, and yet still so very close.

I closed my eyes as the well of memories—memories that were not mine, but I nonetheless felt—poured over me. Even at this distance, my suit's scopes could pick up the huge nest bases—continent-sized, sprawling over land and sea. Green and blue mixed in equal measure; gigantic kelp-beds crossing the hemisphere, swamplands merging with shallow seas. In the deep alien forests, the Krell observed, aware through their connection with the Deep that war was coming. The Great Nest bases were hives of activity, as every bio-form capable of fighting was mustered.

"It's…kind of beautiful," said Zero, dragging me from my thoughts. "No Alliance eyes have ever seen this place, up close."

"Is main fish world," said Novak. "Yes?"

"This is where it all started," I muttered.

"People have worked, fought, died, to find this place," Zero said. "And now we're here, trying to save it. Feels like this should be more of a moment or something."

"Moments are for people like Secretary Lopez," I said. "We're just getting a job done."

I felt fear. Real, tangible fear. The Krell Deep Ones knew what was at stake, and they knew Harbinger was coming for them.

P initiated a private mind-link with me.

<If Warlord reaches Ithaca Prime, and specifically the Deep Ones,> it said, <they will be irremediably infected. The entire Krell species will fall to Harbinger.>

I know, P, I said, answering privately as well.

<If this occurs,> P went on, <we do not think that the anti-virus will be an effective remedy.>

How can you tell?

<We have accessed Science Division's mainframe. The predictive models are…concerning. We are certain that the anti-virus would be insufficient.>

Then what would our options be, if Warlord does succeed?

A long pause. <There would be two.>

Go on.

<The Aeon could initiate their starfyre weapon. This would erase Ithaca Prime, and the Deep. There would be consequences for the entire Kindred Collective.>

Not good ones, I take it?

<All history, all Deep-knowing, would be gone.>

What's the second option?

<We do not wish to discuss that at this time.>

My suit's sensor-suite pinged an alert.

"I'm reading multiple ships," said Feng. "Many, many signals, in fact."

The Black Spiral fleet infested the Kalliper Belt. Despite the heavy losses that the Spiral had suffered, there were still hundreds of ships here. Like fleas on a dog, they jumped between the asteroids, using them as cover, advancing on Ithaca Prime. Many did not even bother to shield their identification tags, and we read their data remotely. From stolen military transports to corporate leisure cruisers, these ships had come from all over the Alliance. Infected Krell bio-ships sailed with the Spiral fleet. Those vessels were bloated and swollen with Harbinger virus, and trailed bio-matter as they limped onwards towards their target. All in, I identified over three hundred possible hostiles hiding in the Kalliper Belt.

"Well isn't that just great..." Feng complained. "How are we supposed to find a single ship among that mess?"

<It is taken care of,> answered P.

The thruster unit of my drop-capsule kicked in, and I jinked portside. The sudden acceleration was jarring, but I saw what had happened. A single ship was highlighted on my HUD, and was now our objective. The *Iron Knight*. Warlord's ship.

"What did we ever do without you, huh, P?" I asked.

<Not very much,> P answered.

"Can the Black Spiral fleet see us?" I asked. "Are these stealth bands, or whatever they are, actually working?"

"You're still running dark," said Dr Saito, over the comm from the SOC. "The Spiral won't be able to find you unless they conduct a visual check."

Given the utter mess that was the asteroid field, and the ongoing conflict, the chances of that were slim to none. That was slightly reassuring, if nothing else.

"Priorities then, troopers," I said. "We get onto the ship. We find Lopez. We exfiltrate her."

"How are we going to do that?" Feng asked, his voice vibrating as his capsule initiated another wave of thrust.

"We'll improvise," I said. "Use whatever craft we have available locally."

"That would be your best option," Zero agreed. "Maybe they have a dropship, or perhaps an evacuation-pod?"

"We'll look out for one. Coming up on the objective."

"I see it," said Feng.

Knife-like, we slid through the Kalliper Belt and made for the *Iron Knight*.

CHAPTER TWENTY-THREE

EXTREME PREJUDICE

The drop-capsules shed the final layer, and I took over thrust with my EVAMP.

"Touching down," I declared, over the comms. "Stay in formation, Jackals."

I grasped the *Iron Knight*'s hull, activating the mag-lock grips in my gloves and the soles of my boots. Feng landed next to me, with practised ease. Novak did his best, but sort of tumbled along the hull, grunting as he snagged an armour plate and finally came to a stop. Behind his armourglass visor, he looked pasty green and nauseous, with wet spittle on his lips.

"I have not been sick," he insisted.

"Well, that's an improvement," muttered Feng.

The *Iron Knight* was a medium-class transport ship. Millions just like her flew Alliance space lanes, shipping cargo to and from the Core Systems. This ship, however, had been substantially upgraded. It wasn't the original *Iron Knight* that Commander Dieter had once flown—that ship had been a proper military starship—but Warlord had obviously named it in memory of the lost vessel. That image of Commander Dieter, her face looming large behind the glass of the airlock hatch, came back to me.

"We need to get inside, and fast," I said.

"Agreed," said Feng. He'd unshouldered a demo-charge, and was already priming it to breach the *Knight*'s hull. "Just tell me where to blow a hole, and I'm good to go."

"No," I said, shaking my head inside my helmet. "We can't risk losing atmosphere. Lopez is in her real skin." I selected an airlock, further along the hull, and flagged it on our battle-net. "We'll take the hatch."

Feng immediately moved on the location, using long loping strides, one boot always in contact with the hull. He popped open an emergency access panel next to the airlock, and unpacked a hacking tool from his belt.

"This won't take long," said Feng. "The access codes aren't even protected."

Novak moved up too. He gazed out across the Kalliper Belt, sweeping the vista with his enhanced vision.

"The *Svetlana* is out there," Novak said, his voice quiet and surprisingly calm. "Vasnev is here. She must've delivered Lopez."

"Eyes on the prize, Novak," I said. "Remember our talk."

He grimaced and nodded. "I remember."

"Hatch breached," declared Feng.

Through the inner lock, we emerged into a storage bay.

"We're in," I whispered into my communicator. "We're on the *Iron Knight*."

"Copy that," Zero said.

Déjà vu swept over me as we entered the ship. The Jackals had first seen the *Iron Knight* during the operation on Daktar Outpost when they had been new recruits. The squad had attempted to rescue Major

Sergkov—who had become our commanding officer, for a time—from the Black Spiral. Ghost memories teased at the edge of my consciousness. So many had been lost in this war: Major Sergkov, Captain Carmine, Commander Dieter...

Zero dragged me out of it. "Is your position safe?"

"Appears to be. No immediate response to entry."

Graphics demonstrating the ship's layout were projected onto my HUD. The *Iron Knight* was a decent-sized ship, but as with most vessels of this type, only a small proportion of her mass was dedicated as living space. I painted those areas for possible investigation. Meanwhile, my bio-scanner also activated. There were life-signs all around me. That gave me crew numbers. Other, more specific data also filtered across my HUD.

"I have Lopez's location," I said. Her bio-ID chip blazed on my scanner, indicating not only her position but also her vital signs. Her heartbeat was steady, within acceptable tolerances. "She's alive. They're holding her in a compartment towards the aft."

"What's your immediate location?" Zero asked.

"We're in a storage bay."

Aboard the ship, we were now in artificial gravity. Novak had popped on his suit-lamps, and was panning them over the darkened interior of the locker. Stacked crates and boxes filled the chamber. There were muted lights in the dark, accompanied by the gentle hiss of operational cryogenic tech.

"Holy Christo..." Feng said, as Novak's beams illuminated one corner of the bay. "We...just hit the motherlode."

Feng and Novak's bio-signs spiked as I saw what they had found. Gooseflesh crept over my simulated skin, and revulsion crested in my chest.

"You should get moving," Zero suggested.

"Hang on," I said. "We're going to be here for a few minutes. We have a job to do, before we recover Lopez."

I pulled the sidearm from my thigh-holster. A PPG-13 plasma pistol: an old classic. Checked the ammo loadout, and the spare power cell at my belt.

Novak unslung his plasma rifle. "What do you want us to do?"

"We clean up our own mess," I said, nodding at the cryogenic tanks. "Quietly and quickly."

Task done, Novak opened the storage bay doors, and we slipped into the corridor beyond. My bio-scanner confirmed that the immediate area was empty, which gave me a moment to plot our next move.

We knew where Lopez was located, but Warlord could be anywhere on the ship. Our Pathfinder combat-suits still carried a full complement of drones, and we could map the ship with those. I didn't want to risk using them though, because a drone could give away our position. Dr Saito's stealth-tech was so far masking our bio-signs. We had the element of surprise, and I wanted to keep it that way.

The bulkheads were studded with glow-globes, set to minimum illumination, which gave the place an eerie twilight feel. Here, away from the horror show of the war, the air smelt of cooking, and of body odour. The Spiral and their allies were committing universe-wide xeno-cide, and yet life aboard the *Iron Knight* went on as it always had. Did these bastards truly realise what they were doing? I had my doubts. I remembered the discussion that Feng and I had, after the attack on Sanctuary. En masse, the Black Spiral didn't really understand Warlord's goal. He said the right things, promised the impossible. People listened, and heard what they wanted to hear. That was the human way.

"We're approaching the aft compartments," I said to Zero.

"We read," she replied.

Lopez's life-sign was close, but so were other life-forms. I tuned my helmet's audio receptors and listened to the conversation between several men in the next chamber.

"...*won't matter any more*," said one. The words were in Russian, and were translated in real-time by my suit's AI. Everything came back to me in an electronic drone, but the original words sounded slurred, perhaps a little drunk.

Novak recognised the language. I caught his eyes in the dark, and nodded at him to remain still. This was as good an indication as any that Major Vasnev was either on this ship, or certainly in this region of space.

"You don't understand," said the second man, in Standard. "He is the One Truth. This isn't just some silly adventure for me."

"*He gives creeps*," said the third man, also in Russian. "*Is not man any more.*"

That could only be a reference to Warlord. I tightened the grip on my pistol.

"*There won't be anything left but Warlord*," said the first man. "*He will see all true believers through. Dominion will come.*"

There was a clatter of metal on metal, the splash of liquid in a cup. A jubilant cheer from the group. That was followed by an angry sigh. I'd recognise that petulant voice anywhere. It was Lopez.

"*I wish we could kill the girl*," said one of the group. "*Or...at least do something with her.*"

There was a round of hoarse, alcohol-tinged laughs.

Lopez didn't react, because she didn't understand Russian, but it did make me wonder what condition she was in. My hand dropped to a grenade in my webbing, and I realised that I was stroking it: desperate to use some ordnance, to kill some shit. The sim body was raging with hormones and combat-drugs. No. I'd have to do this quietly, quickly, and with minimum collateral damage. I might be in a sim, but Lopez was here for real. Her skin wasn't expendable.

"We're in position," I said. Licked my lips. "Get ready to do this, Jackals."

Novak slid a mono-knife from the sheath on his chest. "You want I should go in first?" he asked.

I nodded. "You take point. I'll go next. Feng, you cover the corridor and take out any stragglers."

"Solid copy," said Feng.

"Here goes."

The hatch peeled open, and the chamber immediately reacted.

Two gangers-turned-mercenary wearing tactical flak vests, sitting around a metal table. Playing cards, with credit chips piled between them. Three tin cups, an opened bottle of alcohol. A third man, wearing a beat-up survival suit. Younger than the others, with a Proximan look about his features.

The gangers went for sidearms holstered on their hips, while the Proximan dashed across the chamber.

"Alert! Alert!" that one yelled, fingers grasping for a control box on the wall. "Alert! Alert!"

Headsets were piled on the table. No comms with the rest of the ship. That control box was their only lifeline.

Novak saw it too. He vaulted the chamber, knife slashing in a deadly arc. He caught the tango in the shoulder. The oversized combat blade activated, and the wound it cut through the hostile's survival suit sprayed arterial blood across the chamber. The body went down, and Novak went with it. Slashing again and again for good measure.

I raised my pistol and fired once at the first ganger. The plasma bolt hit the tango in the torso, sent him toppling into the table. A column of smoke rose from the charred crater that had been his chest.

The third man grabbed the bottle from the table, and threw it at me. Reflexively, my arm went up. The glass shattered against my suit, sending droplets of alcohol across the room. It only succeeded in irritating me. The ganger upended the table, using it as a makeshift shield. He drew his pistol and rolled behind the barricade.

Feng charged forward, foot against the thin metal. Fired twice. Once in the body, once in the head. The tango slid against the bulkhead, life-signs extinct.

By rights, it shouldn't have happened, but another figure appeared at the hatch. A Spiral disciple, clad in a hard-suit, carrying an assault rifle. Maybe attracted by the noise, perhaps coming to check on the prisoner: it didn't really matter. The woman's face went rigid as she assessed what had happened.

"What the—" she began.

Novak whirled about. His knife cut another arc.

The woman's finger closed on the trigger of her rifle. A spray of AP rounds hit Novak in the chest. At such close range, the volley of bullets punched right through his null-shield, and then his armour.

"Novak!" Lopez yelled.

Novak's body spun and noisily impacted the upturned table. His vitals flatlined on my HUD. USER NOVAK, LEON: EXTRACTED, my suit told me.

The woman looked almost surprised by the success of her shot, and momentarily paused in the doorway, before bringing her rifle around to open up again. I put her down with a single plasma bolt to the head. Her corpse folded in the hatch, gun clattering to the deck.

"Christo…Everyone will have heard that."

Gabriella Lopez sat behind an observation-field, like the one we had used to imprison Riggs aboard the *Valkyrie*. She was being held in a small sub-chamber, sitting on an upturned cargo crate.

"You okay, Lopez?" I asked her.

"I am now, ma'am."

"You injured?"

She shook her head. "No."

I looked her over with my suit's remote scanner-tech. She still wore her Alliance Army uniform, which was bloodstained, but my scanner confirmed that nothing was broken that couldn't be fixed. Barring some superficial lacerations to the forehead, Lopez looked in reasonable shape. She dropped off the crate, and stood in front of the obs-field, eagerly looking out into the rest of the chamber.

"You can get me out of here now," she said.

"Of course."

Feng activated the field controls, and the energy barrier dropped. There was no audible alarm, which was good, and my suit didn't detect any silent warning tech either. Lopez bolted out of the cell, stepping around the corpse Novak had just made.

"We're sprung," I said, warily. "Get that body in here, Feng."

"Affirmative," said Feng. He hauled the Spiral woman's body into the chamber, leaving a smear of bright red blood across the deck. "Someone is going to see this."

"We don't have time for a proper clean-up," I decided. "Glad to have you back, Lopez."

"I'm glad to be back. Where exactly are we? I felt the ship moving under thrust. They took me from the *Svetlana* to here."

"To cut a long story short: you're on Warlord's ship, the *Iron Knight*, in an asteroid belt around Ithaca Prime."

Lopez's eyes widened. "Ithaca?"

"We brought the Aeon here, but the Spiral were waiting. They're fighting alongside Shard warships. Unless we can stop it, the entire system is going to fall to Harbinger. That's a highly summarised version of events, but you get the picture."

"It'll probably do for now," agreed Feng.

"We've re-joined the fleet, and we're skinned up aboard the *Defiant*."

"In contravention of your father's orders," Feng grimaced.

Lopez didn't look surprised by that, which struck me as another example of the strange relationship she had with the Secretary.

I made uplink to Zero. "Z, we have Lopez. We'll exfiltrate her, then commence the search for Warlord."

"Solid copy," came Zero's static-tinged reply. I could hear the relief in her voice.

"What's your status?"

"Not good. Heavy losses all around. The fleet is burning up around Ithaca Prime, but Secretary Lopez is pushing on."

"Novak's extracted," I said.

"Received," Zero replied.

"Keep an eye on him. Is the SOC secure?"

"For now," was the most she could promise.

"All right. Don't worry about Novak. I'll sort it when I get back."

"Copy that."

"Jackals out."

"Zero out." I turned to Lopez. "Get armed. We could run into trouble."

Lopez reached for a pistol, one of the weapons dropped by her guards. She checked the loadout, nodding to herself, and racked the slide. Then reached for another pistol, doing the same, tucking the second weapon into the small of her back.

"You can never have enough firepower," she said, "especially when it's cheap-ass, mass-manufactured Russian shit."

"I can still remember when you used to be afraid of guns," Feng said.

Lopez smiled wanly. "A lot has changed since then. Is P okay?"

"It's fine," I said. "Tougher than it looks, and all that."

"I hear you."

"It came out of the chrysalis, and it's better than ever."

Still, I noticed something. When I reached out to try to connect with P, it wasn't responding. The sensation wasn't the same as when P had been in hibernation; more that P didn't *want* to answer me.

"What's our plan of retreat?" Lopez asked.

"We'll head for the evacuation-pods," I said, "and launch one into the belt."

Feng deployed into the corridor. Lopez followed me out, moving fast but with caution. Through one deck, down a ladder-shaft to the next. Across the crew quarters, picking the right moment to move, hiding when necessary. That was no easy task, wearing full armour. The combat-suit was big, and not made for stealth. It made noise when it moved, from the whine of hydraulics to the thump of boots against the deck. Still, we did okay. The Black Spiral weren't soldiers, and they obviously thought that they were safe out here, hidden in the asteroid belt. Unless, or until, someone went to check on Lopez and her guards…

A thought nagged me. Riggs might be on this ship. I was almost within touching—*killing*—distance, and the idea that he could survive this encounter pained me. Almost absently, I realised that I'd marked the location

of the medical bay, where the Sons or the Spiral or whoever, had likely set up Riggs' simulator. Was I going to
leave that technology intact? But a glance back at Lopez
told me that I had to focus on what actually mattered.
Riggs could wait. There would be other chances.

Really? the voice of doubt argued. *Because you keep
saying that, and Riggs keeps getting away…*

"The evac-pod bay is ahead," Feng said.

The corridor was quiet and still; half a dozen circular
portals in the bulkhead, each leading to a pod. I covered
Lopez as she approached the first hatch, peering inside
the letterbox view-port.

"Open the door," I ordered, sweeping the corridor
with my scanner. "Keep the area covered, Feng."

There were life-signs around us, but not in the immediate vicinity. Several clustered on the deck above…
They've found the empty cell, I realised.

Feng sealed the corridor, shutting the hatch behind
us. The panel that controlled the lights in this sector was
unprotected, and he activated that too: throwing the pas-
sage into darkness. Emergency warning labels on the
deck lit, providing Lopez with enough illumination to
see by. Then Feng took up a position at the neck of the
corridor. Ready.

The evac-pod hatch hissed open, producing a warning chime that echoed down the corridor. Although
there was no one else around to hear it, the noise made
me wince. Lopez reacted in the same way. A wave of
stale atmosphere escaped from the open pod.

"It's clear," said Lopez.

"Great. Get inside."

Four plastic crash couches were arranged in formation, facing a basic control panel, and an open view-port.
Lopez hustled into the pilot's seat, pulling at the harness

straps. Her breath produced a plume of white vapour as she breathed out.

"Shit, it's cold in here," she complained.

"You Proximans are all the same," I said, eyes both on her and on the scanner on my HUD. "Always with the cold. Just get on with it."

"Are we compromised?"

Bright bio-signs were converging around us.

"Yes," I answered. No point in dressing it up. "Initiate the launch sequence."

Lopez wasted no time. She put her pistol on the dashboard and began to cycle through the launch codes. Military or civilian, evacuation tech worked in much the same way. The pod launched, and then the craft's transmitter sent out a mayday code to anyone listening. Alliance Army infantry were taught the essentials during Space Tech training, and there was very little skill involved. I could see Lopez checking off the necessaries in her head...

"Seal the pod, Lopez," Feng said, reading his own scanner. "They're almost on us. Do it now!"

"What's the delay?" I asked.

"I don't know! The launch sequence won't start!"

Bio-signs were everywhere now. *Fuck. Fuck. Fuck.* Voices through the air-shafts. The clatter of boots on the deck. Feng was crouched further up the corridor, covering the approach. I glanced in the other direction, which led deeper into the *Iron Knight*.

"The launch codes are blocked." Lopez looked up at me, face grim. She scrambled with the harness again, pulling herself free. "This isn't going to work."

I opened a comm-channel to the *Valkyrie*. "Zero, do you read? Zero, come in!"

"We copy," said Zero. Her voice was so lost to static

now that I could barely hear her. "What's happening? The *Iron Knight*'s weapons systems are going active, and her drive is igniting."

"We're in trouble. Heavy resistance, inbound. The pod launch is restricted. Can you run a remote override?"

"I can't do that at this distance," Zero conceded.

"Just try!" I yelled. I wasn't losing Lopez on this ship. "Ask Dr Saito for help!"

"Could you try another pod?" Zero suggested.

If that had ever been a practical solution, it wasn't any longer. Warning lamps flashed above each pod, text blinking in red LED. ACCESS RESTRICTED. No prizes for guessing what had happened there. This was the only way off the ship, and the Spiral knew it. The ship's AI began to broadcast a message: "*This is a security lockdown. Transport on or off this vessel is now prohibited.*"

There was hammering on the hatch at the end of the corridor. Yelling.

"They're here," Feng said, cutting short any further suggestion that we might be able to get out of this by stealth.

"Stay in the pod, Lopez, and keep trying," I said. "Feng: provide covering fire."

The hatch at the end of the corridor opened, and Spiral spilt in. Four targets, armed, armoured.

Feng answered their intrusion with a volley of plasma bolts. The energy discharge seared the area, killing two tangos before they had a chance to evade.

A third yelled "Dominion come!", and opened fire with an assault rifle. Rounds bounced off the deck, ricocheting in the closed environment. My combat-suit's null-shield activated to repel some of the assault.

"Lopez, stay in the fucking pod!" I ordered.

Lopez ignored me. She was at the open hatch, shooting with her stolen pistol.

"If we're dying here, this is my call, ma'am," she said.

I shook my head. "You're too stubborn for your own good."

"That's what Daddy always tells me."

The gunfire intensified. In the flash created by muzzle-flare, bodies advanced towards us. The distance wasn't great—maybe twenty or thirty metres—but the tangos were paying for it in blood. Screams accompanied the report of guns firing, the hiss of plasma tech. I snapped the activator on my grenade and hurled it underarm in the direction of the attackers.

"Fire in the hold!" I yelled.

Feng scrambled to safety.

The frag grenade detonated. The corridor shuddered and bodies were thrown in every direction by the blast. My null-shield flared brightly—a sphere of blue energy forming around me, ablating the incoming frag. The noise was deafening.

Another null-shield—the same as mine—lit at the end of the corridor.

"What the actual fuck are you doing here, Keira?"

The voice pierced the racket, scything through me like a mono-knife. The distinctive outline of a body in a Class III combat-suit advanced through the smoke and debris. An identifier tag danced over the newcomer.

CORPORAL RIGGS, DANEB.

EXECUTE WITH EXTREME PREJUDICE.

"Holy fucking Gaia…" I whispered. "Feng, take Lopez."

"Ma'am…" Feng started to argue.

"*Now!*" I yelled. "Get her out of here!"

Feng didn't argue with me any more. He grabbed Lopez, and hauled ass down the corridor. Riggs let them go. I was quite sure that wasn't out of any sense of decency. Rather, I was his focus. He wore no helmet, but he was in a sim. His eyes narrowed and jaw set; determination etched into his features.

"No fish to protect you this time?" he said.

"I don't need anything, or anyone, to protect me from you."

"This won't—"

There was an ear-splitting crunch throughout the *Iron Knight*'s hull. The deck underfoot quaked violently, the ship's spaceframe vibrating just as furiously. An emergency lamp in the deckhead began to strobe, filling the corridor with red light.

"What the fuck have you done, Keira?" Riggs asked.

CHAPTER TWENTY-FOUR

END OF THE LINE

I managed to remain standing, which was a minor miracle given the force of the impact that the *Iron Knight* had just suffered. A ringing filled my ears, which resolved into a voice.

"I am in hangar bay," said Novak. "Am here to help."

Novak's vitals were resurrected on my suit-sensors. He'd made transition again, and was back on the *Knight*. How and why he had done this would have to wait.

"Feng, get Lopez to the hangar bay!" I shouted, overloud, to compensate for the other noise.

I cancelled a dozen warnings that filled my HUD, searching for only one: Lopez's life-signs. She and Feng were further down the corridor. Intact. That was a better result than I'd expected.

"Solid copy," Feng answered. "Lopez, run!"

Lopez recovered her composure fast and began down the corridor, to another hatch at the far end. Feng popped his Widowmaker pistol to cover their retreat, while I faced off against Daneb Riggs.

Riggs bolted, snarling at me as he gained speed, the

strength-amplifiers in his combat-suit whining as they took his weight.

"I'll find my father, Jenkins," he chanted, voice roaring from the external speakers of his armour. "He isn't dead! You'll see!"

"All this is to prove a point?"

I bounced off the wall, using my EVAMP to gain momentum, and collided with Riggs. Armour on armour, our bodies pirouetted together.

In a sim, Riggs was just as fast as me, but nowhere near as angry. He had his plasma pistol up. Fired. A bolt of blue energy lanced past me, barely missing my head as I turned it aside. I slammed into Riggs' body with my shoulder, driving all of my weight into the impact.

Riggs grunted. He tumbled away, an arm out to break his fall.

"Oh no you don't," I said.

I grabbed him, and pounded my fist into his face. He wore no helmet, and there was a satisfying crunch as something broke. Blood droplets poured from his face, tiny red marbles spraying the walls of the chamber. He yelped in pain. His nose was broken, and probably his jaw too.

He lurched towards me, throwing a backhanded blow at my head. I dodged again, and he hit the wall. Gravity was scrambled now, becoming twisted. Riggs' shoulder-guard smashed against the bulkhead. One arm went limp, and Riggs' howl suggested the pain was intense. I lurched over him, slamming a fist into his stomach.

The armour plating of Riggs' suit gave beneath my powered blow, and he jerked away again. Trying to put distance between us, Riggs spun backwards, bouncing off the far wall, making the most of the fractured gravity.

"I'm done here," he growled, through a mouthful of

blood. Reached for a mono-knife sheathed at his chest, and put it to his own neck. "Be seeing you, Keira."

I let him draw the knife over his own flesh. His eyes widened, mouth slackening. Life left him, in the instant, and his corpse went limp—drifted off the deck in the fluctuating gravity.

That was a classic Sim Ops move. Extract from a damaged body, in order to make transition to another skin.

But the tactic only worked if you had more sims.

There had been operational cryo-tech in the *Iron Knight*'s storage bay. Riggs' skins, on ice. Probably stolen from Sanctuary, during the Spiral's raid.

We'd purged those bodies. Killed them in their tanks.

That was my penultimate gift to Riggs.

I had one more gift to give him before we parted ways for all eternity.

I hoped that he enjoyed it.

The *Iron Knight* was moving.

I could feel its operational drives vibrating underfoot. On a proper military ship, that wouldn't be possible. But the *Knight* was a converted hauler, and despite the after-market upgrades, nothing would change that fact. The sudden acceleration accounted for the shift in gravity, as the internal damper and artificial-G fields failed to compensate.

"Novak? Feng? Do you copy me?"

I yelled the words over the comm, as I ploughed onwards through the ship. Was Lopez safe? Had the Jackals already reached Warlord? I hoped so, but there was no telling. P was still ignoring my attempts to communicate as well.

I'd have to search the place myself. The bridge would probably be too well defended to take on my own. That was what I told myself, at least. I stormed through the decks, heading for a different target.

The *Iron Knight*'s medical bay was exactly where it was supposed to be. I slaughtered my way through every compartment and corridor, dispatching Black Spiral wherever I found them. Doubtless, the tangos would bring heavier weapons to bear soon enough, and with numbers on their side they might take me down. I knew that I wasn't invincible, but it didn't really matter. Novak and Feng were both operational. That gave Lopez the best chance of escape possible.

I had a different job in mind.

I vaulted off another corpse, towards the open hatch that led to Medical. With my improved hearing, even over the disarray that was enveloping the ship I could pick out a voice. I'd never forget it, for as long as I lived— in this body or the next.

"What do you mean, we can't make the uplink?" Riggs screamed. He was panicking, and it was delicious. "Get me into a new body now, you fuck!"

"There are no bodies left!" came the strangled response.

Some higher force guided me. Maybe it was P. Maybe it was just pure determination.

"Hold!" shouted a tech in a dirty-looking medical smock. "You can't be in here!"

"Negative," I said.

I slammed the figure aside. The medic—a man with a face full of tattoos, wearing a black plastic smock that suggested a career involving backstreet bio-enhancements and illegal body-mods—was unarmed and unarmoured. He hit the far wall so hard that his ribcage cracked. With a wet sigh, the man collapsed; bio-signs snuffed from my HUD.

"No more skins, huh, Riggs?" I said. "You can thank me for that."

Riggs' simulator-tank sat in the centre of the chamber. Surrounded by an ad hoc neural-link set-up, doubtless made up of stolen tech. The tank itself glowed blue.

Riggs' eyes flared in disbelief as he saw me.

The simulator's canopy lifted. Fluid poured across the deck.

Riggs was out of the tank. Naked. Vulnerable. He reached for the bench immediately beside his simulator.

Gun.

I launched across the chamber. Grabbed his shoulders with both hands. I knocked the pistol on the bench away from him, out of harm's reach.

"What do you mean?" he gasped.

"I killed your sims while they were still in cryo."

Riggs looked genuinely amazed by that—*why would you do such a thing?*—and tried to squirm away from me. He was physically as slippery as he was mentally.

"Don't do this, Jenk!"

I hurled him against the wall. Riggs, unlike the medic, didn't break. But he did make an almighty crash, and released a satisfying cry of pain. He was a broken toy. I bounded towards him.

"Please!" he squealed. "I only ever wanted to know where he'd gone!"

I held my pistol to Riggs' head. Drove the weapon's muzzle into the flesh of his temple, felt the gun meet the resistance of his bone structure. This would be it. For ever. After all this time, it felt so damned good that it was almost unreal. Adrenaline and rage washed through me. My skin was flushed, my heart a trip-hammer.

"I never meant to hurt you!" he wailed.

More than anything I wanted him to feel what I felt. Wanted him to know what he had put us through, but also that all of this had been in vain. That his father really had died in that nest on Barain-11. The emotion and hurt poured out of me. I don't know how it happened, why it happened, but we connected in that final moment. Whether it was the Aeon, P, or something else: Riggs *knew*. Riggs finally knew. His eyes became dark pools.

"No comebacks, Riggs," I snarled. "This is final."

"I know that you won't actually do this, Keira, and—"

I fired the gun, and Riggs' head exploded.

Daneb Riggs, former Jackal, traitor to the Alliance and Black Spiral terrorist, was dead.

I had no time to enjoy my victory. Another rumble sounded through the deck. Spend enough time on warships, and you develop an innate danger sense: an ability to distinguish whether damage is trivial or significant. The enormous, bell-like boom that echoed through the *Iron Knight*'s spaceframe was very clearly serious. The *Knight* wasn't coming back from this.

"Hold firm," came a rasping voice over the ship's PA. "Dominion comes."

Warlord.

Bio-signs rushed across the ship, converging on the main hangar at the aft of the vessel. I followed the flow and did whatever I could to hold the Spiral off. My communicator was showing an error message—I'd damaged it during the fight, or the *Iron Knight* was causing local disturbance: either was a possibility—so I was in the dark. All I could tell with any certainty was that Lopez was still alive. I only got the basics—heart rate, respiration activity and so on—but that was good enough. She was in the vicinity of the ship. Feng and Novak were still operational too. That was less important, because they were skinned, but it meant Lopez was protected at least.

The corridors were filled with Spiral. Most were wearing armour now, carrying heavier weapons, chanting hymns and war-cries. I popped a few on the way, but received little in the way of return fire. They were focused on what had happened in the hangar.

As I cleared the last corridor, I could see exactly why that was the case.

A shuttle had collided with the *Iron Knight*. The Wildcat Mk 2 armoured personnel shuttle—one of the mainstays of the Alliance fleet—had come to rest at the near end of the hangar. Memories flooded back to me again. Warlord, escaping from Daktar. Now, of course, it looked very different.

The Wildcat's skids were deployed, but whoever was responsible for piloting the ship hadn't done a very good job, and the landing gear had carved three deep grooves into the *Iron Knight*'s deck. Cargo crates, miscellaneous supplies and even a couple of maintenance vehicles had originally been obstacles in the Wildcat's path, but—along with a half-dozen Black Spiral in space armour—they had been crushed beneath the shuttle's bulk.

"Is rescue," came a basso voice, above the chatter of gunfire.

Novak was braced at the shuttle's flank hatch, a stolen assault rifle in one hand, an activated mono-knife in the other. He was clearly in his element, indiscriminately blazing away with the rifle, baring his teeth like an animal.

"How the hell did you get this shuttle in here without blowing the hangar doors?"

"Zero give help," Novak said. "She get doors open. Remotely, or something."

"Where's Lopez?"

"I'm here," Lopez said, appearing beside Novak. She looked about as stunned by this development as I felt.

Novak paused to waste another target. The man clutched at his neck, where Novak had just sprayed a volley of AP rounds. The Russian pushed the body away, and wiped blood across his simulated face. His combat-armour was already drenched in the stuff.

I flinched as slugs bounced off my null-shield, and Lopez momentarily retreated into the cabin. Novak braved the storm, roaring as he emptied the assault rifle's magazine. The attackers were becoming more cautious now, shielded behind troopers wearing hard-suits, deploying plasma rifles. Fired at close range, that sort of ordnance might be capable of puncturing the shuttle's hull.

"We need to get Lopez out of here," said Feng. "This place is hot, and getting hotter."

"The ship took some damage on the way in," Lopez said. "Novak isn't exactly a careful pilot…"

"Is not serious," Novak shouted, above the din of gunfire. "Shuttle will fly fine. Zero can take control again."

An icon in the corner of my HUD flashed—CONNECTION LOST—so I couldn't verify Novak's intel, but there was no way he had flown the shuttle over here on his own. What really swung me, though, was that there was no time to consider the viability of the plan. Lopez either got into the shuttle and bailed out, or she waited here and died. There wasn't much of a contest in that.

"Novak, Lopez: get into the ship," I ordered. "Feng: hold the line with me. We'll cover their retreat, then double back and search for Warlord."

"I don't think that's going to be a problem," Feng said.

His camouflage-cloak whipping around him as though he were in a high wind, the Warlord of the Drift glided through the abject chaos. Removed from time and space, every plasma pulse and rifle round seemed to avoid him.

The dark surrounded Clade Cooper like a shroud; his pet Shard Reapers coiling and recoiling, forming and reforming.

"Lieutenant Jenkins!" he roared, voice a hurricane, amplified unnaturally.

The hangar bay shuddered. Not with any physical, explainable force, but with Warlord's presence. I recalled the same localised space-time disturbance when we encountered Warlord on Darkwater Farm. Whatever was powering Cooper's ragged shell of a body had grown in ability since then.

I'd taken cover near the Wildcat's nose cone. Warlord seemed to spur the tangos on, and the shuttle's hull rang with incoming gunfire. Plasma pulses scorched the outer canopy.

"Get the Wildcat airborne!" I screamed, into my comm.

The Wildcat's engine activated, and simultaneously a missile fired from one of the racks beneath the ship's stubby wings. That exploded against the far bulkhead, showering a dozen Spiral tangos with debris, and catching Warlord in the after-blast. A wave of heat washed over me as a fireball enveloped the end of the hangar. Feng was beside me, an arm up to protect his face.

"…leaving!" came Novak's voice.

REMOTE PILOT SYSTEM ACTIVATED, my HUD flashed. I guessed that was Zero, taking control of the shuttle. I *hoped* it was, at least.

"Go, go!" I yelled.

The entire deck listed. The shuttle tilted sideways, metal shearing as it slid. More bodies were crushed. Its thrusters kicked in, the transport pivoting to reach the hangar bay doors—

The *Iron Knight*'s spaceframe released a tortured roar. Something deep inside broke. The damage caused by the Wildcat's impact was too much, and her gravity-well was giving up. I'd seen this before: knew the signs of a ship's demise better than anyone. Next came—

Explosive decompression.

"*Novak!*"

The shuttle tumbled out into space. The hangar bay doors had given way, and the *Iron Knight* was breaking up. The unplanned and uncontrolled decompression was enough to do that. She was only a transport ship, after all.

Feng hung on to a cargo rail, his rifle still in his gloved hand. He'd had the foresight to remain sealed into his suit. I thought-commanded my mag-locks, and ducked low. Debris slammed into me and a blizzard of bodies whirled by. Some alive—equipped with respirators or sealed suits—but many more dead. Already feeling the frozen kiss of vacuum. Eyes boiling, air pulled from their lungs. Sucks to be Spiral.

An alert flashed on my HUD. Among the blackened mess that was the end of the hangar bay—where the Wildcat's ordnance had impacted—*something* persisted.

"*...readings!*" came Zero's panicked voice. "*Still alive!*"

Warlord emerged from the tangled mess of girders and fused steel. He lifted his corpse—that was surely all that was left of him—from the deck on a tide of black energy. The Reapers whipped around him, forming into the faces of everyone I'd lost during this fucking war. A sphere of nano-particulate shaped in front of him, and he hovered there, surveying the devastation.

"Oh come *on*!" I yelled. "Just die already!"

Warlord's exo-suit was self-repairing. Shadow matter crept over the armoured plates. Where external extenuators and man-amp cabling had been damaged, the Shard made good. Energy crackled over the dead man as he rose from the wreckage. He swept his gaze in my direction.

"Dominion comes, Jenkins," he said.

Doom and horror dwelt within his dead, dead eyes. Warlord's voice was majesty. The hangar was a whirl-wind of debris. The *Iron Knight* was breaking up. Hot and cold washed over me. Friction.

"...*Iron Knight is going down!*" screamed Zero, as though she were living it herself.

CHAPTER TWENTY-FIVE

DEEPER STILL

Beep. Beep. Beep.

TAKE EVASIVE ACTION. TAKE EVASIVE ACTION. USER EXTRACTION IMMINENT. TAKE EVASIVE ACTION.

Beep. Beep. Beep.

The warning chime sounded through my earbead. Words scrolled across my HUD, and were communicated via the neural-link.

The *Iron Knight* had crash-landed.

No, that wasn't right. Not crash-landed. *Crashed.* Taken a direct nosedive into the planet's surface. I moved my arms and legs, and realised that I was still operational. All four limbs worked, although my left leg was partly crushed, and sharp pain vibrated all along my left side. There was more where that came from; just breathing sent hot splinters across my chest.

I'm on Ithaca Prime, I realised. *I'm actually on the Krell homeworld.*

I lay on my back, and through a thatch of hull ribs and assorted debris the sky—a strange, alien sky—was visible. Something had fallen across my body, partly pinning the combat-suit. Testing my suit's man-amp, I lifted the twisted metal spar and sat up.

The wreckage of the *Iron Knight* was all around me. The ship had come down hard and fast, and broken up during atmospheric entry. The heat-shielding had taken the worst of the friction, and some damage had probably been avoided by the null-shield as well. Still, the simple fact that her energy core hadn't cooked off was impressive. My position was open to the elements, and a light wind stirred fires among the wreckage, columns of smoke polluting the horizon. It was something like local daytime, and Ithaca Prime's sun was breaking through the clouds. Despite the apparent hour, several multi-hued moons—the Jagged Moons—were visible too.

I staggered to my feet, careful not to place any weight on my left leg. *Fuck, my head hurts*, I thought. My armour automatically administered combat-drugs and an almost suicidal dose of analgesics. But if it kept me going, I was good with it.

The *Knight* had made planetfall among the Great Nest, the biggest Krell conurbation on Ithaca Prime. The ship's innards trailed maybe a kilometre across a landscape consisting of bio-structures and coral spires. The *Knight*'s main bulk had impacted a dome-like structure that was so big I couldn't make out the outer perimeter. I recognised this as much like the nest we'd assaulted on Vektah Minor, except on a bigger scale. Across the Great Nest, Krell were rousing from hiding, coming to investigate the noise and confusion.

A living city spread around the foot of the dome, wreathed in dense mist, reaching as far as I could see. Swamp, kelp-beds and spawning stations interspersed the apparently random terrain. This was a Krell city, but the term meant nothing to a species that shared a collective consciousness. Things like jellyfish floated across the sky, fizzing with bio-energy. Spires of coral and bone jutted from the swamp-lands at the edge of my vision. I was sure that to something, this all made sense, but certainly didn't to me. The alienness of the bio-scape was disorienting.

It was then that the importance of this moment hit me. Perhaps I'd been wrong about something, I realised. Maybe moments weren't just for politicians and senior brass. This was my moment. This was the first time a human had set foot on Ithaca Prime. The Krell home-world yawned before me. I allowed myself a short sigh of relief.

The face-plate of my helmet was badly damaged, and a web of fractures divided my vision. I cancelled the medical alerts and focused on dragging myself out of the burning wreck. Through the maze of twisted metal to higher ground. My Pathfinder suit was barely functional. Many armour sections were dented and concave, and that left leg was history. I dragged it along behind me. Looking back over the wreckage, I decided that only a simulant could have survived a crash like that. Several bodies—Black Spiral tangos, their suits adorned with intricate eternity swirls and scripture—lay among the remains, but none of them gave off a bio-sign.

"Feng?" I called, using my suit-speakers. "You still operational?"

I found his body torn in two by a piece of jagged hull plating. His PPG-13 plasma pistol was still holstered at his thigh, and he had two grenades in his chest webbing. I pocketed those, for no reason other than routine. I was probably going to have to extract myself, so they might come in handy.

A new alert flickered across my HUD. UPLINK DETECTED, my suit told me.

"Do you read me, Zero?" I asked. "*Defiant*, come in. California, in the blind."

No reply. I tottered onwards, pistol in hand.

I reached the edge of the crater and looked out across the city. The Krell were streaming from their positions now, flooding the lower echelons of the Great Nest. Huge weapon-emplacements were visible at the perimeter of the bio-dome. They still pointed into the sky, watching for what might fall from space next.

"Do you copy, Zero? California transmitting. We've won. Warlord is gone." No one was listening, but that was fine. I was content to reel off my story, while the swell of pain built in my chest, and I came to terms with my next extraction. "Maybe you should call down an anti-viral warhead on my position, just to be sure. Tell Secretary Lopez he can thank me later, and that I accept cash payments as well as medals."

I winced as a burst of white noise filled my earbead.

"...*receiving!*" came Zero's panicked voice. "...*boarding ship! Don't know...can keep you...operational!*"

A Krell tertiary-form lay dead on the ground beside me. It was massive, uninfected, and wearing ornate bio-armour. Carrying a stave-like weapon that was coated with black blood...The alien's big, blank eyes glanced back at me, reflecting my battered image, and—

A flicker of movement behind me.

I rolled sideways, barely evading the spear of black light that sliced the air.

"You have *got* to be shitting me!" I screamed.

Warlord rose from out of the wreckage. Palms open, messiah-like, his helmet gone now.

"You killed Daneb Riggs," he said. His voice was dry and rasping, each word on the verge of descent into a coughing fit. "He was like a son to me."

"You fucking lied to him!" I shouted. "You turned him against the Alliance, and all for nothing!"

An explosion bloomed overhead. The Krell weapons emplacements around the Great Nest opened fire, sleeting living ammunition across the horizon. Shrieks and booms filtered up to us, as activity erupted in the lower regions of the city, and around the foot of the bio-dome.

Warlord snarled. "Marbec Riggs was my brother. He would forgive me for what happened. He would understand, even if you don't."

Warlord moved so fast that he was almost a blur. He was out of the *Knight*'s wreckage, and over me. Automatically, I turned aside, rolling across the broken surface of the bio-dome. Warlord's powered fist impacted the ground beside me. The coral surface cracked, and Warlord's hand went through it. Again and again, he slammed his gauntlet into the ground, with more force than his damaged exo-suit could generate. Shard nanotech infused his every move.

I got to my feet, and through the jagged splinters of my visor, aimed my pistol. Fired, just as the bio-dome gave way. Warlord and I collapsed through the ensuing hole. The structural damage Warlord had inflicted on the dome's outer surface was enough to create a wider fissure, and a huge chunk of the *Iron Knight*'s hull came down too.

"Zero!" I yelled, as I dropped into the nest. I took the fall on my hands and knees. I surely wouldn't forget the pain that lanced through my left leg any time soon. "If you can hear me, fire the anti-viral!"

The inside of the nest was a warren of passages and chambers. It would've taken a normal human decades to map them out, and to decipher the route through to the lower levels. The biological madness of the Krell wasn't prone to rhyme or reason. Then again, neither was

Warlord. As the ship's hull settled around us, the nest creaking and groaning, Warlord knew exactly what his target was.

"Stop this!"

Warlord slammed a fist into the floor again. Shard Reapers danced around his torso, and slid through the deck. As Warlord withdrew his fist from the damaged coral floor, I was reminded of just how dangerous he had become. His abilities had been growing, developing, shifting ever since we'd first faced off on North Star Station.

I scrambled left. Whirled about-face to take on the man who had decimated the Alliance, and would decapitate the Krell. The man who would bring back the Shard, and the Dominion. Here he was, as vulnerable as he was ever going to be. I fired the pistol.

Of course, "vulnerable" was a very relative description.

Warlord snarled—more animal than man—and twisted aside as plasma seared the spot where he had been standing. The speed at which he moved was impossible, incredible. He was everywhere, and nowhere. His ragged cloak swirled around him, the camo pattern spilling darkness, shedding viral cells. I could feel his illness, and this close I could see it too. His haggard, scarred face was twisted beyond recognition: a man consumed by what he had brought back from Barain-11. Silver flecks danced beneath his skin, warping the flesh.

I fired my EVAMP. Surprisingly, that worked, and I powered closer to Warlord. I threw a fist into his face with enough strength that it would've killed a warden-form. Warlord merely took the blow, and tumbled through the network of living passageways we found ourselves in.

Attracted by the intrusion, Krell primary-forms spilt from the shafts at the edge of the corridor. They wore heavier armour, their limbs weaponised to perfection. Aware that I wasn't the danger, they ignored me and headed straight for Warlord. A dozen of them descended in a tide of razor-sharp talons.

Warlord merely raised a hand. A black spear erupted from his palm, puncturing the first attacker in the head-crest. The body whirled about, soundlessly. The next attacker almost reached Warlord, but he slammed a fist into the creature's face. The third was stabbed by more dark light. Streamers of black oil filled the air, comprehensively demolishing the Krell attack.

Onwards through the nest we fell. Coral growths randomly sprouted from the walls, from the ceiling. Everything here was alive, organic. Corruptible. The walls were ribbed, dripping with moisture, fleshy coating covering every surface. Pools of stagnant briny liquid, squirming with Krell fry, pocked the uneven floor. The further we descended, the darker it became, the structure lit only by the dim glow of fungus.

I bounced after Warlord, taking pot shots with my plasma pistol. The Krell kept coming, sending more and more against Warlord. He tossed corpses aside, besting everything the Collective had to throw at him.

Then he fumbled. The ground was wet here, and a secondary-form blazed Warlord with a shrieker. The pitched wail of the living flamer unit filled the air, and Warlord was a second too slow to avoid the wave of napalm. It kissed his torso and face, and he roared in anger and pain.

I took my chance. I slammed a powered foot into Warlord's shin. His own armour clattered noisily, and he yowled again, stumbling back. It was satisfying to know that for all of his power, all of his strength, he still felt pain.

But he recovered fast. His armour still burning,

Warlord scrambled away from me. The Krell warrior saw an opportunity too, and aimed its shrieker, the muzzle of the bio-weapon dripping ichor and flame. Warlord nonchalantly threw his hand in the alien's direction, and it was decapitated by a Shard Reaper that sprang from his palm.

That was the last of the opposition. Warlord paused, evaluating his surroundings. Satisfying himself that this was his objective. He knew this place, and I did too. Knowledge unpacked itself in my head.

"This is the resting place of the Deep Ones," said Warlord.

We were in a cavernous chamber. The ground was uneven and irregular, but it gradually declined towards a pit. That was maybe thirty metres in diameter, and filled with impenetrable darkness. Without even trying, I knew that no physical illumination would cancel that dark. The lack of light was a deliberate concealment, because what dwelt at the bottom of that pit didn't want to be seen. *Couldn't* be seen.

Science Division and Command had labelled these creatures the Krell High Council. In reality, there was no suitable description in the human lexicon. The Deep Ones—the progenitors of the Krell Collective, the controlling mind of the entire species, and the embodiment of the Deep—were no more a council than the Krell were really fishes. They were the ancient personification of a collective species and the lynchpin for the entire existence of the Krell. The Deep Ones were the source of the psychic pain that stained this planet. They knew that Ithaca Prime was dying, and that if the planet fell, so too would the Collective. Their fear was palpable.

Whatever physical form the Deep Ones took, it occupied the shaft. How far the tunnel went, I didn't know. Whether any Krell bio-form had ever returned from their pilgrimage to the well of shadows, I couldn't say. All I knew with any certainty was that Warlord had to be stopped from making contact with the Deep Ones.

He crouched at the lip of the well, glancing between me and the darkness.

"You are on your own, Lieutenant," he said, his own voice a sibilant, dying mess. "Dominion comes. You fought admirably. You did your best, but there is nothing left for you to do but let this happen."

The ground rumbled, quaked, and a nearby coral shelf came away. It fell into the cavern. The impact caused a chain reaction; more coral outcroppings breaking up, slamming into one another. A keening cry filled the air. The Deep Ones shivered in the dark.

<We feel their pain,> came P's voice, suddenly back in my head. <This must end.>

Long time no speak, P, I broadcast back. *Ready the warheads. Fire every anti-viral you've got on my position. I'm going to take care of Warlord.*

For all the good it would do me, I primed a hi-ex grenade with one hand and aimed my pistol with the other.

"Step away, Cooper," I said. "I'm not going to let this happen."

"Why are you even trying to save them, Jenkins? Look at what they are." Warlord gestured towards the pit. "They are pathetic, dead things. Shivering in the dark."

"I'm not even going to pretend to understand them," I said, "but I do know the difference between right and wrong. Whatever happened to you, Cooper, this is *wrong.*"

"The Deep Ones don't care. I can feel them in my head. They don't even understand what is happening."

"I think they understand just fine," I said as calmly as I could. "Who are we to judge the existence of an entire species?"

"I am," Warlord said. "The Shard will wipe them from existence, for eternity."

"And us, too, right?" I said. Through my breached helmet, the stink of burning coral and singed flesh was almost overpowering. "Do you really want that?"

"It doesn't matter."

"Would your wife and children want it?"

Warlord's face froze. "They are gone, but they will be remembered. *I* will remember them. This will be their legacy."

Warlord smiled with his thin lips. The scar tissue on his lower face distorted the expression. The veins under his skin were bulbous, and lesions crept up the collarring of both his exo-suit and his neck. He was a walking Harbinger bomb.

"I brought the virus back from Barain-11," Warlord said. "It was what Command, what Military Intelligence, wanted. Command could've saved my family, Jenkins. Sim Ops should have been there when the invasion came."

"Command didn't know this was going to happen," I said. "Command didn't know that you were going to turn into *this*. They wanted a weapon, but they didn't know it would do this to you."

"They always want a weapon, Jenkins. Always. Something bigger, better, stronger, faster."

"I'm not going to pretend I won't kill you," I said, edging closer to Warlord, holding out the grenade, "but you can still redeem yourself. You can change this. Call off your attack, and step down. The virus is making you do this, turning you into something that you're not."

The smile broadened, but Warlord's body twitched. Shard Reapers danced around his torso, snakes that jumped in and out of reality. The Krell habitat shook again, and an explosion from somewhere above shook the structure.

"The virus hasn't done anything," Warlord said. "That responsibility falls on one man."

"Who?"

Another step forward. I was desperately trying to make contact with P again. It either wasn't listening, or the Deep Ones were causing some sort of psychic disturbance.

"Rodrigo Lopez," he said. "The Senator, as he was then. He made me into this. He endorsed the mission, and he sent the Iron Knights to Barain-11."

"That's not true," I said. "That—that can't be true."

"I can give you every name you want. Major Vadim Sergkov was my commanding officer. Commander Vie Dieter was to be responsible for our exfiltration." He choked a sob. "Jandra Cooper was my wife. And Marbec Riggs my best friend. Daneb Riggs was Marbec's son, the boy he left behind."

I was virtually standing over Warlord now. In my head, I calculated the likely blast zone of the explosive grenade. The yield might be enough ... Warlord reached down to touch the gelatinous floor, his palm against the living tissue, one leg outstretched. Poised.

"You lied to Daneb Riggs," I said. "You twisted him against the Alliance. Against *me*."

"Maybe I am sorry for that," he said. "But he isn't the only person I've lied to in order to get here." Warlord's presentation shifted suddenly, and the hard edges returned. "None of that is my fault. Lopez created me. It's all on him. He was the one who brought me back from the dead. *Resurrected* me."

Warlord's back was to the opening of the pit. From there, the Deep Ones screamed, their collective despair filling the cavern. There were no words, no formed expressions, in the wall of alien emotion. Being this close to the vast xeno intelligence was almost overwhelming, and I struggled to concentrate.

Come on, P! Answer me!

"He needed a weapon, Jenkins," Warlord continued. "You know yourself that he tried to shut Sim Ops down. He needed something new, that he could control and make his own."

A chill ran down my spine.

"I was the symbiosis of Shard, Krell and human. Except, when it comes to it, there's not enough room in one body for that mess."

"Maybe I can help you."

"Now who's lying?" Warlord said. He stood. "There was a time, long ago, when I wondered if perhaps you— or someone like you—could. But then I remembered the help that Sim Ops had been to my family..."

"That was different. Had the Army known, they would've sent help."

"That's exactly the point. They *did* know, Jenkins. They knew that the war-fleets were coming to my home, and they let it burn." A distant, vacant look descended over Warlord's shattered face. "Logistics. Numbers. They sacrificed my homeworld for a victory elsewhere."

He backed up. Arms out now. A mere step from the edge of the pit.

Answer me, P!

"You're insane," I said. "That isn't how things happened, Cooper."

"On my honour as an Army Ranger," Warlord said.

"That means nothing. You're not that person any more."

"But why would I lie? I know that there's no coming back from this. I either die here, my objective achieved, or you kill me. This is *exactly* how things happened."

I saw my chance and took it. I vaulted forward, all my strength in my right leg. Grenade outstretched, into Warlord's body. I punched through the blizzard of angry darkness that swirled around him.

"You were stalling, right?" he said, as I pulled him close, body around the grenade. "It's okay. So was I."

Warlord and I fell backwards into the pit.

The grenade detonated, but it didn't matter any more.

By the time he reached the bottom of the pit, there was nothing left of Clade Cooper except for Harbinger.

CHAPTER TWENTY-SIX

HARBINGER REALISED

The neural-link broke.

Normally, when that happens it's a cold, calculated process. Although some operators describe life flashing before their eyes, or memories suddenly coming to the fore, that's never happened to me. Science Division had comprehensively debunked this phenomenon as a reaction to intense trauma; the human mind playing tricks, trying to make sense of the simulation process.

Which made what happened all the stranger. In the micro-second it took to extract from the simulant, images burst into my head. Real-time captures of the war. I knew what I was seeing was real, and I had no doubt as to the reliability of this information.

Space around Ithaca Prime was a clusterfuck of activity.

There were no battle lines any more, no fleet formations. The Alliance fleet was in ruins. Warships were scattered across the Kalliper Belt, around the Ring of Thorns. Several of the larger ships were still firing—unleashing devastating fusillades with their plasma cannons and rail guns, releasing swarms of missiles—but the activity was disorganised, without leadership. The theatre was littered with the wreckage of starships and evac-pods. Cries for help reached across the void, but went unanswered.

The infected Krell war-fleet circled Ithaca Prime. Space was laced with a network of Needler attack ships and Stingray troop carriers. Infected ark-ships, their original Collective now long forgotten, sat in high orbit.

As P had predicted, the Black Spiral's fleet had been largely consumed by the invasion. Those few ships left picked off damaged Alliance assets, conducting attacks of opportunity.

Then there was Ithaca Prime itself. The target of this conflict, Ithaca's vulnerability was exposed. The Deep Ones' influence was pervasive and their corruption was visible from space as a stain on the face of the planet. The Great Nest had begun to desiccate and wither as Harbinger took root. The very planet was reacting to the infection. The surface of Ithaca Prime was a swollen mass of activity. Whirlpools and vortexes blighted the oceans. Vast bio-structures broke up. Even in orbit, Krell warships had started to falter—some dropping to the planet below, others withdrawing from the defence of Ithaca, unsure of what they should now do.

The Shard warships prowled deep space like predators on the hunt for prey. Their black outlines were only occasionally lit by nearby explosions, or when they released their offensive technologies to annihilate a vessel that got too close. The Shard ships closed on Ithaca with calm, mechanised precision.

My focus shifted to the Aeon fleet. Only five vault-ships left, and those were beleaguered. They were being overwhelmed by the sheer volume of enemy fire, from every direction. One of the vessels was being circled by a dozen infected bio-fighters, its hull punctured in several places. The ship trailed debris, as it sporadically returned fire with its energy weapons.

<This is not lost, Soldier,> came Wraith's voice. <It can be undone.>

Are you putting these images into my head? I asked. *Is this more of your mind-manipulation bullshit?*

I felt, rather than heard, a laugh. <Yes, Soldier. It is. We can end the Black Spiral. We can cease their threat, but it will not finish what has been started on Ithaca Prime.>

What are you going to do? Activate the starfyre?

<This is an option, but it will expunge the Deep. It is the Great Destroyer.>

I thought about that for a long moment. The memory of an entire species, lost. Gone in an instant. The black blot—a nightmare Rorschach pictorial—had spread further. It was threatening to envelop the whole of the Great Nest.

If there is another way, we have to try that first, I said.

<Pariah knows. It will lead you. We will ready our weapons.>

Even as I watched, a fifth Aeon ship was devastated by Krell bio-fire. The vault-ship's lights went out, and like its brethren, it broke up in the void. Triumphant, the wing of Needler bio-fighters moved on to a fresh target.

The remaining Aeon fleet collected together, sailing towards Ithaca Prime. Their collective might was focused there now. Wraith was on one of those ships, and her mind touched mine again.

<Go now. There is not much time.>

I opened my eyes in my real skin and extracted to find that the Simulant Operations Centre was on fire. Literally.

Novak wore a respirator and was spraying a halon

dispenser across a damaged section of bulkhead panelling.

A fragment of background noise entered the comms: "...*fire control on D-Deck! Fire control, immediately*..."

"Get Jenk out of the tank!" Zero yelled, her voice a constant in my earbead.

Zero sat at her terminal, trying to work amid the chaos. She typed rapidly, her eyes scanning lines of data as new information popped up on her tri-D screens. Feng worked at a terminal beside Zero, attempting to assist her. Meanwhile, Lopez still wore the uniform we'd rescued her in, and had armed herself with a Navy-issue sidearm. I was glad that she had got back in one piece.

"You heard the lady!" Captain Ving said, hurrying me on. "Give us a sitrep, now!"

Ving popped the catches on the tank and dragged me free. I quickly shook off the post-extraction confusion.

"The *Iron Knight* made planetfall to Ithaca Prime," I said, words tumbling out of me. "Warlord has reached the surface. I tried to stop him, but he made contact with the Deep Ones." I paused, hesitant to voice the last words aloud. To say them would make them real. "Harbinger has reached Ithaca Prime," I said.

P watched me. This close to the alien, I realised that it knew this already.

<We are sorry it has come to this,> said P.

"Get dressed," said Dr Saito, tossing me a fresh set of fatigues. "I'm not sure if—"

The *Defiant* rumbled around us, and everyone paused for a moment. Something keened within the ship's hull.

"What the fuck was that?" Ving asked. "Have we been hit?"

Zero typed even faster. Surveillance feeds appeared on her screens. There were vid-feeds from across the

Defiant, covering her portside docking bays and access corridors.

"Another ship has got through the *Defiant*'s defences," Zero said. She shook her head in disbelief. "We have hostiles across the vessel. More boarders."

"*More?*" I asked.

"We've already had our fair share of problems in the SOC," said Captain Heinrich. His ordinarily well-presented uniform was dishevelled, and a dark bloom spread across his left shoulder, the colour spreading through the fabric.

"You've been shot, sir," I realised, the surprise impossible to conceal from my voice. "It—it looks serious."

Captain Heinrich nodded grimly, clutching his own sidearm in both hands. "Yes, I have," he said, "and I can't say I like it much."

"Repetition doesn't make it any easier," I said.

Captain Heinrich grimaced, but also couldn't help smiling. His face was bathed in sweat. "Can't say it's an experience I'd like to repeat. One of the Spiral got me, while I was defending the SOC."

A siren cut through the background rumble that filled the *Defiant*, and the AI's voice cheerily declared, "*Evacuate ship. This is not a drill. Evacuate ship. This is not a drill.*"

Dr Saito ignored the siren, and leant over Zero's position, reading from her terminal. "The planet is experiencing some sort of cataclysmic shift, caused by the Harbinger virus. It's infecting everything down there."

"Where are the Aeon?" Captain Heinrich asked.

<They are moving into position around Ithaca Prime,> said P. <They are preparing to activate their weapons.>

"They...they told me that they could use the starfyre," I said, "but if they did, it would wipe the Deep for ever."

"We see this on way into Ithaca system," said Novak. He'd armed himself with a mono-knife, but exactly where he'd acquired the weapon from wasn't clear to me. "It will destroy planet too, yes?"

"What about the anti-viral warheads?" Zero asked, desperately searching for another possibility. "We can't let them do this. There has to be a way to stop it."

"We could get into an evac-pod and leave it all behind," Ving offered. "That's what most of Sim Ops has done."

But as I looked at his face, I knew that it wasn't a serious solution. "I know you won't do that, Ving," I said. "Whatever has gone down between us, whatever you think of the Krell: you're better than that."

Ving exhaled slowly. "All right. The warheads, then."

<They will not work,> said P. <Warlord is the Harbinger virus. He carries an improved strain. It has been evolving inside him since his original infection.>

"We have to at least try," Zero argued, her eyes still on the monitors. Some of the screens had gone dark now. "The planet is dying."

"Then what other option do we have?" Feng asked.

<There is another way,> broadcast P.

"I'm all ears," said Ving.

<We are the anti-virus,> P said. <We can remedy the infection.>

"How will that work?" Zero questioned.

<We were the original source of the anti-viral,> P explained. <We carry the solution inside of us.>

"So how can you stop this?" Ving challenged. "You're just one body, fish." He gestured at Zero's tri-D screen, which showed the devastation developing across Ithaca Prime. "There's a whole planet of infection down there."

<It does not matter,> said P. < If we reach the Deep Ones, we can undo the damage.>

"You are the second option," I said, remembering what P had told me during the drop to the *Iron Knight*. "We talked about using starfyre, then you said there was another possibility."

<Correct,> said P. <We will go to Ithaca Prime.>

"Then that's what we'll do," Captain Heinrich said, grunting as he readjusted his injured shoulder. "We can take a dropship, and bring the pariah-form to the surface."

P shook its head, barbels shivering. <No. We must do this alone, via drop-capsule. This is the only way.>

"Then you'll need access to the drop-bay," said Zero. "That sector of the ship is filled with boarders. The Spiral..." She swallowed. "And something else."

"Go on," said Feng. "This surely can't get any worse..."

Zero bit her lip. "The *Svetlana* has docked with the *Defiant*."

Novak watched the scene develop with a cold detachment. "Vasnev has boarded," he muttered.

"Remember what we said," I told him. "The mission comes first."

"Why is Vasnev here?" Lopez asked. "Has she come back for me?"

"Probably," said Novak. "It is what I would do. Major Vasnev wants to make good her mission. You are value to her, yes?" He waved a hand in the air. "This is all one big mess. Profit must be salvaged from what is left."

Lopez nodded and wrapped her hand a little tighter around her pistol. "Then let her come. We'll see what she makes of me."

Clade Cooper's final words—his revelation that Secretary Lopez had been behind the mission to Barain-11, and then his transformation into Warlord—echoed in my mind. But there was a time when I could act on that, and it wasn't now. On another of Zero's screens, the

Aeon vault-ships had come together in a tight formation. The closer proximity seemed to amplify their powers, creating localised time-space disturbances on the
scanner-feeds.

"What do we do?" Captain Heinrich asked. I realised, after a moment, that he was directing the question at me.

"Get back into the tanks, Jackals," I said. "Our sims
are in cryo-storage, right?"

Zero nodded. "I've decanted four, ready for deployment. Someone will need to escort P across the ship."

<We do not need assistance,> P protested.

"While that's true, P," I said, "we can't take risks."

"I'll do it," said Ving.

"In your real skin?" I asked.

Ving shrugged. "It's not like I've got anything to lose.
We'll meet you in the drop-bay."

"I'm coming too," said Dr Saito. He had his pistol
unholstered. "I can lend some additional fire support,
and I can manually approve the launch codes."

"We can't do that from here?" I asked.

"Not any more," said Zero. "The launch codes are
subject to a Command override."

Secretary Lopez, I thought bitterly. He was surely
safely ensconced in the CIC, or had already launched in
an evacuation-pod. He could be another windfall for the
Sons of Balash, if they caught him, although he would
probably charm or buy his way out of their custody.

"I'll stay here," Captain Heinrich said, "and cover the
SOC. I would only slow you down."

The blood loss from Heinrich's shoulder was significant, and just as colour was leaking across his uniform,
it was draining from his face. If I had been a gambler, I
wouldn't have put money on Heinrich pulling through

this… To Heinrich's credit, he didn't request back-up or complain about his fate. This had changed him, as much as any of us. The old Heinrich had been shed like a dead simulant.

"I should stay too," said Novak. "Captain is hurt. He cannot do this on his own."

Heinrich opened his mouth to argue, but lacked either the strength or conviction to argue. He nodded. "That's probably a good idea," he said.

"We can follow your progress via the surveillance cameras," Zero suggested.

The surveillance feeds showed a running battle between the Spiral, and what was left of the *Defiant*'s security forces. As Zero cycled through locations, it became apparent how badly damaged the ship was. Most of the Sim Ops bays were abandoned, and almost all of the evac-pods had been launched. Like rats fleeing from a sinking ship, the strike-force was running. Captain Heinrich hadn't even suggested making contact with General Draven, because there was no point. There was no chain of command any more. Quite possibly, this was the biggest rout in all of Alliance history.

<We must do this, now,> P said.

My data-ports throbbed in time with the shaking through the *Defiant*'s hull. Wraith's cold consciousness grazed my own, and encouraged me onwards.

"Mount up, Jackals."

"Transition confirmed," I said. "You read me, Z?"

"Affirmative. Jackals are in the green."

I pulled myself free from the charging dock, and the combat-suit instantly responded. Feng and Lopez did the same. I activated my mag-locks, prepped my plasma rifle.

"I've painted your rendezvous point," said Zero. "Captain Ving, Dr Saito and P have just left."

A map appeared on my HUD, and I focused on it. There was the SOC, several decks up, and cryo-storage, where we were located. We'd jumped the length of the *Defiant* in an instant, avoiding hostile forces. The boarders were mainly located around the portside docking bays, although some had breached the main corridor that formed the ship's spine. There were still pockets of resistance throughout the ship, but I didn't know for how long the Alliance forces would be able to hold out. P was currently making good progress through the starboard storage hold, its location indicated by a blip on my bio-scanner.

"Tell Dr Saito and Captain Ving not to die," I said. "Not until they reach the rendezvous, at least."

"I'll pass on the message," Zero said.

"We'll attract the Spiral's attention, and keep them off P's tail," I said. "It should keep the hostiles busy."

"I've plotted P's group a route through the service tunnels," Zero assured me. "I don't think the Spiral will find them, unless they're specifically looking for them."

"All right. Keep an eye on Novak. He's vital: if the Spiral or the Sons of Balash reach the SOC, this will be over."

"He understands," said Zero.

"California out," I said. I turned to Lopez and Feng, who had now prepped their weapons and were waiting for me. "Are you both ready for this?" I asked.

"Absolutely," Lopez answered.

"For sure," said Feng.

"We'll use whatever we've got to reach the rendezvous, and then the drop-bay. No mercy, no regrets."

"No mercy," repeated Lopez, with a grim smile.

"We make as much noise as we can," I said, "and keep the Spiral off P and Dr Saito. Maximum carnage."

Feng stroked his plasma rifle. "Now that, I can do."

On my command, the blast hatch from cryo-storage opened. The corridor outside was already stitched with gunfire, the atmo laden with heavy smoke.

I picked a target and started shooting.

The M125 plasma rifle throbbed through the palms of my combat-gloves.

The Black Spiral undeniably had one thing in their favour: as far as they were concerned, they had won the war. These people had nothing else to live for, so they threw themselves at Alliance forces with the single-mindedness of the Krell Collective. Nothing else mattered, because their plan had succeeded.

Feng and Lopez were on point and focused. We stormed the corridors in a blizzard of plasma.

"Grenade left," Lopez said.

She pumped her rifle. A hi-ex grenade slammed into the body of an armoured target, at the end of the corridor. The tango fumbled for a split-second, before the explosive detonated. The deck rumbled, warning sirens screeching overhead. Feng put a volley of plasma into more hostiles, ensuring that none would dare follow. The close quarters combat was furious and lethal.

"Ease up on your gunfire," I said. "We're approaching the drop-bay."

My HUD showed that P was just behind us, using an alternative route. I felt its presence in my head, and affirmation that the alien's group was still alive.

"I'm almost out of charge," Feng said.

"Catch this," Lopez replied, tossing him a power cell for his plasma rifle.

Feng deftly caught it. Ejected the old cell, and slammed the new one into place.

"You almost look like a professional," Lopez said. "That was my last cell. You better make it last."

Feng grinned. "Or what? We all die of the Harbinger virus?"

"I kick your ass when we get back Coreside," Lopez said.

"It's encouraging that you even think we're getting back Coreside..." I said. "Take that corner, Feng."

"Solid copy."

I slid back, covering a side corridor with Lopez. She pumped another grenade from her underslung launcher, then paused to watch as it exploded. Several enemy life-signs vanished from my HUD. The hail of shrapnel caused by the frag munition showered us both, but our null-shields neutralised the danger.

"What?" she asked, turning to me. "You're looking at me weird, ma'am."

I shook my head. "It's nothing."

Lopez lifted a perfect eyebrow. "It doesn't feel like nothing. You did say to make some noise."

"I know. As I said; it's nothing."

It wasn't nothing. It wasn't nothing at all. I toyed with the idea of telling Lopez what Cooper had told me. Would she want to know what her father was, I wondered? He'd been disappointed in her, and her decision to join up with the Simulant Operations Programme. She was very different from him. She was a Jackal. But she didn't need to know, not yet.

"You sure everything is okay?" she asked.

"I'm sure. Come on, drop-bay is ahead."

There was an open blast hatch ahead of us. The words PRIMARY DROP-BAY were stencilled on the far bulkhead, glowing brightly through the miasma of smoke and debris that choked the corridor.

Under normal circumstances, the drop-bay was fully automated. Simulants were ferried from cryo-storage into drop-capsules, and then loaded into the waiting launch tubes and fired into space according to the targeting solution provided by the CIC or the SOC. As a result, except for maintenance personnel this sector was out of bounds to most crew. The compartment had the feel of a factory floor to it, with multiple gantries overlooking the tubes, and storage compartments for redundant drop-capsules. The latter resembled metal coffins, waiting to receive corpses. I'd never actually been into this bay, and the place had a creepy vibe about it. Red light strobed the vacant gangways, the ranks of robotic loading arms. Our intrusion seemed to throw the whole bay off. The nearest semi-autonomous arm paused, its single red-lensed eye fixing on me, waldo-grip cycling open and closed in protest.

"Do you copy, Zero?" I asked. No reply. "Feng: are you reading Zero?"

Feng kept his rifle up, covering the many possible hiding places that surrounded us, but answered, "No, ma'am. I lost her signal at the last junction."

"Marvellous."

"Do you think it's the Spiral?" Lopez asked me. "They seem to have a thing for jamming technology."

"Maybe."

I panned my rifle over the compartment's interior, searching for targets. There was heat and motion in here, caused by the robotic loaders, and it was fouling my bio-scanner. But whether the Spiral were disrupting comms or not, they couldn't stop me from reaching out to P. I detected its aura, moving at the edge of the compartment.

"P's here," I said. "Watch our six."

"Copy that," said Feng.

"Lopez, overwatch on the entrance."

"Affirmative."

There was a thunk, as a service hatch at the end of the bay came open. P uncoiled its bulk from inside the cramped corridor, using all six limbs to pull itself free. Dr Saito followed closely behind, still clutching his gun. Captain Ving was last out. His face was scrunched in disgust, and he gasped for air as the trio emerged.

"Everything went to plan, I take it?" I asked.

"No hostile contacts," Ving confirmed, "but in those tight passages, the fish stinks."

"You get used to it," I said.

Dr Saito swept the drop-bay with his pistol. "Is the area secure?"

"Enough," I said. "We took out several hostiles on the way down here. The boarders aren't very organised. This feels like an attack of opportunity, rather than a directed operation."

Dr Saito gave a brisk nod. "What with the loss of Warlord, the Spiral's leadership is lacking as well."

"Could be," I said. "Fall in behind me. The control console is this way."

With Feng still covering the main gangway, and Lopez standing overwatch, I escorted the team across the drop-bay. The compartment was still in darkness, and my bio-scanner threw error messages back at me. The deck rumbled again as we made our way to the control console. Dr Saito reached for a safety rail, pausing while the vessel took the vibration.

"That felt like more than a ship docking..." Ving muttered. "I think we got hit."

My suit-lamp illuminated the manual launch control console. It looked beyond the understanding of most Navy personnel, let alone a Science Officer specialising in xeno-biology.

"So, Saito, operating the launch programme of an Alliance Navy warship is another of your many skills?" I asked.

"One of several personal interests," Dr Saito said. He didn't look at me, but instead wiped his hand over his smock, then found a combined DNA and palm-print reader. Frowning to himself, he put his hand on the scanner. "The Watch has many faces," he said, as he worked.

P monitored the doctor's progress, the antenna that sprouted from its backplate writhing softly.

"This is just like the Vektah Minor drop, P," I said, my rifle on my hip. "Straight down the pipe."

<Dr Saito has the coordinates of the crash site,> said P. <We must be deployed directly to that location.>

"I want you to take care down there."

<Are you concerned for our safety?>

"Of course I am. You're one of us, P. A Jackal."

P touched a clawed hand to the Jackal-head marking on its forehead. <We are, Jenkins. We always will be.>

"We'll mop up the Spiral on the ship," I said. "Once we're done, we'll send a dropship down to the surface, as quickly as we can. Just hold tight."

<You misunderstand, Jenkins-other.>

"What do you mean?"

It struck me, in that instant, that something was wrong here. Something was very wrong. P had been trying to shield its mind from me. Wraith's alien presence crackled around P, as though she were trying to communicate with me, but P was restricting her from doing so.

Dr Saito interrupted the moment by slapping his pistol down on the launch terminal. "I think we're ready,

P. I've worked around the command restrictions." A launch tube at the far end of the bay hissed open, hydraulics whining, pressurised atmosphere escaping in a white mist. "The automated loader has prepped a drop-capsule for that tube."

<Affirmative, Doctor,> said P.

"I only wish that we could—"

Dr Saito's words were cut off, as a bullet whined past my head, and sliced straight through his stomach.

CHAPTER TWENTY-SEVEN

THE MISSION COMES FIRST

I immediately went into combat mode.

More shots peppered our position, and I grabbed Dr Saito's forearm. We went prone behind a metal crate. The bay illuminated with gunfire, as rounds struck metalwork and slammed into the deck. The sound of multiple weapons firing on full-automatic overlapped.

"P, get down!" I ordered.

P rolled into cover, leaping over an open drop-capsule, avoiding injury. Ving dropped too, although I couldn't see whether he'd been hit or not.

Dr Saito immediately began to hyperventilate. Beads of sweat popped up all across his face, and he shook violently. Both hands went to the wound in his gut, fingers interlinked over the injury.

"You've been hit, Doc," I said.

"You're telling me," said Dr Saito, through gritted teeth.

"Stay still and don't panic."

Dr Saito's Sci-Div smock was already heavily bloodstained, red pouring between his fingers. He looked at me with glazed, distant eyes; an expression that I had seen too many times before. His grimace, teeth flecked with blood, was almost as familiar.

"I . . . I'm . . ." he said. "Don't worry about me."

More gunfire sprayed the area. The attackers were using heavy weapons; I recognised the electric whirr of rotary cannons, the noise the barrel makes when it spins. Panning my helmet across the bay, I picked out three targets.

"What've we got?" Ving said, above the roar of the guns.

"Multiple shooters at the end of the bay. Big guns."

"Anti-simulant guns?"

I nodded, although I knew that Ving couldn't see me from his position. "Likely. They're loaded for bear."

"Ain't that great," said Ving, sucking his teeth. "Just when I was beginning to think we might get out of this alive . . ."

"I wouldn't ever go that far," I said, avoiding looking down at Dr Saito. His back was against the cargo crate, but he'd slid down to the deck now, and was gasping for breath. "Not where the Jackals are concerned."

"Who's shooting?" Feng said. He was further away from the attackers, covering the entrance hatch with Lopez.

Both Lopez and Feng's bio-signs were stable, and neither had been hit. I picked out their positions maybe thirty metres away, concealed behind robotic loaders. They were in cover, for now.

"Unknown hostiles," I said. "At least three."

"More inbound," said Lopez. "I'm reading multiple tangos approaching the hatch."

"Give me an estimate."

"Thirty," said Lopez.

I checked my plasma rifle. The cell was almost depleted;

I had maybe a half-dozen pulses left. My Widowmaker sidearm had perhaps six shots left.

"Ammo check, troopers?" I asked the Jackals.

"Three pulses," said Lopez.

Feng swallowed over the comm. "Twelve."

"What about you, Ving?"

"A full clip," said Ving.

He popped up above the lip of his crate and fired a volley of shots into the dark. He was chased back into cover by the enemy's response. Explosive rounds impacted the console behind him, noisily demolishing the panel.

"I wouldn't try that again, sir," I said.

"I don't think that I will," Ving agreed.

P bristled beside me. Despite its size, the xeno hugged the floor. Tiny flecks of debris pocked the alien's carapace.

<We must act now,> P insisted. <We can feel the Harbinger virus's progress. Wraith is in position; her forces cannot wait.>

Wraith's consciousness pricked my own again. Without knowing how I knew, I could detect the movement of the alien vault-ships. They were concentrating their efforts on holding off the Shard warships. Soon, they would be overwhelmed…

"We need to get P into the capsule," gasped Saito. "I…I can't activate another."

The launch console was wasted. It had been chewed up by gunfire, and even if I could get Dr Saito upright in order to operate it, there would be no point in trying. That left us only one option.

"The active tube is at the other end of this bay," I said. "That's exactly where the shooters are located."

"I didn't…didn't know they would be here," said Dr Saito. His body shuddered, and his eyes fluttered open.

<Dr Saito has expired,> P said.

I nodded grimly. "Shit."

Heart attack, caused by blood loss. Not unexpected, given the size of the wound in his stomach. Dr Saito's hands were still clutched over the injury. His features had gone vacant and slack.

The gunfire paused. Heavy boots plodded across the overhead gantry, as the attackers took up new positions.

"I advise you to stand down," came a voice. "This is not a fight you can win. You're outnumbered and outgunned."

"Ah, crap," said Ving, as he recognised the speaker.

"This ship is now under my control," said Major Mish Vasnev.

She stood on the upper gantry, overlooking the drop-bay, carbine slung over her shoulder, dirty silver hair hanging around her face. Every bit as menacing as when we'd last seen her aboard the *Valkyrie*.

"What the fuck are you doing here, Vasnev?" I shouted back. "This is an Alliance warship. You're out of your depth."

Vasnev's face settled into an irritated expression. "I go where I please." She repeated, "Stand down."

Her gangers wore heavy hard-suits, reinforced space armour. I plotted the progress of one, as he prowled the upper catwalk, providing close protection to Vasnev. The cannon he used would've been cumbersome for a simulant in combat-armour, and the ganger only carried it with the assistance of a torso-mounted man-amp. As I watched from a gap between cargo crates, I saw another shooter come into view, equipped with the same weapon.

"What've they got?" Feng asked me.

"It looks like they've plundered weapons from our

armoury," I concluded. "At least two heavy gatling cannons."

"They're using armour-piercing hi-ex munitions," Lopez added. "Those rounds are punching through plate steel."

<We must act now,> P insisted.

"Don't do anything rash, P," I said. "Those rounds will go straight through you, as well."

Vasnev stalked the gangway, sweeping her gaze across the many and varied hiding places that the drop-bay presented. To get to the active launch tube, we'd have to go beneath her position ...

"Even now, the Black Spiral and my Sons approach," Vasnev said. "This will be easiest if you provide the girl, and the fish."

"Fuck you," Lopez yelled back, over her suit-speakers.

<We are not going with her either,> said P.

"I know that you are in these simulants, *da*?" Vasnev said. "So I can do as I wish to them now. Then my Sons will find your station, and take your real skins."

"Why do you want our alien?" I asked.

"The fish will attract high bidder. Directorate, Pacific Pact: wherever. They will want to know of cure for virus."

Bio-signs coalesced around the edges of the drop-bay. I could hear chanting from the approaching Black Spiral.

Vasnev pressed her hands onto the safety rail, leaning over the drop-bay. Her gunmen were masked, wearing heavy respirators. They flanked her on either side like an honour guard.

"Every disaster presents opportunity for profit..." she started. "This is chance for my Sons to flourish."

"It's FUBAR," I said. "Warlord has done it. Ithaca Prime is dying. There won't be anything left when Dominion comes."

Another bio-sign popped into existence behind Vasnev. Was it another of her gangers, perhaps ensuring that her retreat from the bay was covered? I glanced in P's direction, and asked that question with my mind.

<It is not,> P answered me. Silent understanding passed between us.

Vasnev barked something in Russian at one of her death squad. The ganger loped sideways, trying to outflank us.

Now! I commanded.

In the dark behind Vasnev, a shape formed. Bulky arms, sweat-slicked skin. Tattoos.

Leon Novak lurched across the platform. A knife in each hand, a silent, wicked grimace plastered across his face. His boots barely touched the deck, as he dropped down behind Vasnev. He was a flash of motion and blades.

One went into Vasnev's back. The whites of her eyes grew, visible even across the drop-bay, and she snarled.

"Go, go!" I yelled.

Feng and Lopez were up. Plasma rifles firing. Pulses strobing the drop-bay.

The ganger to Novak's left sprayed the deck with gunfire from his cannon. Rounds churned up the metalwork, piercing crates and punching holes in empty drop-capsules. Feng went down, his armour peppered with AP rounds, null-shield failing under the weight of fire. But Lopez picked off the shooter with a precision plasma shot. The pulse punched through his torso armour and exploded out of his back. Corpse and cannon toppled from the gantry, slamming to the deck ten metres beneath.

"Behind me, P," I said.

I weaved between loaders and crates, determined to reach the active launch tube. P used all six limbs to scramble over obstacles. The second ganger opened fire with his cannon, indiscriminately spraying the bay with life-extinguishing gunfire. I felt something pierce my suit, and the pain was sharp enough that I gasped, but not enough to put me down. The psychic resonance of P taking a hit was more jarring.

Vasnev reached for the wound at her back with one hand, touching gloved fingertips to blood. The blade had gone into her ribcage, through armour plating. Novak's shoulders rose and fell as he faced off against her, half observing us as we made the dash beneath. He was rage incarnate, the anger pouring out of him.

Vasnev crumpled to the deck, on her knees in front of Novak.

"Do not need skins any more," Novak said to Vasnev. He wiped blood across his tattooed face. *His face.* His real face. Novak wasn't in a simulant. "I do this for real."

"Leon Novak…" she purred. "Look at what you have become."

"I am Jackal," Novak roared. "I am Vali's dog!"

"Leave her!" Lopez yelled. "Cover P and the lieutenant!"

The Black Spiral burst into the compartment. Their roaring voices echoed around the chamber, their cries audible above the churn of gunfire. The second ganger was adjusting his aim, and had me and P in his sights. Another bullet sliced the back of my calf. The round went through my armour, and made a golf-ball sized wound in the muscle. P faltered beside me, jerking as it too took impacts.

"We'll get you down there, P," I said. "Just keep going."

The open drop-capsule was metres away. We kept going.

The mission comes first.

Novak turned from Vasnev, who was still alive, but in a state of shock and disbelief. He pounded towards the lone gunman, sweeping his mono-knife in a long, deadly arc. The ganger was so focused on us that he didn't notice Novak's attack until it was too late. Novak sliced again and again and again. The cannon was silenced.

P reached the drop-capsule and folded its bulky body inside. The alien was wet with blood from a dozen wounds. Its apparent invulnerability was just a mask.

"Good luck down there," I said. "We'll be right behind you with a pick-up."

P shook its head. <There is no need.>

"Don't get all gallant on me."

<You misunderstand. We are the solution, Jenkins. We always have been. The Aeon, the Pariah Project: all of this has been for a purpose.>

I was silent. Realisation hit me and my blood froze.

<This is the alternative to the starfyre protocol,> P said. <The Aeon will use their quantum-weaponry to distribute our consciousness throughout the Deep. We will join with the Collective, and the Harbinger virus will be eradicated. Our immunity will become the Collective's immunity.>

"But... but you'll be—"

<Terminated. That is correct.>

"No. We'll tell Wraith to use the starfyre!"

<The Deep will be purged. The Kindred will cease to exist, for all intents.>

"You don't have to do this! You can exist outside the Deep. All Krell can!"

<Correct,> P said. <But the Kindred would lose their knowing. That would destroy them—us—as a species.>

I slammed a fist into the drop-capsule's outer canopy. "No! You can't do this! You're a Jackal! You can't do this."

<This is the only way. The anti-viral is not effective. We can end the war. Here, now.>

Lopez was firing her plasma rifle, Ving his pistol. The bay was shouting and chaos and horror. The *Defiant*'s deck quaked again, as the ship took another impact. Out in space, Wraith's vault-ships resisted another round of dark-matter pulses from the Shard ships. And on Ithaca Prime, the Harbinger's stain spread further, seeping into the very core of the planet. These things were projected into my head—by P or Wraith, I couldn't tell—and I knew that they were true. I also know, as much as I hated to admit it, that P was right.

"You'll be destroyed!" I said, trying one last time to change P's mind. I couldn't stop the emotion from breaking in my voice. Not that it mattered what I said. P was in my head, and it knew what I felt. It knew what I wanted, and still this wouldn't change.

<We were designed to stop this war, Jenkins.>

The deck listed. Gravity warped. Something ruptured in the *Defiant*'s hull.

<Goodbye, Jackals.>

There was nothing else that I could say or do to stop this. With resignation, I saluted. "Be seeing you, fish."

<Always.>

The drop-capsule entry hatch slid shut with a low whine. The launch sequence commenced immediately.

"We can't hold them off any more," said Lopez, over the comms, the desperation blatant in her voice.

The attackers—Christo only knew how many of them there were—had circled them, breaking in through the hatch, taking spots behind the hard cover of robotic loaders and missile racks.

"We will help," Novak said. He tossed aside the dead ganger, the heavy cannon clattering on the gang walk. "There is still—"

Bang.

Vasnev was on her knees, dying, bleeding out. But she clutched a heavy pistol in her hands, and aimed it at Novak. The Russian ganger dropped.

"*Novak!*"

Vasnev grinned down at me. "I am the leader of this—"

Lopez felled her with a single shot from her Widow-maker pistol. Right through the head.

I slid against the deck, numb with loss, unable to comprehend what had happened.

"Confirm on launch. P is gone."

P's capsule arced through space.

Out of the *Defiant*, and the increasing cloud of debris that circled the dying ship, and then towards Ithaca Prime. The drop-capsule's second-stage thruster unit activated. It gained speed as it jinked past more space wreckage, avoiding gunfire and energy pulses. The AI compensated for P's increased weight.

P used all its abilities to understand what was happening. The drop-capsule's cams provided some information, but P gleaned much more through its own preternatural senses. Although it had seen the world in dreams, P had never witnessed Ithaca Prime with its own faculties, and what it saw pained the alien. The planet's green-blue prospect was currently blighted by bands of dark corruption. P computed the landing coordinates for the centre of that mass, into the heart of the Great Nest. It sensed the location of the Deep Ones, and on some molecular level knew that was where it must go.

The war raged in orbit around Ithaca Prime. The Black Spiral's disparate fleet was scattered, but still dangerous.

Infected bio-ships chased down Kindred war-fleets. The remaining Alliance Navy assets were rallying, but they were too few in number to do much good.

\<Are you ready?\> asked Wraith.

The Aeon vault-ships were in position, their orbit fixed over the Great Nest. Their quantum-weaponry was alive with energy.

\<We are,\> answered P.

\<May we make an enquiry of this Kindred?\> Wraith said.

\<You may, Aeon.\>

\<Are you frightened?\>

P did not answer immediately, but then said, \<No. We do not fear what is inevitable.\>

\<We rail against death, Kindred. We do not go gently into the dark. Are we to believe that you embrace it?\>

The drop-capsule punched through the upper layers of Ithaca Prime's atmosphere. P detected the increase in ambient temperature inside the craft, as friction heated the outer shell. There was a quickening of the alien's pulse, which—if asked—it would have explained as a simple by-product of the changing atmospherics.

Except, P realised, *there will be no one to ask. Not any more.*

\<We go willingly. For the good of the species.\>

\<You will cease to exist, as Soldier says.\>

\<This is inevitable. It is the way of all organics.\>

Wraith's vault-ship was hulled in a dozen places. It fired a quantum-beam at the nearest Shard warship and watched as the machine absorbed the impact. There was not much time left for any of them, truth be told. Only the machines persisted. P knew this too. It was a galactic truism, and always would be.

\<Will you miss her?\> Wraith asked.

<We will. She was a true friend.> P closed its eyes. The drop-capsule rumbled around it now, and P could sense that it had made atmospheric entry. The Harbinger virus lapped at the capsule's armour. <Ensure that she is safe, Wraith.>

<We will do what we can,> said Wraith.

The many minds echoed. That was the first time P had heard them reach agreement on something.

<We are in position,> said P. <Goodbye, Aeon.>

<Goodbye, Kindred.>

P hit the face of Ithaca Prime.

There was a stabbing, piercing whine of white noise over my communicator.

Then silence.

The absence had returned to my head, but this time it was so much worse. The finality of it made me shake.

"What the fuck just happened?" Captain Ving said, as he rose from cover.

"P is gone," I repeated. "It made planetfall. This... this was always the plan. Between P and the Aeon, at least."

"I'm not talking about the fish," said Ving. "I mean the Spiral."

Lopez stirred too, now. She kicked at a body, which lay gibbering on the deck. The man wasn't dead, but was clutching his head, repeating something over and over again. Lopez bent down and picked up the tango's pistol, pinching it between her finger and thumb like it was dirty. She tossed the weapon out of the tango's reach.

"They're all like it," said Ving. He picked his way through the carpet of chattering wrecks and approached me.

"Dominion come... Dominion come... Dominion come..." the group muttered.

"They were chanting this a moment ago," said Lopez.

She grimaced. "Something they were welcoming has just become something they're frightened of."

"It was Wraith," I said. "Maybe."

I got to my feet, careful not to place any weight on the injured leg. Fresh blood oozed from the gun-wound inflicted by Vasnev's ganger. That wasn't the only wound I'd suffered during the gunfight, but it was the worst. My combat-suit was administering a steady stream of painkillers to keep me from going under. I checked my bio-scanner and saw that all hostiles in the area had frozen.

"If it was," Ving said, "then that's one hell of a weapon the Aeon have there..."

"Figures," said Lopez. "Mind-manipulation was their thing on Carcosa."

I scrambled up the gantry to find Novak, but before I'd even knelt down beside him, I knew that he was dead. The bio-scanner didn't lie. Novak's body lay still on the gantry, not far from Vasnev's. This was their ending, intertwined in death, just as they had been in life. *You did Vali and Anwar proud*, I thought to myself. There was something bittersweet about that. Not for the first time, I considered how hollow hatred was. I should've felt the swell of triumph, the endorphin rush of victory...

But there was nothing. Nothing but an overwhelming sense of loss.

I unlatched my helmet and threw it to the deck. Fiddled with my communicator. The white noise burst had ceased. I thought-commanded a line back to the SOC.

"Do you read, Zero?"

"I copy," came Zero's voice. "Are you all okay down there?"

"We're operational, if that's what you mean. Dr Saito is dead."

"Do you want me to send Feng back out?"

"I don't think that's necessary. P's launched."

"I know. I read its progress from here."

I glanced up at the bodies on the gantry. "Novak's dead too. We'll meet you in the SOC. Stay locked down until we get there."

There was no need for that last order. There were tangos everywhere, but they had been reduced to quivering wrecks. Universally, they were curled up on the deck, crying and wailing about the Dominion. What they had once dreamt of had become their nightmare. We met no resistance at all as we picked our way across the ship.

Zero, Feng and Captain Heinrich were poised over Zero's terminal, watching vid-feeds.

"We tried to stop Novak from going after you," Zero started. Fresh streaks of tears marked her cheeks, and her eyes were watery. "Is he really gone?"

"He is," I said.

Feng absorbed the grief in a different way, but looked as devastated. That was the only way to describe what had happened: devastation. We'd lost so many of our number.

"He was a trooper, a friend," said Feng. "A good man."

"The right kind of wrong," Lopez muttered.

"No one could've stopped him," I said. "We couldn't have done it without him."

"I'm very sorry for the loss of your trooper, Lieutenant," Captain Heinrich said. The gunshot wound must've stabilised, because he was still ambulatory. "I'm sure Private Novak would be very interested to know what he assisted in achieving. The Black Spiral fleet is in complete disarray. I've never seen anything like it."

The Spiral's ships were drifting through space without purpose. Some had entered terminal decline around Ithaca Prime and were burning up in the upper atmosphere.

Others were being chased out-system by the revived Krell war-fleet, which was quickly rallying around the homeworld.

"Whatever P did," Zero said, "it worked. Look at this."

Ithaca Prime had been cured. The Harbinger virus had created a band of shadow across the equator and polluted the Great Nest. Those sections had now turned a vibrant green, as though something had turned back the infection. Equilibrium had been restored.

"At a cost," I said. "P is gone."

"How did this happen?" Captain Heinrich asked, shaking his head. "*Why* did this happen?"

"The Aeon were going to purge Ithaca with their starfyre weapon," I explained. "But that was always the option of last resort. P knew that. So it entered the Deep. It had natural immunity to the virus. Now the Krell have that immunity, too."

"This was what P was planning," Zero said, working through that theory, "when it went into hibernation…"

"Maybe even before then," I said. "It knew. It has probably always known. Which was why Warlord sent Vasnev after it."

Lopez sighed, her eyes fixed on the tri-D images. "P is one with the Deep now."

"We couldn't have done it without the Aeon," I said. "Their Q-tech did what P was made to do; allowed it to fuse with the Deep."

The Aeon vault-ships hovered at the edge of the *Defiant*'s scanner-range. They were pursuing dark shapes that moved out-system. The Shard warships wouldn't make it beyond the Reef Stars. The machines were licking their wounds, if such a thing were possible.

A chime sounded over the *Defiant*'s internal address system.

"Lieutenant Jenkins?" came a familiar voice. It was

General Draven, from the Command Centre. "Are you still operational?"

"I'm here, sir."

"I take it what just happened was down to you?"

"No, sir. Pariah takes that credit."

"We could do with some help in the CIC."

I swallowed. "What's left of the Jackals will report for duty."

CHAPTER TWENTY-EIGHT

SIGNING OFF

We cleaned up the ship. Maintenance teams recovered the dead. Support drones rescued evacuees who had either abandoned ship, or survived attacks on other Alliance vessels. The Aeon sent another Scuttler swarm to assist with repairs, turning the *Defiant* from a wreck into a vessel capable of the journey home.

Throughout the Black Spiral's attack, General Draven had remained in the CIC, locked down with most of his command staff. It wasn't particularly comforting to know that the senior brass had survived the war, but there you go. This had been history since time immemorial. Secretary Lopez—architect of the war—had disappeared. His ship, the *Destiny*, had vanished during the closing phase of the conflict. How he had escaped a locked-down CIC still puzzled me, but it would have to wait. We had other things to focus on.

Back in my real skin, I took in the view from the observation deck. Ithaca Prime gazed back at me. This planet was revised, improved. It wasn't the same world that the Alliance fleet had first encountered, but it was still the Krell's homeworld. The Harbinger threat was over and Warlord's plan had failed. The Black Spiral were finished, once and for all eternity. A new dawn commenced across Ithaca, and across the Maelstrom.

Daneb Riggs was finally gone. Warlord and Vasnev too. But Novak was dead. Dr Saito was dead. Most of Phoenix Squad was dead. Commander Dieter was dead. I closed my eyes and let the memories roll over me. For the first time in a very long time, my data-ports didn't hurt. I neither wanted nor needed to make transition. There was hurt inside me, though. It was the ache in my head, that yawning absence I felt where the mind-link with Pariah had once been. Where Novak once lived.

"Who wants to live for ever?" I whispered. "Good journey, all of you."

There was a cough behind me. Zero, Feng and Lopez stirred at the elevator entrance.

"Can we join you, ma'am?" Zero asked.

"Be my guests."

Zero pulled out a bottle of something clear and obviously alcoholic from behind her back.

"What's this, Zero? Do you have a secret drinking habit or something?"

Feng put an arm around Zero. "It's news to me."

"No," Zero said, shaking her head. "I found this in with Novak's things. It's Kronstadt vodka."

Zero opened the bottle. The scent of over-proof alcohol was almost overwhelming.

"Do you want the first drink?" she invited.

I nodded and knocked back a mouthful. I cringed, and nearly spat it out. I passed the bottle to Feng, who did the same.

Lopez's face dropped a little. "I'm not sure that I feel much in the mood to celebrate."

Feng's eyebrows lifted in surprise. "We just saved the

entire galaxy from the Shard, Lopez. Didn't you hear? The Spiral are on the run. The Shard look like they've gone, and the Krell infection was cured the moment that P touched down on Ithaca…"

"That's just it," Lopez said. "The Shard *look* like they're gone. We haven't investigated every infected star system yet."

I nodded. "They're gone, Lopez. I can feel it."

"Another of your feelings," Lopez said, a little dismissively. "Can you be sure that everything you're getting from the Aeon is accurate?"

"I can be sure. I don't know how, but I can be sure. I don't feel like celebrating, either, but this is what Novak would've wanted."

"Novak…" Lopez said, her voice barely a whisper. "I can't believe that he's gone."

"He took down Vasnev with him," said Feng. "He got what he wanted."

"It's more than most of us can say about life," I said.

The scent of vodka filled the chamber, setting off a different kind of yearning in me. It had been a while since I had a damned good drink, but Kronstadt vodka certainly wasn't it.

"All of this," Lopez said, drinking the neat vodka, "was my father's fault."

I'd told Lopez the truth about Warlord, what he had told me about Secretary Lopez. She carried that weight on her shoulders now, and it was a private burden. Even if Rodrigo Lopez was deprived of his title and stripped of his authority, there was no way that High Command or the Proximan government would ever accept responsibility for the Warlord Project.

"It'll blow over," I said. "Your father is in hiding, but someone will find him."

"I don't care about him," Lopez said. Her voice was rock hard with determination, and I didn't doubt her for a second. "He brought this down on our heads."

"Don't think about it. It wasn't you. You did the Lopez dynasty proud. Sleep at night knowing that."

"I'd like to know whether he really did endorse the Warlord Project," Lopez said.

I grimaced at Zero. She swallowed, nervously, shoulders tight.

"I take it that you've been inside the mainframe and looked at those files, Z," I said. "Do I even need to ask?"

Zero gave a slow nod. "What Warlord said: it checks out. Rodrigo Lopez did endorse the Barain-11 mission, and Clade Cooper's orders were to bring back a sample of the Harbinger virus."

Lopez let out a long and painful sigh. "Well, that's just great…"

"The files are on lockdown, but I've copied them already." My wrist-comp pinged, as Zero sent me a local link to the data. "You should keep a back-up, in case something happens to that data."

"Thanks," I said, although in truth that probably made me a target as well.

"The Secretary's yacht launched when he realised that Warlord would be face to face with you," Zero said. "I guess he thought the risk of being revealed was too great."

"Coward," Lopez spat.

"I'm getting the feeling that you don't much like your father…" I said.

Lopez pouted back at me. "You're a genius, ma'am."

"So," Feng said, "what are we going to do now?"

"Go back, and probably get chewed up by Command, regardless of what we achieved," Lopez muttered. "That's life."

Ever the inexperienced drinker, Zero knocked back

her vodka with a repulsed expression on her face. She quickly passed the bottle to Feng.

"That reminds me," she said. "I found this, ma'am, in Dr Saito's locker."

Zero produced a data-clip from her fatigue pocket. Unmarked, the plastic chip was unexceptional and in pristine condition.

"What is it?" Feng asked, frowning.

I activated the clip with my thumbprint, and it unlocked. Wesley Saito had specifically keyed it for only my use. I swiped the device over my wrist-comp. A message popped up. EYES ONLY: KEIRA JENKINS. Data scrolled across the small screen. I smiled as I read the message.

"Ma'am?" Lopez queried.

"It's nothing," I said.

The journey back to Sanctuary Base was short and painless. The Shard Gates were under Alliance control once more, and the remnants of Operation Perfect Storm made use of them. The Aeon followed us part of the way, but departed thereafter. Their drive signatures were virtually untraceable, which was fine by me. Wraith's presence still lingered in my head for a long time after the fleet left.

Sanctuary Base was in the clutches of a celebration like no other, and Jenkins' Jackals were greeted as heroes. The other surviving Sim Ops squads received a similar welcome. A tide of news-casters descended on us, eager to hear of war stories and reports of the Aeon. Several news-feeds were broadcasting images that looked nothing like the actual xenos we'd encountered, and depending on which channel you watched, the Aeon were either galactic saviours or an unpredictable new threat. For my part, I thought they were a little of both.

No one reported on Pariah. No one reported on Novak. Those weren't stories that the Alliance public wanted to hear.

After our official debrief, the Jackals were summoned to attend General Draven's office.

"It's over," said General Draven. "Officially, all hostilities are ceased."

I stood to attention in front of the general's desk. Back ram-rod straight, eyes forward. Six days had passed since our return to Sanctuary. The Jackals stood with me.

"I'm glad to hear that, sir."

A map on General Draven's smart-desk showed the progress of the cure. From Ithaca Prime, immunity had developed outwards in an ever-expanding spiral. Now, most of the Reef Stars were reporting immune responses.

"If progress continues at this rate," said Director Mendelsohn, "then we can expect even the border systems to be Harbinger-free within the next few months." He shrugged. "Perhaps even sooner. How has this happened?"

"I...I think that I can explain, if it helps," said Zero.

"Go on," said Draven,

Zero licked her lips. "Well, P—the pariah-form, I mean—was a singular entity developed as a closed-network access point to the Deep."

"Right," said Draven. His eyes had already started to glaze over, as though he were even now losing interest in the specifics of what Zero had to say.

"Dr Skinner's files, from North Star Station, made clear that was Pariah's purpose. Being an outcast gave it immunity to the Harbinger virus."

"How does that account for what happened at Ithaca?" Draven interrupted.

"With respect, sir," Zero said, apologetically, "it doesn't account for it: it explains it. Pariah's connection with the Deep was selective. It had developed in a way that no other Krell mind had. It was both part of the Collective consciousness, and separate from it."

Draven nodded, although he looked unconvinced.

"When Pariah was introduced to the Deep," Zero continued, "its consciousness—and its immunity—became part of the Collective. The Aeon used their quantum-technology to distribute P's consciousness across the Deep."

"It triggered an immune response," I said, flatly. "And now it's gone."

"We already know that the pariah-form has been lost," Draven said. "The remaining fleet scanned Ithaca Prime before we left."

"If any of you have information as to the asset's whereabouts," Director Mendelsohn started, "then you are under an obligation to inform Sci-Div immediately."

"Understood, sir," Lopez said, her voice dripping with accusation. "But P sacrificed itself for our good."

"The Black Spiral's network has collapsed," said General Draven. "When Pariah touched down on Ithaca Prime, their fleet fell apart."

"Explain how this happened again, please," said Mendelsohn.

Wearily, I gave my report for the tenth time. "The Aeon projected visions into their minds. Visions of life under the Shard, of their supposed Dominion."

General Draven leant forward, his elbows on his desk. His brow was creased in either irritation or anger, and he breathed out loudly through his nose.

"And how do you know this, Lieutenant?" he asked.

"The entity codenamed Wraith told me so, sir. Until recently, we were still in communication."

"I don't know why you doubt this," Lopez interjected. "You saw the captives for yourself."

General Draven glanced down at the images scattered

across his desk. Hardcopies of the Black Spiral prisoners, locked in cells aboard the *Defiant*. Every one of them had given the same report. For all intents, their minds had been destroyed by the Aeon's contact.

"The Aeon specialise in mind-manipulation," said Feng, backing me up. "We experienced this on Carcosa."

"On the subject of the Aeon," said Mendelsohn, "where have they gone?"

I shrugged. "I'm sure that it's not the last we'll hear from them, but I have no information to offer Command on that subject."

General Draven removed his service cap, and ran a hand through his grey hair. His moustache twitched. "You escaped Alliance custody during a time of war. That can't go unpunished."

"We ended a war," I said. "We lost good people doing it."

"They did," said Captain Heinrich. He had been standing at the back of the chamber throughout the debrief, quietly listening. I hadn't even noticed him. "I'd like to request that the lieutenant be considered for a promotion. The Jackals should be lauded for their efforts during the conflict. They deserve medals, not reprimands."

"I'd second that," came another voice. Captain Ving stood beside Heinrich, an unlikely ally to the Jackals. "The Jackals, and Lieutenant Jenkins in particular, showed exceptional valour in the face of impossible odds. These are some of the best troopers I've ever served with."

General Draven rolled the idea around in his head for a moment. "I'm far from convinced, but in light of your contribution to the war effort, and the fact that your actions were instrumental in the cessation of hostilities, I'm going to let this go."

"I'd like to ask a question myself," I said.

"Go on."

"Do you know where Secretary Lopez has gone?"

General Draven pursed his lips, then said, "The official line is that his ship went missing in action during the final stages of the Ithaca campaign. *Destiny* is a government asset; it has a fast Q-drive and a full stealth package. The Secretary—although, as you're also no doubt aware, his title is under review by Congress—simply disappeared."

That was hardly a satisfactory state of affairs, but pressing General Draven on the issue wasn't going to get us any new information.

"There will be a full state funeral for those who lost their lives during Operation Perfect Storm," General Draven said. "Captains Heinrich and Ving have persuaded me that should include Leon Novak."

Captain Heinrich's expression was distant and fixed. His arm was still in a sling and he was on the mend, but he didn't look like the old Heinrich. Like Ithaca itself, he'd been changed by the experience.

"Thank you, sir," I said.

"He's entitled to that, according to his status."

"What do you mean?" Lopez asked. "He was an indentured life prisoner."

"No," said Draven, lifting an eyebrow. "He wasn't. At the end, he was a free man."

Feng frowned as well now. "I think you have the records mixed up..."

"We don't," said Captain Heinrich. He paused, sighed, reading from a service document. "Leon Novak worked off his sentence after Kronstadt."

"He didn't tell any of you that?" Draven asked.

"No," I said. "He didn't."

I heard Zero sniffing beside me. "So he could've gone free?"

"He could've done, but he didn't want to," said Captain Heinrich. "He voluntarily signed up for continued service. I think he stayed, in the end, because of the Jackals."

I nodded, remembering Novak. He'd told me more than once that the Jackals were the only family he had left. In the end, he'd died protecting us, and putting the mission first. Despite the sadness that revelation brought, I couldn't help smiling to myself. Novak might've kept that from us, but he had died free.

"You're dismissed, Jackals," said General Draven. "I'd like to see the lieutenant alone."

The Jackals filed out of the room and I waited behind. Once the squad was gone, I allowed myself to relax. Rolled my head around my neck. General Draven glanced down at the old-fashioned brown paper envelope on the corner of his desk.

"I don't have to accept that," he said. "I could veto it."

"We're not at war any more," I argued. "I served out my service commitment a long time ago."

"I'd like to formally request that the lieutenant reconsiders her position," said Captain Heinrich. "You're a damned good officer, Jenkins. It'll be the Alliance Army's loss."

"There's still a lot to do," General Draven explained. "Those Shard ships need to be accounted for, and the Gates need to be properly secured."

"They're under Alliance control," I countered. "And the Shard warships were destroyed by the Aeon."

"Let's not even get started on the Aeon," General Draven said. "High Command wants to send a task force to secure the Aeon's assistance in case something like this happens again."

Captain Heinrich nodded. "Our head is above the parapet, Lieutenant," he said. "The Shard know that humanity is out here. We need to be ready if they ever come back."

"The best defence is offence, right?" said Ving. "They're talking about sending an expedition beyond the Shard Gates. We can take the war to them."

I'd heard those rumours; discussions about assembling another battlegroup, dedicated to exploring other star systems beyond the Milky Way, and seeking out Shard territories for a retaliatory strike. Hot on the heels of the victory at Ithaca, many troopers were excited about the prospect of another conflict.

But it wasn't for me. "I've thought about this a lot," I said. "I'm not interested."

"I know that I've given you a hard time," Ving said, more sympathetically than he'd ever spoken to me before. "I'm sorry for that, but you're made for this job."

"Don't worry, Ving," I said. "It doesn't have anything to do with you. In the end, I'm kind of glad you didn't die."

Ving smiled. "You too, Jenkins."

"I don't think that we're going to change her mind, Captain," said Draven. He reached for the envelope, and unsealed it. Printed in red along the header were the words FORMAL LETTER OF RESIGNATION. My thumbprint marked a box at the bottom of the sheet.

"Last chance to change your mind," said Captain Heinrich.

"I'm sure," I said.

"We can arrange for the data-ports to be removed if you'd like," General Draven offered.

I thought about that for a moment, but shook my head. "No," I said. "I'll keep them. Never know when they might be useful."

The ports didn't ache like they used to, not any more. They were more like dead metal in my arms, in my thighs and neck. Inert.

"What will you do?" Captain Heinrich enquired.

"I have another job."

"Really?" asked General Draven, as he formally signed off the paperwork. "And where might that be?"

"Nowhere you'd know, sir."

EPILOGUE

Six months had passed since the disaster at Ithaca, and former Secretary Rodrigo Lopez had felt every week, every day, every hour.

The thing about going into hiding, Lopez thought to himself, was that it was inconvenient. Damned inconvenient. There were places he had to be, things he had to do. But he could do none of them holed up in his Gaia-forsaken shithole on the edge of occupied space.

The hotel room was always too cold, not the way Proximans liked it at all. The air-conditioning never worked properly, and the humidity was all wrong. It was disgraceful that the place even dared to call itself a five-star resort. The Three Trees on Reigel-3 would be getting a piece of Lopez's mind, once he cleared his name. Reigel-3, it had to be said, wasn't known for its opulence, and Lopez had been slumming it for too long.

"What's the hold-up?" Lopez asked, angrily, as his bodyguard searched the apartment.

"It's a big suite, sir," said the guard. His name was either Dimitri, or Demiter. Or maybe that was the last bodyguard. "I have to check every room."

"Can you do it any faster?"

The bodyguard stared at Lopez levelly. The man was barrel-chested and tall, the beneficiary of a powered

subdermal endo-skeleton. When Lopez had hired him
for close protection work, the man's stat-sheet had read
more like the report on a walking firearm. The pistol in
his left hand never seemed to leave it, mainly because it
was bio-grafted to the tissue of his palm.

"There are lots of people who want you dead right
now, sir," said the bodyguard. That was what he called
himself, but Lopez knew that in reality he wasn't much
more than a mercenary. "Including your daughter, if I
recall correctly. Now please stand aside and let me search
every room."

"Fine. Just get on with it."

The main chamber was all chrome and glass, overlooking the blue-red jungles that encroached on the perimeter
of Reigel-3's main city. Lopez had the penthouse suite.
During his time in government, he'd acquired dirty materials that gave him leverage on certain parties. The owner
of the Three Trees Hotel chain happened to be such a
person. The man probably considered Rodrigo Lopez
a friend, and thought that he was doing him some great
service by allowing him to use the penthouse. To Lopez,
this was just another step back into government.

"Suite is secure," said the bodyguard.

"About time," said Lopez.

He slung his attaché case down on the black-glass
smart-table. Opened it with his palm print, and pulled
up a chair. The case housed a complicated tachyon-relay
station—about the only safe way Lopez could communicate with those off-world—and it immediately booted
up. Tri-D waveforms danced across the table's surface as
the case made uplink. A face formed out of green light,
and eventually resolved from static into something more
distinct.

"Is that you, Rodrigo?"

"It's me."

"Good to hear from you."

"I wish I could say the same to you."

Director Yarric Mendelsohn's image fluttered in and out of existence. The tachyon-relay used an enormous amount of power, bouncing its signal across half the Alliance, then back again. It was virtually untraceable, much safer than the hotel's open comms-channels.

"I'm taking a huge risk by speaking to you," said Mendelsohn.

"I think that we can agree the risk to my safety is far greater," Lopez snarled. "If my sources are correct, most of Military Intelligence, as well as a good deal of the Secret Service, are looking for me."

Mendelsohn's jowls twitched. "It's true."

"Have they interrogated you yet?" Lopez asked.

"Not yet. I've been careful."

"How careful?"

"Very. The Warlord Project has been deleted. Not just local data, but everything from Delta Primus as well."

"Good." Lopez sat back in his chair, and looked at his polished nails. "I'm considering handing myself in, once we're satisfied I'm out of the loop. Living like this isn't living at all."

Mendelsohn paused, as though he wasn't quite sure how he was expected to react to that, but then said, "It is probably infinitely better than jail time, sir."

"I know that," said Lopez, "but if you've done your job properly and the data is deleted, there will be nothing to link me back to the Warlord Project. It'll be the word of an insane terrorist against mine."

Mendelsohn nodded. "I can promise it's been deleted. There's nothing left to link you to the programme."

"Good. Excellent. When I get back on the horse, Mendelsohn, there will be a place for you in government. I'm sure of it."

"I hope so, sir."

There was a sudden *thunk* from the next chamber. Lopez's face crumpled in annoyance. Bodyguards were noisy, messy individuals.

"Please, do keep quiet! I'm trying to conduct a call in here."

No answer.

Did his skin prickle with fear? I wondered. I hoped so.

"Dimitri?" he asked. "Did you hear me?"

The tachyon-relay died, the link cut. The chamber was plunged into silence; not even the noise from the street outside threatened the penthouse suite. This was a series of chambers fit for politicians, for rulers. Silenced glass and room access were a must. Features that were supposed to be positive suddenly became anything but.

In his expensive Proximan loafers and thousand-credit slacks, Rodrigo Lopez padded through to the next chamber. There was a bed in there, made up with the finest Proximan spider-silk sheets. His eye followed the curve of the bed frame, and he gasped.

Dimitri's gun. No longer in his hand.

"Who's in here?"

Lopez bolted for the exit door. There was an emergency security console on the wall, DNA and palm-print encoded. He could use that, call in security. This sort of thing really wasn't good enough for a five-star resort...

He swiped his palm over the reader. Resolve and determination hardening. He was Secretary of Defence for the entire fucking Alliance!

"Uh, uh," I said.

Lopez froze with his palm still on the reader. It didn't matter, anyway, because the security feed had been cut.

"No one's coming," I said, leaning in so close that he could feel my lip against his earlobe. He still smelt of that expensive cologne, but now it reminded me of corruption more than power. "You're on your own, Lopez."

I wedged the muzzle of my pistol into his neck, at the top of his spine. He released a high-pitched gasp.

"Who are you?"

"You don't even remember who I am?" I asked. "Turn around, and let's see if that jogs your memory."

He did as ordered, hands up at all times. I stood there, wearing a black bodysuit, laced with tools of my new trade. Pouches for security readers. A grapnel-head. A portal null-shield generator. I have to say, the new suit fitted me pretty well. It was figure-hugging in all the right places. Lopez, however, didn't look particularly impressed.

"You were my daughter's commanding officer," he said. "I ... I can't remember your name."

"Jenkins," I said. "Keira Jenkins."

"What the hell are you doing here?"

"Putting right an injustice," I answered.

The gun in my hand was matte black, fixed with an electronic silencer.

"Whatever happens in this room is between us," I said.

"And what is going to happen?"

I aimed the gun at his chest. "As I said, I'm putting right a wrong."

"You're a soldier, Jenkins, not an *executioner*."

"Ithaca changed all of that."

"If you think I did wrong, then call it in," Lopez said. His hands lowered, fractionally. His face sort of shifted as well, the twitch of a smile at the corners of his lips. "See what Military Intelligence think of it. If you have evidence, then fine, let me see it."

The pistol still pointed at Lopez, I reached over and

activated the local recorder on my wrist-computer. A voice drifted out of the unit's small speaker.

"*...if you've done your job properly and the data is deleted, there will be nothing to link me back to the Warlord Project. It'll be the word of an insane terrorist against mine...*"

Lopez's smile cracked.

"That isn't how it sounds," he insisted.

"I still have a copy of that data. I know what you did. I know that you endorsed the Barain-11 mission. I know that you approved Science Division's work on Clade Cooper."

"That was Director Mendelsohn—"

"It was you. It was always you. And when the project got out of hand, you tried to burn it."

"Listen, to yourself. This is crazy!"

"No, you listen," I said. "Hear these names: Captain Miriam Carmine, of the UAS *Sante Fe*. Commander Vie Dieter, of the UAS *Valkyrie*." I tried to remain calm, tried to do this as professionally and coldly as I could, but my voice still broke. "Private Leon Novak, of the Jackals. Pariah."

"That last one isn't on me," Lopez argued. "It was a fish, a science project gone wrong. You can't expect—"

When the pistol fired, it was whisper-quiet. The round went straight through Lopez's chest, and out the other side of his body. Embedded in the wall behind him. Just for good measure, I fired twice more. One in the body, one in the head.

Rodrigo Lopez fell to the floor.

I breathed out and stood over his body for a long moment.

"Watch One," I finally said, using my throat communicator. "This is Watch Two. Mission accomplished."

A familiar voice answered. "Well done, Watch Two. Pick-up inbound in two minutes."

"That's too long. Can't you get here any sooner?"

"Some days there's no pleasing you, Watch Two," came the Detroit-accented reply. "I'm getting too old for this."

ACKNOWLEDGMENTS

As ever, I'd like to thank friends and family for helping me create this book. I couldn't have done it without you all!

Louise has provided me with invaluable feedback and been there through the many drafts of this book.

I'd like to express my gratitude to my agent Rob Dinsdale, as well as Anna Jackson, James Long, Priyanka Krishnan, Joanna Kramer and Nick Fawcett from Orbit.

Thanks to everyone who has bought and read my books—you guys are what really make this worthwhile, and you're all great.

extras

orbit

meet the author

JAMIE SAWYER was born in 1979 in Newbury, Berkshire. He studied law at the University of East Anglia, Norwich, acquiring a master's degree in human rights and surveillance law. Jamie is a full-time barrister, practising in criminal law. When he isn't working in law or writing, Jamie enjoys spending time with his family in Essex. He is an enthusiastic reader of all types of SF, especially classic authors such as Heinlein and Haldeman.

For a glossary of military terms used in this book, visit www.jamiesawyer.com.

Find out more about Jamie Sawyer and other Orbit authors by registering for the free monthly newsletter at www.orbitbooks.net.

if you enjoyed

THE ETERNITY WAR: DOMINION

look out for

VELOCITY WEAPON

The Protectorate: Book One

by

Megan E. O'Keefe

Dazzling space battles, intergalactic politics, and rogue AI collide in Velocity Weapon, *the first book in this epic space opera trilogy by award-winning author Megan E. O'Keefe.*

Sanda and Biran Greeve were siblings destined for greatness. A high-flying sergeant, Sanda has the skills to take down any enemy combatant. Biran is a savvy politician who aims to use his new political position to prevent conflict from escalating to total destruction.

However, on a routine maneuver, Sanda loses consciousness when her gunship is blown out of the sky. Instead of finding herself in friendly hands, she awakens 230 years later on a deserted enemy warship controlled by an AI who calls himself Bero. The war is lost. The star system is dead. Ada Prime and its rival Icarion have wiped each other from the universe.

Now, separated by time and space, Sanda and Biran must fight to put things right.

CHAPTER 1

The Aftermath of the Battle of Dralee

The first thing Sanda did after being resuscitated was vomit all over herself. The second thing she did was to vomit all over again. Her body shook, trembling with the remembered deceleration of her gunship breaking apart around her, stomach roiling as the preservation foam had encased her, shoved itself down her throat and nose and any other ready orifice. Her teeth jarred together, her fingers fumbled with temporary palsy against the foam stuck to her face.

Dios, she hoped the shaking was temporary. They told you this kind of thing happened in training, that the trembling would subside and the "explosive evacuation" cease. But it was a whole hell of a lot different to be shaking yourself senseless while emptying every drop of liquid from your body than to be looking at a cartoonish diagram with friendly letters claiming *Mild Gastrointestinal Discomfort*.

It wasn't foam covering her. She scrubbed, mind numb from coldsleep, struggling to figure out what encased her. It was slimy and goopy and—oh no. Sanda cracked a hesitant eyelid and peeked at her fingers. Thick, clear jelly with a slight bluish tinge coated her hands. The stuff was cold, making her trembling worse, and with a sinking gut she realized what it was. She'd joked about the stuff, in training with her fellow gunshippers. Snail snot. Gelatinous splooge. But its real name was MedAssist Incubatory NutriBath, and you only got dunked in it if you needed intensive care with a capital *I*.

"Fuck," she tried to say, but her throat rasped on unfamiliar air. How long had she been in here? Sanda opened both eyes, ignoring the cold gel running into them. She lay in a white enameled cocoon, the lid removed to reveal a matching white ceiling inset with true-white bulbs. The brightness made her blink.

The NutriBath was draining, and now that her chest was exposed to air, the shaking redoubled. Gritting her teeth against the spasms, she felt around the cocoon, searching for a handhold.

"Hey, medis," she called, then hacked up a lump of gel. "Got a live one in here!"

No response. Assholes were probably waiting to see if she could get out under her own power. Could she? She didn't remember being injured in the battle. But the medis didn't stick you in a bath for a laugh. She gave up her search for handholds and fumbled trembling hands over her body, seeking scars. The baths were good, but they wouldn't have left a gunnery sergeant like her in the tub long enough to fix cosmetic damage. The gunk was only slightly less expensive than training a new gunner.

Her face felt whole, chest and shoulders smaller than she remembered but otherwise unharmed. She tried to crane her neck to see down her body, but the unused muscles screamed in protest.

"Can I get some help over here?" she called out, voice firmer now she'd cleared it of the gel. Still no answer. Sucking down a few sharp breaths to steel herself against the ache, she groaned and lifted her torso up on her elbows until she sat straight, legs splayed out before her.

Most of her legs, anyway.

Sanda stared, trying to make her coldsleep-dragging brain catch up with what she saw. Her left leg was whole, if covered in disturbing wrinkles, but her right…That ended just above the place where her knee should have been. Tentatively, she reached down, brushed her shaking fingers over the thick lump of flesh at the end of her leg.

She remembered. A coil fired by an Icarion railgun had smashed through the pilot's deck, slamming a nav panel straight into her legs. The evac pod chair she'd been strapped into had immediately deployed preserving foam—encasing her, and her smashed leg, for Ada Prime scoopers to pluck out of space after the chaos of the Battle of Dralee faded. She picked at her puckered skin, stunned. Remembered pain vibrated through her body and she clenched her jaw. Some of that cold she'd felt upon awakening must have been leftover shock from the injury, her body frozen in a moment of panic.

Any second now, she expected the pain of the incident to mount, to catch up with her and punish her for putting it off so long. It didn't. The NutriBath had done a better job than she'd thought possible. Only mild tremors shook her.

"Hey," she said, no longer caring that her voice cracked. She gripped either side of her open cocoon. "Can I get some fucking help?"

Silence answered. Choking down a stream of expletives that would have gotten her court-martialed, Sanda scraped some of the gunk on her hands off on the edges of the cocoon's walls and adjusted her grip. Screaming with the effort, she heaved herself to standing within the bath, balancing precariously on her single leg, arms trembling under her weight.

The medibay was empty.

"Seriously?" she asked the empty room.

The rest of the medibay was just as stark white as her cocoon and the ceiling, its walls pocked with panels blinking all sorts of readouts she didn't understand the half of. Everything in the bay was stowed, the drawers latched shut, the gurneys folded down and strapped to the walls. It looked ready for storage, except for her cocoon sitting in the center of the room, dripping NutriBath and vomit all over the floor.

"Naked wet girl in here!" she yelled at the top of her sore voice. Echoes bounced around her, but no one answered. "For fuck's sake."

Not willing to spend god-knew-how-long marinating in a stew of her own body's waste, Sanda clenched her jaw and attempted to swing her leg over the edge of the bath. She tipped over and flopped face-first to the ground instead.

"Ow."

She spat blood and picked up her spinning head. Still no response. Who was running this bucket, anyway? The medibay looked clean enough, but there wasn't a single Ada Prime logo anywhere. She hadn't realized she'd miss those stylized dual bodies with their orbital spin lines wrapped around them until this moment.

Calling upon half-remembered training from her boot camp days, Sanda army crawled her way across the floor to a long drawer. By the time she reached it, she was panting hard, but pure anger drove her forward. Whoever had come up with the bright idea to wake her without a medi on standby needed a good, solid slap upside the head. She may have been down to one leg, but Sanda was pretty certain she could make do with two fists.

She yanked the drawer open and hefted herself up high enough to see inside. No crutches, but she found an extending pole for an IV drip. That'd have to do. She levered herself upright and stood a moment, back pressed against the wall, getting her breath. The hard metal of the stand bit into her armpit, but she didn't care. She was on her feet again. Or foot, at least. Time to go find a medi to chew out.

The caster wheels on the bottom of the pole squeaked as she made her way across the medibay. The door dilated with a satisfying swish, and even the stale recycled air of the empty corridor smelled fresh compared to the nutri-mess she'd been swimming in. She paused and considered going back to find a robe. Ah, to hell with it.

She shuffled out into the hall, picked a likely direction toward the pilot's deck, and froze. The door swished shut beside her, revealing a logo she knew all too well: a single planet, fiery wings encircling it.

Icarion.

She was on an enemy ship. With one leg.

Naked.

Sanda ducked back into the medibay and scurried to the panel-spotted wall, silently cursing each squeak of the IV stand's wheels. She had to find a comms link, and fast.

Gel-covered fingers slipped on the touchscreen as she tried to navigate unfamiliar protocols. Panic constricted her throat, but she forced herself to breathe deep, to keep her cool. She captained a gunship. This was nothing.

Half expecting alarms to blare, she slapped the icon for the ship's squawk box and hesitated. What in the hell was she supposed to broadcast? They hadn't exactly covered codes for "help I'm naked and legless on an Icarion bucket" during training. She bit her lip and punched in her own call sign—1947—followed by 7500, the universal sign for a hijacking. If she were lucky, they'd get the hint: 1947 had been hijacked. Made sense, right?

She slapped send.

"Good morning, one-niner-four-seven. I've been waiting for you to wake up," a male voice said from the walls all around her. She jumped and almost lost her balance.

"Who am I addressing?" She forced authority into her voice even though she felt like diving straight back into her cocoon.

"This is AI-Class Cruiser Bravo-India-Six-One-Mike."

AI-Class? A smartship? Sanda suppressed a grin, knowing the ship could see her. Smartships were outside Ada Prime's tech range, but she'd studied them inside and out during training. While they were brighter than humans across the board, they still had human follies. Could still be lied to. Charmed, even.

"Well, it's a pleasure to meet you, Cruiser. My name's Sanda Greeve."

"I am called *The Light of Berossus*," the voice said.

Of course he was. Damned Icarions never stuck to simple call signs. They always had to posh things up by naming their ships after ancient scientists. She nodded, trying to keep an easy smile on while she glanced sideways at the door. Could the ship's crew hear her? They hadn't heard her yelling earlier, but they might notice their ship talking to someone new.

"That's quite the mouthful for friendly conversation."

"Bero is an acceptable alternative."

"You got it, Bero. Say, could you do me a favor? How many souls on board at the present?"

Her grip tightened on the IV stand, and she looked around for any other item she could use as a weapon. This was a smartship. Surely they wouldn't allow the crew handblasters for fear of poking holes in their pretty ship. All she needed was a bottleneck, a place to hunker down and wait until Ada Prime caught her squawk and figured out what was up.

"One soul on board," Bero said.

"What? That can't be right."

"There is one soul on board." The ship sounded amused with her exasperation at first listen, but there was something in the ship's voice that nagged at her.

Something…tight. Could AI ships even slip like that? It seemed to her that something with that big of a brain would only use the tone it absolutely wanted to.

"In the medibay, yes, but the rest of the ship? How many?"

"One."

She licked her lips, heart hammering in her ears. She turned back to the control panel she'd sent the squawk from and pulled up the ship's nav system. She couldn't make changes from the bay unless she had override commands, but…The whole thing was on autopilot. If she really was the only one on board…Maybe she could convince the ship to return her to Ada Prime. Handing a smartship over to her superiors would win her accolades enough to last a lifetime. Could even win her a fresh new leg.

"Bero, bring up a map of the local system, please. Light up any ports in range."

A pause. "Bero?"

"Are you sure, Sergeant Greeve?"

Unease threaded through her. "Call me Sanda, and yes, light her up for me."

The icons for the control systems wiped away, replaced with a 3-D model of the nearby system. She blinked, wondering if she still had goop in her eyes. Couldn't be right. There they were, a glowing dot in the endless black, the asteroid belt that stood between Ada Prime and Icarion clear as starlight. Judging by the coordinates displayed above the ship's avatar, she should be able to see Ada Prime. They were near the battlefield of Dralee, and although there was a whole lot of space between the celestial bodies, Dralee was the closest in the system to Ada. That's why she'd been patrolling it.

"Bero, is your display damaged?"

"No, Sanda."

She swallowed. Icarion couldn't have...wouldn't have. They wanted the dwarf planet. Needed access to Ada Prime's Casimir Gate.

"Bero. Where is Ada Prime in this simulation?" She pinched the screen, zooming out. The system's star, Cronus, spun off in the distance, brilliant and yellow-white. Icarion had vanished, too.

"Bero!"

"Icarion initiated the Fibon Protocol after the Battle of Dralee. The results were larger than expected."

The display changed, drawing back. Icarion and Ada Prime reappeared, their orbits aligning one of the two times out of the year they passed each other. Somewhere between them, among the asteroid belt, a black wave began, reaching outward, consuming space in all directions. Asteroids vanished. Icarion vanished. Ada Prime vanished.

She dropped her head against the display. Let the goop run down from her hair, the cold glass against her skin scarcely registering. Numbness suffused her. No wonder Bero was empty. He must have been ported outside the destruction. He was a smartship. He wouldn't have needed human input to figure out what had happened.

"How long?" she asked, mind racing despite the slowness of coldsleep. Shock had grabbed her by the shoulders and shaken her fully awake. Grief she could dwell on later, now she had a problem to work. Maybe there were others, like her, on the edge of the wreckage. Other evac pods drifting through the black. Outposts in the belt.

There'd been ports, hideouts. They'd starve without supplies from either Ada Prime or Icarion, but that'd take a whole lot of time. With a smartship, she could scoop them up. Get them all to one of the other nearby habitable systems before the ship's drive gave out. And if she were very lucky...Hope dared to swell in her chest. Her brother and fathers were resourceful people. Surely her dad Graham would have had some advance warning. That man always had his ear to the ground, his nose deep in rumor networks. If anyone could ride out that attack, it was them.

"It has been two hundred thirty years since the Battle of Dralee."

if you enjoyed
THE ETERNITY WAR: DOMINION

look out for

FORTUNA

The Nova Vita Protocol: Book One

by

Kristyn Merbeth

Fortuna *launches a new space opera trilogy that will hook you from the first crash landing.*

Scorpia Kaiser has always stood in the shadow of her older brother, Corvus, until the day he abandons their family to participate in a profitless war. However, becoming the heir to her mother's smuggling operation is not an easy transition for the always rebellious, usually reckless, and occasionally drunk pilot of Fortuna, *an aging cargo ship and the only home Scorpia has ever known.*

But when Corvus returns from the war and a deal turns deadly, Scorpia's plans to take over the family

*business are interrupted, and the Kaiser siblings
are forced to make a choice: take responsibility for
their family's involvement in a devastating massacre,
or lie low and hope it blows over.*

*Too bad Scorpia was never any good at
staying out of a fight.*

CHAPTER ONE

Fortuna

Scorpia

Fortuna's cockpit smells like sweat and whiskey, and loose screws rattle with every thump of music. I'm sprawled in the pilot's chair, legs stretched out and boots resting atop the control panel forming a half circle around me. A bottle of whiskey dangles from one of my hands; the other taps out the song's beat on the control wheel.

Normally, this is my favorite place to be: in my chair, behind the wheel, staring out at open space and its endless possibilities. I'm a daughter of the stars, after all. But I've been in the cockpit for nearly eight hours now, urging this ship as fast as she can go to make sure we unload our cargo on time, and my body is starting to ache from it. Scrappy little *Fortuna* is my home, the only one I've ever known, but she wasn't built for comfort. She was built to take a beating.

My shift at the wheel wasn't so bad for the first six hours, but once the others went to bed, I had to shut the door leading to the rest of the ship, and the cockpit soon grew cramped and hot. No way around it, though. I need the music to stay awake, and my family needs the quiet to sleep. Someone needs to be coherent enough to throw on a smile and lie their ass off to customs when we get there, and it's not gonna be me.

I yawn, pushing sweaty, dark hair out of my face. Envy stings me as I think of my younger siblings, snug in bed, but recedes as I remember they're actually strapped into the launch chairs in their respective rooms, with gooey mouth-guards shoved between their teeth and cottony plugs stuffed up their ears. I don't know how they manage to sleep with all that, but it's necessary in case of a rough descent, the likelihood of which is rising with every sip of whiskey I take. *Fortuna*'s autopilot can land the ship on its own, but it tends to lurch and scrape and thud its way there, with little regard for the comfort of its occupants or whether or not they hurl up their dinner when they arrive. Some pilot finesse makes things run more smoothly.

Given that, I'd normally avoid too much hard liquor while at the wheel. But as soon as Gaia came into sight, anxiety blossomed in my gut. Now, the planet fills my view out the front panel and dread sloshes in my stomach. It's a beautiful place, I'll admit that. Vast stretches of water dotted with land masses, wispy clouds drifting across, like a damn painting or something. Historians say that after centuries of searching for humanity's new home, the original settlers wept with joy at the first glimpse of Gaia. I, on the other hand, always go straight for the bottle strapped to the bottom of my chair.

Beautiful Gaia. Rich in alien tech and bad memories. Ever since Corvus abandoned us to fight in his useless war, even the good ones from my childhood have turned bitter.

"Damn," I mutter, and take another sip. I've once again broken the rule I invented in the early hours of my boredom. Every time I think of my older brother, that's another drink. It's a tough rule when my memories of Gaia are so deeply entwined with memories of him.

I was seven when we left Gaia. It's been twenty years since we were grounded there. And after a brief stop on Deva, where Lyre was born, we spent another six years on Nibiru, while she and the twins were still too young to live on the ship. Those were better years, when we spent our days playing and fishing in the endless ocean and our nights sleeping in a pile on our single mattress. Yet even then I could never shake my anxiety that Momma wouldn't come back one day, and I'd be stranded again. I never felt safe like I did on *Fortuna*, never stopped waiting for someone to notice I didn't belong. The days on Gaia wouldn't loosen their hold on me.

And every time I see the planet, it all rushes back to the surface. Memories of Corvus's smile; of digging through trash for food; of playing tag with him in the narrow streets of Levian, the capital city; of huge alien statues staring down at me with their faceless visages.

Memories of Momma wearing hooded Gaian finery to blend in on the crowded street and saying, *"It's just a game, Scorpia,"* as she showed me the best way to slip my hands into someone's pocket without them noticing. When she taught me my first con, dressing me up like a little lost Gaian child, she said, *"It's like telling a joke, but you're the only one who knows the punchline."* Guess Momma didn't anticipate that once I started, I wouldn't be able to stop thinking that way. Or maybe she didn't think I'd live long enough for it to matter. I probably wouldn't have, if Corvus hadn't been around to get me out of trouble. Corvus, who was never any good at lying, so he went to school while I learned to be a criminal.

"Damn." I sip again. Through the viewing panel, Gaia looms closer.

As I wipe my mouth, I glance over the expanse of screens and gauges and lights all around me, tracking the radar, fuel tank, and various systems. The numbers are blurry, but the lights are all the soothing red of Nova Vita, which means everything is running fine. Good enough for me. I take another swig, and choke on it as the ship shudders.

It's not a particularly menacing rumble, yet the hairs on the back of my neck stand straight up. I let my boots thud to the metal floor one after another, dragged by the ship's artificial gravity, and frown at the panels. Nothing on the radar. It could be some debris too small to pick up, a cough in the machinery...or a cloaked ship. It's rare for us to have company out here, when interplanetary trade and travel have all but ground to a halt due to the tense relations between planets. Rarer still near Gaia, whose border laws are tightest of all. But it could be those pirate bastards on the *Red Baron* hounding us again. If they picked up cloaking tech, we're in trouble. Not for the first time, I wish *Fortuna* was outfitted with weaponry for self-defense—but of course, weapons on ships are illegal, and we'd never be able to land anywhere in the system if we had them. With current laws, the planets are wary enough about ships without the added threat of weapons on them.

Indicators are all a solid red. There's not so much as a blip out of place. Still, my skin prickles. *Fortuna* is saying something. I slap the button to shut off the music, tilt my head to one side, and listen to the silence.

The next rumble shakes the whole craft.

The bridge goes dark. Every screen and every light disappears. My sharp intake of breath echoes in the darkness.

"Fortuna?" I ask, as if the ship will answer. I clutch tighter to the whiskey with one hand and the wheel with the other as my muddled brain tries to work out what

else to do. I've dealt with my fair share of malfunctions, but I've never seen the ship go dark like this.

The lights blink back online. A relieved laugh bubbles out of me, but cuts off as I realize all of my screens are crackling with static.

I smack a few buttons, producing no effect, and turn from one end of the control panel to the other. My eyes find the system indicators on the far right. Life support and the engine are still lit red, signaling that they're online and functioning. But navigation is the shockingly unnatural green of system failure. Radar is green. Auto-pilot is green.

The ship has everything she needs to keep flying, but not what she needs to land.

"Aw, shit." Judging by the fact that we haven't been blasted or boarded yet, this isn't the *Red Baron* or any other outside interference. It's an internal malfunction. I flash back to my sister Lyre begging for new engine parts on Deva, and curse under my breath. Our little engineer is usually too cautious for her own good, but it seems she was right this time.

I take a final sip from my bottle, cap it, and tuck it between my boots. Once it's secure, I reach toward the neon-green emergency alarm button on the left side of the control panel. At the last moment, I stop short.

Hitting that button will send alarms screaming and green lights flaring through the ship, cutting through my family's earplugs and waking them from their strapped-in-for-landing slumber. My ever-scowling mother will be here in less than a minute, barking orders, taking control. And at the first sniff of whiskey in the cockpit, she'll relieve me from my duty and send me to bed.

Fortuna will stay in orbit until everything's at 100 percent and I've passed a BAC test...which means we'll miss the drop-off on Gaia *and* the side job I hoped to pull off beforehand.

And I'll be the family screwup. Again. One step further from ever amounting to more than that, or ever prying my future out of Momma's iron grip. One step further from *Fortuna* belonging to me. I can already hear her usual speech: *"You're the oldest now. You can't keep doing this shit."*

Plus, this side job is important. There's not much profit in it, but I can use all the credits I can get after I blew most of my last earnings on Deva. I can't deny I'm looking forward to seeing the pretty face of my favorite client, too.

And, of course, I want to see Momma's expression when I tell her I pulled off a job on my own. I know that she was grooming Corvus to be in charge one day—Corvus, who was always so obedient and ready to follow in her footsteps—but he's been gone for three years now, fighting in the war on his home-planet. We all have to accept that he's not coming back. Instead, Momma's stuck with me.

This deal I set up is the perfect chance to prove that's not such a terrible thing. And once the ship falls to me, I'll finally have a place in the universe that's all my own. A home that nobody can kick me out of. I'll get to make my own decisions, be in charge of my own life. I'll keep my family together and make things better for all of us, like Corvus always promised he would before he abandoned us.

But if we don't make it in time, this will just be one more disappointment on the list.

I sit back in my seat, running my tongue over my teeth. I'll have to land the ship as planned. Even if it's bumpy, and even if Momma smells the whiskey on me once we land, she can't give me too much shit if I get us planet-side intact and on time.

It's a damn nice thought...but it's been a long time since I landed the ship without autopilot. And, lest the blurry vision and stink of whiskey in the cockpit aren't enough to remind me, I'm drunk enough that I could get jail time for flying a simple hovercraft on most planets. There's no law out here to punish me for operating a spacecraft under the influence, but down there the law of gravity waits, ready to deal swift and deadly judgment if I fuck this up.

"So don't fuck it up," I tell myself. I suck in a slow breath, blow it out through my nose, and hit the button to connect to Gaian air control. Static crackles through the speakers, followed by a booming robotic voice. I wince, hastily lowering the volume.

"You have reached Gaian customs. State your registration number and purpose. Do not enter Gaian airspace without confirmation or you will be destroyed."

I know the automatic Gaian "greeting" by heart, and I also know it's not bullshit. As a kid, I saw many unregistered ships shot out of the sky before they got close to landing. The locals would cheer like it was some grand fireworks show. I always felt bad for the poor souls. If they were entering Gaian airspace illegally, they had to be desperate. Using the opportunity to pick some Gaian pockets felt a little like justice.

"This is pilot Scorpia Kaiser of merchant vessel *Fortuna*," I say into the mic, working hard to keep my words from slurring into one another. "Registration number…" I run a finger down a list etched on one of my side panels, and blink until the numbers come into focus. Of course, the Gaian registry is the longest number of them all. Damn Gaians and their regulations. "Two-dash-zero-two-one-eight-eight-dash-one-zero-three-six," I say. "Registered to Captain Auriga Kaiser, Gaian citizen. We're delivering freeze-dried produce from Deva."

It's not the whole truth, but it's not a lie, either. If customs agents peek into our cargo crates, they'll find neat packages of fruits and vegetables dried and sealed for space travel. The good shit is well hidden. We're professionals, after all.

"Checking registration," the robotic voice says. There's a pause, followed by a click. "Checking landing schedule." Another pause, click. "Ship two-dash-zero-two-one-eight-eight-dash-one-zero-three-six, you are cleared for entry. Noncitizens are not permitted to travel beyond the landing zone. Entry elsewhere will be considered a hostile act. Welcome to Gaia."

"Yeah, I'm feeling real welcome," I mutter, severing the radio connection. But the recording has provided a good reminder of what's at stake here. If I crash, we all die. If I land so much as an inch outside the legal landing zone, same shit. I roll my shoulders back and slip the safety belts across my chest, clicking them into place and yanking the straps tight. "Okay, *Fortuna*," I say. "Hope you're ready for this. It's gonna be a rough landing."

I fish in my pocket for the gooey lump of my mouthguard, chomp down, and shove the control wheel forward.

Follow us:

/orbitbooksUS

/orbitbooks

/orbitbooks

Join our mailing list
to receive alerts on our
latest releases and deals.

orbitbooks.net

Enter our monthly
giveaway for the chance
to win some epic prizes.

orbitloot.com